By Andrew M. Greeley
from Tom Doherty Associates

All About Women
Angel Fire
Angel Light
Faithful Attraction
The Final Planet
God Game
Irish Gold
Irish Lace
White Smoke

Sacred Visions (editor with Michael Cassutt)

Andrew M. Greeley

Summer at the Lake

FORGE

A TOM DOHERTY ASSOCIATES BOOK

New York

F
Gree

SUMMER AT THE LAKE

This book is printed on acid-free paper.

A Forge Book
Published by Tom Doherty Associates, Inc.
175 Fifth Avenue
New York, NY 10010

Forge® is a registered trademark of Tom Doherty Associates, Inc.

Design by Bonni Leon

Library of Congress Cataloging-in-Publication Data

Greeley, Andrew M.
    Summer at the lake / Andrew M. Greeley.—1st ed.
    p.   cm
    "A Tom Doherty Associates book."
    ISBN 0-312-86082-X (acid-free paper)
    I. Title.
    PS3557.R358S86   1997
    813'.54—dc21   96-6566
                                                                 CIP

First Edition: June 1997

Printed in the United States of America

0 9 8 7 6 5 4 3 2 1

For the Saint Angela Class of 1942, in gratitude for a magical golden reunion. Our classmates, Jane and Leo and Chuck, were there too. But since they exist only in the world inside my head and not in God's world I was the only one who saw them.

They loved the reunion too.

Where're the Catholic sun does shine
There's music and laughter and good red wine
At least I've found it so
Benedicamus Domino!

—Belloc

Summer is y-cumen in
Ludè sing, cuccu!
Groweth sed and bloweth med
And springeth the wudè nu—
Sing, cuccu!

Awè bleteh after lamb
Lowth after calvè cu:
Bulluc streteh, buckè fereth,
Meriè sing, cuccu
Cuccu. Cuccu
Well singes, cuccu:
Ne swik thu never nu!
Sing, cuccu, nu! Sing cuccu!
Sing, cuccu! Sing cuccu nu!

—Friar Thomas of Hales

Prologue

Patrick

He'll meet her out on the road at the foot of the hill by the tree where the accident happened. The first time he's seen her since my Ordination almost a quarter century ago. He says he's just going out for a breath of fresh air, but that fools no one. He came back to Chicago to renew a love affair that's been dead for thirty years. A second chance. They'll probably mess up the second chance like they did their first chance.

My best friend and the woman I've loved since she was in eighth grade.

Obscene fantasies fill my mind, actions in which I'd never engage with her in the real world. Does she know how much I desire her? Does she know that my imagination now automatically undresses her? Women usually know, don't they? She *must* know. Yet she glows whenever she is with me. So she does not object.

Is it not my turn? Have I not taken care of her through the years? Did I not urge her to leave her sociopathic husband? Do I not have some rights in the matter? Have I not been a priest long enough? Is it not time to break away from the insane Church and its stupid cowardly leaders?

The smell of blossoms is overpowering tonight, like the empty flower car returning from a cemetery.

I had my turn too and I lost my own first chance. It's only fair to give him his second chance before I take mine.

If I'm really serious about leaving the priesthood and I'm not in some dumb mid-life crisis.

It's all fantasy isn't it? Jane and I could never be lovers, could we? Surely not.

Am I sure of that? I don't know. I'd like to find out.

Anyway I must give the two of them my best possible advice. They are entitled to their second chance without my trying to spike it. The Lake seems sinister and brooding tonight, dark and restless out there. Water. Baptism. The symbol of life and death and new life. It meant life for Leo and Jane once. Then death. New life? Maybe.

What does it mean for me?

Three times I might have possessed Jane—that evening here at the house, the day she told me she was pregnant, and that dazzling night in Rome. What I thought was respect overcame my desire. Now I wonder if I am a coward just like Leo, a wimp who is also an occasional hero.

I can tell that I am still special for her by the way she smiles at me and the lilt in her voice when she talks to me. I'm not out of the running yet.

Does anyone know how I feel? Even my preternaturally perceptive sister-in-law?

I don't know. Only once did she speak to me about my feelings towards Jane and that was long ago.

Leo

In those rare moments when I am honest with myself, I have to admit that I accepted the offer from the University and returned to Chicago because I had heard that Phil had walked out on Jane. Finally. Yet I've made no attempt to see her until this improbable stroll on a May evening with the odor of spring so dense on the night air that it reminds me of the pungency of that luxuriant Brazilian rain forest I was in a couple of years ago, the smell of rapacious fecundity.

Will I find her? Will she find me?

Will the old magic still be there? Or, as seems more likely, will we find that at the age of fifty—almost fifty for her—we are not the same persons we were at the age of twenty? Will an encounter, even on a lovely and romantic night, dash cold water on the foolish dreams we had when we were young?

That's the likely scenario. Academic that I am, I analyze and reanalyze and come up with the same conclusion: You can't go home again.

But why else am I here but that I am trying to go home again?

The place has changed, the road is paved now. The subdivisions are crowding in from the other side of the Lake. The streetlights are newer and brighter—old gaslights long since gone—but the road seems darker, perhaps because the trees are so much taller and the foliage so much thicker. The Old Houses have been remodeled and repainted and look faintly modern and commonplace instead of elegant and romantic as they once seemed to me. The glitter and the romance have vanished. Or were they ever here? Do not we humans spread a nostalgic sheen over the site of our adolescence and our first love and make it more dazzling in our memories than it ever was in reality? And don't we thus run a risk of profound disillusion when we discover how ordinary it is when we try to come home again?

She is likely to have changed too. Plain Jane instead of Magic Jane. Maggie, who is her ally, insists not, but she is a prejudiced witness.

What if she hasn't changed? What if it's gasoline that gets poured on the embers instead of water?

Will the fury and the guilt of the past come back to haunt us again? Or the ghosts that lurk on this road, the ghosts of dead friends? Can I have her, if I want her, without putting those ghosts to rest?

Will I have to find out what happened that night?

The last time I saw her was at Packy Keenan's ordination. She already had two children and was probably expecting a third. She looked terrible. I was still trapped in my fury and was barely civil.

When we meet tonight, if we meet, will I be anything more than barely civil? I feel the rage stirring within me again.

Jane

I know what I'm doing. Unless Leo has changed completely, he'll wander towards the tree where our friends died and I'll meet him there. He will be expecting me. He always was an incurable romantic even when the romance was with death.

Only a few days before the accident, he had asked me to marry him, more or less. I didn't say no, but like a fool I didn't say yes either. I talked about a lot of foolish objections and problems with our families of which I didn't even realize I was aware. Then on the day of my twentieth birthday I betrayed him. He never forgave me. Instead he ran out on me just at the time when I needed him the most.

He's the only one who thought he made a fool out of himself. The others all thought he was a hero. When I heard what he said at the jail, I was terribly proud of him.

I would have married him before he went to war on a day's notice if he'd asked me. He didn't ask.

What will he think of me? An old woman—almost fifty, worn out by an unhappy marriage, unable to satisfy her husband sexually, and unable to save two of her kids, and probably a third? I was pretty good-looking at twenty but that was long ago.

Not counting doctors, three men have seen me naked—my husband who quickly lost interest, another man whom I unintentionally terrified before I was married, and Leo. He didn't see much in that fragmented moonlight, but I think he liked what he saw. If he should get another look at me, will he still like me? Or will he be disappointed?

Will he guess that I think a lot about ending my life? He always knew what was going on inside my head.

He was so sweet at Packy's Ordination, same gentle smile and so nice to young Phil and poor Brigie, my two lost kids. And as friendly to me as though we'd seen each other the day before. He didn't look like a man whose soul had been torn apart by war.

Maggie Ward Keenan, who thinks she knows everything, says that Leo and I should have a Catholic summer, one in which we allow the summer heat to rekindle the warmth of the love that once existed between us. She quotes a liturgy from some place about the bride being buxom and bonny in bed. Well I suppose I'm buxom enough but not very bonny in bed. Not much practice in a long time.

I tell myself that my husband is wrong when he says that he fools around because I'm not very good in bed. But I wonder often whether maybe he's right. Would I have been any better a lover with Leo?

Or with Packy? If he had not been committed to being a priest I might have married him after Leo died. That night in Rome ten years ago we were so close . . . I must not think about that.

Would I be any better with him if we made love tonight?

Was that an adulterous thought? I would have confessed it a few years ago. Now I'm not sure that Phil and I were ever really married.

Maggie quotes some poet called Friar Thomas of Hales about cuckoos singing in early summer. I don't quite know what that means.

Maybe she's right about being Catholic. We do know in our hearts that our lover is kind of like God to us. I wish I could really believe that. I certainly was not God to my husband nor he to me.

If I invite Lee back to our empty house, would he come? Should I try? Would You want me to?

I bet You wouldn't object all that much. I think You always wanted us to be together.

The scent of the lilacs and the jasmine and the flowering crab apple trees reminds me of the scent of a wedding mass.

Now I wish he'd never come back to Chicago. I wish I was not walking down the hill on this road with its terrible memories, hunting for him like a horny teenager searching for her latest crush.

Leo was my first crush, even before my crush on Packy. I was his first crush too.

I hope he likes me.

Memorial Day/
Pentecost

O Light of surprise divine
Keep in mind how short our time
Our strength and will please renew
Without your help we are lost
Useless fluff not worth the cost
Our only hope lies in you

Heal whatever may be ill
Quicken that which may be still
Soothe our restless, aching hearts
Energize what may be old
Warm whatever may be cold
Bind us who have come apart

Protect us in love with You
Pardon all the wrong we do
Grant us joy that does not cease
Give us life's last reward
Bring us home to you, O Lord,
Grant us everlasting peace

Amen!

ALLELUIA!

1978

Leo

For a few seconds I was terrified.

She had caught up to me under the streetlight. Materializing suddenly in its faint, leaf and branch obscured luminescence like a spirit floating in the summer darkness, a spirit from a past summer that I had conjured out of bittersweet memories, a phantom of lost opportunities come to haunt me and punish me for my sins.

I was spooked only for a moment. Jane was never ethereal enough to be one of the fairie troop.

She kissed me lightly on the cheek, a quick gesture of remote friendship and nothing more. Yet the kiss ignited an inferno of hope—the ever-lurking professor in my brain warned me, the most dangerous of emotions.

Jane was not plain Jane; she was astonishing Jane and dangerous Jane. She was almost the effervescent young woman I had known three decades ago, unchanged in personality from the bubbling little toddler who had bounced down the street in our neighborhood and unchanged in physical appearance from the girl I had held in my arms under the same streetlight in 1948. She wore a cotton print dress with a low-cut, square neck that could have been the same one that she had worn thirty years before. Her body seemed to have the same lithe athletic shape, primed for a tennis match. The pale light or perhaps deft makeup obscured the lines that time must have etched on her round, faintly freckled face. I saw in the dim glow of the streetlight that her brown eyes sparkled with mischief as they always had. Her curly brown hair was still a halo around her head. Her smile was as bright as ever and her laughter as contagious as ever. Jane, touched by time and the tragedy of painful marriage and loss of children, but triumphant over tragedy.

We had met in the lilac-scented dark, by accident we would have said, at a place of love and death and the death of love. Perhaps of murder and the murder of love. But lilacs, I had always thought, were flowers of hope and promise.

"It seems so long ago," her sigh hung like a wisp of fog on the humid night air. "Thirty years."

Thirty years ago sighing was not part of her character.

"Or only yesterday," I replied.

Then, stuffy professor that I was, I added ponderously, "The past is always incarnated in the present."

"I'm sure you're right."

"I used to like it, Jane, when you said I was talking intellectual nonsense."

She sighed again, a hint of weary wisdom, "I've changed my mind about intellectuals, Leo. Sometimes," and her magic laughter returned, "only sometimes, mind you, they know what they're talking about."

I felt the first stirrings of rage in my gut. I fought to keep it down.

My friends had told me that she was the "same old Jane," yet I was not ready for her to enchant me just as she had when I was twenty.

"How much more money do you make now because you are a member of the National Academy of Sciences?" she had touched me lightly on the arm. "What's it worth in hard cash?"

She was grinning wickedly, mocking me, mocking herself, mocking the values of her family, and at the same time congratulating me.

It was election to the Academy that had ended my marriage. My wife and our therapist had bitterly attacked me for not rejecting the honor because of what it did to Emilie. I knew then that no matter how much I wanted to save the marriage it was finished. So too were the therapy sessions. I had called my friend Packy, as I always did when I was in trouble.

"They're the crazy ones, Leo," he had told me. "Get out while you can."

In fact Emilie had moved out when I refused to attend the therapy sessions any longer. "Your precious National Academy of Sciences," she had snarled, "is more important than the wife you've exploited all through your marriage."

That was that.

"Maybe you could get a ride on the Chicago subway with it, so long as you had the money for the exact fare," I replied to Jane, trying to organize my response to the surprise of meeting her again at just this place and control the frenzy that suddenly had begun to flame within me.

There was no reason for me to be angry at her, I told myself. Yet anger was surging up from my gut and threatening to pour out of my mouth.

Had she been waiting for me?

No, that was impossible. She had caught up with me. Besides, she had no way of knowing that I was at the Lake this weekend.

She had hunched her shoulders and giggled as she always had, "I'm sure there's big money in being a university vice president."

"Provost."

"Whatever!" she cackled with glee. "Really big money!"

"Junior partner in a law firm makes more."

She clapped her hands, "Same old Lee. Nothing has changed. *Déjà vu* all over again."

"I'm staying with Jerry and Maggie Keenan for the Memorial Day weekend," I stammered.

I had learned how to control my explosions of rage, to wall them up inside myself, to give no hint of them though they seemed to tear at me and twist me apart.

"You have grown up OK, Lee," she rested her chin in her hand as if considering me. "Not bad for a fusty old political scientist."

It was a humid, windless night for so early in the season. The Lake was listlessly tapping the shore and the smell of flowering trees permeated the air. My anger ebbed, leaving me emotionally exhausted. I had also learned to hide the letdown after my rage.

"And you're prettier than you were when you were twenty, Jane."

It was a typically creative compliment from me, a cliché that I had regretted as soon as I had spoken it.

She slapped my arm lightly. "None of your blarney, Professor Kelly . . . it's the dim light that deceives you."

"It's not that dim and I don't think so."

Then we both became silent, the memories of the dead past throbbing around us.

I almost reached out for her breast just as I had done in 1948. We were both of us flirting with adultery. More or less.

"The same spot," I murmured.

Then she sighed, and somehow in her seriousness both my anger and the possibility of passion renewed evaporated; all that remained was the scent of lilacs and the jasmine and the crab apple trees.

1948

Leo

The nightmare started after I had turned around at the wrought-iron gate of the Devlin house and started to walk back down the road. I had leaned against the gate for some time, trying to figure out why Jane had been so hostile to my suggestion that we should marry.

I gave up the puzzle and started to plod down the road to the Keenans' house. Jane and I could talk it out on the morrow. Then I heard a fearsome roar behind me; a car was careening at full tilt down the road, seventy miles an hour at least. I dove into the ditch and escaped it by a second or two. As it thundered by I realized that it was the Lasalle.

Damn Phil, I thought, why did he and Jim and Eileen borrow the car without asking me. Thank God I had the brakes fixed.

A half block down the road the car spun off to one side into the ditch and then lurched back onto the road, spewing out a stream of gravel in its wake.

The brakes are gone!

I had checked them, had I not?

Yes, but not on the hill!

The car plunged ahead, twisting and skidding like a tornado racing across a prairie. Then it swerved into the opposite ditch, flew into the air in an almost lazy slow-motion gyration and turned over on its back.

Astonishingly it turned upright again, lunged forward, and crashed with a boom into a huge oak tree. The front door on the driver's side swun open and someone hurled out. I was running down the road as fast as my feet would move; but I seemed to be caught in a swamp of molasses.

For a moment there was no sound, only a total and hollow silence. Then with a dull blast, the car blew up and a dirty orange and black flame consumed it.

I kept on running. Phil was stretched out on the highway unconscious only a few feet from the fire. I grabbed his shoulders and pulled him across the highway.

Then I was aware of the terrible screams in the car—Jim and Eileen. I rushed into the smoke, grabbed the rear handle of the car door with both hands and pulled it open. My hands were pierced with pain and I jumped back.

A second explosion tossed me across the road. The screaming in the car stopped. I was alone with Phil's motionless body, watching the fire and listening to the leaves of the oak tree crackle as the fire consumed them and smelling gasoline and a terrible sweet odor that was probably burning human flesh.

Almost certainly Jim and Eileen. The maid had said they came with Phil to take the car.

Someone else was running down the road, Jane in her pajamas. Pink silk pajamas.

"Leo!"

"I'm here, Jane, in the ditch. Stay away from it!"

She jumped into the ditch next to me. "Are you all right?"

"A few burns. I tried to get the others out."

She stared at the dark, ugly fire.

"Leo," she grabbed me, "Is it the Lasalle?"

"Yeah!" I found that I was choking for breath and that my eyes were stinging from the smoke. I hurt from head to foot.

"Who's that!"

"Phil. I pulled him away from the flames."

"Is he dead?"

"He's still breathing, drunk I think."

"You saved his life!"

"Maybe not."

"Who was screaming?" She clutched my arm.

"I think it was Jim and Eileen."

"No!"

"I'm afraid they're dead, Jane," I said dully, "burned alive. I tried to get them out, but I couldn't get there in time."

"How horrible," she clung to me and sobbed. "It can't be happening."

"Go back to your house and call the fire department and the police and the ambulance. Right away."

"Yes."

And, brave woman that she was, she rushed back to her house.

Phil was breathing all right, indeed he was struggling back into consciousness, more drunk than hurt.

"Take it easy, Phil," I said. "You're all right."

"Am I going to die?"

"No, you're not going to die."

"Who was in the car with you?"

"In the car . . . ? Uh, Jane and . . ."

"No, Jane was not in the car."

He frowned. "You're right," he mumbled.

"Were Jim and Eileen Murray with you?"

He shook his head, unable to concentrate. "Yeah, I guess they were. We were coming back from Warburg, we had some wonderful suds. Really great Wisconsin beer . . ."

Then he passed out again.

Drunk again. And he didn't even ask whether the Murrays were still alive.

Time seemed to stop completely. It might have been minutes or maybe a quarter hour or maybe eternity before the first police car, lights spinning madly rushed down the road. Then, perhaps quickly, perhaps not, a fire truck and an ambulance appeared, then another police car.

The cops and fireman shouted confused orders at one another. There was no fire main this far out from town. But someone had the sense to turn on the hose in the fire truck and pour the water from its auxiliary tank on the blaze. It died quickly.

"Pardon me, sir," I said respectfully to the two men from the ambulance; "there's an injured man over by the ditch."

"How did he get there?" the man yelled at me. "Don't you know that you shouldn't move an injured man, you damn fool!"

"Not even away from a fire?"

"You the driver of this car, kid?" a cop grabbed me. "You know what you've done?"

"No, sir," I said wearily, "I'm not the driver. I saw the car go off the road and rushed up to help. Phil was on the road and I pulled him out of the way."

"If you weren't in the car," he snarled, "how come you're burned?"

"Am I burned?"

"You sure are."

"I tried to get the others out."

"Others? There were others in there? How do you know?"

"I heard them screaming. I pried open the back door," I held up my hands, "but I guess it was too late?"

"Why the back door?"

I knew that the cops were under pressure, but I couldn't figure out why I was being talked to like a criminal. I had probably saved a life.

"It's where I was in the smoke. One of them should have been in the back."

"You saw them?"

"No, sir. There was too much fire to see anything."

"How did you know there was someone in the back seat?"

"I think they were two friends of mine, Jim and Eileen Murray."

"The Murray kids! From the Old Houses! Wow!"

These were county cops, not town cops. They hated all the people in the Old Houses. Hated them and feared them, rural poor hating and fearing urban rich. The kids from the Old Houses were spoiled rich kids and Irish too. They thought they could do whatever they wanted and their parents would bail them out of trouble. Nor was this accusation altogether false. Our crowd was often in trouble with them for drinking and making noise in their jurisdiction outside the village limits. Jane and Packy and I were never caught, but Jim Murray and Phil Clare were not so elusive. Their fathers routinely put in the fix.

"Someday," a county cop called Omer whom we had tormented for years had warned us, "we're going to get one of you rich brats and we're going to get you real good."

When I tried to figure out much later why they abused me the next couple of days, I concluded that I was the perfect target—a kid from the Old Houses but a hanger-on, an outsider without clout. They thought they could vent their rage on me with impunity. Not once did they bother to pause to consider that they had misunderstood what had happened.

In retrospect perhaps I can't blame them.

And there was always the possibility that the fix was in. Not to blame me for the accident. But to give the fixers time for a cover-up.

I hated them and I hated the people in the Old Houses for believing them at first. I hated myself for losing my temper and playing the fool.

"Who's the guy they're putting in the ambulance?"

I noticed for the first time that the cop was Omer.

"Phil Clare."

Would the dumb questions never stop!

"Doctor Clare's son! Holy shit! . . . Well I knew something terrible would happen to those spoiled rich brats."

I was too tired and too sick to poke him in the mouth like I wanted to.

"What's your name kid?"

"Leo Kelly."

"You a renter or something?"

"A visitor at the Keenans' house."

"A hanger-on," he sneered.

"What's your occupation?"

"None . . . no, officer, I'm sorry. I'm a little confused. I am officer candidate in the United States Marine Corps."

"No shit!"

"No shit."

"You sure you're not the driver?"

"How could I be the driver?"

"You got burns. He doesn't." He glanced over at Phil who was babbling in the ambulance.

"He was thrown clear. I tried to save the others after pulling him away from the fire."

"I think you're the driver and you're lying to protect your ass. I don't believe a young punk like you could be a Marine, not a kid who sucks ass around Tom Keenan's."

Tom Keenan, Packy's father, was not the richest man in the Old Houses, but he was the most powerful—and the most dangerous to the county cops and hence the one they feared and hated the most.

"He couldn't have been the driver, officer," Jane, dressed now in white slacks and a navy blue sweater, spoke coolly, "he's been with me all afternoon and evening."

"Who are you?" he asked with a leer, hinting at what we might have been doing.

"I'm Jane Marie Devlin. That house at the foot of the hill belongs to my family. I heard the crash and the explosion and came rushing out. Lee sent me back to call you and the fire department."

"Yeah? Well, we'll talk to you later."

"You'd think we'd done something wrong," I said to her.

"They're as confused as we are, poor men."

The surrealistic nightmare continued, as clear in my mind as I write these words as it was at the time. It took me a couple of years to sort out what happened. Then I began to suspect that by the next morning the fix was in and the cover-up was proceeding. I was a pawn not so much to their hatred as to their need to stall for a day to get the cover-up in place. Now I am convinced that was what was happening. But what was being covered up?

More police cars and fire trucks appeared and a crowd gathered. The local priest bustled up. "I've warned you kids about the way you drive," he said to me.

"I wasn't driving the car. I wasn't in the car. There's two dead kids over there, you pious faker, go give them the last rites."

"Leo!" Jane protested.

He fussed and bothered, and hand on his nostrils, pushed into the smoldering rubble and began to rush through the Latin prayers. Jane and I followed him and answered the "Kyrie" and "Amen" at the proper place. He glanced back at us, annoyed to find cooperators. We even said the "Pater Noster" in Latin with him, slowing him down I fear.

"Where are they?" he demanded. "I don't see any bodies."

A fireman gestured at two lifeless heaps, one in the front seat one in the back seat, incinerated corpses which had once been my two friends.

"Dear God, they smell," said the priest.

I grabbed Jane lest she hit the man.

"Anoint them," she ordered.

He quickly made signs of the cross in oil on the pathetic remnants of two skulls and scurried to his feet, eager to find a place where he could barf with dignity.

"The papal blessing," Jane ordered him.

"What!"

"I said give them the papal blessing with the plenary indulgence that remits all the temporal punishment due to sin."

He mumbled the words and staggered away from the wreck. He vomited across the road.

At least a half dozen people came up to me and bawled me out for my reckless driving.

I had had it with being blamed. I merely turned my back on them.

Every time Jane put the record straight. "He was *not* the driver. He wasn't even in the car. He pulled the driver out and saved his life."

No one seemed persuaded.

Looking back at it as an adult trained in the study of human nature I can see there were two ordinary human prejudices at work that night—the older against the very young and the less affluent against the rich. Envy, resentment, call it what you will. It was the first time I ever encountered such generalized hatred. It shocked me into a silence that would last till the next day when I would explode against it.

"You should see a doctor about those hands," Jane insisted and dragged me over to an ambulance.

I followed numbly, too battered and too overwhelmed by death and hatred to think.

"This man was hurt trying to save those in the car," she told the medic who was in charge. "He should see a doctor."

"You the driver of the car?" he asked contemptuously.

I was about to hit the guy.

"Look, asshole, he's the hero who came down the road after the accident, saved one person's life, and tried to save the other two. Now get him to a doctor."

"Yeah?" the attendant looked at her skeptically and then decided that he didn't want to combat the fire in her eyes. "OK, we'll take him in with the bodies."

Jane was about to protest. Then from out of the crowd roared a screaming demon from hell—Jane's mother, reeking of gin, in curlers, hairnet, and a white satin robe, a tiny wreck of what once had been a beautiful and vivacious woman.

"Jane Marie Devlin, what are you doing out here with all this trash! Don't you care what people will say about us! Go to your room this minute!"

She slapped Jane hard across the face, three or four times. "You are a shameless, stupid girl. You'll disgrace our family with this trash. Who do you think you are?"

She hit her a couple more times.

She and Jane were now the center of attention, the smoking wreck forgotten by the crowd in their astonishment at this exhibition of craziness.

Jane disgrace the family? People will never forget this scene.

"You stupid bitch," Mrs. Devlin bellowed. "I'll teach you to disobey me!"

She hit her again, a vicious blow that brought blood from Jane's lips.

There was no fight left in me. It was all a bad dream anyway. It would soon end. As I watched, Jane, tears flowing down her cheeks, became irresolute, hesitated, looked at me regretfully, and then turned and followed as her mother dragged her away by the ear.

I was astonished at how old Mrs. Devlin was. She could not be older than her late forties, yet she seemed twenty years older, tiny, sparrowlike, wizened—a minute, fearsome alcoholic bird of prey.

So that's what greed does to you. It wasn't a nightmare, it was a movie, a bad movie and she was the wicked witch of the west. Pretty soon the good witch of the east would arrive and save me.

No, she couldn't do that. She just had a baby.

Finally they took me to the hospital with the charred and foul-smelling bodies of my two friends. I had found my rosary and, barely able to hold it in my pain-shattered hands, said the prayers mechanically but still with as much feeling as I still possessed.

The intern at the Warburg hospital who put sulfa on my hands and bandaged me up was like all the others. "You certainly were luckier than your two toasted friends in the other room."

"I guess so."

"You drive the car?"

"I wasn't in the car."

"How come you got burned then?"

"I saw the crash and pulled one of them away from the car. I tried to get to the others. Too late."

"Yeah. Big hero, huh?"

"Not with two of them dead."

He did a pretty good job of fixing me up, though my hands would hurt for weeks.

Joe Miller, a cop from town, where the cops were all friendly and knew all the kids and young people by their first names, drove me back home. Joe was a short, stocky man, solid muscle, with thin blond hair, twinkling gray eyes and a friendly smile. He had a way with the kids, knew all our names and who was in love with whom at any given time. So he didn't harass us and we didn't harass him. Not much anyway.

He could have been no more than thirty at the time.

"It was the old Lasalle, huh? Leo?"

"Yeah. He wasn't supposed to take it, he wasn't supposed to drive it that fast down the hill, he wasn't supposed to be drunk."

"Young Phil drunk again?"

"Out of his mind, the smell of booze on him was stronger than the smell of the fire."

"The brakes on the old jalopy OK?"

"I had them fixed yesterday. Winslow. Picked it up this morning. Got a receipt somewhere. Here in my wallet."

"There'll be a lot of covering up, you can count on that. There always is when the Old Houses are involved. The state and county cops think it was you in the car, no matter how often they're told you weren't in it. They will want to blame someone so they can withstand the pressure that's going to build up for quick explanation. You're not a member of one of the Old House Families—and they haven't figured that Tom Keenan takes care of everyone in his house."

That idea kept me going until well into the next day. With Packy's dad on my side, nothing could go wrong. Then I began to wonder if he was really on my side.

"Why do they want to blame me?"

Joe shook his head patiently. "You don't get it Leo. When something goes wrong in one of the Old Houses someone has to be blamed. It can't be anyone who lives in the House and the county cops know that. Everyone knows that. So the cops find someone to blame or they'll be blamed. It's so much a habit with them that they do it automatically. You're available so they'll blame you, at least until they get more time to figure out another victim."

"They can't get away with blaming me, can they?"

"Nope, because I saw you and that little Devlin kid walking down the road a half hour before it happened. After a while, they'll settle down and listen to me. But you know what the county cops think of us . . . that kid sure is cute."

"Yeah."

"Tom Keenan around?"

"He became a grandfather in Chicago yesterday."

"Think I'll give him a call first thing in the morning. You don't look in such good shape. Maybe ought to get some sleep."

"I'm all right. I have to pray for my friends."

"Maybe if you give me the receipt for the car repair I'll take care of it."

"OK."

"Here," he reached for a notebook as we pulled into the Keenan driveway, "I'll give you a receipt for the receipt, all right?"

"All right."

"You don't mind if I phone Tom?"

I couldn't see why that would be necessary, but if he wanted to make the call that was all right with me.

"Sure."

"Can I give him this receipt?" he waved the torn piece of notebook paper at me. "He can make better use of it than I can."

Fine.

Looking back at those events over the years, I realized how much I owe Joe Miller. He knew exactly what was going to happen and how to put an end to it quickly.

Not quickly enough, but that wasn't his fault.

"You take care now, you hear?" he said as he let me off at the Keenans' gate. "Get some rest."

"Thank you, Officer Miller, I'll try."

I didn't try. Instead I poured myself a full glass of Tom Keenan's Irish whiskey, sat on the front porch of the house, stared glumly at the Lake, and automatically repeated the prayers of the rosary.

I also remembered Jane's haggard, haunted face as she looked longingly over her shoulder at me while her mother dragged her away from the scene of the wreck, an expression that admitted guilt and begged for forgiveness. I would see that same face only once more in thirty years—at Packy's Ordination on May 5, 1954. Her son Philip was a sulky two year old that day, her daughter Brigid a cute little infant in her arms with glowing brown eyes like her mother's.

Their mother wore the same mask of guilt and the same plea for forgiveness.

I was still an emotional mess from my POW experience and was incapable of forgiveness.

For which God forgive me now.

I watched the sun go up, put aside the empty whiskey tumbler, and hiked over to the six-thirty Mass. It was after all Mary's Day in Harvest Time and I had to pray for the repose of two souls. I couldn't believe that I myself was in any jeopardy because I hadn't done anything wrong.

The priest rushed through the service in less than twenty minutes.

My hands were now throbbing with pain and my head ached like I had been hit with a hammer. I wasn't sure I was strong enough to make it back to the house.

I stopped by the wreck and made the sign of the cross.

That's when I heard the State cops talk about the broken brakes and pry open the metal box with the counterfeit money. I guess they didn't see me leaning against the tree.

I stumbled against the gate at the Keenan house. A police car and two county cops were waiting for me.

"Where you been, punk?" the big cop demanded

"At church."

"What you doing at church on a weekday?"

"It's a holy day for Catholics. We're supposed to go to Mass."

"Yeah? Well, it's going to be one hell of a holy day for you. We're taking you in for vehicular homicide. You're going to spend a lot of holy days behind bars. Cuff him, Omer."

"You bet, sheriff!"

The little cop brutally slammed handcuffs on my burned wrists. They both laughed at my screams of pain.

1978

Leo

After she was safely out of sight I walked back to the oak tree into which the Keenans' old Lasalle had crashed thirty years before. The Devlin Old House—the first as you drove in from Warburg, the last as you drove away from the village—was at the top of the hill, the tree at the bottom of the hill and the Keenan's Old House—a delightful Gothic monstrosity was about a half mile beyond the tree. Time had long since covered the jagged gash with newer bark, but the outline was still indelibly imprinted on the tree, a fatal scar. I saw again the eruption of flame, a dirty orange burst of light, and heard the screams from those who were dying inside the car. I heard Jane's screams next to me. I felt the heat of the blast as I pulled Phil away from the car. I remember my suspicion even then that he had escaped and the others had not—Jim and Eileen, as it would turn out. I recalled again the smell of burning human flesh, a smell that touched the terrifying memory of burning bodies in the Korean camp. I shivered as I did when I found out that Packy and his sister Joan were not the victims, a guilty joy that those closest to me had not been fried to a crisp.

I saw again the State Police searching the rubble the next day. I heard them murmuring about faulty brakes. I saw them pry out the metal box from the trunk of the car and watched as the cover fell open and the hundred dollar bills streamed out, thousands of them.

"Counterfeit," one cop had told another.

"Damn good fakes," the other replied ruefully.

"Just like they said."

"Who was it supposed to go to?"

"That's one of those questions we're not supposed to ask. Got it?"

"Got it."

What the hell is going on? I had wondered.

It was no clearer to me in 1978 than it had been in 1948 how the tangled passions in two generations of four families were intricately locked into that charred wreckage. There were mysteries within mysteries, puzzles within puzzles.

I knew then I had to solve the mysteries if I was ever to have a happy life. Now thirty years later I still knew it.

Perhaps I should say three families: the Keenans were only on the margins of the drama.

Maggie Ward Keenan was there the last two summers; on the day of the tragedy she was in Oak Park Hospital admiring her newborn girl child— Maria Margarita. What did Maggie think? She was only a kid herself, no older than Jane or I, but with a tragic past of her own. Even then her keen, discerning gray eyes searched out the truth. I had never asked her what she thought had happened. Maybe she had made some of her usually shrewd guesses even then. I was not sure that I wanted to know about them.

Jane and I were also on the margins. Or so I thought then. I was at the Lake as an outsider who was permitted to watch because I was a friend of Packy Keenan. Jane was also an outsider, a daughter of an unacceptable family, crude, uncultivated "Shanty" Irish. She was permitted to watch the drama because of her beauty and energy, which captivated the glittering and glamorous world, as it seemed to me, of the Old House families.

Yet, somehow, in ways that I still could not comprehend, we were at the center of the drama and the tragedy.

I shuddered and hurried away from the tree. I should never have come back here. Never.

Jane

Ought I to write about Leo in these fragments of my novel?

Maggie says that writing fiction is a way to understand your life. That gave me an excuse to do it. I've always wanted to be a novelist. A very famous and successful one, naturally!

I've made up my mind that I'm going to be one. But first of all I have to figure out how to do it. So I've decided that I'll try to keep a journal first. A journal of the past, as best as I can remember it, and of the present when it happens. A journal and a memoir at the same time. Then when I figure out how it works I'll use the journal and the memoir as a resource for the novel.

Even the two greatest autobiographical novelists of the century lied a lot. I wonder if Lee would be impressed if he knew I had read Proust and Joyce. Well, first I'll be good old Jane and then maybe after that I'll become a womanly version of Marcel or Stephen.

Poor dear men.

It was just a coincidence that I started to write these fragments when I heard he was back in Chicago, right?

Who do I think I'm kidding. "Whom" he'd make me say.

Well, I can't keep Leo T. Kelly out any longer. Not after tonight. He is still *so* cute with his red hair as bright as ever despite the snowflakes in it. Packy said he used to wear a beard. He'd be unbearably sexy in a beard.

I love him so much.

Yet I am thinking again about the sin against the Holy Ghost. Holy Spirit. Whatever. These pills I hold in my hand are that sin. Or so the nuns taught us. Is there sin? Is there a Holy Ghost? And if there is, does He care about me? No sign of that. I've turned Him off.

Good old Jane, they all say. Isn't it wonderful how she holds up. Takes good care of herself. Great figure. Wonderful boobs. Great game of tennis. Great wit. You'd never know what she's been through. Always was a remarkable person. Radiant woman, full of life and laugher. Now that she's gotten rid of Phil finally she should settle down with some nice widower and have a happy life. God knows she's entitled to it.

Bullshit. They don't know what it costs to be good old Jane. I can cry my eyes out here but I don't dare weep and rage in public. I don't dare tell anyone, not even Maggie, that I feel like such a terrible failure because I could not keep my husband for myself. His fault maybe, but still I was inadequate.

For him and for Leo and for my kids.

Why don't I swallow these little brown pills? Afraid of hell? Could it be any worse? Afraid that I'll lose my nerve and that they'll pump out my stomach and I'll look like a fool. Poor Jane, she should talk to someone. Maggie Keenan maybe. Her family was always a little strange. Can you imagine her, with all she has going for her, trying to kill herself.

I don't care what they say about me after I'm dead. I just don't want to have to hear it all while I'm still alive. Lucy won't mind my dying, God knows. She'll be glad to be rid of me. But if I bungle it she'll tell me I have ruined her life by embarrassing her. Again. She was such a cute little tyke. It was so hard to bring her into the world. Where did I go wrong with her? Why does she hate me so much? Will I take the pills tonight? I tell myself at the beginning of the day that this will be my last day, that tomorrow morning I won't have to wake up and face it all, I won't have to play my good old Jane game. Then when the night comes and I take the pills out of the bottle and stare at them I lose my nerve.

Leo Kelly. The bastard. He ran out on me when I needed help. Never once phoned me. Went off to Korea and got himself killed without ever once looking back. Damn fool! I'm going to have to tell him that before the summer is over. Whether I sleep with him or not.

Dear God, why did he show up now? One more guilt to face. I should have married him. The chemistry was there tonight, like it has always been. A wrong word, a wrong touch and we'd be in bed together now. That's all I need. A horny old woman in a final fling. It would not be as final as these pills. And it would definitely be more fun. My damn body was ready for the fun.

I say that I don't want to marry again and I mean it. But, since I began to think about an annulment, my sexual feelings are no longer dormant. I fantasize about seducing men, even poor Packy who adores me. Now I want to seduce Leo so badly I can taste his flesh. Horny old woman.

Anyway, I'll compromise. Only one pill tonight so I can sleep. And I'll avoid Leo tomorrow.

Are You satisfied with that compromise, damn You!

Leo

"I'm sure, Professor Kelly," Maggie Ward Keenan looked up from her knitting, "excuse me, *Provost* Kelly, that you know that a Freudian like me does not believe in coincidences."

Maggie and her brother-in-law Monsignor Patrick James Keenan and I are the same age, a couple of years younger than her husband Judge Jeremias Keenan of the Seventh Circuit. A psychoanalytically oriented psychologist, she grew up in Philadelphia, the rest of us in Chicago. Packy and I were seminary classmates until I decided after the third year at Quigley, the high school seminary, that I lacked the personality necessary to be a priest. We were sitting on the deck of the Keenans' lakeside house, sipping Jameson's on the rocks (*very* slowly) and watching the lightning in the distance intermittently turn the Lake into an incandescent mirror. The Keenans' kids and grandkids were all off somewhere celebrating the beginning of summer.

When Tom and Mary Anne Keenan, Jerry and Packy's parents, had wearied of presiding over the endless festivities at their Old House, they turned it over to Maggie and Jerry and moved into the clean and comfortable—and air conditioned—"coach house" fifty yards down the beach. The younger Keenans had done very little to change the old gothic lady, besides putting screens around the porch facing the Lake and creating a new porch, also with screens, on top of the boathouse, which was called a "deck" to distinguish it from the porch of the house. They had added an intricate and not always adequate air-conditioning system; but they had resisted the temptation to tear down walls and create a few large bedrooms out of the rabbit warren of tiny bedrooms on the third floor (including the former servant quarters at the back of the house facing the road). Nor had they replaced much of the old furniture that thirty years ago had been broken down and now perhaps approached antique status. The kitchen, the most important part of the house for planning parties, had been modernized, the "ballroom" floors resurfaced and the rest of the house had been left pretty much as it was—a home designed for informality and relaxation and not for propriety or even privacy when coming out of one of the showers, which at times worked better than at others times but never very well.

"She didn't know I was up here for the weekend."

Maggie, a small pretty woman, with vast eyes, a quick tongue, and uncanny instincts, sniffed derisively. "No, and it would never occur to her that the good Monsignor here would invite his once-again bachelor friend to the Lake for the Memorial Day weekend. Nor that the aforementioned friend would wander down the same dimly lit street in which the two of you had nuzzled each other in the days of more demanding hormones."

She was wearing a light summer dress, gray as usual, her husband and her brother-in-law were in chinos and knit sport shirts—presumably returned earlier in the evening from golf at the Club. The air was still and now a bit ominous. Clouds had covered the stars. The Lake was tapping light against the foundation of the boathouse as it often did when a storm was in the air. The heavy smell of late spring still hung all around us.

"I haven't noticed hormones diminishing," the Judge, a big handsome man, silver-haired like his brother the Monsignor, with gentle eyes and a slow smile like his wife, observed. He was much like his father, Tom Keenan who with his wife Mary Anne, the adopted parents of my youth, were in Taos with their daughter and her children. Jerry was a little less obscure than his father in the style of communication favored by old time Irish political lawyers. But not much less obscure.

"We're both married," I protested, not too vigorously.

I was well aware—too well because the situation had been explained to me at least three times by Packy—that I had never been able to persuade Emilie to have our marriage validated in church and we were legally divorced. Jane's civil divorce would be final by the middle of the summer and her canonical annulment would probably come through in early autumn. There was not much in the way of civil or canonical obstacle to a little summer romance. But it was useful to pretend that I saw such problems, if only to restrain somewhat the enthusiasm of my friends for getting Jane and Leo together again.

"Your wife has divorced you." Packy, a six-foot-five, silver-haired ex-basketball player and "new-style Monisgnor" (if the term isn't an oxymoron) jabbed a finger at me, being careful not to spill any of his precious Jameson's. "And you were not married in the Church and she's getting an annulment, not that I believe much in those things."

"She doesn't have either a divorce or an annulment yet."

Packy shrugged. "Everyone gets them these days."

"That doesn't seem fair."

"Yes, it does. We now understand that for a marriage to be a sacramental union—one that reflects the union between Jesus and his Church—a certain amount of maturity is required. Marriages that break up generally do so because of immaturity one side or the other . . ."

"Usually both," his sister-in-law interjected.

I didn't bother to argue, as I usually did when priests tried to explain this to me, that the Church had done a bad job explaining its new approach to divorce to the laity.

"And there's no question," Packy continued, "that Phil Clare is about as immature as anyone can be. He's been unfaithful since the beginning . . ."

"From the *very* beginning," Maggie added.

"He walked out on her," Jerry Keenan summed up the argument, "to shack up with some bimbo in Florida. Again. The divorce is final next month."

"She's taken him back before. I don't want to break up a family."

"Why did you come up this weekend if not to explore that possibility of a second summer?"

"I'm not your patient, Margaret Mary Ward Keenan!"

She chuckled. The others roared.

"It's the feast of Pentecost," she argued. "You shouldn't fight the Holy Spirit. She doesn't like it."

"Fove quod est frigidum," Packy said piously.

Warm up what is cold, huh?

"I'm being blamed for not committing adultery with a woman I have not seen for thirty years."

"Minimally for not beginning the process of seduction," Maggie nodded. "Not that the poor woman is likely to resist."

"Poor woman," I exploded, "Jane seems fine to me."

"Good old Jane," Maggie sneered. "Isn't it wonderful how she holds up? Takes such good care of herself. Great figure. Great game of tennis. Always good for laughs. A philandering husband who has destroyed her sense of sexual worth, brutish brothers, a son killed in Korea, a daughter vanished into a commune, a second son who is a Yuppie prig, and a daughter who hates you—and none of it bothers good old Jane."

"It doesn't seem to."

"Some day we will wake up to find that she's ended permanently the burden of being good old Jane."

"Kill herself? Jane's not the kind."

"Don't bet on it! She's had to pretend all her life. Adult children of alcoholics grow weary of pretending. And her alcoholic and avaricious and twisted mother was much worse than her father. She ruled the roost with fear and no one in the family dared to resist her drunken tantrums.

"Good old Jane has assumed responsibility for everyone else since she was a child—including you and the rest of that crowd back in the forties. It was too much even then."

I didn't argue. I had always thought myself that in part Jane's radiance was a cover-up. But she certainly wasn't the kind who might kill herself. Moreover I had already contended with one troubled woman whom I had desperately tried to save. I didn't need another.

"And there's everything that happened back in the forties," I said.

"Ah yes," Maggie Ward nodded solemnly. "That's the problem isn't it?"

"It's not written in the stars," Packy said softly, "that you have to make the same mistakes again."

"I didn't make the mistakes."

"The hell you didn't."

"And I'm not afraid of making them again."

"The hell you're not."

"If you weren't," Maggie intoned the words of solemn judgment, "you would be with her now and not with us."

At the moment it seemed like a pretty good idea.

"There was killing in the summer of 1948," I murmured. "I don't want there to be any killing this summer."

"Do you honestly think you could have stopped it?" Maggie asked.

"Besides, you're not going to be called off to Korea this time," Jerry Keenan added.

"No way out," Packy concluded, sealing my fate. "No way out."

I refilled the drink Jerry had put in my hands when I joined them on the deck and tried to change the subject. "I suppose everyone fantasizes that their youth was a time of shimmering lights and glorious wonders, a special time and a special place and special people. I suppose our crowd wasn't all that much different from any other group of kids growing up in the forties."

"Wrong," said Maggie Ward Keenan, her knitting needles clicking furiously. "Totally wrong. I came as an outsider, as you may remember, and I was immediately impressed with the fact that it was a special place and a special time and special people. Magic. Pure magic."

"What made it magic?" I demanded.

"You and Jane," she responded crisply, "and the luminosity that glowed in everything you touched. You were magic people."

"I find that hard to believe."

"So does she, but you're both wrong. And, Leo Thomas Kelly," Maggie added, "don't you dare deny that you went out looking for her tonight."

"I did *not*."

"Then why did you go to the one place where you were certain to find her if she were looking for you?"

Patrick

Besides my family, they are the two most important people in my life—a woman I have loved since 1941 when she and I were both thirteen and would have hoped to marry if I had not become a priest, and the other a man with whom I shared the anxieties and the playfulness of middle adolescence. Two marvelous human beings, admirable in every way, doomed from the beginning by forces outside of themselves they could not control. I was at the seminary in December of 1950 when the news came of Leo's death. My dad called them and asked them to tell me. The Rector refused. "A lot of young men are dying," was his reply. "We don't do any favors for young men merely because their family has money."

I received the letter from Mom two days later, the day before the Memorial Mass. I begged the Prefect of Discipline to let me attend the Mass. He refused flatly. "We don't even permit anyone to leave the seminary for the funeral of a grandparent or an aunt or uncle. We cannot do it for a mere friend."

"He's not a mere friend," I snapped. "He's the closest friend I ever had."

"You will not bring him back to life by leaving the seminary."

"Why do you have this rule?"

"Cardinal Mundelein wanted it this way. He did not want seminarians riding back and forth to Chicago."

"Cardinal Mundelein has been dead for fifteen years!"

"Thirteen," he corrected me.

My father who had, and has, enormous clout in Church and State did his best, even talking to the Cardinal's secretary on the phone. (The Cardinal, he told me, was probably taking a nap, his favorite pastime.) "If we do it for one," the Monsignor apologized, "we'd have to do it for everyone."

"Then why not do it for everyone?"

"Cardinal Mundelein wanted it this way."

"He's been dead for thirteen years!" Dad had a better sense of time than I did.

"I know," said the young Monsignor sadly.

So I did not see Jane till our two week vacation at the end of January—Cardinal Mundelein did not want seminarians going home at Christmas time. Didn't we have everything we could possibly want at the seminary?

She was incoherent the one time we talked, grief and guilt stricken. And unbearably beautiful.

"I killed him, Packy, I killed him. If I had married him when he wanted to marry me, he'd still be alive."

"Jane, that's not true," I held her in my arms while she sobbed.

"Yes, it is. I betrayed him."

"She's a sponge looking for guilt to absorb," Maggie told me later. "It's the down side of being an Irish matriarch."

Maggie kept me informed by mail of Jane's deterioration until I was summoned to the Rector's office.

"Who is this Maggie person who is writing to you?" he demanded.

"My brother's wife," I replied. I did not volunteer any of the details of our search for Maggie Ward because I knew the Rector would not appreciate the story.[1]

"She has strange ideas about psychology."

"She's a psychologist. Just earned her Ph.D. and is finishing up her internship."

"Doesn't she have any children?" His feigned surprise hinted that perhaps my brother and his wife were practicing birth control.

"Three."

"She belongs at home with her children."

"I'll tell her that you said so."

"You will also dismiss her from your correspondents. We forbid you to receive any further mail from her."

The rector loved the word "dismiss"; he savored it as if it were orgasmic.

"Yes, Monsignor."

I hated the seminary and the fools who ran it. But I wanted to be a priest. Putting up with them for seven years was part of the price you paid.

So it was Mom who wrote that Jane was engaged to Phil Clare and would marry him in early June. They wanted me to be an acolyte at the nuptial mass.

They let us out of the seminary just a week before the wedding.

"Jane," I begged her, "it's too soon. You can't make a decision this important while you're still grieving."

"I'll always grieve." Her face was hard, her voice cold.

"So will we all, but give yourself some time."

I had rehearsed my lines carefully. I would tell her that I loved her and wanted to marry her. Forget Phil Clare who was a shallow creep.

Before I could act out my little drama, she said, "I'm pregnant, Packy. I don't care about anything any more. I wish I were dead. But since I'm not dead, I might as well marry Phil."

I criticize Leo for being indecisive, but I was just as indecisive as he was.

"That she's pregnant doesn't change anything for you, does it?" Maggie asked me later that day—the only time in all the years we've known each other that she hinted she knew about my love for Jane.

"Not really," I replied.

I don't know whether it did or not. Maybe I would not have declared

---

[1] *The Search for Maggie Ward.*

my love even if she had not told me she was pregnant. Or maybe she would have turned me down.

So, as much as I loved her, I decided to hang on at Mundelein.

I knew then that it was the right decision and I still do some of the time. But I feel guilty about Jane. Was there another way I might have saved her?

How does Qoheleth put it, "My mind has carefully observed wisdom and knowledge. So I applied my mind to know wisdom and knowledge and folly. I realized that was a chase after the wind."

So do I chase after the wind when I try to figure out their story. Now for some reason that You alone know, You have decided to give them a second chance. How clever of You. Will it work this time?

I don't buy the idea that it was Leo's "death" in Korea that doomed their love the first time. Nor the auto accident thirty years ago. My charming sister-in-law doesn't buy it either. "Over identification with the internalized mother," she says. "They'll have to resolve that first, Jane more than Leo." Her mother was a real prize. Given a choice between a sneaky, conniving, dishonest way of attaining her goals and a straightforward and direct way, she would invariably choose the former because she enjoyed being sneaky, conniving and dishonest, especially when she was drunk, which was most of the time during the last years of her life.

The mothers were real prizes all right. Both wanted respectability for their family, the battle cry of Irish women for hundreds of years I suppose. Ita Devlin thought she could win it by wealth and power and the right marriages. Delia Kelly thought her kids could earn it by hard work, educational success, professional careers. So she pushed her kids unremittingly when she didn't have to and never quite had time to love them, especially since she feared that, if you spoiled kids with too much love, they wouldn't work hard enough to be successful. Funny thing, they both achieved their goals, only they didn't realize it. And they both died sour and bitter women. Delia's kids are all successful professionals and she died with every one of them hundreds of miles away, having fled her constant harassment. Ita's kids are all respected, affluent even, in their own worlds, respected—which the boys were not thirty years ago. And she died cursing them for their failures.

Dear God, how do You tolerate such tragedy, how do You endure it, why do You permit it?

Delia loved her kids enough so that, despite her constant pushing, they could become mature adults, even Pete whose smartest move was to leave the priesthood where he never belonged in the first place. She didn't love them enough to leave them alone, poor woman.

Ita?

Ah, there's the tragedy. She was a lively and appealing woman, gorgeous in fact, who turned bitter through the years—bitter and alcoholic and maybe evil.

She was always tricky. Dad told me that she was the kind that would stop payment on a forty dollar check for, let us say, a carpenter because it would cost five dollars for the stop-payment and she'd save thirty five dollars because the carpenter wouldn't bother to try to collect from her. It was a cheap petty trick but she got away with it for years before tradesmen would demand payment in full before beginning work for her.

I remember when they bought the house up here in 1940 and invited us over for dinner. Mom and Dad had been told that they were vulgar and corrupt, but were too polite to turn down the invitation. I managed to tag along because I had seen Jane from a distance and wanted to see her up close. Her parents seemed all right to me. He was a big, black-haired Irishman with a genial smile and a warm handshake. He didn't say much because his wife talked all the time, mostly about how much all the finery in the house cost. But he had a warm laugh that made you want to laugh with him.

His wife was very pretty, sexy even, in an intense and diminutive way. She was, it seemed to me, awfully young to have three sons older than I was. She looked like she might be Jane's older sister, and not much older because Jane was already as tall as her mother. She was, as far as I could tell, a lot of fun—energetic, witty, charming. I thought she was tiny in comparison to my tall parents but she filled the house with her laughter and vitality. And what I now realize was, perhaps, unconscious sexual invitation.

Jane paid no attention to me but watched her mother perform with mute adoration. I was permitted to sit at the dinner table, but Jane was banished to the kitchen to eat with the servants. I didn't think that was fair, but I kept my mouth shut and kept my eye on the kitchen door just in case I might get another look at my new love's gorgeous face.

The house was at the top of the hill, the last of the Old Houses. Indeed according to some it was not truly an Old House because the village line ended just beyond our place. It was newer than the others, a sprawling imitation of a nineteenth century Irish or English country house. Looking back, I suppose it suited Ita as a replica of the "Big House" near which she had grown up. Moreover it was decorated and furnished in every detail as a late Georgian country house ought to be furnished. As Dad later said, "Lord Mayo himself would not have lived in any place more Georgian than that."

"Except for that ugly statue of Our Lady of Knock in the master bedroom," I piped up.

"How do you know it's Our Lady of Knock, dear?" my mother asked.

"When no one was looking I checked the inscription on it. Ugly."

My parents laughed somewhat uncertainly. They were never quite sure who or what I was at that age. Neither was I. I figured they'd all be a welcome addition to the summers at the Lake, particularly Jane. I'd heard that her brothers were jerks, but I wasn't afraid of any male my age or a few years older. I was, I told myself proudly, a big tough kid myself with a powerful right punch. The punch was not bad, but I was never very tough.

The brothers were rarely in evidence at the Lake, hidden perhaps as ugly family secrets.

"He doesn't seem like a thug," my mother said as we walked home.

"If he is, Mary Anne," Dad replied, "—and all my information is that if he is—that little woman drives him to it."

"She is certainly lovely and very, well, vivacious."

"A charitable name for it . . . They'll never fit in here," my father said firmly. "Too bad. We could use a few honest crooks instead of those who pretend they're not crooked. But she tries too hard. They just won't make it."

"I suppose not," my mother sighed. "If she talked less about how much things cost, she wouldn't seem so vulgar, especially since everything is in such good taste—even if it is someone else's taste."

"It wouldn't make any difference. Some kinds of vulgarity are accepted up here and some are not. I'm not sure they're any worse than Phil and Iris Clare, but they are vulgar in an acceptable way and the Devlins in an unacceptable way."

"What do you think of Jane, Patrick?" my mother turned to me.

"Who?"

"The daughter."

"I didn't notice her."

They both laughed.

Jane was certainly cute in those days. But there were a lot of pretty girls around and we were too young to distinguish between someone who was pretty and someone who was beautiful and likely to remain so. What fascinated me was her voice, rich like cello music and thick like dark chocolate, a voice that promised fun and affection and happiness. Kind of like Katherine Hepburn's voice, but not so affected—and definitely a Chicago voice, which Hepburn's was not.

In a room full of young people you could distinguish her voice and the matching laugh. Whenever I hear it on the phone, my throat still tightens and my heart beats a little faster.

We invited them back to our house. Jane didn't come. I listened from the porch. I can't remember exactly what was said but it was a very uncomfortable evening. Mrs. Devlin wanted us to sponsor them for the Club. Dad agreed; but they were voted down and then ignored us ever after.

Except Jane who made terrible faces at me in Church on Sunday and grinned happily. Shyly at first, we became friends.

The Devlins moved to our parish sometime after I went to Quigley Seminary in 1942. They had not been accepted in their old parish and they weren't accepted in the stable, affluent River Forest suburb of that era either.

I guess they weren't accepted at any of the places they tried to get in. Or in the parish women's society at which Mrs. Devlin worked so hard.

"Poor thing," my mother would sigh about her.

Jane and I became tennis partners and good friends. She was the first girl I kissed and, she insisted vehemently, perhaps too vehemently, I was the first boy she kissed.

I don't know when Ita Devlin's ambition for respectability turned to rage. I don't know when she determined to win respectability by piling up more wealth and choosing indisputably respectable spouses for her children. I don't know when her heavy drinking turned into alcoholism. I don't know when Jane's adoration for her mother turned to hatred—mixed with fear. But it all started I think that summer of 1941, a few months before the Japs bombed Pearl Harbor.

Thirty-seven years ago. If I'm to believe Maggie, Jane was virtually locked into tragedy even then.

"It might have been different, Pack," she says. "She could have escaped but she didn't have much of a chance."

"Does she this time?" I ask her.

"God knows," she replies.

Through the years my longings for Jane have been mostly romantic. Now they have become hard sexual hungers, mixtures of exquisite erotic fantasies and almost irresistible impulses to tenderness. I want to hold her in my arms and exorcise all the demons that make her such a contentious woman.

I might make a fool out of myself. She might laugh at me. Or be terribly shocked by me. She likes me but I've always been a priest for her, even before I was a priest.

Just the same, I love her and want her. Desperately. Yet I owe her and Leo their second chance.

All my efforts to help would be chasing the wind. I guess I have to leave it in Your hands. Yours and Leo's.

If You don't mind my saying so, he's an unpredictable ally.

So are You as far as that goes.

So I'll give You and Leo one more chance. If it doesn't work out, it will be my turn. Just like it was in 1952.

Leo

The Korean came at me again with the club, a beatific smile on this round, bland face. You will sign now. You will admit war crimes. You will confess your guilt. Then we will take care of your wounds. I refuse. He hits me repeatedly. Then he throws me out in the snow. I grow numb from the cold. I am going to die. He comes back, his head cased in a giant parka and bent against the wind and the falling snow. You will sign now, he demands. I agree.

Then I wake up, shivering from the cold. It is many minutes before I realize that I did not sign. I did not betray my country.

For whatever that is worth today.

Leo

I came home from Korea in late August of 1953 with a stack of medals—including the Navy Cross for my bravery as a prisoner and the Medal of Honor for my rear guard action near the Chosin Reservoir and the X Corps retreat, the latter awarded posthumously because the Defense Department reported me killed in action in that last fire fight. For reasons I do not understand even today, I had ordered my men to fall back while I manned the last machine gun at the bridge as the Chinese swarmed down the road. My men survived. I killed a lot of Chinese. I still dream about them, though not very often any more. They always die silently, peacefully. It is the Koreans in my dreams who torment and try to kill me.

I didn't like the Marines and still don't. I never bought their ideology even when I was a member. I resented the interruption in my carefully nurtured career plans the Korean war created. If you ask me about the Marines I'll tell you how much I hated them. Yet I acted like a gung-ho Marine on that bitter cold December day in 1950. When President Eisenhower gave me the medals after I returned from Korea in 1953, an emaciated, quivering ex-POW, he said I was a real Marine in every respect.

I replied, no sir I'm not. Ike thought it was humility and said, Yes you are, son, yes you are.

Packy says the same character trait leads me to accept administrative and government service roles when all I want to do is my own research. Maybe he's right. Well, there was more than a sense of duty that brought me back to the University last autumn.

I was a time bomb of anger when I came home, angry at the Koreans for what they had done to me, angry at my family and Jane for believing me dead while I was alive and suffering. I knew even then that my rage was irrational. It was not their fault that the Defense Department had made a mistake about me. They had also written off General Hodge, the American commander in Korea, as dead and he was very much alive. I had no claim on Jane. She was within her rights to marry Phil Clare when she thought I was dead. Yet after years of therapy I still blamed her. Only after I married Emilie did I realize that my anger was less at Jane than at myself for losing her.

I don't talk about Korea much. I don't think about it much either. I only dream about it. Maybe less now than I used to. I opposed Vietnam from the beginning, unable to believe that we'd make the same mistake twice in a generation. The dreams were especially bad during those years.

In the first sweet and tender years of our marriage, Emilie tried to reason with me about my dreams, which she could not understand. In later years she said she tired of being kept awake by my guilt over my "war crimes," as she called them, against the people of Korea.

Someone knocks at my door. Laura in her Notre Dame sleep T-shirt. Like me she is staying at the Keenan house for the Memorial Day/Pentecost weekend.

"Are you all right, Daddy?"

"Fine."

"I heard you scream. Korea dreams?"

"I guess . . . when did you get in?"

"An hour or so ago. Jamie Keenan picked me up at O'Hare. I phoned him from Geneva. See you in the morning."

I had persuaded Laura to try a year in Switzerland to get away from the fights between me and her mother. She liked it enough to stay for two years. I was now half hoping that she would want to come to Chicago and live with me. But I certainly did not want to interfere in her life.

Sixteen years old, a high school junior and she flies in from Switzerland, summons a young man to pick her up, and directs him to drive her to the Lake from the airport. Maybe I've done something right in my life.

Leo

In the afternoon after lunch with Laura and the Keenan clan (Packy had returned to his parish for Sunday Mass or Sunday Eucharist as they now call it), dressed in sweatshirt and swim trunks, I abandoned the Indy 500 race on the radio and went walking on the beach in search of Jane. Or more precisely in search of Jane's body, which I wanted to inspect more closely. Having admired her in tennis clothes I wanted now to see her in a swimsuit. I admitted to myself that I was engaging in the lustful activity of a sexually aroused male. I knew that my woman colleagues at the University would say that I was objectifying Jane. Just then, however, I did not much care what they would say.

I was not, I told myself, your ordinary horny male predator. I had been faithful to my wife through our marriage and was still faithful to her, though we were now officially divorced in the eyes of the State and never married in the eyes of the Church, because I respected the marriage bond even when it was terminated—perhaps like Jane in this respect still in part of my soul an "old fashioned Catholic." Moreover there was always available to me, should I choose, the slave market of graduate school women. Though I had never used them, I know all the magic words that make such seductions seem to both the victim and the exploiter not only politically acceptable, but indeed acts of high revolutionary virtue.

However lustful I might be, it was not a new lover I was looking for, but an old one that I had lost.

After Jane and I had beaten Jerry and Maggie that morning, Laura had appeared looking for a match. Jane, to whom I had introduced her had volunteered to be the victim. It was a match to remember—two tall, graceful, women with sizzling serves and wicked backhands competing for each point.

"Poetry in motion," Jerry had said.

"Ballet," I had added.

"You understand the complicated psychological agenda in this match?" Maggie asked.

"They're negotiating about me."

Occasionally it is necessary to put Madame Shrink down.

She sniffed in reply.

Laura finally won 7–5. She and Jane walked off the court arm in arm.

"She's better than I was at her age," Jane told me.

"If Daddy hadn't worn you out, you would have creamed me," my daughter replied modestly.

"So how did the negotiation end?" Maggie whispered in my ear.

"I lost."

She sniffed again.

When I began my stroll down the beach, a northeast wind had swept away the heat and the humidity of the previous night and the weather was now more appropriate for the Memorial Day weekend in middle western America, pleasantly warm but not hot, a promise of summer rather than its reality, a day for lolling on the narrow and artificial sand beach, which the village renewed every year between the Club and the Old Houses. But you did your lolling with a sweatshirt or a jacket handy in case the wind picked up again. While only a few kids dared to dash into the chill waters of the Lake, now whipped into delicate white foam like lingerie lace by the wind, it seemed that everyone in the village, in varying degrees of undress, had crowded together on the beach, absorbing the sun's assurance that summer was indeed at hand, if not quite present among us.

My stroll was a pleasant, not to say triumphant, procession. People I had not seen for a quarter century and more shook my hand and welcomed me back. They congratulated me on my appointment, wondered if I were planning to buy a house in the village, some mentioned the National Academy, as if perhaps it were some kind of Masonic lodge. One or two even wondered what a provost actually does.

"Keeps the natives on the reservation," I would reply enigmatically if not inaccurately.

A few asked if I had seen Jane yet, a presumptuous question given our past, but their memories of that evening thirty years ago were probably vague. I am, after all, a student of human behavior. I should understand that details of such events are promptly forgotten.

I replied honestly enough to the question. She had beaten me at tennis that morning and therefore nothing had really changed. No one mentioned Phil. *Ne nominetur inter nos.*

Only one man, an athletic fellow a few years older than I whose name I did not remember, dared to touch on the key question.

"They never did figure out what happened the night the Murray kids died, did they Leo?"

Probably a lawyer.

"I never heard that they did," I answered, "but I've been away a long time."

"Some folks said it might have been murder."

"I often wondered about that possibility myself. But it was a long time ago."

"No statute on murder."

"So my law faculty tells me."

He nodded sagely. "Well, anyway, good luck on the new job."

"Thanks. I'll need it."

I did not interpret his remark to be an accusation against me. I was, after all, a war hero and a university vice president. We both knew, he had implied with the nod of his head, who might be to blame.

I didn't know. I didn't have the slightest idea.

In all fairness, however, if there had been a murder, I was as legitimate a suspect as anyone else. Indeed I had the receipt to prove that I had seen to fixing the brakes. But I could have loosened them again, could I not? It was my car, after all. Or rather the car I was driving that summer.

The humans who had arrayed themselves on the beach or were strolling along it came in all the ages and sizes and shapes of humankind. I consoled myself for my own loneliness with the thought that one of the advantages of turning fifty was that you could enjoy a much greater variety of womanly attractiveness than when one was twenty, not that when I was twenty young women would have dared to wear the skimpy bikinis that seemed to be standard issue these days.

Maggie, wearing a sweatsuit and massive sunglasses with white rims, glanced up at me from behind her copy of the *New York Times Magazine*. "Find her yet, Doctor Kelly?"

"Played tennis with her this morning, Doctor Keenan."

"So I understand. You'll find her under that large red beach umbrella maybe fifty yards in that direction."

"Where is your good husband?" I replied, ignoring her exercise in mind reading.

She shrugged indifferently. "On the golf course with his good brother . . . I hear you're not having supper with her at the Club tonight."

"In the middle ages they would have burned you as a witch."

"Arguably."

As predicted, Jane was sitting on a deck chair near the red beach umbrella, wearing a skin tight black swimsuit and reading one of the Barchester novels. She was, I decided, well worth objectifying.

"How much money can you earn by reading Anthony Trollope?" I demanded.

"Not much," she closed the book and, finger in her place, rose languidly to her feet, "not unless you are a tenured professor in English literature and they don't earn much do they, Mr. Provost?"

Maggie's comments about Jane's body were an understatement. I sunk deeper into objectification. Before the summer was over, my most exploitive *persona* whispered in the back of my head, you're going to make love with that woman, you're going to take off her clothes and play with her lovely breasts and arouse her hunger and then overwhelm her with your love.

I replied with the silent question of what would happen after that, enough to shut the fantasy down temporarily. To Jane I said aloud, "A provost is committed ex officio to the doctrine that all academics earn too much money and meet too few students."

"A boss in other words . . . Provost Kelly, this is my son Charles and his wife Belinda and my daughter Lucy . . . the Provost, kids, used to hang around here when he was young. People remember him because they never forget redheads, even when they become provosts."

Maggie Keenan had described Charles and Belinda as Yuppie prigs. They were in fact very polite junior partners at an important loop law firm whose name they repeated several times in reverential tones in case I was not aware of its importance. They both wore white slacks, light blue shirts, and dark blue jackets in defiance of the more informal garb of the rest of us—and perhaps in judgment on Jane's maillot. At least Chuck had not worn a tie. They treated me with enormous respect since they were both graduates of our law school and I was therefore a "very important" person in their world, though not as much as if I were the dean of the law school. Lucy, lying on her stomach in the sand, straps detached from her bikini ignored me completely.

The Yuppies returned to the Sunday *Times,* he to the financial section, she to "The Week In Review." Neither would, I was sure, waste their time on anything as frivolous as the Magazine. Lucy rose from the sand and, straps trailing behind her, flounced down the beach in disgust. At me I presumed. Her mother ignored this outburst.

Lucy reminded me of her mother at the same age, though somehow she did not seem knitted together quite as well, more slack and less tautness in her fresh young body.

Jane swept a towel around her shoulders and accompanied me a few steps down the beach. Her head was even with my shoulders, five feet nine inches, a tall and graceful woman with flecks of gray in her tight brown curls. And erect nipples pushing against the fabric of her swimsuit. The result of the wind, I assured myself.

"I think I said last night that you are prettier now than when you were twenty."

"Some sort of Shanty Irish blarney like that." She hunched her shoulders in her old mischief movement.

I noticed that she was wearing a small Celtic cross around her neck, a successor to the brown cloth scapular of three decades ago. Did she know it was a symbol for sexual intercourse, I wondered. Now was not the time to ask.

"Can I revise that comment?"

She tilted her head up at me. "To improve on it?"

"Well, I think so."

She giggled. "Same old imp."

I had never been an imp, had I?

"I'd now rephrase it to read that you are more erotically attractive, far more so in point of fact, than you were thirty years ago."

"Gulp," she laughed, a flush spread over her face and down her chest. "Is that an academic compliment, sort of thing you hear from a professor?"

"Only from a provost . . . I fear my women colleagues would say I was objectifying you."

"You started doing that on the tennis court this morning, which is one of the reasons why it was so easy to beat you. But, like I always say, a little bit of objectification is all right," she giggled again, "in the proper context."

"A beach on the Sunday before Memorial Day, I would argue, is the proper context."

"I agree," she grinned up at me. "Though not the context for a detailed explanation of the content of that evaluation . . . anyway, thank you, I am flattered as my purple complexion shows . . . and isn't it amazing how this man," she gestured with the Trollope novel she was still carrying, "can fill a book with sexual tension without ever explicitly mentioning sex."

My love had matured into a clever and intelligent woman, far more skillful than I was or ever would be at navigating through a pleasant but potentially embarrassing conversation.

"I've often wondered," I joined her game, "whether the tension was as apparent to the readers in his time as it is in our time. Could they think about sex as explicitly as we do?"

She waved the book at me in disbelief. "Now you *are* being a stuffy professor. *Of course* they knew. Maybe even enjoyed the tension more because they didn't have Freud to explain it all away . . . anyway," she turned back, "I'm sorry you can't make supper tonight."

"Another weekend."

"If you're invited."

We both laughed.

She had beaten me in the exchange as she had long ago. I didn't mind.

You will definitely fuck her before the summer is over, my demon reappeared.

Watch your language!

Well, you will.

Maybe.

She was at least ten years older than the mysterious (or seemingly mysterious) women who were part of my real and fantasy life in the early forties at this same lake. Was she more erotically attractive now than they were then?

Impossible question. They were not persons to me in those days, well not fully persons anyway. Bodies with stories attached, tragic stories perhaps. Mysterious stories certainly. Moreover they had not seemed vulnerable as Jane did now. As she always had even as a girl. Unbearably pretty and so fragile, for all her comedy and laughter, a Belleek figurine that you don't want to drop.

I was, nonetheless, very happy with myself when I returned to the Keenans' for a shower and a preprandial drink. My better self, well, my professorial self anyway, told me that I was a male predator, horny from prolonged celibacy, on the prowl for a vulnerable woman. I was, the professor said, more interested in sexual intercourse (he *never* uses the word "fuck") than trying to straighten out a relationship from the past.

Even though I had in a momentary loss of nerve declined her supper invitation, I had, you see, already accepted the charge of my hosts, which I had denied vigorously less than twenty-four hours previously, that I had come to the Lake for Memorial Day to see if my love for Jane Devlin could somehow be revived.

Revived, I said as I buttoned my shirt, it never died.

Leo

"That is you, isn't it, Leo?" The cop got out of the sheriff's red and white car and walked up to me—a short, stocky, bald man with a big grin.

"Joe Miller!"

We shook hands warmly.

"You haven't changed much, Leo."

"Neither have you, Joe. You're sheriff now."

"Yep. Won it fair and square in a lot of elections. Might retire some day soon. So you've come back home, huh?"

I had stopped at the drugstore in the village to buy sunglasses for the ride home. I never remember to bring sunglasses with me to the car.

"Is this home?"

"Only at home you wouldn't get a ticket for parking illegally like you just did."

"Go on, Joe Miller doesn't give tickets to strangers for that."

He threw back his head and laughed. "Well, don't tell too many tourists that, huh?"

"Anyway, this isn't your jurisdiction."

We were walking toward my black Volvo, a provost's kind of car.

"It is now, we combined the village and country police twenty years ago."

"A little late for me."

"Still got that on your mind?" He hitched up his khaki pants. "It was a long time ago. You were the hero after they got things sorted out. You saved that worthless Clare kid's life. You never did come back, not till now."

"Not till now."

"And you're going to stay around?"

"Maybe."

"Well, that's better than a flat-out no."

"What happened back then, Joe?"

"Leave it alone, Leo," he shook his head in warning. "It's over and done with and it was a long time ago."

"Two of my friends were killed."

"I know. But you won't be able to bring them back to life. Or . . ."

"Maybe I have to figure out what happened."

He shook his head again. "Dangerous, Leo. Very dangerous."

"There was a cover-up."

"*Of course* there was a cover-up. A solemn high cover-up. But you can't uncover it now."

"What was the cover-up about, Joe? Do you know?"

He opened the door of my car, which I had not locked. "You'd be surprised how many cars get stolen in this village."

"You didn't answer me, Joe."

"Same old Leo," he grinned and shook hands with me. "Well, I will answer you. I'm not sure. I have my ideas but I'm not sure."

"Will you tell me about those ideas?"

I got into the car and rolled down the window.

"When I'm sure—if I ever am."

"If I find out, will you confirm it for me?"

"Leo, it's not worth it."

"Will you confirm it for me if I figure out whose money it was?"

He watched me somberly.

"Yeah, Leo. I will. I figure we owe you that."

St. John's Night

Four happy days bring in
Another moon. But, O, methinks how slow
The old moon wanes. She lingers my desires
Like to step dame or a dowager
Long withering out a young man's revenue.

W. Shakespeare
A Midsummer Night's Dream

Leo

"Do you know what night it is?" Maggie Ward Keenan relaxes on the bench at the side of the tennis courts and complacently slips her racket into its press.

I have returned to the Lake in the third week of June, in great part because Jane had called me in my office at the University and renewed her invitation for a Sunday night supper.

"Shortest night of the year. St. John's night."

"Also *Midsummer Night*. 'Lovers and madmen have such seething brains, such shaping fantasies, that apprehend more than cool reason ever comprehends. The lunatic, the lover, and the poet are of imagination all compact.'"

"Theseus is a fine one to talk," I respond, showing off my recognition of the quote.

"Precisely, he will that very night take his willing Hippolyta to bed. And arguably enjoy her more than his young friends will enjoy their brides."

I see what is coming.

"Arguably."

"Do you know what St. John's night was like in medieval Europe?"

"I wasn't there."

She sighs impatiently, as she must with recalcitrant clients on her couch.

"Men and women went out into the woods for love—hence Shakespeare's themes in the play. Children to dance and sing. Young people to flirt and court and maybe play with one another's bodies. Serious lovers to experiment at love. Married men and women for the privacy that they did not have in their crowded little homes during the winter cold. The woods would be awash with love. Summer time was and still is, a time for love."

"Not very good Catholics," I say, hoping to turn her away from her lecture to a theological discussion.

"Were they not? Even Joan of Arc told her inquisitors without any sign of guilt or shame that she had sung and danced by the ponds. Old Celtic custom put to Christian use. Catholicism, despite our gloriously reigning Pope, believes in love and in the goodness of the human body."

"So it doesn't mind people fooling around?"

"It doesn't mind human love, Leo, as you very well know. And if passion leads people too far, it was always understood down in the villages and the parishes that the passion itself is not wrong. Rather it hints at how God feels."

"Yes ma'am."

"You should have a Catholic summer, Lee," she nods in agreement with her own dictum.

That line stopped me. Yet I had come back to Chicago with something like tonight's opportunity in mind, had I not?

Not really.

Yes, really.

The University had made cautious inquiries about whether I would want to apply for the provost position. I was assured that of course there was a national search and there could be no guarantee that I would be the final choice. But . . .

That "but" in our business is the all-important word. The tone with which it is said tells you everything. The "but" that I heard said, "if you want it, you can have it."

I asked for time to think it over. Why should I leave Harvard and my research for a thankless job in a city that had too many bad memories for me?

The politician in me if not the political scientist thought the job might be fun, so long as I did not take it too seriously and become pompous. Well, more pompous than I already am.

But I didn't want to go back to Chicago.

Then I met Chuck O'Malley at a meeting of the board of the National Endowment. Chuck was the other redhead in our class, a whimsical little guy who made teachers laugh in spite of themselves. He had always claimed, with his self-deprecating grin, that all he wanted to be was an accountant. Now he was one of the most famous photographers in the world.

"How's herself doing?" I asked him.

He sighed. "More beautiful by the day. It is a terrible thing, Leo Thomas Kelly to be married to a beautiful woman." He grinned. "Until you consider the alternatives."

"Give her my love."

"I will indeed. She has already sent hers and insists that you must come back to Chicago."

"Ah."

"Phil Clare has finally walked out on Jane."

"Indeed."

"His latest lover insists on marriage. Unlike many of the previous occupants of this role, this one has prevailed. The woman I sleep with says that this time Jane will not take him back. She's applying for an annulment."

"So."

"My bed partner adds that it is high time."

"I should think so too."

I wondered why I had not heard from the Keenans about this development. Perhaps they were waiting for matters to become final.

Well, it meant nothing to me. I was not going back to Chicago for Jane Devlin.

No way.

During the lunch break I called my contact at the University and told him that, while I hardly thought I was the man for the job, I would be willing to apply for it.

Right.

Patrick

I decided against spending Sunday afternoon of the longest day of the year at the Lake. It was my turn to take calls at the rectory. While I could have persuaded one of the other priests to trade with me, I really didn't want to have to observe the developing relationship between Leo and Jane.

Someone said once that celibacy is hardest on Sunday afternoons in an empty rectory. Especially in late spring, I would add. Or early summer as it was becoming this weekend.

I am by all accounts a happy and successful priest, pastor of one of the best parishes in the Archdiocese before my silver jubilee, loved by my people, admired by my fellow priests, with prospects of becoming a bishop once our crazy Cardinal dies or is removed.

No one knows, not even Maggie who knows a lot, how tired I am and how I have come to hate my work and hate the assholes who are running the Church, especially the little old self-pitying Pope who messed up the impact of the Vatican Council with his damned birth control encyclical ten years ago and the paranoid sociopath who has pretty well destroyed the Archdiocese. How can you want to be part of an institution led by such pathetic human beings.

They even make the twelve apostles look good.

I'll always be a Catholic, but I no longer think I'll always be a priest. I swore ten years ago when everyone was quitting that I'd never leave the priesthood. Now I'm not so sure. Even if Leo does not marry Jane and even if Jane rejects me, I want out.

Or do I?

Maybe, like my young associate says, all I need is a vacation, a real vacation and not a day now and then at the Lake.

The only hope I see for the Church is in the laypeople. But my own parishioners whom I love most of the time are now driving me up the wall. Some leave the priesthood because they want sex, some because they want companionship, some because they want children. When I leave, if I leave, I'll depart because I want to be left alone.

Leo

"The old place change much, Leo?"

I had arrived early for my dinner at the Clubhouse with Jane—the punctuality my mother had drummed into me sometimes survived the sloppy habits of the professorate—and was looking around in astonishment at a place I had once considered magic.

The Clubhouse, built during the 1890s and remodeled every decade after that except during the Great Depression, was a mix of heavy oak, broad picture windows looking out on the Lake now purple in the late twilight of the shortest night of the year, thick maroon carpets, and sparkling white tablecloths with very old china and silver. As a kid I thought it might be the most glamorous place in the world. Now I realized that its hodgepodge tastelessness lent it a certain amount of quaint charm.

Gone from the ceiling was the great revolving ball at least two feet in diameter made up of scores of mirror tiles that reflected the colored stage lights in the four corners of the room during the formal dances. It was like whirling stars. Probably they used strobe lights now.

The formal dances at the Club were for me the most magical events at this magical place—stars shining above a jet black lake, a gentle breeze blowing in the open windows stirring ever so lightly the curtains and the women's hair, handsome men in summer formals, beautiful women in dresses that revealed a lot of shoulder and breast, big band music, the murmur of soft, cultivated voices and occasional discreet laughter. Magic, pure magic. Or so it seemed to me then.

And the most magical element was Jane, the most beautiful of all the women, the one whom I knew eventually I would love and who would love me.

"It seems to have changed a lot," I said to the older man who was standing next to me, the same one who had spoken to me on the beach about the deaths of my friends. "Or have I romantic memories from my youth?"

He chuckled, a big man, wearing white slacks, a navy blue blazer and a Notre Dame blue and gold tie—elaborate garb for a clubhouse from which all the old formality had been exorcised. His hair was white, his rugged face red, and his shrewd blue eyes missed nothing. I remembered his name, Steve Lanigan. "They mess with it every once in a while, but it's pretty much the same place, a WASP dowager trying to live up to the ideals of elegance of the upper crust of the Irish middle class."

Not a magic fairy castle that it had once seemed.

"I was interested, Steve, in what you said the other day about the accident. It was a long time ago, but . . ."

"But you still want to know what happened to those poor kids. And you know and I know that it wasn't an accident."

"Right."

"Having supper with Jane?"

"Who else?"

"A good idea. Poor woman deserves a real man for a change." He nodded solemnly. "It might be dangerous to dig around too deeply. Not everyone who had reason to want that money is dead, know what I mean?"

"Oh?"

"Mind you," he winked, "I'll not mention any names . . ."

The perennial style of the Irish politician who wants to give the illusion of telling you a secret when he's really not revealing anything.

"But," he went on, "there were certain parties here that needed money a lot, a certain doctor maybe, to protect a certain investment that might have been made."

"And?"

"And there were certain well-connected people who might have been able to put him in touch with those who had the money, know what I mean?"

"Tino Nicola."

"I'll name no names," he winked again. "Everyone knows that the certain doctor was not much of a man and these other parties led him around by the nose, know what I mean?"

"I think so."

"Something went wrong. A lot of money changed hands. Then everyone shut up."

"They did indeed."

"You know what happened to a certain party's family? They went up in smoke."

He meant the Nicolas, Angie's family.

"So I heard."

"And the party is still alive and as dangerous as ever."

"And still connected?"

He nodded. "Still connected. And still crazy and still dangerous. Know what I mean?"

He wasn't telling me anything I didn't know, but he made it sound ominous.

"Sometimes you have to know the truth," I said. "No matter how dangerous it is to find out."

"True enough . . . here comes Janey. Still a lovely woman isn't she? Be careful, Leo."

"I will," I said. "Or at least I'll try to be careful."

Coming across the lobby, Jane was so beautiful that she could drive a man to almost any risk. The magic castle was gone but the fairy princess remained.

Leo

"So what did you mean erotically attractive?" she demanded with a crinkly smile after we had ordered our drinks (two Jameson's, straight up—the way it ought to be consumed, despite the Keenans). "I want further details."

She had swept into the dining room of the Club like an empress on a royal visitation. "Non-smoking as always, Charles. Professor Kelly does not approve of women smoking."

"Men either."

"You have grown more tolerant," she had hunched her shoulders in the familiar expression that accompanied a giggle. "I quit when I was carrying my first baby."

"I promised never to smoke again if I came home alive from Korea."

For a moment we were both silent, realizing that we had stumbled on dangerous rocks.

"Didn't give up the creature?" she asked lightly.

"No way."

She was wearing a white dress, brief at both top and bottom, with a gauze-like pale blue scarf around her shoulders, a cover that merely enhanced the picture.

"A little too cool for this," she had waved her hand dismissively as she pecked me on the cheek, "but I figured it might be the only dinner date I'd have all summer."

"I doubt that," I had said.

"You still don't play golf?" She had waved at the eighteenth green outside the picture windows of the lobby of the Club, a mixture of Decadent Georgian and Scandinavian Pseudo-Modern.

"Only tennis and squash, the latter a professorial sport. I guess I could play golf with this hand," I had lifted my left hand, the last two fingers of which had been left in Korea. "But it didn't seem worth the effort."

"I'm sorry, Lee," she had been terribly flustered. "I guess I forgot."

"No problem, Jane. Most people don't notice. I guess I cover up pretty well. I figure that it's a nice reminder for me of how lucky I was."

"Lucky?"

"I didn't leave any more of me in Korea."

She had been silent while I had ordered our drinks and then, confidence restored, she demanded an explanation for my ill-advised comment on the beach a couple of weeks ago.

"I'm sorry for that comment," I said, truly regretting it at that moment. "It sort of slipped out."

"Nothing has ever just sort of slipped out of your mouth, Leo Thomas Kelly. We both know that . . . did you mean that I looked like I'd be a good fuck?"

I winced as I always did at such candid obscenity. "I don't doubt that for a moment, Jane. But . . ."

"But professors don't put things quite that way . . . oh, thank you very much, Joseph. That's right. No ice. Professors don't drink ice in their Irish whiskey."

"What I meant," I fell back on language, the last refuge of the scoundrel if he happens to be a professor, "was that you are pure delight to the aging male eye because you suggest that pleasure and joy of every sort need never end."

"That sounds almost religious," she peered at me suspiciously, "like I'm grace or something."

"Surely that," I toasted her. "Surely that. Besides you have wonderful breasts."

"Genetic luck," she held her tumbler cautiously, not ready to return the toast but pleasantly flushed just the same.

"The total person is not luck."

"OK," she laughed and raised her glass, "to grace."

"Capital G or small g?"

"Both." She swallowed a large draft of Jameson's and choked on it. "See what you do to me with your terrible dirty talk!"

"I'm afraid that I've never been very good at saying the right things."

"Huh?" She put down her tumbler. "You gotta be kidding. You were always clever with words, an accomplished flatterer even in fifth grade."

"I was a shy quiet boy whom no one ever noticed."

"You really believe that, don't you?" She was examining my face carefully.

"I don't think there's any doubt about that."

"I won't argue," she waved away my self-image as patent foolishness, "except to say that you are wrong. Everyone thought you'd be a good priest because you were such a good talker. And how could we not notice all that red hair. I'd say that you had a terminal case of Blarney then and now. Erotically appealing, indeed!"

I felt my face grow warm. She had selectively misperceived the past. I had become articulate only in the classroom and only after my marriage to Emilie. Yet her admiration for me was both pleasing and acutely embarrassing.

I was in the swamp in which I often find myself with women, both attracted by the mysterious cave they offer (metaphorically as well as literally) and also frightened of it. I talk a good line but they scare the hell out of me.

It does not follow that I am inadequate at lovemaking. Whatever went wrong in our marriage was not in that area, not at first. Rather the problem is that I don't know how to combine firmness and tenderness in the appropriate amounts, a rare art at which, in my observation, most men are not very good and in the exercise of which most women are very demanding.

So, naturally enough, I suppose, Jane and I talked not of love nor of sex but of our marriages. While I was legally divorced and she was not, not yet at any rate, she was more definite that her marriage was finished.

"Phil's not a bad man," she said, with a shake of her brown curly hair, "but he's an incurable chaser. He simply can't stop it even when he tries. If I know Phil, he's cheating on her already. The next step is to want to come back to me. But it's too late for that."

Jane's tone, as she recounted the story of a quarter century and more of marriage to Phil Clare, was composed, matter-of-fact, as if she were narrating someone else's problem. She displayed no anger, only a mild impatience with her husband's infidelities. I began to suspect that Maggie Keenan's diagnosis of the high costs of Jane's living up to her own image might be valid. I could not, however, picture this tall, graceful, self-possessed woman ending her own life. Quite the contrary, her good humor now seemed to be alloyed by tragedy transcended. She was not only an attractive woman, I decided, but an interesting one.

However, her glow faded a little as she talked about her two lost children. She was no longer the vivacious woman who had so charmed my daughter. Even the most radiant, as I had preached at Laura, suffer tragedy.

(Laura: "You should have seen her in the shower. She's simply gorgeous, Daddy. And sweet too. You shouldn't let her get away."

Me: "It sounds like you're objectifying her."

Laura: "No way! And you know what I mean!")

Young Phil had been killed by a Vietcong mine the second day he was in Vietnam. Brigid had been in and out of communes and drug treatment centers. Jane had not heard from her for two years and was not even sure that she was still alive.

"Charley and Lin are dull Yuppies, I know," she smiled affectionately about them, "and I suppose they'll eventually get around to providing me with a grandchild or two. And Lucy is a moody teen. But, dear God, Leo, they're relatively normal. Phil wanted to be a hero like he thought his father was in the Big War and Bridge wanted to save humanity."

"And neither succeeded?"

For a moment a far-away look—pain, grief, unfinished mourning—lingered in her deep brown eyes.

"I still love them both. I'll always miss them." The sadness vanished from her eyes. "But life goes on and I treasure my normal children."

Maggie, I told myself, is wrong. This lovely woman has managed to put it all together—a neat balance of vitality and a sense of the tragic.

We returned to the subject of our marriages.

She was, Jane insisted, a traditional Catholic on the subject of marriage. If you had made a mistake, you learn to live with it, make the best of it, stay together for the sake of your kids and your immortal soul, hope that your spouse will finally grow up. Maybe that was a mistake. Maybe if she had threatened to walk out on Phil after the first time he would have shaped up. Maybe she had not been altogether fair to him.

He was, she repeated, not a bad man. He had just never grown up. She had to deal with all the tragedies, Philip's death in Vietnam, Brigid's rebellion and disappearance into a commune, the death of his parents, and the joys too, like Sister Norine's wonderful work in Belize. She had to go to the wakes and funerals because he was afraid of breaking down at them or so he said. He was afraid of aging. He wanted to be perpetually young; he dyed his hair, wore cosmetics, went on radical diets and then put the weight back on again. He did not work. He never really had worked, probably didn't know how. Even when he had his own firm, he rarely did anything, but left the work to his partners who probably robbed him blind. Her brothers Mickie and Dickie paid him a handsome salary from the Devlin firm after his own business had gone under and would do so forever. A sad and unhappy man, but not a bad man, not deliberately bad. Just a hurt little boy.

"Peter Pan syndrome," I murmured.

"And I was his always patient and sympathetic Wendy . . . I don't think I was all that bad in bed . . . whenever he slept with me, which wasn't often. I think he was probably more interested in conquests than sex as such."

This time he had gone one step too far. He had actually filed for divorce. All right, she had said, if he wanted to be free of her because his "Sheri" wanted to be wife as well as mistress, fine, she would accept her own freedom. Now as the divorce was almost final, his lawyers were hinting at reconciliation. He and Sheri had probably discovered that he did not have all that much money. He had run through his vast inheritance. He couldn't touch her own investments as well as her very prosperous travel agency, not even the house in Lake Forest or the one here at the Lake. There were rumors of a government investigation of his involvement in some kind of inside information scandal in his defunct brokerage firm. If there were anything like that, he certainly hadn't made any money from it. His salary from her brothers was not nearly enough to sustain his life-style. So he wanted her to support him—and probably Sheri too. No way.

Sure?

She hesitated. Not absolutely. Lucy was on her father's side for a while. Jane was not sure where she is now. Mickie and Dickie wanted a reconciliation for the good of the family, by which they meant the family firm. Monsignor O'Malley, the pastor emeritus of their parish, the priest who had officiated at their wedding, had pleaded with tears in his eyes for "Christ-like" forgiveness. But she had enjoyed a few months of emotional freedom after twenty-seven years; she did not want to return to the old burdens.

"Judgment, please?" She smiled appealingly at me, vulnerable to my response.

"Huh?"

"What do you think of my story?"

"Why should it matter what I think?"

"It does. Please."

"I don't think it was ever a real marriage. You were married. He wasn't."

"That's what my priest says. He says I have a perfect case for an annulment. I don't know that I should bother. I won't marry again. I've tried it once and that's enough."

"You will be pursued avidly."

"That won't be new," she lifted a bare shoulder from which the blue gauze had slipped. "I'm pretty good at saying no."

"Who's your priest?"

Laughter and the old smile bounced back. "You shouldn't have to ask."

"Pack?"

"Who else?" She blushed.

"He agrees that you won't marry again?"

"I told you I was an old-fashioned Catholic . . . now am I going to hear your story?"

I could hardly wait to tell her. Yet I was frightened at the prospect of revealing my failures. She had persevered with a spoiled little boy. I had lost a brilliant and gorgeous adult woman and I still wasn't sure how.

I did not begin with our first romp in my office. I was contemptuous of my colleagues who seduced attractive graduate students and I did not want to seem to be guilty of the same offense myself. In retrospect maybe I was not the seducer. She did take off her own blouse after all.

On the other hand I had felt proud, immensely proud of my conquest. Emilie was the most beautiful graduate student any of us at Stanford had ever seen. I'm sure others had tried before me to capture her in the slave market that graduate schools have become. I won the prize, beautiful and brilliant, the brightest and most promising in her cohort—even if she was having trouble finishing her dissertation, a long, complicated theoretical comparison of Pareto and Gamasci.

Good Catholic that I was, I had made up my mind from the beginning that I would marry her. Emilie LeBeau was the descendent of French Canadian dirt farmers who had migrated to New England to work in the mills. Less devout than they or maybe not so scrupulous, she had no objection to marriage though she seemed less compulsive about it than I was—though she adamantly refused a Church marriage. "I'm finished with all that religion shit."

Marriage did not help her to make progress on her dissertation. Since I was an empiricist busy developing the mathematical model for explaining election results (what else would you expect from an Irish Catholic with

Chicago roots?), I was not much help to her. Indeed like most theorists she had little respect for my nose-counting, number-crunching work.

After I had put myself back together again in the middle fifties, my academic career was rapid, if not quite brilliant. I did my doctorate at the University, moved on to Stanford, and obtained tenure at the end of my first three-year term. The profession marked me for great things. It never occurred to me that my wife, with more native intelligence than I possessed, would consider me a competitor or envy my success.

I know better now, but the competitive spouse was a rarity in the early sixties. Even if I had understood the problem I don't know what I could have done, but I have the uncomfortable guilt that there must have been something I should have done, long before it was too late.

My surges of anger continued through those years, but I kept them between myself and whoever my therapist was at the time. I never turned it on Emilie. Maybe I failed her because I spent so much emotional energy containing my anger.

I did not tell Jane about my anger.

She finally ended, not finished, the dissertation, and gave it to me, triumphant in what she thought was a brilliant Marxist analysis (Marxism was just becoming popular again, especially in the Bay Area) and impatient with my less than enthusiastic response. It was, though I did not tell her, so much garbage. But we managed to move it through the department. I took an appointment at Santa Barbara, full professor for which I would have had to wait a couple of more years at Stanford, because they were willing to hire her as an assistant professor.

She had six years to produce a book and a couple of articles, a relatively easy task it had seemed to me. Instead she produced Laura in 1962, as adorable a little girl child as one could have imagined.

Laura, however, became the scapegoat for her mother's academic failures. Because of Laura Santa Barbara gave her another year to publish something, but her seven years ran out. At the end of the sixties she had published one article in an unimportant European journal, submitted several more to other journals (none really prominent), and written most of a book that had yet to find an academic press that was interested in seeing the rest of it.

In the meantime I was flying back and forth to Washington to consult with the Hubert Humphrey campaign. (He did not follow my advice, backed up by data, to disown the war. If he had, Richard Nixon would never have been president and we would have a much different country than we do today). I was aware of her resentment but didn't take it seriously. I also realized that I was playing the role of mother as well as father to Laura but didn't know how to respond to that problem either.

I learned later of the rumors that she was having affairs with my faculty colleagues. To this day I don't know whether the rumors were true. They probably were.

Santa Barbara couldn't possibly give her tenure under the circumstances, whatever promises her lovers, should there have been such, might have made. They offered her a five year appointment as a lecturer, which she turned down with hysterical tears.

So we went to Brandeis where she did get tenure as part of the package deal for me. I accepted the job only for her sake, but she didn't seem grateful. Looking back on it, I should not have expected gratitude. I should have been sensitive to the problem of a woman who knows her university wants her only as a means to win her husband. I don't know that I should have also been aware that my success made me (and Laura) the problem. Emilie had begun to feel that her only identity was as Leo Kelly's wife. My move to Harvard four years ago didn't help, although our home in Chestnut Hill was closer to Waltham than to Cambridge. Fool that I was, I thought it might be better if we were at different schools.

I wrote position papers for the Carter campaign and tried to persuade the rednecks around him to reach out to the Catholic "ethnics." My only success was in a spate of late campaign ads in which Catholic Poles endorsed him. No wonder they defeated the man who had pardoned Richard Nixon by a little more than two percentage points. I was offered a State Department post but turned it down because I felt I had to stay with Emilie and Laura. I did make a couple of trips for the Carter crowd to international monetary conferences (a sideline I had picked up) but accomplished nothing.

As I look back on our marriage I am aware that I repressed the signs and the symptoms of trouble as well as my rage. I did not know what to do about them and, dummy that I was, I didn't understand that in her mind I had become the problem. As Packy would say later, "at her age in life, many bright and well-educated women begin to think they have wasted their talents. They look around for someone to blame and their husband is the first available target."

"That doesn't mean he's not to blame."

"Nor does it prove that he is to blame."

It was after Brandeis had denied her promotion to full professor for the second time (and this time I heard early the rumors about her sleeping around but ignored them) that she told me in a furious rampage that she wanted to be her own person and that she was leaving me.

Fool that I was, I was utterly astonished. I begged her to reconsider. She wailed that she was tired of everyone dismissing her as "Leo Kelly's wife" and stormed out of our house, leaving Laura, who was then going on fourteen, to me.

I begged her to come back, to try to save the marriage, to find a marriage counselor.

Emilie was a very confused woman at the time. She did come back (and fought constantly with Laura) and we did go to a marriage counselor, one that Emilie had chosen. I later learned that the counselor was a radical feminist who specialized in attacking husbands. I put up with her because I thought there was still some chance of saving the marriage.

As I recount this story—which I told as best I could to Jane—I realize that it probably sounds self-serving despite my efforts to describe our marriage objectively. Perhaps I did even turn Laura against her mother as both Emilie and the therapist claimed. I don't know. I know that I tried desperately to save the marriage and that I searched my past as honestly as I could to see whether I had contributed to Emilie's career failure.

That exercise was counter-productive and quickly labeled as "self-serving." I was not faulted for my lack of support for her, I was faulted for my own success. I didn't know there was a race between Emilie and me and that I had exploited her to win it. I still don't know that. I torment myself with efforts to understand what went wrong, where I failed, how I could have sustained her.

"Forget it," Packy told me on the phone. "You did your best according to your own lights. You can't undo the past even if you made a lot of mistakes. Hasn't she made it clear to you that she doesn't want the mistakes undone? She does not want to be married to you any more, isn't that clear?"

"She may change her mind."

"Not likely. Hasn't she moved in with a sociologist from Brandeis?"

"A man who hasn't published an article in ten years."

"You got it."

As I said before it was my election to the National Academy two years ago that led to final rupture of our marriage. I even offered to turn it down if she wouldn't move out, an offer that both she and the therapist loudly scorned.

One of the minor reasons for coming back to Chicago was that she became violently angry whenever we encountered one another at academic events in the Boston area.

"Will you *please* stop following me around!" she would wail and burst into hysterical tears.

Pack is right. The marriage is dead. I failed as a husband. I wish I could locate the precise time when it started to go wrong. I wonder now if the beginning of the end was that hot spring day in my office at Stanford when she took off her blouse. I guess I'll never know for sure.

Not in this life.

"Verdict?" I asked Jane when I had finished my story, as sanitized as I could make it.

"The poor woman," she replied, tears in her warm brown eyes.

"Oh?"

"She's a farmer's kid whose parents probably couldn't speak English. She discovers that she's bright and slips into the academic world where she doesn't really belong. She's terrified of failure and marries a husband who will protect her from failure. He doesn't, because finally he can't; naturally she blames him for not being omnipotent like she thought he was."

"Maybe you should be the social scientist."

"Just common sense," she dabbed at her eyes. "I feel so sorry for her even if she is a stupid little fool."

"And me?"

"*You?*"

"The verdict on me?"

"Oh, not guilty on all counts," she patted my hand. "What else? Now let's order supper."

Leo

"That isn't big band music is it?" I asked my date.

"Sure it is," she grinned. "Glen Miller. 'Moonlight Serenade.' Romantic enough for you? Lots of old folks here at the Club on weekends. Want to dance?"

"Wouldn't it create great scandal?"

"Probably." She stood up and took my hand. "So what? Everyone knows that you academics don't have any morals anyway . . . you're as good a dancer as you ever were." She buried her head against my shoulder.

"I was never a good dancer, Jane."

She looked up in surprise. "Sure you were."

All right, you don't argue.

We danced through three numbers, close together like young lovers. Like the young lovers we had been the last time we had danced at the Club in 1948. Angie had been my date that night; Jane was Phil's.

She was still dazzling, lines on her face and neck notwithstanding. She smelled of spring, lilacs and orange blossoms.

"Did I say erotically attractive?"

"Um-hum."

"Can I add to that observation?"

"Um-hum."

"I almost said 'Intellectually interesting' . . ."

"That would be nice."

"But that sounds too professorial."

"Um-hum."

"Though it's certainly true . . . so I'll say 'an utterly fascinating woman.' Is that acceptable?"

That was, I suppose, seduction talk, though I meant it as absolute truth.

"Um-HUM!" She drew me closer, her breasts firm against my chest and pressed her head more vigorously on my shoulder. "You're as sweet as you ever were."

I did not dare contest her statement. But no one had ever thought me sweet in my youth. Shy, silent, morose perhaps, at least on occasion. Mean and stubborn surely. But hardly sweet.

I plunged recklessly ahead with a professorial pontification. "A woman really doesn't begin to be interesting till she's forty. Not that it necessarily happens even then. I hasten to add that most men don't become interesting either."

She withdrew her head from my shoulder and looked at me suspiciously. "What do you mean?"

"By that time," I raved on, "a woman is confident of her sexual appeal and skill, she's had enough experience to understand what life is about and how really inferior in a charming sort of way men are. She knows how to manipulate a man so his only response to her is obedient adoration. She has faced a certain amount of tragedy and comprehends the dark dimensions of life. Source of life that she is, however, she knows that the power within her is stronger than death . . . oh, yes, she's very interesting and will only become more so."

The band stopped playing. We stood on the floor hand in hand waiting for the next number.

"I'm not sure," she studied me intently, "whether that's wisdom or bullshit."

"A bit of both. You see, however, how the conquest of a woman like that is one of the world's greatest challenges."

The band began again and we returned to the dance.

" 'Blue of the Evening,' 1942," she murmured. "You speak from experience about conquest of such a woman?"

"Certainly not. Professors usually don't."

"It's an experience you'd like to have?"

"In theory. In practice such an opportunity would scare the living daylights out of me."

"I doubt it," she sniffed impatiently. "What about those beautiful women we knew around here when we were growing up. How many of them became interesting?"

"Packy's mom, for sure. Iris Clare. Elizabetta Nicola too, some of the time."

"Like Angie is now?"

"So I'm told."

The memory of the four exquisite matrons of those days reduced us to silence—and perhaps some mourning—for the rest of our dance.

Later, when we were about to leave the Club, she handed me the keys to her Mercedes. "You'd better drive."

I had walked over to the Club, expecting that she would drive me back to the Keenans' after supper.

"You seem perfectly sober to me."

"Two drinks before I came here, one at supper, half a bottle of wine. You drive."

I'd had needed only one drink to work up my nerve.

"All right."

"I'm not a drunk, not like my parents or like my brothers used to be."

"I wouldn't think that for a moment."

In the Mercedes she asked softly, "Do you still think Phil was responsible for the death of those poor kids?"

There it was, the haunting question, the monumental barrier between us, much higher and thicker than my caution and her disillusion with marriage.

Eileen and Jim Murray were "kids" now—what they had been when they died, part of another generation.

"Not any more," I said. "I agree with you. There is no harm in him. He just never grew up."

In saying that, I had come to believe it. Even the night before I would not have been so positive. Later that summer I would ask myself the question again.

During our ride from the Club back to Lake Shore Drive I told her Maggie's theory about St. John's night, giving the latter a due reference as befits someone with academic ethics—and a prudent judgment that Jane might have heard the lecture already. I left out any hints that it ought to be Catholic summer *for us*.

"I've heard that kind of stuff from her too," she said. "But it's true isn't it? We kind of knew all along didn't we that love was all right and our bodies were all right? I mean with all those ceremonies—First Communion and May Crowning and Midnight Mass and Ash Wednesday and Candlemas day, all those things—we had to believe that creation was good."

"Too bad they didn't tell us."

She thought for a moment. "Maybe they were afraid we'd enjoy love too much."

"If man and woman are supposed to be God for one another, maybe we would have."

"It's a shame all right, Lee. Our lives might have been different. I don't mean yours and mine, I mean everyone's."

"Yeah."

For the rest of the ride we were silent, each of us perhaps living with the memories of our failures—to one another and to those we had married. We were two lonely people, mournful about our mistakes, hungry for affection, mindful of the passion that had once existed between us, conscious of our mortality. Vulnerable, anxious, attracted, frightened. Moreover her inhibitions, if there were any, had been relaxed by the "drink taken" as the Irish would have said. The wind had died, the night air was soft and gentle. The smell of summer still filled the night—or was it only her perfume? Her children had all returned to the city because of the storm that was promised that evening.

I could have her. Now. Tonight. After thirty years of waiting. What would be more natural than that we should fall into each other's arms? Faint heart never won fair lady. I am congenitally fainthearted.

"Are you sure you can walk down the road to the Keenans'?"

We were standing, hesitant and awkward, both wondering what would come next, at the door to her house, the old "Devlin House," the same granite "Old House" just beyond the edge of the village from whose yard I had been banned thirty years before. Now I had been permitted to drive through the open gate without comment. In the dim light of the lamp over her back door I noted banks of white peonies around the foundation of the house and a couple of blooming crab apple trees.

"I need the exercise and it's a lovely night." I almost added that it was a night as soft as a lover's touch. That would have done it for both of us.

"It is that." She hesitated, key to her house in hand. "Were you looking for me the night we met a couple of weeks ago?"

"Of course . . . and you?"

She laughed. "Naturally."

I put my hands on her shoulders, disturbing the symbolic scarf. "You and I will have many things we must discuss before this summer is over, Jane."

I rested my thumbs on the tops of her breasts.

"I know that." Her eyes filled with tears and she sagged under my hands. "I know that, Lee."

We kissed each other, at first affectionately, not passionately, and then our lips lingered together, as if savoring a familiar and intoxicating taste. She was crying and I was close to it.

She broke away and slipped into the house, closing the door softly.

If she had invited me into the house at that moment, I would have accepted the invitation.

She did not, so I walked down the road to the Keenans'.

As I say, congenitally fainthearted.

Leo

The next day I did what professors do best, I analyzed. A good analysis is usually at least as satisfying as action, sometimes more so.

The storms that had threatened the night before had finally arrived and chased summer away. The sun ventured out of the clouds on occasion, looked at the gray, angry Lake, and darted away for its own protection. The longest day of the year dawned cold and gray. So much for Maggie Ward Keenan and her Catholic summer of warmth and love. I woke up with a mild buzz from the drink and I suppose from the woman. So I went down to the "ballroom" (under usual circumstances a comfortable parlor with TV, stereo, and a gorgeous view of the Lake), glanced at the surging gray waters, and opened the previous year's minutes of faculty senate meetings— best cure for insomnia since sheep—and began to analyze, not the faculty senate, but what had happened in the previous twenty-four hours.

I was the provost of a very great University. In many ways, as we would say, the best in the country, and I must therefore as a matter of strict obligation create around myself an atmosphere consonant with that role. She had not, as far as I knew, even graduated from college. She administered a travel agency of all things. I was sure it was a high quality travel agency, but still she would feel very ill at ease in the culture of the High Academy with its brilliant conversations and its profound and often allusive knowledge. Wouldn't she?

My daughter bounded into the parlor of the Keenan house where I was alone with faculty senate and my memories. She was dressed in yellow oilskins from head to toe.

"Sensational day for sailing," she pirouetted around the room. "Totally sensational."

"A little dangerous?"

"Twelve knot winds? Don't be silly, Daddy. It's perfect."

"So long as you're careful."

Pompous professor discharging parental responsibilities.

"Did you have a nice time with that cute Mrs. Clare last night?"

A question that pretended to be innocent when it was anything but innocent.

"I wouldn't call her cute."

"I would . . . well, how did it go?"

"Not very far."

"*Daddy!*"

"Actually, we had a very nice time."

"And?"

"And nothing."

"I heard you danced with her."

"Your pompous old father dance with a beautiful woman? Slander! I bet they told you it was totally old music. Gruesome."

"Huh . . ." My child was not amused, definitely not. "I saw Mrs. Clare again today. She was out running. She's really dazzling, Daddy. Sweet and gorgeous and like totally intelligent."

"Yes, I know."

"I mean really attractive." She stopped and hovered over me, shedding her oilskins in the process.

"Laura, you sound like you're trying to make me a voyeur in the woman's locker room at the Club."

She threw back her head and chortled gleefully. "*Daddy!* You are like *totally funny!*"

"If there is one thing, my dear, that a provost of a great university cannot be, it is even partially funny."

She thought that was pretty funny too.

"*Well,* she does have wonderful boobs!"

"I need not enter in fantasy a woman's shower room to make that determination."

More laughter, slightly ribald, from my sophisticated sixteen year old.

Then she became serious. "I've met her daughter, you know, Lucianne."

"Yes."

"I kind of like her."

"I would have described her as a brat."

"*All* teenagers are brats, some of the time."

"*D'accord* as they say in the language of your school."

I would not divert her from her assessment of the Clare family by my feeble attempts at wit.

"She's had a hard time."

"So have lots of kids."

"We got along all right. She kind of likes me too."

I wondered where this line of chatter was going. It turned out that it wasn't going anywhere. Whatever point she had intended to make, she had made.

"Do you ever notice Mrs. Clare's eyes, Daddy?" She sat down next to me, hands on her knees.

"Brown in color, I believe."

"You know, she's always so energetic and enthusiastic, like you know someone bubbling with joy?"

"Always was that way, as best as I can recall."

"Until you look at her eyes. Daddy, they are so sad, the saddest eyes I've ever seen."

I thought my heart would break. Exit analyst, re-enter lover.

"She's had a hard life, Laura."

"Yeah, I know." My daughter rose and drifted vaguely toward the door. "Almost as hard as yours."

I waited till I heard her opening the fridge in the kitchen and reached for the phone book. I punched in Jane's number, but there was no answer. I tried to phone her intermittently the rest of the day until I finally gave up on the weather and on the phone and, bidding the Keenans good-bye, drove back to my apartment near the University. I took the route through Warburg, which would bring me by Jane's house at the end of the hill. I even stopped and peered through the gate, hoping she might materialize. Neither she nor her car were in the driveway.

I had missed an opportunity.

An opportunity for what?

Precise object discreetly unspecified.

But the summer, our gratuitous second summer, our warm and sunny Catholic summer in which we were to become sacraments of God for each other, was young and there would be other opportunities, would there not?

Jane

Head still aches. Not as bad. Maybe I'll sit in the whirlpool and imagine that he's with me. Stop that! I didn't see him while I was running. Met his daughter. Very friendly kid. She was with Lucy. They seem to get along. Strange combination. He hasn't called. I won't call him. Well, not today anyway. I suppose he will have to figure out what happened when poor Jim and Eileen died. Knowing him, he'll want to put everything in order. I won't let him get away this time like I did last time. Even if I have to be shameless. What did the people at the Club think of us last night? I bet the tongues were wagging! And the phones ringing this morning. A lot of them probably thought we looked cute and it was high time I had a little fun. My brothers will call me before the day is over. They'll be real careful because they'll remember how I blew up at them when they tried to talk me out of the divorce. But they will think it is scandalous for me to be dining and dancing with an old lover when my divorce isn't final and I haven't made much progress on the annulment process yet. I'll hint that we did make love. That will drive them up the wall, them and their goody-two-shoes wives. They're nice women all right and they cleaned up the family act, but *so* proper! I suppose I should pack the things I'll be bringing home. Sleeping pills? Well, I might need one some night. Please don't let my grace slip away again. Why shouldn't I sit in the whirlpool and daydream after I'm finished packing?

Leo

"Maggie," I knocked at the door of the attic room she used as her office when she was at the Lake, "can I interrupt with a serious question?"

She looked up from her Radio Shack TRSDOS computer, a slight frown on her forehead. Then she smiled. "Sure, this article is dull. One of my rainy day articles."

She was wearing gray slacks and a matching sweater, a perfect fashion picture even in her rainy day work room. She waved me to a chair, almost as though I were a patient.

"I never asked you this before: Who tampered with the brakes in the old Lasalle the day Maria was born? I had them fixed; someone else unfixed them."

She turned away and stared out the tiny window; rain was drumming against it. Nothing worse than intermittent driving rain on a summer Sunday.

"I don't know, Lee," she shook her head disconsolately. "I knew something terrible happened up there before Mary Anne told me. I had a hard time with Maria—but she's certainly worth it isn't she—and I wasn't feeling up to par."

Small woman that she was, Maggie had trouble with all her kids and they were all worth it, including the child she had lost to crib death when she was seventeen, before she met Jerry Keenan and came to Chicago.

"It was all confusion in my head," Maggie continued. "Has been ever since. . . . Do you really think you have to solve it before you win the fair matron?"

"What do you think?"

"I wish I could tell you that it's not important any more."

"Packy says that."

She nodded solemnly.

"I don't even know where to start."

"And it could be dangerous not to simply let the dead bury their dead?"

"You think it might be, Maggie?"

"Yes," she said simply. "Though I don't know why. Maybe because everyone is so mysterious about it. But you might have to do it anyway. Like that poor Proust person, you may have to rewrite the past to make sense out of the present.

"He didn't think that's what he was doing."

She shrugged her tiny shoulders. "But of course he was."

Call me Marcel.

Patrick

They both called me on the day after the weekend. The two of them kidded with me about "conflict of interest" but in such a tone of voice that I knew they didn't want me out of the picture. Their accounts of the weekend were similar, herself's far more sensitive and insightful than his, but that figures.

If they only knew about my real conflict of interest . . .

Jane trusts me more than she trusts him; she tells me things she'd never share with a husband; she even admits strong sexual desires for men since she dumped Phil.

Does she desire me? She didn't say she did, but wasn't there a hint of that? Perhaps if I had raised the issue?

I'm thinking like a fool!

They're still in love, an adolescent passion recurring in adult bodies, not that any of us ever banish adolescence for long. A new possibility offered them for this "second summer" as they both called it. How will they cope?

What a strange mix of hero and wimp Leo is. Wait till he finds out that she is writing a novel or a memoir or a journal about growing up during the forties. About him, unless I miss my guess.

"Yeah, Keenan here . . . Benedetto, comme sta? Yeah, I'm all right I guess. How's the scheme coming to get rid of our nut case Cardinal? What's the Roman gossip?"

"The matter has already been settled discreetly the way such matters should be settled. Soon there will be an Apostolic Administrator. You can guess who it will be, I'm sure. The present man will lose all his powers. The Pope is sending Baggio to inform him. Baggio, as you know, chaired the commission that investigated him. The present man will resign for reasons of health."

"Don't bet on it."

"Pardon me, Patricio?"

"You'll have to carry him out at gunpoint. I hope the man on the fifth floor is more ready for a fight than he usually is."

Silence.

"Let us hope it does not come to that, my friend."

It will come to that.

I've had a peculiar priesthood, one that many of my fellow priests envy. I worked for five years in a new suburban parish on the southwest side of the city and had the time of my life with the young families there. I was not particularly happy when the man that was then Cardinal, a tall, soft-spoken, extremely intelligent man, summoned me to his office.

"Pat, the seminary authorities have described you as stubborn, contentious, and arrogant."

"They ought to know, Your Eminence."

He smiled ever so slightly. "They say you have a first-class mind but you are proud of your intellectual abilities, and prefer your own opinion to that of the Church."

"You could make a case for that interpretation."

"They say your problem is that your family is very rich and you've been spoiled."

"We're professional class, Eminence, at the most. The Rector and the Prefect of Discipline don't know from rich. They're what we would call Shanty Irish."

"And you're" he actually grinned, "uh, curtain?"

"You mean Lace Curtain. No, we're what they call Country Club Irish, out of one bog and into another."

We both laughed.

"I need someone who can think for himself," he sobered up instantly. "The Church is going to face some tough moral questions in the years to come, especially in the matter of sexuality. I want better advice on moral theology than I'm presently getting—a comment that I trust you will keep in confidence."

"Of course, Eminence." I shifted uneasily in my chair, not sure what was coming but not liking it. "I'm not a radical. My problems in the seminary were about freedom not about theology. Yet I have to say candidly that five years in our parish have convinced me that we have to change our birth control teaching."

"Ah?"

"We give our young laypeople three choices—impossibly large families, no sex, or no sacraments. It's a cruel choice."

"You think so?" He rolled his pen carefully across his desk, watching its movements rather than my face.

"If marriage is a sacrament, husbands and wives should make love often so as to reflect the constant passionate love of God for his people."

"The natural law?"

"I don't see—and neither do a lot of people in my parish—how it's natural for husbands and wives to sleep in separate bedrooms."

"You convinced me, Pat, that you're the man for the job. I'm asking you whether you will go to Rome to study moral theology for me. I will need your advice in years to come."

"*But* the Jesuits teach morality at the seminary."

"Not necessarily forever. It's up to you, Pat. I won't insist. I'm asking, not telling."

"I understand."

"Take a few days or even a few weeks to think about it."

"Not necessary, Eminence. Count me in."

Neither of us knew what "in" would mean. He would be dead in six years to be replaced by a fat, stupid monster. I would be caught up in the excitement of the Vatican Council and the tragedy of the birth control encyclical.

The Thirties

Jane

The little girl and the little boy stood on the corner waiting for the Good Humor truck. I'm the little girl of course. They kept their distance from one another. The little boy, his red hair glowing brightly in the summer sun, pretended the little girl wasn't there. She *ought* not be there because this wasn't her corner. She had no business hanging around *his* corner. They were no more than eight so it must have been no later than 1936, perhaps even 1935. Milk trucks and garbage wagons were still horse-drawn. Only a few blocks from where they lived the streetlights were still gas lamps, lighted each evening by a lamplighter (though extinguished automatically the next morning). Peddlers still shouted "RagsOLARN" in the alleys. On some hot summer nights the smell of the stockyards, many miles away, would drift in on the wind. "Three Little Pigs" was a favorite movie with all the kids and in the school yard they would shout, "I'll huff and I'll puff and I'll BLOW your house down!" Grown-ups would hum, "The Music Goes Round and Round and Comes Out Here!" At the Lake they would show "Girl of the Limberlost" at the hall every summer. The kids knew some of the lines and facial expressions by heart. The pool at Charles Dickens Playground was where everyone went in the afternoons. Or so that time reappears in memory. Probably the sounds and the sights and the smells of different years bunch together as the little girl, now an "old woman" recalls that day when the Good Humor truck turned the corner at four-fifteen just as it had done every day in the summer since the beginning of time. Or so it seemed to her. To me. Whatever.

The truck would arrive at her corner ten minutes later. But the cute little boy with red hair wouldn't be waiting at her corner.

Careful, cautious person that she was even then, she had scouted him out that summer and knew that he was usually the first one on the corner waiting for the truck. But only rarely did he buy an ice cream bar.

That, she thought, was strange. Why wait for an ice cream man if you did not buy any ice cream?

Sure enough, right on time, the white truck, bells ringing and music box playing, turned the corner and parked under a giant old oak tree. Kids swarmed out of the houses and crowded around the truck. The ice cream man, who seemed very old then, but was probably only in his early twenties, joked with the kids, calling them all by name.

"Are you going to buy an ice cream bar?" she asked the little boy, even then not afraid to be bold.

He shook his head.

"Why not?"

He shrugged, as if he were not interested in ice cream.

"Why wait for the truck if you don't want ice cream?"

He shrugged again.

"I have two nickels." She held out her hand. "I'll buy two ice cream bars."

This was part of her carefully prepared strategy to trick the quiet little boy into a conversation. In fact she had four more nickels in the pocket of her skirt, but that was beside the point.

"No," he said flatly, his green eyes sparking fire.

"I can do whatever I want to," she announced, proud that she had coaxed a word out of him. Even if it were only one word and that one negative.

You didn't get much choice in ice cream bars in those days—vanilla with chocolate, chocolate with chocolate, and orange ice. A hedonist even then, she bought two chocolate with chocolate.

"Two, Janey?" the Good Humor man laughed at her. "Really hungry today, huh?"

"I like chocolate," she replied, honestly enough.

"Not even at your own corner?"

She felt her face warm. She did not want him to know about her plot.

"Couldn't wait for the chocolate."

The little boy was sitting on the curb, watching the frenzy around the Good Humor truck. She sat next to him.

"S'ter says it's a sin to waste food."

He grunted.

"I can't eat two chocolate bars."

He grunted again.

She held the bar out to him.

He looked at it, looked at her, and then took the bar. His piquant, funny little face lighted up in a smile.

"Thanks. I probably could eat two chocolate bars if I had to."

"*Well,* you only get one."

They both laughed and sat down to the serious task of demolishing their treats.

The next day he was waiting for her.

"I have two nickels today." He held out a grubby little paw as proof. "My turn."

She had plenty of nickels but was smart enough not to argue.

"That's very nice."

He grinned impishly, a grin she would never forget.

So he bought the bars. She thanked him politely.

"You're welcome, Jane."

"You know my name."

"Everyone knows your name."

Again, they sat next to each other on the curb, companionably this time, and polished off the ice cream.

Did they talk to one another? They must have because they were both talkative kids. But her memory fails as she tries to recapture the conversation.

The next day she was at the corner waiting for Leo and the Good Humor man. The Good Humor man came as he always did. But Leo was not there. He never returned to the corner all summer long.

Later she would hear that his mother had told him not to play with her. She couldn't believe that but when she saw him in the school yard in September, he would not talk to her.

Leo

The Devlins treated life like it was a barroom in which a brawl was about to erupt.

The men in the family, father and three sons, were big and heavy with dark black hair, low foreheads, and frowning faces. Even in church on Sunday morning, they clenched their fists and glowered. Ita Devlin, the mother of the family, was a frail looking little woman, very pretty but with thin, tight lips that seemed always ready to erupt in a stinging and obscene denunciation of anyone who stood in the way of her family, especially when she had been drinking.

"They're thugs," my father would say, "rural criminals from County Cork, a disgrace to Ireland, not much better than tinkers."

"The woman has the filthiest tongue I've ever heard," my mother would agree. "Monsignor shouldn't let her in the church on Sunday morning."

We were respectable, you see. My parents were not immigrants like Joe and Ita Devlin. They both had graduated from high school. They didn't have much money during the Great Depression, but my father had a secure job as a clerk at the Pullman Company office building on Michigan Avenue and my mother was an officer in the parish Altar and Rosary Society. Neither of them drank or swore or engaged in barroom brawls. All of their (eventually five) children, of which I was the oldest, would go to college and professional school. I would be the priest in the family, the priest that every Irish and Irish American mother in those times wanted in her family. They did not exactly push me into the seminary. Rather they assumed I would go there, an assumption beyond question because beyond discussion.

"When you're a priest, Leo," mother would say and then add an injunction like, "you certainly will not rush off the altar at the end of Mass like you were in a rush to get to the golf course."

I would remain silent in the face of such an injunction. Or perhaps say something like, "I don't play golf."

To which Mom, always requiring the last word, would say, "Priests really shouldn't play golf. They should do their work and say their prayers."

So I was not supposed to be interested in girls. Future priests could not act like other kids.

Especially a girl whose parents were described to me (not without reason) as "heavy drinkers" and whose brothers were swilling down booze even when they were in eighth grade—a practice not unknown in those days or subsequent days, as much as the good people of the neighborhood would pretend to be shocked each spring when beer bottles appeared on the rectory lawn.

My parents were handsome folk, he not as pompous as he often sounded and she cheerful and even funny when she was not worried about her kids—which was most of the time. In her wedding picture she is tall and striking and quite self-possessed. The last time I glanced at it I realized how much she looked like Jane—not in specific details but in general shape and posture. The realization frightened me.

The Devlins were also rich and we were if not quite poor at least impoverished. The Devlins had migrated to America in 1921, one step ahead of gunmen, it was said, from both sides in the Irish Civil War of that time. Their three sons—Herbie, Mickie (for Michael Collins), and Dickie (for Richard Mulcahy, successor as commander of the National Army)—were born in short order after their arrival and then Jane in 1928, the same year as I was born. Even as boys they were frightening—big, mean, hard kids who delighted in beating up on younger and weaker victims—though they usually avoided their victims' big brothers.

"Carbon copies of their father," my mother would snort.

"They'll end up in jail," my father would predict.

Dad was wrong, none of the Devlins ever went to jail, though later they escaped it by the skin of their teeth and, it was said, because of liberal bribes paid to police, prosecutors, and judges.

How did recent immigrants become rich in such a short time and especially during the Great Depression?

They came with some money, according to rumor stolen from the funds of one of the military groups in the Irish Civil War. They bought a coal company that was on the edge of bankruptcy and turned it around by hard work, political bribes, and violence—usually with fists—against their competitors. They made deals with the city government and the unions and won big contracts both from the city and from companies that were afraid of having their windows smashed and their employees beat up. They branched out into gasoline stations and bought two restaurants, and took over a couple of "family taverns" in another neighborhood (lower on the social scale than ours) all of which ventures were successful even in the Depression because many people thought it prudent to buy their gas and their dinners and their booze from the Devlins.

Maybe some were charmed just a bit by Ita's songs and laughter, bubbling enthusiasm, and reckless good looks. But, if they weren't, there were other reasons to keep the Devlins happy.

They bought one of the largest houses in the parish and wore expensive clothes (which, it was said, did not fit them). The whispers of the late thirties said that they were second only to Doctor Clare's family as the wealthiest parishioners. And the Clares spoke to none of the rest of us.

Most of us didn't like the Devlins very much, though some of us (*not* my family) admired their fierce competitiveness and envied their success.

"No matter how much money they have," Mom would comment, "they'll never be anything but Shanty Irish. Crude, rude, and uncultivated. Not a bit of respectability."

"They are totally lacking in refinement," Dad would agree. "Money can't buy cultivation."

"Or manners."

"Or good taste."

His first observation was certainly true then. I'm not so sure that the latter was true, then or now. As a University officer I must concede that if you give enough money to us we are perfectly willing to certify you as respectable, no matter where your money comes from.

The idea that, contrary to all the facts, the Devlins might be respectable gained currency in 1940 when they bought a house at the Lake at the end of the road and not far from Clares. Apparently the Clares even spoke to them, adding to the cachet of respectability.

My mother dissented. "I don't think the Clares are all that fancy either."

A month or two before she would have said just the opposite. Bad money, it would seem, does drive out good money.

The parish was of mixed mind about the fights that Herbie, Mickie, and Dickie seemed to be in almost every night after they graduated from our grammar school. The joke was that some cops both in Chicago and Oak Park were getting rich on bribes paid to bail out the "three stooges," my contribution to parish vocabulary.

They heard the rumor that I was the source of the label and sought pretexts to pick fights with me. With one exception I responded by the same tactic the X Corps would use at the Chosin Reservoir. I redeployed to the rear—in other words, ran like hell. Since I was faster than the Devlins, they never did get a chance to slug me. Later at the Lake, they would have loved to have found me without Packy Keenan in tow (I was, in fact, usually in his tow). But they were afraid of Packy's dangerous right fist, as was anyone with some amount of sanity. After a year or two of coming to the Lake I was as big as they were and arguably twice as mean—I had become very mean as soon as I had the strength to back it up—they avoided me. Then they stopped coming to the Lake except on weekends, because their mother insisted they weren't working hard enough.

For all their pugnaciousness, the three Devlin sons were in no hurry to join the military after Pearl Harbor. They waited till the draft caught them and then never left the United States, though in later years they would brag about their military accomplishments. Herbie, the oldest and the dumbest, was reported to have a particularly cushy job as a personnel clerk at the Navy Department, shuffling files. Despite the super-patriotism of their father ("Teach them yellow bellies a lesson!") he and his sons flourished on their own little defense industry, the black market: "We didn't have a chance at prohibition so now we're entitled to catch up on with the Dagos," Joe would explain to anyone who would listen. "If we don't take the money, someone else will."

Then came Jane Devlin, the distantly worshipped goddess of my youth, arguably of my whole life. How that family produced Jane is a genetic mystery. There is a tendency, I believe, to glamorize the lovely young women with whom we grow up. When we look at graduation pictures many years later, we discover that while they are attractive enough, they are not as extraordinary as they seemed to us when we were all young together.

Even granting that propensity, Janie was still special. One looks at our class of 1942 picture, suspecting that she will seem merely pretty and discovers that, no, the memory is correct, she is radiantly beautiful; tall, slender, neatly shaped, lovely round face about to burst into laughter, tightly knotted curls—nothing unusual about the components perhaps, but a devastating package. She exudes a vivacious allure that seems ready to jump off the yellowing photo and tempt you, make you laugh, enchant you.

I remember the day they took the picture. Janie found it difficult to stand quietly in one place and be silent for more than ninety seconds. With some help from Chuck O'Malley who knew when and how to play the straight man, she kept all of us, including the photographer, the nuns, and the Monsignor in laughter through the whole hot, uncomfortable session.

My mother glanced at the picture and then tossed it aside abruptly. "They ought not to let that Devlin child in the picture with respectable children. Look at her. She's the spitting image of her mother."

I looked at the picture and saw no resemblance. Now I realize that the resemblance was strong though Jane was already taller than her mother and, as they would have said then, "much better developed."

"She's an attractive little thing," my father said.

"Attractive is as attractive does."

Jane got away with her games. No one in authority ever begrudged Janie her energy or her wit, her quick tongue or her animated disregard for rules. S'ter (whoever might be S'ter in a given year) would perhaps try to be angry at Janie's mischief but her outrage when Janie took the class away from her would always melt in laughter.

"That young woman will never amount to anything, not with a family like hers." My mother would insist. "She'll end up a tramp."

It was not the common opinion. The parish adored Janie and conveniently covered up her origins. Jane was never disloyal to her parents or brothers. Rather she seemed oblivious to what they did or what the rest of us thought about them, although she seemed to adore her mother—if one were to judge by the way she hung on her every word when they walked home from Mass every morning.

"Seemed" is the operative word here. Janie was a "deep one."

"Someday, Jane Devlin," one of the S'ters said, "I'll figure out what really goes on inside of that bright little head of yours."

"It's empty, S'ter. Just the other day you said I was an empty-headed lame-brain."

We all laughed. Janie was skillful at remembering just what S'ter said and using it in repartee against her.

S'ter flushed but was not angry. "That's true too."

Janie was by far the brightest kid in the class, even brighter than Chuck. She may also have been the deepest, though that judgment reads back into an earlier time evidence that I subsequently acquired.

So she seemed in those days to have everything—looks, brains, money, popularity. Everyone in the parish seemed to know her and like her. Jane Devlin was our radiant princess of whom we all were proud. If any of the other kids felt envy toward her they were smart enough to keep it to themselves.

Too good to be true?

Surely. But allowing for all the facts, still pretty damn good.

There were edges of sadness around her even then. Her brothers had all gone to Fenwick—judged in those days to be the elite Dominican school—for their first year in high school and were summarily ejected before their freshman year was finished. Thereupon they went to St. Philip's or St. Mel's—middle and working class institutions—where they did not last the second year. They "finished up" at Austin, though it is doubtful that any of them ever graduated. Joe and Ita had their doubts about wasting money on a girl's high school education and announced that what was good enough for their sons was good enough for their daughter. Wave the flags for Austin High, boys.

Horror swept the parish. Our luminous heroine deserved better. Sister Superior spoke to Joe and Ita in vain. Then she spoke to the Monsignor. He laid down the law in the firm tone of a west of Ireland canon. All right, Jane would go to Providence High for two years. After that the Devlins would determine whether any further education, Catholic or public, was worth the money. They told the Monsignor over and over that they could never understand why Americans wasted money on the education of young women whom, after all, God had designed to be wives and mothers.

The Monsignor, to give the devil his due, did not back down. It was Trinity, a women's Fenwick, and not Providence, and for four not two years. Trinity was a school for spoiled rich kids, the Devlins replied. The Monsignor denied that myth and insisted. Trinity was to some extent college preparatory; Jane should have a chance to go to college. Beaten but sullen, the Devlins withdrew.

The battle was not a private fight: the Devlins had two levels of speech—loud and louder still. The whole parish listened with dismay.

"No matter how much money they have, they are cheap and disgusting," my mother said often during those tense days.

"He's a gombeen man," my father agreed.

I think they accurately reflected the sentiments of the parish at the time of the controversy.

Through it all, Jane said not a word. Nor did anyone dare ask her. Her serenity and laughter were undisturbed.

"It's almost like she doesn't know it's happening," Chuck O'Malley said to me.

"She knows."

"She doesn't show it."

"It's called class."

"Yeah."

"She's got enough for the whole family."

"Yeah," he admitted.

In those days I did not wonder about how much energy went into denial mechanisms or what the psychic costs of denial might be.

I worshipped her from a great distance the very first day of first grade. I doubt that we ever spoke to one another, save perhaps for a "*Hi*" when my crowd and her crowd would, through some miracle of providence, emerge from the local movie house at the same time. She barely knew I existed. Moreover my mother had forbidden me to have anything to do "with that little Devlin snip." Such a prohibition would have had little effect, in all honesty, if Janie Devlin didn't scare the hell out of me.

My worship turned to desire, pubescent lust I suppose, as we progressed through grammar school.

A boy knows that the bodies of his girl classmates are different from those of adult women. He even realizes at some theoretical level that the girls will eventually mature into women, but the wonder of that phenomenon when it comes overwhelms him (as will the transformation of his daughters many years later). The typical boy hides his astonishment behind crude obscenities, which are perhaps his only escape. The girl becomes an object to evaluate in foul and clinical detail, a response to the terror of womanly sexuality, a terror some of us never outgrow.

I'm sure we were especially astonished—and delighted—by Jane's transformation from cute girl to devastating woman. But so great was our awe of her that we kept our dirty thoughts to ourselves. Since I planned to be a priest I went to none of the eighth grade parties in 1942, just at the time when the United States was turning the tide in the Pacific War at Midway Island. Even if I had wanted to attend the parties—and I'm sure I did—Mom would not have permitted it.

"Why should a future priest want to engage in such immoralities?"

The report on Jane from the parties was that she was a great kisser, but you couldn't go any further with her. I felt proud of her. She continued to fill my dreams, as I'm sure the dreams of every male between thirteen and eighteen in the parish.

It was during that summer that I told off one of the Devlins for the first time. Dickie, the youngest and a couple of years older than us, cornered me and warned me about Jane.

"Don't you dare even look at her, punk, do you understand me?"

As best as I can remember, I replied something on the order of, "Fuck you, asshole!"

I almost never used that kind of language.

Oddly enough he backed down. So bullies are really cowards, I reflected. Interesting.

I continued to look at Janie from a safe distance, especially at Mass every morning. No matter how late the party she always managed to be at Mass. As a future priest, awakened by my mother, I too was there every day. I was sure no one woke Jane. I managed to sneak out the side door and avoid conversation with her. I fear, however, that she rather than God was my main interest at Mass. Dear God, I'm sure I prayed, she is so lovely!

As every academic must, I have struggled through some of Marcel Proust. I am well aware of the dangers in trying to search for times lost. Or, as we say in my discipline, the dangers of selective perception. How different was the reality of my early maturity from what I have described? I have no idea. Maybe someday I will be able to ask Jane how she remembers me. It might be a very risky question, however.

My later love for her surely blurs my recollections of her at thirteen, going on fourteen. Perhaps I add a glow to Jane Devlin that was not there, or there only in my mind. I think, however, the general impression I have tried to convey is accurate. My friends from that era have similar memories, complete with glow. Especially Packy Keenan who was at least as much in love with her as I was.

I wonder if he still is, not that it matters.

I thought I would never see her again after the summer of 1942 was over. She went off to Trinity (and great success there) and I to the seminary.

I would see her often during the early 1940s by pure alphabetical chance. My first day at Quigley I met Patrick Michael Keenan, an event that perhaps changed my life and one that certainly guaranteed that I would encounter Jane Devlin many times in the next six years.

Jane

I promised myself that I would not break down at grammar school graduation. In seventh grade I was disgusted with the hysterics of many of the girls after they had filed out of church. My mother thought the weeping girls were a disgrace. "No refinement." I wanted to be refined, though my efforts at "acting like a lady" were usually unsuccessful. I warned my classmates that we would not do the same thing. We would instead rejoice that we were finally out of Saint Ursula and free from the nuns. Only babies were sad about getting out of grammar school. I was not the first one to break down. But when others began to weep, I couldn't keep myself under control. The graduation ceremony was heavy, sad, poignant. The friendships of all those years would have to end. We would never be together again as a class. It wasn't graduation that made us melancholy, it was growing up. We wanted to be kids forever. The boys could pretend to be tough. We girls knew more clearly than boys that graduation was a sad event. So we wept.

Pain welled up from the depths of my soul, pain of which I had not been aware. It surged to the surface like a flood rushing out of control. My discipline disintegrated and I collapsed into hysterical sobbing.

Later I would read and comprehend the bittersweet lines written about a girl named Margaret, "It is the blight man was born for / it is Margaret you mourn for."

Then the boy with the red hair and the beautiful and gentle green eyes came up to me and put his arm around my shoulders. Not Chuckie who was consoling Rosemarie who hadn't even graduated. But Leo.

"It's all right, Janie," he said. "It's all right. Cry your eyes out. Most of us wish we could cry the same way. Don't worry, you'll have a long and happy life and eighth graders of your own."

Even in memory that insight seems staggering. His prediction was wrong, however: there has been little happiness in my life.

"Thank you, Lee," I leaned against his solid shoulder. "I'm glad you understand."

So I was free to draw back from hysteria and control my weeping.

Smiling like I was a daughter of whom he was proud, he kept his arm around me till my tears had trailed off into sniffles. He offered me a handkerchief to dab at my eyes.

"Thank you," I said, smiling up at him self-consciously.

"My pleasure," he laughed. And we both laughed together.

He ignored my brothers who were glaring at him and, I thought, winked at Father Raven, who was beaming.

"You're so grown-up, Lee," I sighed.

"I have a long way to go to catch up with you, Janie," he replied, squeezing my shoulders and then releasing me.

So it ended.

If it ever ended, which it probably had not and never would.

The 1940s

Leo

"Patrick James Keenan," the big kid said, "usually known as Packy. What's your name, Red?"

"Leo Thomas Kelly," I replied. "I'm glad you're name isn't Kennan."

"How come?"

"Because then I'd be sitting in front of you."

"Why would that be bad?" he grinned, suspecting what I was about to say.

"Then I'd have no place to hide."

He chortled gleefully.

In that instant Packy Keenan and I became life-long friends. He was and is, without any doubt the most important male friend in my life. With the exception of Jane and Laura and maybe Emilie, he was and is the most important person in my life.

"Where you from?" I asked.

"St. Mark's," he shrugged as though a River Forest origin was not important.

My mother would approve. I was choosing my seminary friends from boys "with a nice family background."

"You?" he continued.

"St. Ursula."

That name ought to have meant a lower middle class parish, not worth comparing to the affluent St. Mark's. Instead his eyes widened.

"So you'd know Janie, huh?"

"Who doesn't know Janie?"

"A real hot number," he shook his head. "Enough to make a guy think twice about celibacy."

"We shouldn't let girls disturb us."

"Ha!" he exploded. "If someone like Janie doesn't disturb you, you're not a human male . . . hell, Leo, we don't give up marriage because we don't like women. No dedication if that were true."

Thus did he absolve me from my mother's constant injunction to avoid liking girls.

"Naturally," I said glibly. "How could anyone not like Janie."

"Especially in a swimsuit," he nodded appreciatively. "Especially one of those two-piece things."

"Where did you see her in a two-piece swimsuit?" I demanded, astonished at my own emotions of jealousy.

Janie was mine, I didn't want this big, handsome, black Irish kid from River Forest ogling my Janie.

"At the Lake. Her brothers are jerks, but she's wonderful. Spectacular tits, huh?"

"I didn't notice."

He clapped me on the back, "The hell you didn't."

"You have a house at the Lake too?"

"Right down the street from them. They're terrible people, but she's an angel," he sighed, "a glorious angel. And a great kid besides."

"Absolutely. Maybe we can found a Jane Devlin admiration society here at Quigley."

He glanced around the classroom, always half dark because of dim lights and narrow gothic windows, with fake nervousness. "We wouldn't want any of the faculty to find out about her, would we now?"

"Absolutely not . . . you know Philly Clare too."

"I'm not bragging about that," he said. "That drip thinks he has a monopoly on Janie. And no one has that."

"The Clares are important people in St. Ursula."

"They think they're important everywhere . . . hey, maybe you can come up a couple of weekends next summer and we can organize that Janie fan club. Memberships strictly limited to the two of us, right?"

"Right!"

Before we could continue our conversation, the Latin professor came in, smelling of after-shave and whiskey and I was left to fantasize about Jane in a two-piece swimsuit at the Lake, as pleasant a fantasy as was possible inside the gray preparatory seminary.

Packy and I were close friends from that day forward. We discovered that we had a lot in common besides Jane, including a love of off-beat whimsy, like the Janie Devlin fan club. We studied together, played basketball together—especially after I grew a foot or so and was able to catch Packy's quick passes and lay them into the basket.

We traveled to Quigley together each morning and home each evening, laughing most of the way at our teachers. Most Quigley students from River Forest took the Lake Street L downtown and the subway up to Chicago Avenue and the Q. However, Packy's mother, one of the most elegant women I had yet seen, used to drive him over to Division and Austin where Packy would meet me. We would ride to Central, take the Central Bus to Chicago Avenue and hang on for dear life as the "red rocket" bumped down to Quigley, which was on the then dull and seemly Rush Street.

I learned that Packy had a sister named Joan whom he didn't like and an older brother Jerry whom he adored—and about whom he worried because he was in Navy pre-flight as part of the V-5 program at Iowa. Each day when we walked down Rush Street from Chicago Avenue and saw the V-12 "ninety day wonders" double timing from their residence in Luis Towers (now Loyola University Downtown) over to Northwestern's Abbot Hall on the lakefront, Packy would frown. Casualties among aircrews he told me were sometimes a hundred percent. Only one man had survived Torpedo Squadron 8's disastrous failure at Midway.

Packy's father was a lawyer with political connections—Democratic, which was unusual for River Forest in that era. His mother was active in a lot of "Red Cross things."

"She's a very pretty lady," I said cautiously, feeling that such an observation was not only appropriate but necessary. "Indeed if the word doesn't offend you, she's a knockout."

Packy laughed at that but seemed pleased with my praise of his mother—as well he might be. "You notice good-looking women at every age, don't you, Leo?"

"Don't you?"

"Yeah, but a lot of guys don't."

"Worse luck for them."

We both laughed at that.

I wondered if his mother wore a swimsuit at the Lake but dismissed that as an inappropriate if not irrelevant question.

If he meant his invitation to the Lake on a couple of summer weekends I had a lot to anticipate.

Jane

She pretended to be surprised and a little disgusted when she met them on the village dock, a multistory boat pier and amusement hall with pinball machines, soda fountains, and juke boxes—one of them at that moment blaring "Moonlight Becomes You." Two seminarians, she protested; that's all that a dull summer needs. But she hugged and kissed them both, as though that were typical behavior among fifteen-year-old friends in 1943, which it certainly wasn't. The boy with the black hair laughed appreciatively. Her old friend with the red hair, now so tall and strong that she hardly recognized him, absorbed her body and soul with his response to her kiss. No one had ever kissed her that way before, not even in the dark at the Rockne movie theater. Now he was doing it in public with everyone watching. She didn't care.

"We should have invited you to the kissing game parties," she said breathlessly. "Or do you only kiss like that in daylight?"

"Depends on the girl," he had laughed.

"Only the easy makes?"

"Only those I want to kiss."

Ohmy!

"What the girl wants doesn't matter?"

"Sure it does," he brushed his clenched fist lightly against her jaw. "I read the invitation in her eyes."

Ohmy, ohmy!

"Listen to him!" Patrick had hooted derisively.

"Maybe you should take him back to Chicago!" she sniffed, knowing that it was the last thing she wanted.

She had been waiting to see them together all summer long. Her two favorite boys in all the world. Both destined for the priesthood. All right if God wanted them, that was His right. She didn't doubt about the boy with the black hair and the easy laugh. He had priest written all over him. About the other boy with his smoldering green eyes and his quick tongue and his intense gentleness she was not so sure. Even less after he had kissed her. You could, she supposed, like to kiss girls and still be a priest. But that much?

What would she do if he tried to kiss her again while he was at the Lake?

She would not permit it.

Don't be silly. Of course she would permit it.

Up to a point.

So she would trust that God knew what He was doing but still look out for her own interests.

As her father had taught her. "Trust everyone, Janie girl, but cut the cards just the same."

"You'd better believe that," her mother had agreed with the mean laugh that was becoming more frequent in their house.

Aloud she said, "Patrick, do you think we could teach this big goof how to play a decent game of tennis? Then we could play mixed doubles with Eileen Murray."

"Difficult but not impossible task."

Mixed doubles were reasonably safe. Not that she trusted Eileen all that much. She was really boy-crazy.

Almost as bad as I am.

Patrick

I knew in less than five minutes that I was no longer Jane Devlin's best summer beau. She smiled at Leo and he melted like butter soaked in maple syrup. He admitted on the ride up to the Lake that he'd actually spoken to her only a couple of times and insisted that if it were not for his red hair she wouldn't even recognize him.

Leo smiled back, a big, amiable grin that suggested not the slightest hint of shyness. She pecked at his lips, a daring move in public in those days and he devoured her with a kiss that took her breath away.

Now we'd say there was instant chemistry between them.

I was so fond of Leo that I really didn't mind him taking Jane away from me in that moment. Since I was going to be a priest, he was welcome to her.

I stuck to that opinion for the next half dozen years, though I admit that there were occasions when I wavered—especially when Leo seemed to hesitate in his affection for her, not trusting his emotions.

In recent years he often claims that he analyzes life to death because he is a professor. The truth is the other way around. He became a professor because analysis is his favorite way of escaping decisions.

I'm a fine one to talk.

Leo

"We're delighted to have you as a guest." Packy's mother kissed me on the forehead. "Packy is so fond of you. It's nice we'll have two seminarians here for a week or two."

"I'll try to keep him out of trouble," I said, feeling my face flame. "But it won't be easy."

"Trouble is his middle name, Mom!" Packy chortled.

We were under a warm sun on the lawn in front of their house, surely the biggest home I had ever seen in my life, and, as I remember it, the Lake was calm. I had fantasized since Packy's first casual invitation about what his mother would look like in a swimsuit. The reality was much more appealing than my fantasy. I was acutely embarrassed by what I was sure were my exploding eyeballs. Mary Anne Keenan noticed my admiration—what woman wouldn't—and was amused and pleased by it. Graceful in all things, she accepted my reaction and immunized me from embarrassment.

Did she know how clinical are the hungers of a boy in his early teens, how objectifying they are, to use the fashionable term of the ideology of the present? Did she know that images of her totally naked would haunt him for the rest of the summer?

Then I took consolation in the thought that she didn't know what was going on in my dirty imagination. Now I realize that of course she did and was not in the least troubled by my lustful fantasies, as other women would be or pretend to be.

Do I read my subsequent reactions to trim and full bodied women in tight blue strapless swimsuits who are turning forty into that horny fifteen-year-old's filth-crazed brain? At that age in life are not the males of the species interested only in the kind of womanly allure that would later grace the centerfolds of *Playboy*?

Maybe.

Yet I clearly remember being overwhelmed by Mary Anne McCarthy Keenan, her shoulders and legs still wet from the waters of the Lake, kissing my forehead and, in the process, as she stood on her tiptoes, granting me a generous view of her superb breasts.

Even now I hope I didn't gulp too loudly.

Those three summers from 1943 to 1945 blur in my memory. I spent most of the first two pushing a lawn mower for the Chicago Park District. In 1945 we had to attend summer school because of a crazy decision of the faculty, worried about a hostile reaction to draft-free seminarians from the laity whose sons were dying on Iwo and Okinawa. But there are few memories of either the lawn mower or the classroom from that era. All I can recall are images of the Lake, images perhaps shaped by nostalgia for the summer of 1948 when Jane and I loved and lost one another.

Our side of the Lake, as I came to call it, though nothing in it was mine except my friends, had been settled first, at our end before the turn of the century. Indeed some of the sprawling Victorian homes with their gables and turrets and porches and balconies dated to the first summer settlements of the late 1880s and early 1890s before the Columbian exposition in 1893. Each of the Old Houses, as they were called by everyone, boasted a neatly manicured lawn rolling down the hill to the Lake and a freshly painted gazebo and pier—usually with a motor launch of some sort, steam first, then internal combustion (idle during years of the War). On the road side of the house there would usually be a park of trees, all carefully maintained and landscaped and protected by a wrought-iron fence and gate with the family name scrolled always on the gate and sometimes on the fence too. Art deco swimming pools, with pillars and porches and fountains and classic statues graced some of the homes—though not the Keenans'. (Tom Keenan: Who needs a pool when you have a lake that's warm for three months?)

Servants, more often white than black, cut the lawns, raked the sand driveways, cleaned the cars, painted the fence and the pier and the gazebos and seemed ready, usually with what seemed like cheerful grace. This was, I thought, the world of the really rich, a fairy land for a kid who had lived in a two-flat until 1939 and then a bungalow, which was too small for five kids.

Then I thought the homes were the most elegant houses in the world, the kind of places I read about in English mysteries or ghost stories. Later I would realize that they were in horrendous bad taste (and the people who lived in them for the most part new rich). Still later I would agree that they are interesting museum pieces from the Gilded Age and the Mauve Decade.

The Keenan house, as elaborate as any and more grotesque than most, was part home and part parish rectory for me. As Maggie would say later, the Keenans were in fact a kind of neighborhood, a kind of parish, a kind of church.

The Keenan house was arranged for comfort, not for show, and its many small rooms set up for guests, the rooms painted in different colors (mine was robin's egg blue!) with a tastefully matched and framed print on the wall to create a touch of elegance. Somehow there was always an extra room for a guest, usually with an extra bath.

"Save the expensive furniture," Tom Keenan would proclaim, "for River Forest and put the plumbing in here."

It seems in retrospect that I spent most of those very hot and humid summers (as I recall them) at the Lake. With Packy and Jane and their friends I walked the streets, darkened even at midday by giant oak trees and illumined at night by faint streetlights that only enhanced the inviting secrecy of the gloom. In fact, I suppose that in my middle teens I was not at the Lake any more than ten or fifteen days at the most—a couple of weekends and a week at the close of summer.

I drank Coke and smoked cigarettes (a habit abandoned when I was in Korea) and listened to the juke box in the amusement center at the municipal pier while I argued and bantered with and worshipped Jane. She taught me how to dance and danced contentedly with me and Packy until the older boys like Phil Clare and the G.I.s home on leave discovered her. Even when they did, she still danced with us some of the time.

"Should seminarians dance with girls?" I asked Packy one morning as we hiked home from church.

We honored as best we could our obligation to daily Mass.

"Depends on the seminarian and on the girl."

"Huh?"

"It's all right if I dance with Devlin, but not all right if you dance with her."

"How come?"

"She's only a good friend to me. You're gaga over her."

"Bullshit."

"You should see the look in your eyes when she's around."

"Yeah?"

"Yeah."

"I enjoy looking at every pretty girl."

"Or woman."

"Or woman," I amended myself—for Packy had also noted my interest in his mother's luscious friends.

"But it's different the way you look at Jane."

"I'm sure she doesn't think so."

"Hell she doesn't."

"So I shouldn't dance with her?"

He shrugged. "How do I know!"

"You said it wasn't all right."

"That doesn't mean you shouldn't do it. Besides," he grinned broadly, "she's gaga over you."

"Impossible!"

I let it go at that. Anyway there wasn't much chance that I'd turn her down when she would grab my hand and announce, "OK, Lunkhead. It's your turn for another lesson. Eventually, we'll make a good dancer out of you."

"Fat chance," Packy would chuckle.

I would play tennis with her and Packy and either Packy's sister Joan or Eileen Murray, both of whom I thought were pretty and giggling blondes, but excellent tennis partners and agreeable kissing partners. (Not as good

as Jane, obviously.) I turned into a pretty good tennis player, which I still
am, capable of beating most faculty colleagues of my own generation, but
I was never good enough consistently to beat my teacher.

"Better stick to basketball, Lunkhead," Janie would inform me as she
wiped the sweat off her face. "You'll never be as good at this as I am."

She also taught me to swim and to sail in the Keenans' old dinghy and
to paddle a canoe—water skiing had yet to come to the Lake and there was
no gasoline till 1945 for powerboats. She absolutely refused to attempt to
teach me how to play golf.

"You are too clumsy for them to permit you even on the first tee at the
Club."

I was not all that clumsy, not towards the end of those early summers at
the Lake. But she boycotted the golf course, though not the tennis courts
or the swimming pool. Although she never quite said it, she would not
play there even with the Keenans because the Club rejected her family's
membership application every summer (until after 1950 when, by common
agreement of the "old-timers," as Maggie Ward Keenan later told me, all
standards were abandoned).

She rarely mentioned her family and we almost never saw them. They
were busy, as my own mother suggested, staying out of the war and making
money.

She also taught me how to kiss, an activity in which I was completely
untrained. I became if not a proficient kisser at least a determined and not
unsuccessful one. I set about those summers to conquer every reasonably
attractive girl to whom I could find access. It must have been at least 1944
or maybe even 1945 because among my conquests were Angie Nicola and
Eileen Murray, both younger than we were and I can't imagine trying to
kiss an eighth grade girl.

I encountered little more than token resistance in these amorous adventures. Now looking back in embarrassment, I realized that among the young
women at the Lake a kiss, especially a passionate one, from Leo Kelly had
become a mark of social success.

Jane must have known about these infidelities of mine, but she never
complained, perhaps because she was proud of her pupil.

I was careful not to engage in these escapades when Packy was around.
I'm sure he knew about them—his sister Joan was one of my failures—but
he never mentioned them. Many years later I asked him why he had not
remonstrated with me.

"None of my business," he grinned wickedly. "Besides by contemporary
standards, all you guys were capable of were pretty tepid explorations."

"Tepid?"

"Yeah . . . did you confess them?"

"Sometimes . . . couldn't get a straight answer about whether they were sinful."

"You now think they were? God would reject you because of them?"

"Course not . . . part of growing up."

"I wish that was all we had to worry about these days."

"You didn't mind my trying to make out with Joan?"

"I figured it might be good for her."

I never mentioned my erotic encounters to the spiritual director at the seminary. If I had, they might have asked me to leave long before I finally did.

Yet it was not for women that I left when I finally did. And over the seminary authority's protest, not with their sigh of relief.

Jane, clad almost always in tennis whites when she wasn't in a delectable (as it seemed then) two-piece swimsuit, was the unquestioned leader of our little band of "wild kids" as we came to be defined by the adults who heard our noisy laughter and found our beer bottles on their lawns in the morning.

Only after my Pentecost conversation with Maggie did I realize that her leadership was in fact an assumption of personal responsibility for all of us—even to insisting that we all wear the Carmelite brown scapulars around our necks, so that we wouldn't die without a priest.

"Or," she said in the interests of strict orthodoxy, "that you won't need one. Either way God takes care of you."

She was younger than some of us and a girl, but by virtue of her energy and enthusiasm—combined, as these qualities were, with her startling beauty—she still was boss. When she said, "Lets . . ." we all fell into line without question.

"Let's swim in Birdbrain's pool."

"Let's sail in Amadon's boat."

"Let's give Lunkhead another tennis lesson."

"Let's roast marshmallows on Goofy's grill and sing songs from 'Oklahoma' all night long."

"Let's take Angie down to the Rose Bowl and buy her a malt that is as big as she is. It's her birthday."

"Let's make Eileen sing for us, she's better than all of us put together."

She blessed the males of the group with nicknames that questioned our intelligence, our good taste, and out ability to take care of ourselves. None of us minded.

Packy—"Amadon"—was assigned the role of senior confidant, the one with whom she would have serious and private discussions. Already he had become her personal priest. Vociferous and comic at gatherings of seminarians, Pack was usually quiet and reflective with our summer crowd, as though he were an anthropologist from another world watching closely the strange culture of the local natives.

Phil Clare—"Birdbrain"—was her "date," for whatever fancy parties or dances might become available. Big, handsome, blond, and overweight even then, Phil was likable and harmless—and in truth not very bright. He was three years older than us, a Fenwick grad in 1943 bound for Notre Dame instead of the army because of weak eyes. I noted that his eyes were not so bad that he had to wear glasses on the golf course at the Club, where he spent all his time when he wasn't with us.

He was already a prodigious consumer of beer and even more of a loud-mouth, albeit an innocent one, after his second bottle. He and Jim Murray introduced beer into our group. The rest of us, however, were afraid to drink any until Jane reached for her bottle.

Eileen and Angie, a year younger than us and "too young" to drink, carefully imitated Jane's drinking, which never exceeded one bottle, save on very hot nights. Packy limited himself to one bottle, regardless.

As for me, Jane made my limit clear: "Lunkhead, no more than two bottles or you'll be so high that you'll fly back to Chicago."

It was solid advice. Son of two abstainers, I heard a buzz halfway through the second bottle. My capacity has since increased.

In those days I consoled myself that the only reason she dated Phil was that she would not be welcome at the Club dances or in the homes of the rich unless she was in the company of Doctor Clare's only child, spoiled only child I might have said to Packy.

"Green eyes has green eyes," Packy guffawed, permitting himself one of his occasional epigrams.

I kept my jealousy in check by reminding myself of Phil's remark after a dance at the Club.

"Devlin doesn't put out much, does she?"

"Frigid," I replied, calumniating my love.

Jane and I were at best tolerated by the affluent people who lived in the "Old Houses," I felt, with a fine sense of self-pity, she because she was so pretty and I because I was a friend of Tom Keenan's son. In fact, my self-pity was wasted. Adults were immune to social class differences among our crowd. Even when they learned that "that gorgeous young woman" was a Devlin, they were not prepared to hold it against her.

"She's such a lively child and so sweet."

The silent implication was that she was so unlike her family.

Whether Jane felt she was on the fringes I did not know. She never invited the rest of us to her house, however.

It was to the pool next to Doctor Clare's big Victorian house that we would flee on hot afternoons when the Lady Jane (as I called her) determined that the waves in the Lake were too high for our late afternoon frolic. The pool was shielded from the Lake by evergreen trees and built in a classical decor with nude statues and fountains and columns with doric capitals.

"Looks like the decline of the Roman empire to me," I whispered to Packy.

"Decline and fall," he replied. "With Mrs. Clare around, maybe after the fall."

We did not seem to disturb Phil's svelte blonde mother who reclined on her chaise lounge in a white strapless suit, sipping on a martini, next to a fountain in which stood a mostly nude granite Greek maiden. (Well, she might not have been a maiden, as far as I knew.) She was always half-tuned but never more than half-tuned. Packy was the only one to whom Iris McDonnell Clare spoke, perhaps because he was the only one whose name she could remember.

"It's so nice, Patrick, to see you and Philip and your little friends having so much fun."

"Yes ma'am," Pack would say with a perfectly straight face.

"Great ass on that woman, huh?" Jim Murray asked me.

"Pretty good tits too," I agreed.

"What are you too whispering about?" Jane would demand furiously— she tolerated no secrets in our little gang.

"Dirty boy talk, Milady," I would reply.

"Stop it!" She would splash us angrily; and as boys that age have done ever since the species discovered swimming, we would strive to dunk her. I doubt that there have been many young women in the history of the species who fought back with greater strength and determination.

We would be distracted from these efforts only by Mrs. Clare's departure from poolside, an exercise in bodily movements as she rose from her couch and donned her robe (left open) which would distract a male of any age.

"Let's go get a sundae," Jane announced climbing out of the pool and grabbing a towel. "I'm hungry."

Did I really love Jane even then? Was there more than just exploration and experimentation in our kisses? Eventually there surely was, a lot more. But in the early forties while the War, hardly noticed, rolled on in such strange places as Guadalcanal and El Alamein and Stalingrad and Anzio and Normandy and Saipan did I love her even then?

I don't know. For all the rich details in my memory I can't answer that question. I know that she had become a friend and I enjoyed being with her. Where else, I might well ask today, does love begin?

So the memories flood back—sweat, sand, Coca Cola, and eventually beer; hot days and dark, humid nights, popcorn, a dangerously tilting dinghy, warm waves; the jukebox, war songs that we didn't associate with fighting and dying like "Don't Sit under the Apple Tree with Anyone Else but Me" and "There'll be Bluebirds over the White Cliffs of Dover," and "Praise the Lord and Pass the Ammunition" and "I Left my Heart at the Stage Door Canteen"; blistered feet, hot dogs covered with mustard, the pungent aroma of young bodies, the taste of dank air, soft and willing lips, firm young breasts.

And Jane.

My most powerful and poignant memory is of the dark. City boy that I was, I did not know night. At the Lake the immense oaks reduced starlight and even moonlight to a faint glow. The occasional patch of light in a window during the week and the dim, leaf-obscured streetlamps only added to the mysterious peace of the night. The summer smells, lake, beach, oak trees, garbage, were particularly intense in the dark and seemed to hang immobile on the curtains of humid air.

And Jane and I would be together, hand in hand, walking down Lake Shore Drive in the village and turning into the unpaved road to the Old Houses, silent ourselves in the enveloping silence, straining to hear a freight train in the distance, utterly alone in a world that was ours and only ours. As the years slipped away, we were more content to hold hands in the silence and required fewer kisses and caresses. Or maybe the physical affection was less important.

I cannot remember what we said, if we said much of anything at all. I remember only feelings of overwhelming tenderness, the like of which I would never experience again.

I assume we said that we loved one another and meant it, though in the early forties we could have only the vaguest notion of what love was and were in fact enjoying an adolescent crush, transient, flimsy, ephemeral.

Perhaps.

Or perhaps even in the summer of 1943 the two of us were already caught up in the love of each of our lives, an ember that still smolders, an ember in the ashes waiting for someone to pour gasoline on it.

I would learn what real darkness was like only in Korea. It was cold not warm, hell not an antechamber of heaven.

I also recall vividly the lust of those times for Mrs. Keenan's friends, the women who watched (with I thought notable lack of interest) from the pier the day of my first arrival. In those matrons, as I now realize, one might find the origins of the mystery that still haunts me.

I don't know when I first became conscious of the mystery, but it was before the accident in 1948. Very early, on the first day when I was able to take my eyes off of Packy's mother to ogle the other three on the pier, I realized dimly that something was wrong.

I still am not quite sure what it was.

Leo

"What's wrong with them, Packy?"

"Who?"

"Whom."

He nudged me with a sharp elbow. "You'd make a great English teacher."

I think it was the June of 1944. The car radio was playing "Meet Me in St. Louis, Louis," Allied troops had landed in Normandy. It seemed that the War would go on for a long time. I was worrying about whether I ought to stay in the seminary. I was uncertain that I had a vocation to the priesthood and I didn't want to use the seminary as a draft deferment. Packy and I were driving toward the Lake in the bulky, chunky LaSalle that seemed now to be his car.

"Our crowd's parents."

"Oh, *them!*" Packy shifted uneasily.

"Yeah."

"Too much money and too little sex."

"Especially the women."

He didn't take his eyes from the road.

"Especially the women."

"You read too many novels," Packy laughed. "What good does all that reading do you? How much money will it help you to make?"

I felt my face grow warm. Packy was kidding me again about Jane.

"If I leave the seminary, it won't be because of her," I replied uneasily.

"You're thinking of leaving?" His voice was casual, too casual.

"I'm not sure."

Bing Crosby filled the silence with "Toora Loora Loora."

Although she and I lived in the same parish I had seen her only a couple of times and then from a distance during the school year. At the Lake we were constant companions in public and passionate lovers in secret—though only for a few weekends and maybe the week before Labor Day. At home we were strangers. At the Lake, away from my mother's close supervision, I became another person. If Jane thought the transformation was odd, she did not say so. Perhaps she was as eager to hide our love from her family as I was to hide it from mine.

I didn't know whether she saw Phil Clare or not during the school year though I jealously assumed that she did. After all, I reasoned grimly, she went to Trinity and he had attended Fenwick before he went off to Notre Dame and his family moved from River Forest (which was on the West Side) to Lake Forest (which was on the North Side of the City and was the most exclusive of Chicago suburbs). Friendly enough with me at the Lake, indeed very friendly, Phil never did seem to realize that I lived in the same parish he did, even when he saw me coming out of church after Sunday Mass.

Our conversation ended.

I was uneasy at the thought that old people made love—and the Nicolas, Murrays, and Clares were by definition old. None of this was any of my business. Yet there was something strange about the three handsome couples, a tension I had sensed the first day at the Keenan house when Mrs. Keenan introduced me to her three friends who were lolling on the pier, women who were bored at best by their own children and couldn't care less about one more noisy adolescent.

I recall the day now, a vivid and erotic first impression of how the Catholic rich lived at the Lake on a summer day during the War. Giddy, slightly tipsy, high-pitched conversation that ended abruptly when Mary Anne Keenan brought us down to their freshly painted, brilliantly white pier next to their boathouse—also freshly painted. Half empty martini glasses, suntan lotion, white pier furniture, a big umbrella, a faint scent of alcohol, and lots of pampered womanly flesh: Iris Clare, sleek and trim in a strapless outfit; Elizabetta Nicola, a perfect little figurine in a daring (for then) black two-piece swimsuit; and Martha Murray, lush and earthy in a gray garment that was as much corset as it was swimsuit. Unlike Packy's mother the others showed no sign of having been in the water. Their swimming garb was for display, not for use.

Dazzled by the scene—which would have made an excellent if faintly satirical painting—and eager to escape from it lest my hot face reveal my lustful thoughts, I still felt even then that there were strange emotions leaping back and forth among the three women.

Sexual emotions at that; and of the sort that were beyond my youthful comprehension.

In retrospect I realize that much of the tension might have been the result of the fact that three beautiful women at the height of their sexual powers were living most of the summer without men. Their husbands would join them at the summer house on Friday night or perhaps even late Saturday afternoon and return to Chicago on Sunday evening. Not much intimacy.

Packy's father usually drove up on Thursday evening and returned on Monday morning. Lawyer's hours he would joke. Four nights provided a lot more opportunity for love I would later understand.

However, most women in summer resorts lived without their husbands for five or six nights of the week and they did not seem to be driven by the demons I sensed in Mrs. Keenan's three friends.

All three families were rich beyond my imagination, second and third generation wealth that had been untouched by the Great Depression and that was growing rapidly because of the War. Their huge rambling "Old Houses," Gothic, Victorian, Georgian, and Dutch Colonial, were on the top of hills with neatly tended lawns rolling down to the Lake shore and their piers—at each one of which bobbed an ancient and during the war rarely used powerboat. There were at least three servants at each house, all of them white, and at the Clares and the Nicolas a black chauffeur. Doctor Clare insisted on living in the old family home (built by his grandfather in the 1890s long before the bungalow belt invaded the area) in our neighborhood, before he moved to River Forest and then Lake Forest. The Nicolas and the Murrays were from Kenilworth, the most affluent of Chicago suburbs. Their daughters attended the Convent of the Sacred Heart and their sons Loyola Academy, which were the best in Catholic high schools. They drove Packards and Cadillacs, wore expensive clothes, traveled to Florida in the winter and crossed the Atlantic on the Queen Mary before the War.

Doctor Clare, a surgeon with a national reputation, was chief of staff at Passavant Hospital, a third generation successful Irish Catholic doctor who had made it into the medical establishment. A short slender man with a pencil mustache, weak chin, and long brown hair, he was always pleasant, a well-groomed and impeccably dressed M.D. with a flawless bedside manner. He spoke to everyone, even his son's friends, with the bland good humor that, I imagine, he would have used in the room of a terminal cancer patient.

"Phil Clare," Tom Keenan observed, "is not your ordinary surgeon. He doesn't think he is God and he doesn't demand that his family worship him."

"He even manages to find time to visit them occasionally," Mary Anne Keenan observed in a rare burst of sarcasm.

Astonishingly, Doctor Clare knew who I was. The red hair I suppose.

"I'm told your father plans to go into real estate after the War, Leo," he said to me one day while I was waiting outside their grotesque red brick Victorian house to pick up Phil for a tennis game.

I had heard vague hints of it around the house. My mother was adamantly opposed, afraid that our limited resources would be swallowed up when the Depression returned.

"If the Depression doesn't come back."

"Oh it won't come back. There's a lot of pent-up demand and the money to back it up. Those who are ready for the expansion after the war will make a lot of money."

I noticed for the first time that his small blue eyes, shrewd and hard, belied his reassuring bedside manner. Pirate's eyes.

"It wasn't that way in 1920," I said, continuing my mother's approved wisdom.

He laughed and patted my head, "The late forties won't be the early twenties, count on that."

My father did risk that the late forties would be different and changed our family fortunes, though we never did buy a house at the Lake.

I also noticed that night that Iris's eyes were as vague as her husband's were focused. I might have wondered if, despite her slim and appealing loveliness, she was much of a challenge to him.

Martin Nicola ("Tino" to his wife) seemed to me to be the kind of man who appeared in a Tuscan painting, about which I was learning in my quick visits to the Art Institute—a tall, elegant aristocrat with flashing black eyes who might have been a friend of Lorenzo de' Medici or Cesare Borgia. His parents were from Lucca in Northern Italy and had settled in Highwood north of Chicago, an enclave of immigrants from Parma and Lucca. They had been almost instantly successful in a restaurant and food supply business that he had inherited and built into a powerful food distribution network.

"Martin," Tom Keenan remarked expansively one night after supper, "is not exactly your local fruit peddler. He's on the board of the Chicago Opera and the Art Institute. And he's not connected at all to the Outfit—though of course he knows them."

"The Outfit," Packy swallowed half a steak in a single hungry bite, "doesn't mess with the Lucese. They're afraid of them."

"They sure are. Some sort of racial memory."

"Mr. Nicola reminds them of Cesare Borgia," I said, not looking up from my scoop of mashed potatoes.

General laughter at the resident comic.

"Or Niccolo Machiavelli?" Mr. Keenan asked

"Or Savonarola."

"I don't think, Lee, he'd burn anyone at the stake, but I take your point."

"I hope you're not comparing Mrs. Nicola to Lucrezia Borgia, Leo?" Mrs. Keenan smiled benignly at me.

"No ma'am. More like Maria D'Este."

"I don't think, my dear," Tom Keenan barely controlled his laughter, "we want to know who she was. Better that we leave Leo's fantasy life alone."

"For sure," Jane, who often ate with us, chipped in.

More general laughter.

For all of that I would not have wanted "Tino" Nicola as an enemy.

He had access to a seemingly limitless supply of elegant liquor. "So you like the Barolo wine, Irish?" he would ask me. "Pour him some more, Elizabetta. Perhaps we civilize him, no?"

We were sitting in the gleaming "sunroom" of their palatial Queen Anne Old House, surrounded by flowering plants, white wicker chairs and couches, and chattering parrots.

"Would your parents mind, Leo?" Mrs. Nicola paused over my goblet. "I would not want to offend them."

"No ma'am. They taught me never to refuse free booze."

Jane guffawed and pushed her goblet in the direction of Mrs. Nicola and the bottle. "Barolo, Leo," she said primly, "is *not* booze. Please don't embarrass us."

It seemed a happy house; Angie and her little sister were happy kids who appeared to be immune from parental wrath.

One hot evening she "borrowed" a bottle of Cord apricot liquor from her father's cabinet and brought it to a marshmallow roast.

"My papa says this is wonderful."

"Angie!" Packy exploded, "you'll get in terrible trouble when he finds out."

"No, I won't, Patrick," she insisted. "I'll tell him tomorrow and he'll say at least I have good, if expensive taste."

I took the first sip from a paper cup in which it was perhaps a grave sin to put such sublime booze.

We finished the bottle, with half the credit for this accomplishment belonging to me.

"Take my hand, Lunkhead," Jane instructed me later in the evening.

"Yes, Milady . . . why?"

"Because otherwise you won't find your way back to the Keenans', maybe not ever."

"I'm fine. The only trouble is this squadron of P-47s that is buzzing around in my head."

"Look *out* for that rock!"

The next day at the tennis court Angie smiled smugly. "I told papa and he said just what I knew he'd say. He asked me if you liked it."

"Did Irish like it?" I echoed what I knew her old man had said. "What did you tell him?"

"I said that Irish was acquiring a little civilization but still had a long way to go."

Jane whooped enthusiastically at my humiliation.

It is still possible, if you have sufficient clout with a liquor dealer, to find an occasional bottle of Cord. I keep one in my office at the University—rather against the rules to tell the truth, and offer a small sip of it, with a conspiratorial wink, to everyone whom we appoint a distinguished professor. If they have the taste to sigh blissfully, I know that besides a scholar we have found ourselves a true humanist.

James Murray Sr. (father of Jim and Eileen) was perhaps the richest of all. He presided over a brokerage firm in the loop and owned a chemical company that worked three shifts providing unspecified materials to the war effort.

"Profiteer, James," Tom Keenan had laughed at him, half-fun, and full earnest, as my mother would have said.

"Lawyers are doing all right too, Thomas." Mr. Murray would raise his glass of gin (no martini for him) in salute. "May we all prosper and live long enough to enjoy it."

The older Jim Murray, whose grandfather had sold arms to the Union Army during the Civil War was a genial Mick with silver hair and a red face, a handsome if somewhat dissolute-looking man with a loud tenor voice, quick wit and all the charm of a precinct captain who might also be the local undertaker. Oddly enough and despite three generations of wealth, he would have been a fine match for Jane's father, a touch of the gombeen man in both of them.

"Cut the cards with him," I whispered to Jane.

She giggled. "You bet."

He drank too much as did Jim and Eileen's mother Martha, too much even by the relaxed standards of the wealthy Irish Catholics at the Lake in those days. Jim and Eileen seemed to be following in their parents' path. The parents, unlike Jim who became even more melancholy after his second beer, were happy drunks. Their laughter and song merely became louder as they progressed along the road to incoherence.

"How does he ever manage to be so successful on the stock market," Mrs. Keenan would demand, "when he must have a hangover every morning?"

"Darned if I know," her husband shook his head in mystification. "There are not many firms that survived the Crash as well as his did."

"Flair, instinct, genetics," I offered.

Everyone at the Keenans' dark oak dinner table looked at me as though I had two heads—though by then they were used to my nutty comments.

"A thousand years of survival in British misrule," I continued, slopping up the remnants of my vegetable soup.

"And when the flair runs dry?" Tom Keenan was watching me intently.

"Boom," I imitated with my hand a plane crashing on the table.

"You could become very dangerous as the years go on, young man."

"You're telling us," Jane agreed. "Lunkhead sees too much."

"He's harmless," Packy said in weak defense of me.

Even the servant hovering behind us (the husband of a married pair who "took care" of the Keenans not only during the summer but all year round) laughed at me.

"He certainly thinks he's a ladies' man," I was pushing my luck, but what the hell. "Those expensive tailored suits and that cologne, which must cost a hundred dollars a bottle . . . and he's always flirting with women, even with children like Milady here."

"LUNKHEAD!" that worthy screamed at me.

"It's just part of his silly little game, dear," Mary Anne Keenan reassured me. "He's harmless."

"Don't bet on it." Her husband was frowning thoughtfully. "Don't bet on it . . . and I wonder, Master Kelly, what you say about us behind our back."

"That you have to be the kindest and most generous people in the world to feed hungry urchins like me and this woebegone Devlin child every night."

They all laughed, even said urchin whose eyes were already demolishing the cherry pie that was awaiting us for dessert.

The Keenan house was my parish, you see. In it I could I be myself the way I could never be at home.

Those three families, (four counting the Keenans, which sometimes I do and sometimes I don't) were the beautiful people of my youth, talented, wealthy, handsome, powerful. They dazzled, fascinated, obsessed me. I knew that I would never be like them, never own a house at the Lake, never live the way they lived. And, I would often add in my thoughts, never be unhappy like some of them seemed to be.

I remember in particular one formal dance at the Club. It must have been in 1945 because Phil Clare was there in his officer's uniform—his father having obtained for him some sort of supply officer's appointment in the medical corps. Phil came no closer to gunfire than Sheboygan Wisconsin—a couple of hours' drive from the Lake—and hence was available for golf with his father almost every weekend—and for dances at the Club with Jane.

The War in Europe was over and there was a pause before the invasion of Japan, an attack that it was said would cause at least a million American casualties.

The war did not seem to be on anyone's mind, however, that sparkling evening at the Keenans' cocktail party before the dance. The glasses clinked on the porch illumined for the evening by oil lanterns. The women, their light summer gowns rustling as they moved, giggled softly. The men, in white jackets and red cummerbunds, chatted about the coming "postwar" world. Quiet and unobtrusive dark-skinned servants offered hors d'oeuvres, and a pianist played Mozart and Strauss inside in the parlor.

I was there, in my own rented summer formal, because Angie Nicola, a gorgeous sixteen year old and hence eligible for the dance, had invited me as her date. Presumably Jane had set that up. Jane was with Phil, naturally, and Jim Murray with a Protestant whose name I don't remember.

Packy adhered to the seminary rules and stayed away from the dance and the party before the dance. He did not object, however, to my participation.

"Do you feel out of place here?" I asked Jane as I offered her two of the four goodies I had speared from a passing silver tray.

"What are you talking about, Lunkhead?"

She was the only woman at the party whose shoulders were marred by straps, albeit thin ones. She was also and easily the most beautiful woman in the room, looking older than her seventeen years in a pale white loosely hanging gown belted with a narrow strap, which suggested not so much Rome as Athens. Athena rather than Venus. I wanted desperately to kiss her and knew that I was not likely to get a chance.

"These people are rich and we're not."

"Not yet," she lifted her lovely shoulders indifferently. "Besides I think we are."

"It's not our world."

"They're not one bit different from us. Stare at all the boobs in the room if you want, but don't you dare ruin Angie's night by sulking."

"I won't."

I didn't.

"Isn't she beautiful, Leo?" Angie whispered. "Aren't they a lovely couple?"

"Who?"

"Jane of course, who else? Isn't she the most beautiful woman in the room?"

"Adolescent girl child in a high school prom dress that embarrasses her."

"*Leo*," she slapped my arm lightly in protest against this blasphemy.

I was watching Doctor Clare and his wife chat with Phil and Jane at the other side of the dance floor. Iris's dress was the most suggestive at the dance, flaming red and cut almost as low in front as in the back. The doctor doted on his son but I was not sure that he approved of Jane. His keen little eyes saw a coal man's daughter, a beautiful child perhaps, but not quite what he thought his son deserved as a wife. Iris Clare did not seem to mind, but she didn't count.

Or that was what I thought I saw. Or maybe what I read into the scene today with my memories of what I would learn later after I came home from Korea.

"It is not right," I drew my lovely little date closer, "to make comparisons among so many lovely women. Devlin's all right, but you're not bad yourself."

"Thank you, Leo," she murmured complacently. "I'm glad you like me."

In those days I liked them all. But in truth Angie was special.

Doctor Clare and his wife had a spat later that night, perhaps because she danced with many other men, and as the evening wore on her dancing was abandoned. After a quick and sharp exchange of words between her and the Doctor she stormed out of the Club, Phil in tow.

He returned a few minutes later, his broad, solid face furrowed in a baffled frown.

Guided her to the chauffeur, I thought.

I finally danced with Jane.

"I'll take Lunkhead off your hands for this dance," she said to Angie.

"Do I have to?" I protested.

"I want to see whether your dancing has improved."

I must have thought I had died and gone to heaven.

"Yeah," she said, "you are a little less clumsy than you used to be."

"You look very lovely tonight, Jane."

"A compliment?" She looked at me suspiciously.

"An observation."

"I bet."

"A little family fight?"

"You mean Doctor and Mrs. Clare?"

"Whom else?"

"She's such a nice woman except when she's drunk."

"And she's drunk every day by supper time."

"Tipsy, not drunk."

I took Angie home after the dance—in the Keenan Lasalle, which had by now become the group car—kissed her good night and drove back to our house. The Keenan family seemed to be asleep but I was too tense even to think about sneaking into my guest room (of which there were a half dozen). I strolled down to the pier and stared glumly at the Lake, seeing in its dark waters Jane in her long, gauzelike white gown in which she looked like a Greek goddess, a fairy tale princess, a Roman empress. Even if I left the seminary I would never have a shot at her. Her family, I felt sure, was delighted with Phil Clare's attentions. He was hopelessly enchanted by her. If he wanted her badly enough, Doctor Clare would not stand in the way of the match.

They might be married up here instead of back in the parish. They'd have their wedding reception at the Club and I wouldn't be invited. In four or five more years she would be Mrs. Phil Clare.

I kicked a stone and walked back to the house.

It was an accurate enough prediction, although their marriage was in 1951 instead of 1950. I was not invited because I was dead, Jane had wept at my funeral mass.

But I wasn't dead. I was shivering with fever while Phil and Jane were coupling with each other on their marriage bed.

Nonetheless, for all my self-pity on the pier that night, I still felt that I had been at a scene from a romantic novel—handsome men and beautiful women dancing under the stars while a band played idyllic music and multi-colored lights glittered on the waters of the Lake. Maybe a scene from the *Great Gatsby?* Perhaps, though I don't think I'd read that yet. More likely a picture from a Kipling story about the summer season at Simla—if that was the place where the Brits in India went for the summer. The men may not have looked like British officers, but the women all seemed mysterious and wonderful, especially the two princesses who were assigned to my care, one of them with skin sufficiently dark that she might be the daughter of a maharajah and the other perhaps the wife or the daughter of an Irish republican secret agent who had infiltrated into the British Army—for what purpose I was not altogether clear.

Magic, pure magic. Or so it seemed that night.

The feeling of magic faded away, but the memory of its images remained. Remains.

Our lives have worked out just the way I had thought they would that night. But it didn't have to be that way. Even less did it have to be that way a second time.

Jane

I'll have the largest double chocolate malt in the world, the customer insisted, and heavy on the malt!

Mom had demanded that I get a job during the summer because I needed to learn the value of money. I was sixteen, she said, and old enough to learn what money means. The world is a harsh place and you have to work for every penny you squeeze out of it. You've had enough opportunity to run around like a spoiled rich brat, now you have to settle down and find out what life is really like.

I didn't mind working. I liked my job at the Rose Bowl soda fountain on the municipal pier right next to where the boats docked. I liked my cute pink and white dress with its very short skirt; I liked mixing sodas and malts; I liked gobbling the ice cream myself; I liked the fountain with its gleaming marble-top tables and its big mirror and its pink and white walls and its smell of chocolate; I liked the customers—boys and girls and kids my own age and the servicemen and their dates, and older people who brought back a little of their own youth by buying ice cream after the movie; and I liked to make the customers laugh, especially those who were ready to complain because they had to wait for service.

Lunkhead! I screamed at the customer who had ordered the huge malt.

If he were up at the Lake during the week, which was not nearly often enough to suit me, he would often drop in to keep me company when business was slow, sometimes with Amadon and sometimes not.

Amadon would certainly be a priest.

We don't serve disreputable looking people here. This is a high class soda fountain.

High class help. And give me four cookies with the malt.

I did as I was told. On the house, I said when I put the huge concoction in front of him.

You'll spoil me . . . why so glum, chum?

I'm not glum, you're the moody one.

You're glum.

I'm thinking about graduation next year.

So you'll go to college.

There's no point in a girl going to college. She doesn't need it.

Bullshit.

Don't be vulgar. Ma wants me to work for the company until I get married. She says it won't hurt me to learn how the real world works before I settle down and have a family.

Go to college, Jane.

I can't. My family won't pay for it.

Win a scholarship to Rosary.

They won't give me a scholarship because they think my family has a lot of money.

Try for it.

Even if I win it, Pa and Ma won't let me take it.

Tell them that the Clares won't let their son marry a woman who hasn't gone to college.

I'm not going to marry Phil Clare!

Regardless! If you put up a fight your folks will back down, won't they?

Maybe.

He didn't realize how terrible my mom had become.

He leans across the counter, grabs both of my hands, and draws me so close that I can feel his breath, scented with Pepsodent, on my face.

Damn it Jane, he says, take the scholarship exam and go to college.

My legs turn to water, as they usually do when his fierce passion erupts. I can't argue with him. All I can do is agree.

I don't want . . .

Yes you do. Some of the time anyway. That's why you're glum.

His gorgeous green eyes absorb me, depriving me of all resistance to him and all protection against him.

In my fantasy I think again how wonderful it would feel to be naked for him.

You're hurting me, I try ineffectually to pull away.

No I'm not. Take the exam, do you hear me? Then smile at me like you do at all the other customers.

Oh, all right!

I glance around quickly to make sure the Rose Bowl is still empty and then kiss him. He holds my lips with his and then releases me.

I bet you kiss all the customers that way.

Only stupid little boys!

I know what he will do. He will talk to Mr. Keenan who will talk to the nuns at Rosary and, if I win the scholarship, they'll give it to me. So I can go to college if I want.

But I'm still not sure that college for a girl isn't a waste of time. Ma says it is and ma is always right.

Well, no she isn't always right, but we have to act like she is or she breaks up furniture and throws statues and vases at us.

Leo

My father, already embarked on the real estate business that would bring him affluence of which a few years before he would not have dreamed, took my departure from Quigley philosophically, as I knew he would.

I had left the seminary at the end of the summer of 1945 because I said that I felt that I didn't have the personality required to be a priest. The Rector, who liked me, insisted that I did too have the personality, and that I was a natural leader with people.

I'm not sure he was wrong. People have come to me in search of help since my first year as an assistant professor. The real reason for leaving, however, was that the vocation was my mother's, not mine. I admired priests, but I had no desire to be one. Jane had nothing to do with it. Otherwise I would have phoned her as soon as I quit.

"If you're not cut out for it," Dad said, "then you're not cut out for it. There are too many unhappy priests. Better that you find out that it's not for you now instead of then."

My mother wailed for days. She had made so many novenas, she had prayed so hard to the Sacred Heart of Jesus, she had made so many promises to the Virgin Mary. I was breaking her heart.

My brother Pete was ordained in the middle sixties and left to marry a nun two years later. Instead of my mother complaining about a broken heart, she protested about the "silly rule that priests can't marry."

The world changes.

"Well, the war's over," she said to me when she finally dried her tears. "At least you won't have to go into the service."

I suppose that one of the reasons I signed up for the ROTC at Loyola was so that there would be no doubt in anyone's mind, which meant of course my own mind, that I had not been a draft dodger in the seminary.

It was not the wisest decision I ever made.

Fourth
of July

God wants to be thought of
as our Lover.
I must see myself so bound in love
as if everything that has been done
has been done for me.
That is to say, the Love of God makes such
a unity in us
that when we see this unity
no one is able to separate oneself
from another.

—Julian of Norwich

1978

Leo

"Hiyah, Mr. Provost, great to see you again!"

The man who extended a massive right hand to me was tall, trim, and quite bald. He wore a suit that had been carefully made to fit his solid athletic shoulders. His handsome, cheerful face shone in a happy grin.

A distinguished contributor to the University, I assumed. I'd better pretend to know him.

The President should be dealing with such folk, but since I was a native Chicagoan and something of a hero returned to the city, a few folks, including the very distinguished contributor for whom I was waiting in the dark, oak-paneled, prestige-heavy lobby of the Chicago Club, wanted to see me.

I didn't like that part of the job, but it went with the territory.

"Nice to see you again." The face was vaguely familiar.

"Missed you at the Lake on Memorial Day. I hope you're going to be up on the Fourth."

"I will try to make it. I'm not sure Jerry and Maggie will have room for me."

"It's a big house. Didn't the Murrays own it before the Keenans bought it back in 1930?"

"I guess so. That's when the Murrays thought they needed an even bigger place. It doesn't seem to be haunted."

"If herself says it isn't haunted, then it isn't."

Maggie, who was something of a psychic, had never said that it wasn't haunted. But the terrible events that befell the Murrays occurred long after they had sold the house to Tom Keenan and moved out.

In fact, I was of mixed mind about the Fourth—hungry to see Jane again and wary of my own hungers.

"Everyone sure is proud of you. First Catholic to be Provost of the University. That's some accomplishment. We all knew you'd make it big."

Then I knew who it was, Dickie Devlin, Richard Mulcahy Devlin, the very same one who had warned me off his sister on our grammar school graduation night.

"It sounds a lot better than it is, Dickie; there's not much money in being a college administrator."

"Hell, it's not the money that counts."

I felt like I was on a merry-go-round running out of control. This could not be Dickie Devlin.

"I suppose not."

"Look, Mickie and I haven't given anything to that place because we thought it was anti-Catholic. I guess it isn't, huh?"

"No, Dickie, it's not, never was really. Some of the faculty may have been, but the school isn't."

"Yeah, well, we've been thinking of doing something in honor of Herbie . . . he died, you know, too much booze for the liver, didn't quit soon enough like I did . . . so what would it cost for a chair or something out there?"

The merry-go-round would never stop. Never.

"A million."

"That's not bad." He played with a very large diamond on the index finger of his hand. "Could we name it after Herbie?"

"Certainly. Or perhaps name it after your parents in his honor."

We had named chairs after far worse bandits.

"Yeah, that would be a great idea . . . What would it be in?"

Was this thug, former thug, whatever, actually going to write me a check for a million dollars?

"What about Irish history?"

"Yeah, Ma and Pa would have loved that. I'm named after Dick Mulcahy, General Richard Mulcahy, you know, and Mickie, well, he's named after the Big Fella, Michael Collins himself . . . Well I can't say for sure till I talk to Mickie, but I think we can hack it. If I don't see you at the Lake over the Fourth I'll give you a ring."

And I must call the zoo to see about other leopards who had changed their spots.

"You hear about that asshole Phil?"

"I hear he wants a divorce from Jane."

"Yeah, that too. Can you imagine anything so stupid? I mean we tried to hold things together for the kid's sake, little Lucy, you know but what the hell, Janie's had it and I don't blame her. *He* wanted the divorce and he fooled around on their honeymoon."

"Really?"

"It's going to be final next week. We'll keep him on the payroll for old time's sake, but he's finished as far as I'm concerned. I think poor Jane might have taken him back if it wasn't for this latest business."

"Latest business?"

"Yeah, the insider trading thing. It's all in today's *Wall Street Journal.* It's bad enough to get caught doing that kind of stuff these days. It's even worse when you look like an idiot because you didn't make any money doing it."

"Will he go to jail?"

"Nah," Dickie shrugged his huge shoulders, "he'll walk. All the Feds want is his testimony. What really pisses me off is that he involves Janie. She took it pretty hard, poor kid."

"He involved her?"

"Typical asshole move. Says he didn't intend to do anything wrong. Just meant to help people."

"If I remember Phil, that's probably true."

"Yeah, but, tell you the truth, Lee, that wears thin after a while, know what I mean?"

"Indeed it does . . . will Jane be charged?"

"Not likely. The Feds are into harassing these days. But she doesn't need the aggravation, poor kid."

"I agree."

"Those were great times we had in the old days."

"They certainly were."

I could not remember a single encounter with Dickie at the Lake, not a one. I did my best to stay out of his path. Never pick an unnecessary fight.

"Well, she's rid of him at last, thank God. Monsignor Packy says there'll be no trouble about an annulment. Practically all of them are granted these days, which I think is really an improvement, don't you?"

"I didn't need one myself," I said answering his indirect question. "My wife didn't want to be married in church. Then it wasn't important to me. Now it is."

"Yeah, well I always thought Janie would marry you instead of him. It would have been a lot better."

"Perhaps."

"But you were dead."

"So I was."

"Hell, I went to your funeral mass. Never saw so many tears in all my life, especially when they sang that *Ave Maria* you liked so much at the end of the Mass."

"So I'm told."

I had never liked any *Ave* all that much.

"Well, I gotta go over to the Chicago Athletic Club for my workout. You'd think they'd build a gym in this place wouldn't you?"

"It wouldn't be a bad idea."

"See you at the Lake maybe; and I'll be in touch about that chair, know what I mean?"

I thanked him, we shook hands and I collapsed into a couch, still reeling from my carnival ride. Jane's brother had just offered a chair to the University and his sister to me. I was trying with great difficulty to rewrite time lost to give it a different meaning and he had done so effortlessly. Too accurate a memory of time lost is not always an asset.

I'd written a book about the years from 1945 to 1965 called *The Big Change*. It was not too popular when it first appeared after Nixon had been tossed out. It was not fashionable in that era to suggest that anything good had happened before 1965. But now my argument that the era after 1965 was the logical outcome of the enormous social and economic changes in the "postwar" era had become fashionable. I suppose it will become unfashionable in a few more years as a new generation of assistant professors struggle for tenure. I had said that the "postwar" era was the most revolutionary since the time of Andrew Jackson. But that was a global perspective. I didn't expect Dickie Devlin to be part of that revolution.

If it's wonderful how a little money can change a person, it is even more wonderful how a lot of money can change him.

I reflected on the half century of my life. When I was in grammar school we all seemed poor, except the Devlins and the Clares. Then came the war and the years afterward and we spent our time catching up on all the things we missed in the Depression. When Kennedy was inaugurated we were convinced that the American "know-how," which had won the war, would solve all the social problems in the country and the war. Then came Vietnam, the assassinations, the riots, anti-war demonstrations, Cambodia, Kent State, protest marches, Woodstock, the Days of Rage, Watergate, the Nixon pardon, the Arab oil embargo. All the institutions of our society seemed to disintegrate. There was no credibility left. One of my younger colleagues, a self-proclaimed radical with a thousand dollar stereo system in his apartment told me five years ago that the revolution had already occurred and that in a few years the whole of American society would fall into the hands of his generation to remake.

I told him that much more likely there would be a dramatic turn to the right because the ordinary folk thought that he and his kind were dead wrong.

Now I think we both were correct. Most of our institutions have lost a lot of their credibility, but no one is going to change our society very much. So the revolutionaries continue to pile up consumer goods and the radicals talk radicalism and make a lot of money and the rest of us combine suspicion of institution with personal success working for the institutions.

Roaring twenties all over again, maybe.

So Leo T. Kelly, snot-nosed poor Irish Catholic kid from the West Side becomes Provost of the University, thinks of buying a summer home at the Lake, and eats lunch at the Chicago Club.

If I try to do a sequel to *The Big Change*, it will be a much more complicated book.

"You look dazed," the smooth, impressively scented CEO said to me.

I looked up, startled. "I just encountered someone from my past who represented perfectly my thesis about change after the war."

We ascended the spectacular staircase with the polished brass rails to the second floor lobby overlooking Michigan Avenue, a room fit for a Presidential Inauguration Ball.

"World War II?" He was six or seven years older than I and had fought in the war. "Whole different world after the war. Kids today don't understand that. You look like you need a drink. It must have been a hell of an experience."

"It was and I do, even if it's only twelve-thirty."

I had two Jameson's and thanked heaven I had come downtown on the South Shore instead of driving. Back in my office, I was just barely awake for the tenure conflict meeting that awaited me. The unread *Wall Street Journal* lay on my desk through the whole interminable meeting, a torment to my already numb powers of concentration.

The Provost's office at the University, large, dark, opulent, elegant, is designed I think to recall an office in Oxford or Cambridge, something set up in Good King George's time. Actually, the administration building, a solid gray block, is New Deal–ugly in design, perhaps the least handsome building on the University's main quadrangle. As soon as you leave my office, the impression of old wisdom and reverent respect for university traditions disappears into what could be a corridor in an aging hospital or a somewhat run down hotel.

Nonetheless, my office is not the proper setting for a noisy fight because the drapes and the carpets and the wall hangings absorb the voices of the shouters, who, to be effective, must set the Provost's teeth on edge like a ruler on a blackboard, instead of almost putting him into an alcohol induced nap.

The case was a repeat of Emilie's and typical of many other tenure fights we have in the universities these days. It was easy to decide in a certain sense because the merits were clear; only political pressures created a problem. When the merits are in doubt, the problem is much different for it involves truth and not mere prudence.

The young woman was a Berkeley Ph.D. in psychology. She was apparently a good teacher, popular with students, and untiring in her work for them. She was also a radical political activist in a wide variety of causes. These activities would not have been a serious problem (save for some senior busybodies in the Social Science Division) if she had any modestly impressive publications. If you are going to be a radical, I had always said, that's fine so long as you publish too. But this woman had produced less than my former wife. She had organized enough support for herself in the Department to get a one vote majority in favor of a very weak report for promotion and tenure. These kinds of recommendations are a sign to the University that Department is afraid to say "no" and expects the Dean to do so. Our Dean promptly did so. When the professor's "activist" supporters screamed at him, he did what Deans do, he set up a review committee, which of course came through with the expected support of the Dean—thus responsibility for an unpopular decision is spread around and there's no one on whom to focus blame.

Until it gets to the Provost.

There was a lot of screaming in my office that afternoon. I figured that I was escaping from some time in purgatory.

If I thought that the candidate for tenure had a chance of producing important work in the future I might have compromised by arranging for a five year non-tenure promotion, an easy way out if you're not sure. But this young woman clearly had just barely finished her dissertation; teaching and activism were an excuse for her temperamental inability to be a scholar.

The arguments hurled at me were *a*) teaching is as important if not more important than research and *b*) denial of promotion was discrimination against her because she was a Marxist and a woman.

"I quite agree," I began slowly, as Provosts must (you don't want to play the smart mouth Irish Catholic in such a situation), "that teaching is at the heart of this University's mission. It has been so from the beginning. It must be a prime concern when we consider a lifetime appointment (lie, but only a small one). I personally would want to see it become a matter of even greater concern (absolute truth unless the person looks like a future Nobel winner). However, by itself it has not been and can never be the only criterion. I would be more sympathetic to Ms. Lewellyn if there was more evidence of scholarly research in her record. Candidly, I'm afraid I don't see that."

More outcry, including the suggestion that I had engaged in sexual intercourse with my mother.

I let them finish, noting in my head the names of the obscenity shouters for future discreet retribution.

"Ms. Lewellyn knew the rules of the game at this University when she accepted an appointment as an assistant professor. She did not play by the rules. I'm very sorry, but I am not authorized to bend those rules for anyone, no matter how admirable they may be in other respects."

"The Department recommended her."

"A very weak recommendation I'm afraid, not the sort that persuades us that a lifetime appointment would be appropriate."

More obscenities. Then they straggled out of the office.

"She'll sue," said our legal counsel.

"Naturally. A radical lawyer will take the case on contingency."

"She doesn't have a chance in hell."

"It will keep her happy and you busy."

"You realize you'll have to face that radical lawyer in a deposition?"

"It goes with the territory."

And it would go into my record book with the radicals, to be used against me if I was ever considered for a University presidency.

So what.

"So long as you understand," said our law man.

"One of the advantages of having an Irish Catholic provost," I said with my patented leprechaun grin, "is that his sort rather enjoys an argument, especially with a lawyer, and most especially with one who thinks rage is a substitute for disciplined intelligence."

"May the tribe increase."

The confrontation meant nothing of course. It was a ceremony, not unlike the kind our anthropologists observe in some tribes in which conflicts are acted out in dance rather than in actual combat. The protesters knew that I would not overrule the Dean and his committee. They understood the cowardly trick the psychology department had played on the young woman. They knew that she didn't have the credentials for promotion. They knew they were fighting a lost cause. They probably knew that I knew that they knew. The whole affair was a ritual that made them feel good because they could tell themselves they were revolutionaries fighting "the system" and "the establishment." Moreover their protests freed them from the responsibility of doing their own work, which was probably less interesting and certainly less satisfying than "radical protest." They also had the erotic oedipal pleasure of attacking one of the father figures in the University—me.

What better way to spend an afternoon in early summer?

Thus had the intense radicalism of a decade ago deteriorated into bourgeoisie rituals, not unlike churchgoing among Trollope's Victorians or praying over yam gardens on the South Pacific islands.

Sometimes I think it would be a tremendous improvement in the life of a university if the faculty had to work for a living.

Before I could pick up the *Journal* Laura called from Santa Fe asking if it was alright if she flew in for the Fourth.

"At the Lake?"

"If you don't mind."

"Why should I?"

"Will you be there?"

"Now I have a reason."

"Only one?"

"Don't be fresh, young woman."

She responded with impish giggles.

The *Journal* story made me want to join the radicals who had just left my office. Did we live in Nazi Germany after all?

Philip Clare, socially prominent Chicago investment broker, had been a member of a weekly poker club of eight prominent businessmen—other brokers and corporate executives, including two local CEOs—which met in various loop offices and played for high stakes. At these poker sessions, illegal under the laws of the State of Illinois, broad hints were exchanged about future corporate actions that would have a strong impact on the stock market. These hints were enough for several of the participants to make millions of dollars. Mr. Clare had purchased stock in his name and the names of members of his family repeatedly just before the corporate actions. The patterns of his success—which did not cancel out his failures in other investments—attracted the attention of Internal Revenue Service agents who were investigating Mr. Clare's tax returns and had also begun to wonder about the poker club. Further investigation of the investment patterns of other club members revealed that they too seemed to know beforehand of major corporate actions, though they had covered their tracks much better than Mr. Clare had.

The investigators had discovered that Mr. Clare had made more than twenty purchases in the name of his now estranged wife Jane Devlin Clare. Both the Clares are under investigation by a Federal Grand Jury, although government attorneys deny that Ms. Clare is a "target" of the investigation. Ms. Clare's attorney denies that his client had ever purchased or sold stock through her husband's office or that she knew anything about either the poker club or her husband's deals in her name. He also protested an early morning visit of federal agents to Ms. Clare's home in Kenilworth to obtain samples of her handwriting.

I was well aware such was the strategy of the Feds these days: they woke you up at three in the morning, threatened to arrest members of your family, and questioned you like you were already a convicted criminal. They hoped that under such conditions you would not think of calling your lawyer and might make damaging admissions that they could use against you in court.

How like the Gestapo!

Surely Jane was smart enough to hire good lawyers. Dickie had said that she was in no danger of indictment. The Feds had assured the *Journal* that she wasn't a target. There was nothing much I could do to help her even if she was.

Nonetheless, there was no longer any question about it. I would spend the Fourth of July holiday with the Keenans.

Leo

"It was terrible, Maggie." Jane leaned across the table on the terrace of the Club, overlooking the incredibly almost intolerably blue lake, where we were eating lunch. "Lucy answered the door in her sleep T-shirt and these big brutes pushed their way into the house and demanded to see me. For some reason she said I wasn't home and they arrested her for perjury— giving a false answer to a federal agent. Lucy went hysterical and her screams woke me up. They made me sign my name about thirty times on a bunch of index cards and then told us to put on our clothes, they were taking us down to the Dirksen Federal Building for more questioning. I asked them if I were under arrest and they said no but my daughter was."

"Bastards," Maggie muttered. As in our other summer she had needed only a half minute to recoup her good spirits after a close loss on the tennis courts, but she had yet to settle into her professional psychologist mode.

"My colleagues on the Seventh Circuit who let them get away with it are the ones to blame," her husband added.

"Well, we know *they* are all bastards!" She stirred her iced tea like a witch mixing up a brew.

Jerry Keenan, Packy's "crazy" fighter pilot brother was now a model of serenity, albeit disciplined serenity. Not as tall as Packy but with the family silver hair and wide, solid face and broader shoulders than the family priest, he towered over his diminutive wife whom he clearly adored now as much as he had when they were newlyweds thirty years ago.

"On the way downtown," Jane poked listlessly at her fruit salad, "I realized that I had the right to call a lawyer, which they hadn't reminded us of . . ."

"They probably shouted it at Lucy," the Judge said, "and knew she didn't hear what they said."

"And I also realized that my son was a lawyer at a very important firm. So I insisted on calling him. He and Melinda were there in fifteen minutes. My Yuppie son and his Yuppie wife became screaming meanies and made me proud of them. The Feds backed off about questioning us. Then a senior litigator from their firm showed up. He told them that if they intended to use evidence obtained in a pre-morning raid, he'd have all charges thrown out of court. He also asked whether they seriously intended to arraign Lucy on their ridiculous perjury charges, which they knew wouldn't stand up, especially against a juvenile who had been rousted out of bed. They said they only wanted to ask a few questions. He suggested certain . . ." she grinned wanly, "anatomically improbably sexual actions and we stalked out."

"Serves them right," Jerry Keenan nodded in approval. "Then when they found out that poor Phil's imitation of your signatures were clumsy forgeries and that you had never given him any of your investments, they would drop all charges against you if you testified against him before the Grand Jury.''

"I can't believe it," I murmured. "Maybe my radical friends at the University are right."

"The point, Lee," Jerry said solemnly, "is that they didn't get away with it."

"They sure tried to."

"So poor Phil comes running to me," Jane rushed on, impatient to finish telling her story, "and begs me to delay the final divorce decree so I can't be compelled to testify against him."

"That wouldn't matter, would it?" I asked, dumping a large glob of ketchup on my hamburger.

"Of course not," Jane said, "but poor dumb Phil doesn't know that. He tries to explain that he made the investments in my name and intended to give all the money to me when things got straightened out. He probably did too, only things never get straightened out in his life."

Fourth of July sounds—whining whistles and exploding firecrackers were increasing. I winced every time I heard a loud explosion. There was no snow and I wasn't cold, but I was back at the reservoir, killing Chinese by the scores, perhaps by the hundreds.

"I'm getting a little tired," Maggie cut in, "of hearing Phil called poor. He's in the mess he's in now because no one has ever put any reality restraints in his life."

"I am as guilty of that as anyone," Jane said sadly.

"He's marvelously skilled," Maggie drummed her clenched little fist on the table, "at manipulating people to feel sorry for him."

My friends were too upset by Jane's story to do much with their lunches. Typically, anger made me furiously hungry. I dug into my second hamburger.

"So what happened?" I demanded.

Jane was running out of steam, a badly frayed woman whose life-long mask of charm and good humor was fading away.

"So I went back a couple of days later with the litigator—my kids are in estate work, which kind of fits them, doesn't it?—and answered a few specific questions about my own investment practices . . ."

"Which have not been unsuccessful, I gather?"

"Don't talk," she grinned for the first time in our conversation, "with food in your mouth, Lunkhead . . . I've done all right. Anyway they've pretty much forgotten about me, although they won't absolutely guarantee I'm off the hook."

"Typical," the judge murmured.

"Then Lucy goes out and gets drunk the next weekend, which makes the whole thing worse . . . Maggie, is this in the genes? I mean, Herbie died of cirrhosis of the liver and poor Iris's death was at least related to drinking too much. My brothers quit but they were near alcoholics and I think Phil is too. Does Lucy have a chance?"

Only Tino Nicola (and of course both the Keenans) of the parents of our crowd were still alive. They had all died in their late fifties or early sixties, all before their time, all more or less tragically. Lizabetta in an explosion. The Murrays, both drunk, ironically in a traffic accident driving to the Lake. Iris Clare and Ita Devlin of cirrhosis of the liver in their late fifties. Joe Devlin of a heart attack. Four of the six deaths attributable to the drink taken, as the Irish used to say.

What a curse it is. Yet we continue to drink.

"Neither heredity nor environment," Maggie's answer was guarded and professional, "determine completely what we do. Lucy is under somewhat higher risk because so many people in her family have coped with their pain by drinking too much but she's not fated to take the same road they did . . . is she doing well with her therapist?"

"She won't talk to me about it. She's still going and she doesn't miss appointments any more."

"That's a good sign."

"I've had one addicted child, I don't know that I could take another."

Maggie patted her hand. "You'll do all right, Jane. It's good that you're able to talk about these things finally."

Maggie caught my faint wink over my hamburger at her clinical cliché response, and, imp that she is beneath it all, she winked back.

As we talked and ate, I had glanced around the Club and considered it again in the broad light of day and of thirty years of life. It was not the forbidden castle of my early teens nor the magic pavilion of my fanciful Kiplingesque India, nor even a place into which Gatsby might have wanted to intrude. It was merely a summer resort golf course—of middling challenge I suspected—with worn-out tennis courts, a pool that needed repairs, a clubhouse and a terrace where one could eat middling meals and find an occasional glass of Jameson's and a hell of a lot of Irish who were, unlike my companions, drinking too much even at midday.

Had it ever been anything else? Back in those days when Catholics were a tiny minority like the Keenans and their friends and long before they had taken it and the whole resort over almost totally?

Had it once really been the preserve of the super rich as it had seemed to me then? Or once everyone you know has the money necessary to buy a house at the Lake and join the Club, does it by definition stop being magical? Or had they all been just comfortably rich like the natives today and not super rich at all?

Anyway the really rich were now somewhere else and they still had servants.

When the Irish move in and the Italians with them, first thing you know the whole neighborhood changes.

After she had spilled her story, Jane recovered her good humor and dug into her fruit salad. She could put her mask on easily because it was only partially a mask. Much of the Jane *persona* was also the real Jane. The mask however, was, not quite able to cope with a life in which tragedy had loomed so large.

"See you tonight," she waved at me as she rushed off for another round of tennis. "I'm buying the popcorn!"

"I'll buy the ice cream," I shouted after her.

This complex Jane with a tragic dimension in her personality was even more appealing to me. I realized as I walked back down the road to the Keenan house that my physical desire for her body, so attractive in tennis whites, which now permitted form fitting white knit blouses, was almost unbearably intense. Had I wanted her that badly in the forties? Or does age and experience sharpen passion for the desired other even if the hormone count is lower?

Mine didn't seem any lower.

I have said that I can live with celibacy if necessary and have done so for long periods in my life. But now I was free and so, for all practical purposes, was someone I had wanted very much in years past. There was no longer any reason to be celibate, was there?

I put on my swim trunks and joined Maggie and Jerry and their various young people and Laura on the pier. I dove in the water at once and swam what must have been a half mile.

"Firecrackers still bug you, huh, Leo?" Maggie, hanging on the side of the pier with her fingertips asked me as I joined her.

"Only the loud ones. Do they bother Jerry?"

"Not much. But no bullets ever came near his plane. Charmed life."

"He was lucky."

"Walk didn't get her out of your system?"

"Neither the walk nor the swim did much for my bloodstream," I admitted.

She chuckled. "Tread carefully, Lee, my friend, but tread!"

"It looks like I don't have much choice . . . tell me, Mag, is your house haunted?"

"By the poor Murrays, God be good to all of them?"

"Yeah."

She lifted her trim little shoulders. "Every house is haunted, Lee, by the psychic memories that linger there. This place," she nodded towards the beloved Gothic monstrosity on top of the hill, "has more memories lurking around than most but they don't really bother us much, not even me, and if there is a vibration anywhere within a mile I usually pick it up."

"Are they still there?"

"Jim and Marty Murray and Jimmy and Eileen? No, they're not there.

They're in heaven with God. But the memories of what happened are still there, kind of floating around, though of course they died long after they sold the house to the Keenan clan.''

"What kind of memories?"

"Not bad, certainly not scary, just a little sad."

"Could we, uh, get in touch with them, with the memories I mean?"

"Absolutely not!" She jabbed a finger at me. "Don't even think of it!"

"Yes ma'am."

"They screwed around a lot, you know?"

"The Murrays?"

"All of them, except the Keenans of course. I think that all the women slept with Tino at one time or another. And Martha with Doctor Clare too. I'm not sure about poor Lizabetta. She didn't have much willpower and those other two could have talked her into anything."

"Their husbands knew?"

"Poor fools! No, of course not. They thought they were the great lovers."

"You figured this out."

"It was obvious from the first couple of weeks I was here."

"Tom and Mary Anne knew?"

"I never asked them, but I assume they did. They didn't miss much, either of them."

Then Laura and young Jamie Keenan (who was her age) forced me to join them on the Keenan Starcraft for water skiing.

The plastic powerboats with their inboard/outboard motors are much less expensive and much easier to maintain but lack the elegance of the old wooden inboards. The Lake was crowded with boats on a holiday afternoon but Jamie and Laura, she in the most minimal of bikinis, gave a glorious performance on their slalom skis. My own exhibition on two skis was less than distinguished. Nonetheless Laura praised it as "not bad for someone your age."

"Isn't Jamie Keenan, like *totally* gorgeous, Daddy?" she demanded as we walked up to the house together, "and would you believe that he's going to be a *priest!*"

"It runs in the family," I said.

"I guess so . . . I heard that you and Jane beat his parents again this morning."

"Jane?"

"You *know*, Mrs. Clare."

"You call her Jane to her face?"

"Sure, why not? She's like one of the kids anyway."

"Is she?"

"Totally."

"I guess she would be at that."

"Are you going to see her tonight?"

"There's some talk about going to the movies?"

"To see a film? In town? Wow! Really! . . . Will you need the car?"

"We'll walk into town, like we used to do."

"*Daddy!*" she mocked me. "No one ever walked into town, not even in the old days, before the Big Change."

Laura claims to have read my prize winner five times and now to understand me "totally." I doubt the five times, but I do not doubt the understanding.

"It was kinda fun," I said weakly.

She laughed all the louder.

Then we arrived at the Keenans' screened-in porch on which thermopane windows could be placed in the winter. Gothic doesn't have such porches, but when the Irish took over the Old Houses on the hills they promptly built additions without concern for the architecture.

"Can we sit and talk, Daddy?"

"Sure." I felt my throat tighten as it always does when Laura wants a serious conversation.

"I'm going to spend a week or so with Mom in Boston after I finish in New Mexico. Is that okay?"

"Fine. If you want to. Any special reason?'

"Well," she wrapped her beach towel around herself as though a bikini, such as it was, did not seem appropriate for a serious discussion. "She *really* wants me to and I thought it wouldn't do any harm."

"I'm sure it wouldn't."

I tried to sound as casual as I could. Did I fear and hate my ex-wife as much as I felt I did at that moment?

"See, she's worried that you and that school over in Switzerland might prevent me from developing any of what she calls 'feminist consciousness.' So she wants me to meet her friends in Boston and go to a couple of meetings of her 'consciousness' group, you know?"

Convert her daughter?

"If you want to."

"Don't sound worried, Daddy," Laura pleaded. "That stuff's all b.s. Maybe her generation needed it but we just laugh at it. Like, we're feminists before we can talk, you know?"

"I'm sure you're right, Laura. Only don't try to tell your mother that."

"I *won't* . . . the real reason she wants me, Daddy, though she'd never say it, is because she's so lonely. Her latest boyfriend has moved out and some of her students laugh at the things she says about men in her women's studies class and she feels so horrible."

Just at that moment I did too.

"I'm sure she does, Laura . . ."

"She'll never get over it, poor woman. But maybe I can ease the pain for a few days, you know?"

"That's wonderful, Laura. I'm proud of you."

Indeed I was; though she didn't really understand all that she was saying, she had still put her finger unerringly on the truth about Emilie.

"She wants me to call her Emilie, instead of Mom. She says Mom is a word that indicates oppression. Can you imagine that!"

"You call Mrs. Clare Jane?"

"Yeah but she's not my mother." She bounded out of the chair and toward the door of the house. "Not even my stepmother."

"Laura!"

She ducked inside and dashed up the stairs to the bedroom floor.

Then she turned around. "If she ever becomes my stepmother, I'll reevaluate."

"*Laura!*"

"Have a great time at the movies!"

Patrick

In my early years at the parish after ordination I saw little of Jane and Phil and less of Leo. The Clares live about as far away from our "box-on-a-slab" neighborhood as you could and still be in Cook County. She produced her first three children in four years. Lucy came much later—in 1963. I was in Rome for the Council at the time, so I didn't baptize her, though I had introduced her older sister and brothers into the Church. Phil didn't show up at one of the baptisms. From my mother and sister-in-law I heard all the stories about Phil's infidelities. Yet the few times I did see Jane she was the old Jane again, cheerful, self-possessed, gorgeous. I wondered how anyone could cover up tragedy so effectively.

Leo also seemed much better. He was burning up the political science program at the University and grinding out impressive scholarly articles. He never came near the Lake but had supper with us in River Forest a couple of times each winter before he left for California and I left for Rome. We never mentioned Jane.

In Rome I was too much caught up in the euphoria of the Second Vatican Council and then the deliberations of the birth control commission to think much about my friends from the 1940s. I had lost touch with Leo after he went to California and learned of his marriage to Emilie only in a Christmas card. Mom phoned me in Rome after the first of the year to say with a sigh of relief that they hadn't been married in Church. Like Maggie she had never quite given up the idea that somehow Jane and Leo would get together again.

I never really did forget Jane. How could anyone ever forget her? But her life was settled and so was mine.

The Council years were an incredible time. In the seminary we had come to believe that the Catholic Church would never change even in the slightest matter. Then, all of a sudden, the altars turned around, the Mass was said in English, we could eat meat on Friday, birth control and even clerical celibacy became issues that could be discussed freely. My Cardinal had me appointed to the Secretariat of the Council so I could keep an eye on the curialists who were trying to wire things behind the scene.

"I would bet," he told me, "on a Chicago Irishman from a political family any day to outsmart these Italian conspirators."

"So would I," I agreed modestly.

They were exciting days. The council was making history and I was in the thick of the battles on religious liberty and on the Jews, the two big issues for the Americans. Having written my dissertation on the Church's restrained response to contraception in nineteenth-century France ("Don't trouble the consciences of the laity."), I had become the Cardinal's close adviser on that subject too. So he had me appointed as a staff member to the small group of bishops who were supposed to be considering the subject of birth control after the Pope pulled the question off the Council floor—where if it were put to a vote, birth control would have gone the way of the Latin Mass.

When the Cardinal died long before his time I waited anxiously for the appointment of his replacement. I told myself, mistakenly as it turned out, that for most parish priests it really didn't matter who the Archbishop was, but for someone like me who had more or less stumbled into the highly controversial subject of contraception it would make an enormous difference whether I had the support of my own bishop.

At the final session of the Council, the new Archbishop, short, fat, ugly, and boisterous, came to live in the Chicago House, a not particularly modest palazzo on the Via Sardegna, which was where I had a small room up in the attic. After a couple of nights at dinner with him, I realized that the worst had happened to Chicago. He was an immensely clever political operative, but he was crazy—in addition to being a compulsive eater and drinker.

After he consumed several Old Fashioneds and half a bottle of wine, he'd begin to tell stories in which he was always the protagonist and the hero. Sometimes they were stories that someone around the table had narrated the night before. We would glance at each other nervously and then look away.

How could they do this to us, I wondered.

"Now what are you doing here in Rome, Pat?" he would ask me every other night, sometimes more sober than other times.

"I'm on the Secretariat for the Council and on the staff of the birth control commission," I would always reply.

Sometimes he'd say, "That has to change, no doubt about it. The Pope himself told me that."

And other times he'd say, "I heard from the Pope that the commission is going to be disbanded. Can't change on that one."

He'd always add, "I won't leave you here in Rome indefinitely. A priest should be in a parish or he forgets what his stole looks like."

"I hear English-language confessions every weekend in St. Peter's," I would say.

I don't think he ever heard me.

"He's going to order me to come home after the Council is over," I said to Bernard Häring, a Redemptorist who was already one of the influential members of the commission.

"This is what you do," he said to me, winking broadly. "For the last week before he goes home, do not appear at the supper table. Do not let him see you in the house. He will forget about you. He resents any priests in his Archdiocese who gets any attention on any subject. So for a while you must be invisible, eh?"

"Birth control is not a subject, Father, on which it is possible to be invisible for long."

He rolled his eyes. "We will win this time," he said, "the Pope is looking for grounds for a change. We will find it for him."

He could not have been more wrong.

Leo

"I bumped into Dickie the other day."

We were walking down the road into town, holding hands as we had done so long ago. All the summers of the 1940s were just one summer. This was not the sixth or the seventh summer we had held hands on the same road. This was our second summer. A Catholic summer. A possibly numinous summer of a second chance.

She had not resisted when I took her hand. Now it rested compliantly in mine, already a partial conquest, a partial surrender.

The road had been paved, the trees were higher, the farms that had been on the left side as we had strolled into town were now upscale subdivisions. The twenty-minute walk seemed much shorter than it once had. Yet in the dark I had once loved so much, the same laughing, effervescent woman was next to me.

And the same popping Fourth of July firecrackers were exploding all around us.

Should I put my arm around her shoulder?

Not yet. I was not a callow lad, inexperienced in the arts of seduction. One must proceed slowly, judiciously.

Big-time experienced lover indeed. About the craft of pleasing women I knew nothing. Astonishingly, however, she seemed pleased with me.

"Same old Dickie, huh?"

"Do you mean that?"

"You were the one who wrote the book on the big change. Don't you believe your own theory?"

"You read my book?"

"Don't seem so surprised. Of course I read your book. When an old sweetheart wins the National Book Award you have to read it."

"What did you think?"

"I loved it, naturally. Isn't Dickie the perfect example?"

"Unbelievable. He offered us a chair in Irish studies in honor of Herbie. I don't know how seriously he meant it."

"Wasn't that sweet?" She sounded very proud of her brother. "Oh, he meant it all right."

"None of you used to believe in education."

"Except for men and professionals . . . OK, we changed. Nothing like prosperity and for my brothers the right wives to straighten you out . . . did you talk about me?"

"Why would we do that?"

"I don't know, I just thought you might."

She was wearing white shorts and a green and gold T-shirt, which announced to the world that Clare Travels Shamrock tours would take you to the real Ireland. She smelled of very expensive scent, a good deal more expensive than a T-shirt and shorts or a night at the movies merited.

"He seems very fond of you."

"They always were fond of me. Protective too. Maybe not protective enough . . . do you remember how you made me go to college?"

"I didn't make you go to college, Jane. I can't remember ever talking about it."

"You don't remember the day in the Rose Bowl down on the municipal pier when I was working there . . ."

"I guess I forgot that you worked there."

"You held my hands real tight and pulled me half-way over the counter and ordered me to take the Rosary College exam . . . you don't remember that?"

"Vaguely."

"Then you went back to the Keenans' and told Tom Keenan who was on the board of Rosary to tell the nuns that if I won it they should give it to me even though my family had money."

"I'm sure I never did anything like that."

"Yes, you did. I asked Tom years later and he said you did."

She stopped in the middle of the road and, heedless of oncoming cars, kissed me briskly. "You were wonderful, thank you so very much! And get out of the way of that car!"

We resumed our stroll. She was mine tonight if I wanted her. The kiss was in invitation.

I am objectifying her with my lust, I reprimanded my hunger.

No, I responded. I love her and want her.

How can you tell the difference?

I don't have to.

"I can't imagine that I interfered in your life that way."

"You did and it was wonderful . . . I suppose you never wondered about me and my family."

"I couldn't help but wonder. Everyone did."

"For most of those years I was ashamed of them. I knew what people thought even when we were in grammar school: The Devlins were loud, vulgar crooks. I didn't believe all of it and I loved my family, Mom especially before she changed. So I became very good at pretending that I was your all-purpose cheerful kid. I learned how to pretend early. God knows I've needed that skill during my marriage. Good old happy Jane!"

"It wasn't all pretense, not when I knew you."

No . . . not all of it. Maybe all the singing and dancing and laughing is in my genes. But I inherited it from my mother, then she lost it all. She . . . well she became an alcoholic monster of whom we were all afraid and who could make us do anything she wanted. I did have good times, especially here at the Lake."

"I think I can recall that, Milady."

"Shut up, Lunkhead!"

"You were a fairy princess trapped in a castle by a wicked witch."

At that sally she didn't laugh. "Something like that," she said finally.

A metaphor from which I should stay away.

We were quiet for a few minutes, happy with the memories of the good times.

"When I was a little kid I was so proud of my father because he had started out without any money and made a lot. Then I found out what people were saying, maybe when I was in sixth grade, and cried myself to sleep for a week. Then the Jane act started. It's gone on ever since."

"But your brothers changed?"

"Like I say," and her laughter, never far from the surface, bubbled back, "I read your book. Sure they changed. And I understood that a lot of rich Protestants up here got their start the same way and changed the same way. If my poor mother had lived a little longer, she might have been granted the acceptance she wanted. Then she might have sung and laughed again. I know . . . anyway I stopped being ashamed of them and started being ashamed of my husband. There was a time, I suppose, that I covered up for both."

"Makes sense."

"They say that the adult children of alcoholics are unable to tell what is real and what isn't. My father wasn't an alcoholic exactly, though by the time Mom died he was not far from it. But sometimes I'm not sure what is real."

"Have you ever talked about this to anyone?"

"Nope, Lunkhead, this is the first time. Not even to Maggie. I thought I'd better explain some things to you. I was faking most of the time."

"No, you weren't, Jane. You were yourself most of the time. Still are."

"You think?"

"No question."

"I hid a lot."

"Don't we all."

"I guess so."

Then we were in town and in front of the old Bijou and an odd thing happened. For a couple of minutes I was back in Korea.

We joined the ticket line behind a bunch of chattering teenagers. Off to one side, a couple seemed to be arguing, two of your classic hippie types (or they could have been graduate students or even junior faculty at the University). The woman was wearing a long and dirty dress with a floral pattern, a kind of early twentieth-century rural gown. The man, a smelly guy with a long ponytail and a goatee, was clad in a skin-tight T-shirt and jeans. They were superannuated kids, probably dropouts, from the upper middle class mainstream in their late twenties, if they weren't junior faculty. Even from our distance you could smell their unwashed bodies and the pot they had been smoking. Most likely two gypsies on the drug circuit, perpetually stoned, perpetually paranoid. Casualties of the protest movements of ten years ago for whom the drug culture had become the last redoubt of symbolic radicalism. Just like Brigie Devlin who not so long ago, it seemed to me, was a babe in her mother's arms.

The guy pushed us aside. "You took our place in line," he said.

A sudden rage exploded within me. The little punk had become one of my Korean tormentors. I clenched my fist.

"Sorry," I said. "I didn't realize you were in line."

Jane and I stepped back to let him and the young woman ahead of us.

He turned on me, his small eyes blazing hatred. "You're not sorry, old man. You're a shit faced mother fucker."

"Have it your way," I said icily.

"Lee," Jane whispered, "don't get in a fight with the poor kid."

"Shut up, you fucking old crone." The kid glared at her.

"I think you're the one who had better be quiet," I said calmly.

I was back in the prison camp, shivering with the cold, waiting for the guard to hit me in the gut again.

He buried his elbow in my stomach. "Fuck you, old man."

The crowd of teens were now staring at us, forming a semicircle to watch a fight that might just happen.

Other Marines and guards.

I picked the kid up by the shoulders and threw him across the front of the Bijou against one of glass showcases that announced coming attractions. His head smashed the glass. For a moment he lay on the ground, his head and shoulders propped up against the wall.

I was at the peak of my Marine intensity, ready for more hand-to-hand combat. The basic training of the late forties reeled through my head like an old film.

The kid shook his head, and produced a switchblade from his pocket and flicked it open.

"I'm going to kill you, mother fucker."

"Lee, look out," Jane screamed.

As he charged me I kicked him in the groin. He fell back screaming, both hands clutched to his injured vitals. I grabbed his right arm and tossed him to the ground. Then I stomped on his right hand. The sound of his fingers cracking was like more exploding firecrackers.

Everyone was screaming. I heard a police siren coming down the street.

Screeching agony, the kid groped for his knife.

I kicked it away, pulled him to his feet, twisted his arm behind his back, and ordered through clenched teeth, "Someone call the cops."

"We're here already, sir," a voice said. "You're lucky he didn't cut you with that thing."

"Wrong, officer. He's lucky I didn't kill him."

"Marine, by the looks of you?"

"A while ago."

"Nam?"

"Korea."

Weapons were still firing all around us. Reinforcements from the Corps. No, only Fourth of July firecrackers. I struggled to choose one world or the other.

"What outfit?"

"Second Battalion, Fifth Marines."

"Jeez. The Reservoir?"

"Yeah."

I was shivering now, cold roaring down out of the mountains into the prison camp.

"Medal of Honor, Officer Kane," Jane said proudly. "This is Doctor Leo Kelly." Her voice choked, "A professor doctor, not a *real* doctor."

"Glad to meet you, sir."

The cop, a kid about the same age as the screaming hippie, now handcuffed and held by two other cops, actually saluted.

Thank God, I told myself, that my old friend Joe Miller had not seen me make such a fool of myself.

"A pleasure to meet you, sir."

"He pulled a knife, Officer."

"We saw it, Mrs. Clare. We came as quickly as we could but we would have been too late if it hadn't been for the Colonel here."

Korea faded and I was back in America in the era of Jimmy Carter. I looked around the crowd. The hippie girl was clinging to her man, sobbing with him. The teenagers were watching us with wide eyes. Laura and Lucy would have the whole story, substantially enhanced, before the night was over.

On the outside I was the charming provost again. Inside fury was still raging—and with it terror. "Never more than Captain, Officer, and then only before they threw me out. Thank you for coming up with the reserves."

"I'm terribly sorry that this happened to you here. We've been watching these two since they showed up this morning, just waiting for something to happen. We'll take care of them."

"Better get him to a doctor first," I said. "And call their families if you can find out where they live. There may be parents somewhere who care about them. Tell Sheriff Miller I suggested that."

I was coming down off my high, shivering as I always did after combat, the few times I had been in actual combat. My shivering was internal. Outside I was the calm, self-possessed academic.

"You don't want to press charges?"

"Not if they will go into rehabilitation." Jane spoke for me.

"Now," I turned to the ticket seller, "do you think we can have two. Adults, more or less."

"No sir," said the young woman. "It's on the house . . . Hi, Mrs. Clare."

"Hi, Melanie. You should have seen him beat up kids here back in the forties. Lethal Leo, we called him."

"Korea?" She took my arm and lead me inside.

"Yeah. The kid reminded me of a Chinese guard."

"I'll buy the popcorn—*and* the ice cream after. I have clout at the Rose Bowl . . . do things like that happen often?"

"The anger surfaces every once in a while. I never hit anyone before."

She nodded. "Two very large popcorns, Jennifer, drenched in butter, two extremely large diet cokes, two packages of M and M's and two packages of Raisinets."

"Yes, Mrs. Clare." The gum-chewing kid nodded her head and looked at me appreciatively. "Gosh, that was scary out there."

"Nothing to worry about, honey, not with legendary Leo on the job."

To me she whispered, "Would you have killed him?"

"Only if necessary."

"Did you kill anyone in the war?"

"That's what war is about, Jane, killing people."

"Brr . . . How many?"

"Hundreds I suppose, that day I lost my mind and played at being a hero. Chinese. They die very quietly, although they charge at you blowing bugles and screaming. I suppose they know they're going to die. Only one out of three even had guns. Chinese leaders have never cared much about the lives of their people."

"There's so many of them."

"Even when there wasn't."

We walked into the theater, half-filled with young people and families and found a quiet corner.

"You all right now, Lee?" she asked anxiously.

"More or less. I acted like a prize asshole."

"He would have killed you."

"I started the fight."

"No you didn't, he elbowed you."

"I overreacted. Firecrackers bring back all the memories."

She patted my arm. "He was stoned out of his mind and just looking for a fight. Lucky it was you instead of someone who wouldn't have been able to fight back."

"I suppose so."

The lights went down and *Star Wars* began. Third time for both of us. Great flick.

"Leo, you're shaking like a leaf."

"Am I?"

"Yes, you are. How terrible!"

"I'll be all right." I put my arm around her shoulders. "Do you mind?"

"Of course not."

At that moment I would have had as much sexual feeling if I had embraced a tree trunk.

It was however a warm and pliant tree trunk; and as Luke and Han and the Princess and the two androids cavorted around the screen, the tree trunk became a woman with warm breasts even more endearing than they had been thirty years before.

Leo

"Where's Lucy going to school next year?" I asked when we had seated ourselves in a corner of the Rose Bowl.

Jane had ordered "two of the largest chocolate malts in all the world, heavy on the malt."

The young man in the pink uniform shirt behind the old-fashioned soda fountain corner had asked, "Vanilla or chocolate ice cream, Mrs. Clare?"

"Tony, do you gotta ask? I'm an old-fashioned conservative! Vanilla, naturally!"

"I meant," the kid had nodded at me, "uh, your guest."

"He's an old-fashioned conservative too."

After we had collected our treats, Jane led me to an alcove in which we were protected from the glare of the fluorescent lights and the babble of teenage voices.

"I think we're the only adults here," I had said.

"You mean we're not teenagers? I thought we were."

"I even had a teenage fight."

"No, you didn't," she had patted my arm as we sat at the table. "Are you all right now?"

"Sure."

"Did you ever get that mad at Emilie?"

"No. I haven't been that way for a long time."

"But it's all inside you."

"Sometimes."

"Did you ever get mad at her about anything?"

"No, I was afraid the deep anger would explode and I would hurt her."

She pondered that. "That wasn't good for the marriage, was it?"

"No."

"You're angry at the Koreans and at all of us for thinking you were dead. And especially at me."

"I have no reason to be angry at you, Jane."

"Sure you do. I thought you were dead. And I was angry at you for dying and then for coming back from the dead when it was too late."

"It was all over long ago, Jane," I said, not really believing it.

"Is it?" She tilted her chin at me.

"Your fingers are safe."

We both laughed, turning away from dangerous subjects.

But I was not angry at her, not at all.

"You didn't go to church for a long time, did you?"

"Angry at God, too. Childish. Then about ten years ago I started to take Laura to Mass because I figured she ought to have some kind of religion and Catholicism for all its faults was the best available. I realized that you can't leave. It's in your blood. I had missed it all, the art and the music and the ceremony and parish life and the passing of the seasons and the candles and the changing colors of the vestments and talking to the priest after Mass and people swarming around when you need help. So, hell, I was still mad at God but why take it out on the Church! Now sometimes I'm mad at the Church, but no longer at God."

"Once a Catholic always a Catholic."

"Yeah."

"And warm summers for love like Aunt Maggie says?" Her eyes glittered impishly.

"Outdoors and by the ponds."

"No *way*."

"We'll see."

She changed the subject. "They don't give cookies any more like they used to when I was working here. Nothing is the way it used to be. But then you wrote the book on that, didn't you?" She had reached in the large purse she had carried over her shoulder, "So I bring my own cookies. Not homemade, but short breads anyway. Two for you and two for me. Don't dare try to eat mine."

"I can't remember you working here."

"You *can't*? Two summers. Between sophomore and junior years and then between junior and senior years. You used to come in to keep me company."

"I guess my memory of those times is selective."

"Maybe with good reason," she said with an edge of sadness in her voice.

"Do me a favor, Milady?"

"Sure, Lunkhead."

"I'm not proud that I was a Marine."

"I didn't mention it."

"I know. I'm talking about the future, not tonight. Also I'm not proud of the Medal of Honor. It means only that I killed a lot of Chinese kids and maybe broke the hearts of their mothers and their sweethearts."

"And saved the lives of lots of American kids, according to the citations."

"Somehow that kind of calculus doesn't work for me any more."

She considered me with eyes so soft and sympathetic as to break my heart.

"I think I understand, Lee. I won't mention it."

"I'm not a hero. Only a survivor."

"I won't buy that."

We sipped our malts for a few moments in silence. On the jukebox, which was as asthmatic as it had been thirty years ago, the Bee Gees were telling us, "How Deep is Your Love."

Then I had asked about Lucy and school.

"She wasn't doing well at Hardy Prep—that's the Convent of the Sacred Heart now that it's gone coed. They didn't ask her to leave, but I think it was close. I thought we'd try Frances Parker, that's a private school for rich liberals but they take Irish Catholics."

"But actually she's going to St. Ignatius College Prep, as it must be called in these days."

"How did you know that?" Her eyes widened.

"I had a serious chat with my Laura this afternoon. Or rather she had a serious chat with me. Then just before I left to walk over to your house, she stopped me, keys to my car in her hand, and says, 'Oh, Daddy, I forgot this afternoon. I'm probably not going back to Lucerne, if you don't mind that is.' And I ask where she is going if I don't mind. And she says, 'To St. Ignatius if you don't mind. I figure it's time I learn how to be an American teenager. And besides that way I can take care of you.'"

"And you said?"

"I said I don't mind. What else could I have said . . . do you smell a conspiracy?"

"Sure I smell a conspiracy. Do you think it is about us?"

"What else?" I asked.

"They seem to be thick as thieves. Lucy really admires Laura. I can't imagine her being anything but a good influence on my daughter."

"You can guess about what they're conspiring, Jane?"

"Yes."

"Should we try to nip this conspiracy in the bud?"

"How?"

"I could send Laura back to Lucerne."

"Don't do that!" She grabbed my hand.

"Why not?"

I knew full well that I could fly to the moon more easily than I could keep Laura away from St. Ignatius if she really wanted to go there.

"Friendships in these years are so important to people. Like Eileen and Angie and me. If our daughters want to be friends, let them be friends, before it's too late."

"Their conspiracy?"

"What harm can they do?"

We left it at that. I found her smooth, solid thigh and moved my hand up and down.

"Like I said," she continued to sip her malt, "we're acting like teenagers . . . I had to resist a lot of passes when I was working here."

"Not from me?"

"You made your passes elsewhere. I can't remember resisting them. That was because you knew when to stop without being told, which I hope you still do."

"Don't bet on it," I said, squeezing her thigh.

"Lee, *please!*"

But she didn't push my hand away.

Outside as we walked out of the dark streets of the town and down the darker road, I put my arm around her shoulders again. She snuggled close to me.

Firecrackers were exploding all around us. I was able for the most part to ignore them. Except for the big ones. Jane did not notice my reactions because I had long ago learned how to hide my leftover Korean fears. Most of the time.

"We should talk seriously now, Jane."

"I know. I don't want to because I'm so confused."

"I am too."

"Something terrible happened to me," she blurted, "when you died."

"I didn't die, Jane. I was still alive."

"Not for me. When you died the last hope went out of my life. It's never come back."

"Last hope?"

"I lost most of it when Jimmy and Eileen were killed. Then your sister Meg came over to our house just before Christmas two years later, tears streaming down her cheeks, and told me that the Defense Department said you'd been killed in action and that you had been recommended for the Medal of Honor." Her shoulders were quivering at the memory. "I've never had any hope since then."

This was a strange, enormous statement. The woman had married, raised children, become successful in business, maintained a *persona* of bravery and good cheer to the world. Was she confessing despair?

"What do you mean, Jane?"

"When kids are growing up, girl kids especially, they have such bright hopes for all the good things that are going to happen in their lives. Most of us lose those hopes as life goes on, some people manage to cling to them. I lost mine early. Since then I've just hung on."

"Hung on bravely, it seems to me."

I felt her shrug her shoulder. "Fuck bravery . . . look out for the car."

We dodged away from the oncoming headlights.

"I would have waited for you forever, Lee, I really would have, if only they said you were missing. But they said you were dead. So I gave up. Phil wanted to marry me. My folks were pushing me. Iris liked me. Doctor Clare thought I'd settle Phil down. I said what the hell. It might as well be him as anyone else. You were dead."

"Then I turned out not to be dead."

"It was too late. So you were dead for me. When I saw you at Packy's Ordination I already had two kids and was expecting a third. We were both other people. You had the same kind eyes. But you were so different. Not that I had any choice by then. And that's the only time I've seen you, not counting TV, until Memorial Day."

"Am I still different?"

"Not really," she sighed. "Not at all."

I did not know what to make of this odd self-revelation. But it made me love her even more. And want her more passionately.

"If I had been a little more explicit in how I felt about you, it wouldn't have ended that way."

"Even if we were engaged, I would have lost hope and married Phil when they said you were dead."

"I tried to call you before we left for Japan. No one was home at either house."

"It would have been a wonderful memory, but I would have married Phil just the same."

I was not so sure of that. But there was no reason to argue.

"But it's all over now, Jane. We have another summer and another chance. We can change the past by giving it a different meaning."

"You keep saying that, but I don't know that I believe it."

"Why not?"

"I killed Jim and Eileen."

"What!"

"I had a big fight with Phil the night before. He . . . well, he wanted to make love and I turned him down cold. He called me a prick teaser and I hit him. He went off crying. He was so angry at me the next day that he drove the car down the hill at sixty just to show me how angry he was. I knew it as soon as I heard the explosion from the accident and ran over to find you watching the fire and weeping. It was all my fault!"

Now she was sobbing in my arms.

What do you say to a normal, intelligent woman when she has spoken utter nonsense?

If you're a professor turned academic administrator, you try to reason with her. You don't try to understand the deep feelings of guilt and responsibility that underlie her seeming irrationality.

"You didn't tamper with the brakes, Jane. You didn't get drunk over in Walburg before you drove back. You didn't drive down the hill at seventy miles an hour. You didn't act childishly merely because a woman turned you down. It was Phil's fault not yours."

"I didn't have to slap his face," she sobbed, "and tell him he was a stupid pig . . . they were my friends, I was responsible for them. I failed them just like I failed little Phil and Brigie. And probably Lucy too before I'm finished with her."

Such reasoning makes sense only if you view yourself as a matriarch responsible for the lives and loves of all around you. Thank God I didn't say that. What I did say, however, was not much better.

"Did Phil tell you he drove the car recklessly because he was angry at you?"

We had, in unspoken agreement, turned off the road into the small stand of trees, amazingly not yet cleared for construction, which had been our trysting place when we were young. The automatic weapons sound of firecrackers continued but now at a great distance.

"Yes," she said, dabbing at her tears with a tissue.

"Even then, Jane, your husband was remarkably skillful at imposing the blame for his actions on others. Surely you remember that. Surely he did it through the years of your marriage."

"Ex-husband," she sniffed.

"Didn't he?"

"He still does. The other day he came into my office to try to persuade me to postpone the divorce until after the Feds are finished with him, although the divorce is final now. He managed to make me feel responsible for the insider mess in which he has trapped himself."

"You didn't agree."

"Certainly not. He guilts me as cleverly as he always did. But I don't care about guilt any more. I just want to be rid of him."

She became stiff in my arms, furious at her husband. That, I thought, was good.

"So he was doing the same thing after the crash."

"I know that, damn it." She pounded my chest. "But I still feel guilty. I felt guilty even before he tried to blame me. They were my friends and they're dead and I'm alive and it just isn't right."

"I know what you mean. I feel exactly the same way."

She sighed, her emotions spent, and leaned against me. "And Packy says you feel guilty because you didn't solve the crime, if there was one."

"There was one," I said firmly.

We clung to each other, a man and a woman well beyond the middle years of life (as life expectancy charts would indicate), still haunted by deaths that had happened thirty years before. Our guilt was irrational maybe, but it still was a Great Wall in our lives beyond which we could not venture to find peace, and possibly each other.

Then Jane pulled away from me.

I made up my mind. I would have to solve the mystery. There could be no future for Jane and me unless I tore down that Wall and reinterpreted the past to make it different from what it seemed to be. I had no choice.

"Why? Why would anyone want to loosen the brakes in Packy's old car?"

"I don't know, but they did. Al Winslow the auto repair man in town swore that he had fixed them the day before."

"It was odd, wasn't it," she continued, "how everything just faded away. No arrests, no suits, the insurance company settled and that was that."

"After I made a fool out of myself."

"You tried to find the truth."

"Unsuccessfully, I guess . . . but you're right. It just faded away."

"Isn't it strange how everyone is dead. Except us. Only the Keenans—and they don't really count—and poor Angie and her father. Everyone else, parent and child, is gone."

"Phil."

"All right, I forgot him. But he's dead from the neck up."

"People die, Jane. It's part of life."

"So many and so young?"

"It's a bit unusual, but one accident, if it was an accident, accounts for most of it. Maybe all of it. We're not really that unusual."

"It spooks me."

"Me too."

With a foot of space between us, we walked in silence back to the highway and the star-drenched sky.

"I don't want to be involved with a man ever again, for the rest of my life."

"You're too young and too attractive to say that."

"I don't care," she replied stubbornly. "I don't intend to fall in love ever again. I've done it only once and I thought I did it with Phil, but I was kidding myself."

"I was the only one?" We were entering the area of the Old Houses where our crowd had lived so long ago.

"Who else?" she said bitterly.

"But, Jane, we're both still alive and free again or almost free, why couldn't we avoid the mistakes we made the first time around?"

A reasonable and persuasive professorial argument, addressing none of the fears and guilts and perplexities that spooked both of us.

"I don't believe in second chances," she insisted stubbornly. "You make your mistakes and you live with them."

"All right, maybe it's a first chance. Maybe we never had a chance thirty years ago."

That stopped her for a moment.

"Maybe."

"Maybe the same thing would have happened if I hadn't been reported killed in 1950."

"Maybe."

"You're afraid to try?"

Mistake!

"I don't *want* to try."

What do I say now?

We passed a secluded section of beach, ringed by trees and a little marsh. It was the accepted place for skinny-dipping. In an implicit agreement between the police and young people, the former did not patrol it on summer nights and the latter did not make enough noise to disturb the neighbors.

"Remember this place?" she asked, changing the subject.

Our crowd talked nervously about "Skinny-dip Beach" but we never went there as a group. Some of us may have worked up enough nerve to go to the beach very late at night as a couple, but we did not discuss such adventures with our friends.

Jane and I had spent a delirious hour there one humid August night, a starlight night instead of a full moonlight night, worse luck for me. However I did remember it when I read John Updike's word that the naked body of a woman is the most beautiful thing a man will see in the course of his life.

"I think so," I replied.

"Don't give me that, Lunkhead. You remember."

"I remember there was not enough light. Tonight with the quarter moon rising there should be enough."

"There will be none of *that*," she said firmly.

"A man is entitled to his fantasies."

Was the fantasy of your naked woman with you on the side of a lake on a warm summer night part of the tradition of the Catholic summer about which Maggie had preached, apparently to both of us?

Well if Catholic meant that creation is good and the body was good why not?

This summer?

If not this summer, when?

Tonight?

I thought about it.

No, I must not push too hard too soon.

The Lake rippled in the moonlight, little chains of gold trying to stretch from shore to shore. I remembered the moon creating similar ripples on Jane's young body as it peeked in and out of the clouds on that enchanted night so long ago.

"So long as they're fantasies," she insisted primly.

I put my hands firmly on her shoulders. "Fantasies tonight, but before the end of the summer, woman, they'll be more than fantasies, that I promise."

She didn't try to squirm out of my grip. "We're not teenagers any more, Lee."

She was embarrassed and confused, but not angry.

"I don't know about that. I hear they call you 'Jane' instead of Mrs. Clare, because you're, like, just one of the kids."

"That's different." She slipped away from me. "I'm really just a modest Catholic matron."

"Best kind."

"Of what?"

"Wanton, when you finally get them stirred up."

"Silly," she pushed me and we continued our stroll in the darkness. An occasional skyrocket from the direction of the town was exploding over the Lake and spewing its firefly specks of light into the sky.

"What are you humming?" she asked.

"I don't know. I always hum. Do you want me to sing to you?"

I had sung to her that night we had swum at "Skinny-dip Beach."

"Certainly not . . . it's the Bee Gees."

"Better than Fleetwood Mac."

"You couldn't do Fleetwood Mac."

"You're probably right. It's the song they were singing at the Rose Bowl."

" 'How Deep is Your Love?' "

"Appropriate, isn't it, Jane?"

"No." She was not amused.

Then her wit returned. "I'm surprised the Provost knows about the Bee Gees and Fleetwood Mac."

"The Provost has a teenage daughter."

We strolled up the walk from the road to the door of the old Devlin house. Were there haunts there, I wondered. I'd have to ask Maggie whether the vibrations she experienced inside were any more disturbing than plain old normal psychic vibrations.

She brushed her lips against mine. "Thank you for an interesting and exciting evening, Lee." She was her old laughing self.

"And thank you for making it both interesting and exciting." I kissed her, somewhat more firmly.

"My decision on the future is final," she said, putting her key in the door.

"I respect that."

"Good." She opened the door.

Had she not remarked that Lucy was sleeping over someplace? We would have the house all to ourselves.

"But I don't accept it."

She whirled on me. "I *said* my decision is final."

"The rules don't say that I have to give up."

"I don't want to hurt you again."

Was that perhaps the real reason?

"I'm entitled to my own risks. I repeat: your final decision is not my final decision."

She considered that policy statement carefully.

"That's your right, Lee."

She closed the door, the physical door to her house. But she had left another door ajar.

I didn't feel that I had made a complete mess out of the night.

Jane

I slumped against the door, limp, exhausted, and still sexually aroused. Why did I do that? Did I turn down grace again? I've been praying for help, for a sign. There was plenty of help and a bright, bright sign—much brighter than the quarter moon.

I was furious at him, that's why. The bastard has no sense that he deserted me. He still thinks I deserted him and forgives me for it, the self-righteous prick!

All right, why didn't I blow up and get it over with? Why didn't I shout and rant and rave and get it out of my system? I'll have to do it sometime won't I?

I didn't shout because my anger gave me an excuse for pushing him away. I want him and I'm afraid of what will happen if I have him and he has me. So I use my rage as an excuse. If I blow up at him and get it over with, I'll have lost my last excuse. My last protection against love, my last shield against being hurt again.

He's got his own excuses too, but just now I don't give a fuck about them.

Terrible language. I should be ashamed of myself.

But I'm not. He ran out on me and he might run out again.

Leo

Packy was sitting on the front porch of the Keenan house, a pile of magazines on the floor on either side of the old wicker chair. A bottle of beer in his hand, the good monsignor was catching up on back issues of *America* and *The Commonweal.*

"Good date?" he said without looking up.

I popped open my can of beer and sat in the chair next to him, our favorite conversation place in years gone by.

"Does everyone in the village know?"

"I suspect so. They will in the morning after your stunt with the junkie."

"No privacy in this place at all."

"You should know that by now." He tossed aside a copy of *The Common-weal,* contemptuously I thought. "So?"

"So she says she does not want to marry again."

"That's not an unexpected reaction given all the recent events. And you said?"

"I said I accepted that as her final decision—she said it was final—but it did not represent my final decision."

He ruffled his silver hair, "Sounds very professional."

"I suppose so . . . the whole date was not completely professional."

"I'm glad to hear that."

"Packy, I played sensitive and respectful gentleman. I'm not sure that was the best way to go . . . yes, I am. That was what I should have been tonight. No guarantee that I'll be that way the next time."

"There'll be a next time? I thought she said her decision was final?"

"It's not *final* final, Pack. Not yet. I'll have a couple of more shots. It ain't over till it's over."

"Uh-huh. Then if you'll lose, you'll give up?"

"I won't lose," I said, astonished at my own confidence.

He considered me for a minute. "I hope not."

"Why did that accident happen, Packy?"

"Ask God," he said crisply. "I'm only a monsignor."

"I don't mean the theology of it. I mean who loosened the brakes in the old car?"

"What does that have to do with you and Jane?"

"Guilt, Packy, guilt. We both are irrationally but profoundly guilty that our friends are dead and we are still alive. If we can solve the mystery, perhaps we can discharge our obligations to their memories."

"Or to your own neuroses?"

"Maybe. I have a hunch it's a precondition for a renewed love affair between Jane and myself."

He pondered, then nodded. "I understand, Lee, I understand perfectly. Maybe I even agree with you up to a point. But it's been so long ago and almost everyone is dead."

"I know that . . . is there any information about it that I don't know?"

Slowly he uncurled his long frame from the rocker and rose to his feet. He turned and stared at the reflection of the quarter moon on the Lake. There were no more skyrockets, but the firecrackers were still popping away.

"Yeah."

"There is?"

"I don't know what it means, if it means anything at all."

"What is it?"

"The money wasn't counterfeit."

"What?"

"You quoted the cops that found the money in the metal box that the bills were very clever fakes. But they weren't fakes, it turns out. They were the real thing. My dad heard that years later. I don't know where, but he was confident about it."

"What happened to it—there must have been thousands of hundred dollar bills?"

"Fifty packs of one hundred."

"A half million dollars!"

"You social scientists are good at arithmetic."

"Where did it go? Cover-up?"

"Where else? But Dad didn't know to whom. He was as baffled as I am. He also thought it best that we let the dead bury their dead."

"Why do you think he told you?"

Packy turned back from the Lake. "I can ask him. It doesn't follow that he'll give me a straight answer. Irish political lawyers rarely do, you know. It's kind of a genetic imperative. My guess is that he wanted the fact sort of around for a while in case someone needed it."

"Sounds like him."

"He probably doesn't know as much as he'd like to have us think he knows. That goes with the genes too. He might give you something to go on, however."

"You sound like you think the Provost is going to turn detective."

"They do in the English mystery stories, don't they? And for a prize worth less than Jane."

"Is she a prize?"

"Isn't she?"

I finished my beer, poured a shot of Jameson's and retired to the guest bedroom, still robin's egg blue, in which I had spent so many nights long ago. I speculated as I sipped my drink in the darkness about using my prize money for *The Big Change*—which I had invested wisely enough to stay ahead of Jimmy Carter's inflation—to buy a house somewhere around here. Laura would like it.

On the other hand, it was at least possible that I could marry into a house, the old Devlin house, which might or might not be haunted.

As I finished my drink, I strained to sense if there were any psychic vibrations in my bedroom, any remnants of the unfortunate Murrays. I heard only the endless popping of the firecrackers.

Not a hint of psychic vibrations. But then as Maggie Ward Keenan would have said just because I didn't feel them it didn't follow that they weren't there.

Patrick

What the hell is wrong with him? He's obsessed with the mystery of how our friends died and he doesn't understand how important is the mystery of why he stormed out of here in August of 1948 and never came back, never even called Jane until he had his orders for Korea. That's completely crazy. He says glibly that he was ashamed that he had acted like an asshole in the Sheriff's office. Only he had acted like a hero. Maybe a couple of his accusations were off the mark, but no one held that against him. What kind of character defect is it that makes him think those two years don't require a more serious explanation?

If I were Jane, I wouldn't have a thing to do with him until he sees the problem and offers a damn good explanation. All right, she let her mother drag her away that night and still torments herself about it, but that was trivial compared to what he did.

Of course, she could have called him too. He would have melted as soon as he heard her voice.

Idiots.

I'll never forget that day the following summer. Not as long as I live. How could I?

So it was late August 1949. I had been working at one of the homes for children of broken homes to which the Seminary sent us in those days to keep us out of trouble in the summer. I drove up here one late Thursday evening when my term was up, put on my trunks, and swam for a half hour in the Lake. There were no cars in the driveway and only one light on in the house, which I assumed was left on from last week, a bad habit my family had acquired in those days before the energy crisis.

The swim took away the sour taste, which working with those poor kids had created, and I strode briskly up to the third floor and to the shower room across from my bedroom.

Jane came out of the shower room, a towel held precariously above her breasts—and no other clothes.

"Jane!"

"Packy!" She cowered against the wall.

"I didn't know you were here."

"Your family invited me for the weekend. Our house is closed." Her head was bowed and her eyes lowered, as modesty required.

Impulsively I pried the towel out of her fingers. She was the most beautiful sight I had ever seen. She did not try to cover herself or flee. She merely stood there, naked and lovely, head still bowed, and permitted me to drink her in.

I drew her into my arms and held her tightly. She clung to me, a tall, slender, strong woman with wondrous breasts. I felt her diamond hard nipples against my chest.

Then we realized who and what we were and drew apart. I picked up the towel and gave it to her. She deftly wrapped it around herself.

"Amazing," she giggled, "what happens to privacy in a summer home."

"I'm sorry, Jane, terribly sorry."

"Don't be, Packy. I'm not. It was only an accident and not a bad one either. Now if you don't mind I'll go dress somewhat more decently."

"And I'll take a very cold shower."

We both laughed nervously.

Later, fully clad and chastened by our experience, we drank tea in the ballroom. Her first question showed who was on her mind.

"Why doesn't he call, Packy?"

"Why don't you call him?"

"It's his responsibility."

Two stubborn people who thought they had time to get over their foolish anger. Everyone else thought they had time too. I figured Leo would be back next summer—1950.

But they would soon run out of time.

I, however, would never lose the memory of that embrace.

1967

Patrick

Nineteen years later the phone rang in my room at the old North American College on Via Umilita, behind the Gregorian University.

"Keenan."

"Hi, Packy," said that cello-with-dark-chocolate voice, which always made my head spin.

"Jane!"

"None other."

"Are you in Rome?"

"At the Hassler. Nothing but the best for a new travel agent. Would you take me to supper at a nice trattoria where there won't be any American tourists?"

"Polese's," I said, "in the Piazza Sforza-Cesarini, right across from St. Andrew's in the Valley."

"Will Tosca be there? Or Mario?"

"You're showing off."

"You bet . . . I suppose you eat at these uncivilized Italian times . . . eight thirty?"

"I'll be there, Madam Travel Agent."

My heart, I discovered, was pounding vigorously and I wanted to sing. The memory of that encounter on the third floor of our home exploded in my memory. Morose delectation we would have called it in our moral theology class. Nothing morose about it, I always thought.

I had moved out of the Chicago House on Via Sardegna, which the new Cardinal was about to sell anyway, so that I would avoid him. He had ordered me back to Chicago. I told him my appointment to the birth control commission was from the "fifth floor" itself and I could not give it up until released by the "highest authority."

"Highest authority" is supposed to mean the Pope but everyone knows that it actually means a lot of lesser level bureaucrats who use the term to enhance their power.

The Cardinal, who I had come to realize was like running water and followed the path of least resistance, backed off and asked how much I was being paid. He promptly doubled my salary (and the money came the first of the following month!).

Nonetheless, I had realized that Father Häring was right when he said the best thing I could do was to keep out of the Cardinal's sight.

Only a few rooms in the House on Humility Street (now a residence for graduate student priests) had phones, but Keenan family clout had accomplished marvels. I even had my own refrigerator and ice maker, which earned me enormous prestige in Rome.

Jane was gorgeous, an autumn symphony in dark brown—jacket, skirt, blouse, hat—even gloves. The skirt was a miniskirt, indeed mini, mini.

"You know how to tell whether a woman of my generation went to college?" she demanded.

And before I could answer, "Because she wears gloves even when it isn't cold!"

Jane would be forty next summer—as I would too. She looked ten years younger, slim, trim, fit, vibrant. How much of it was an act, I've wondered subsequently. Probably she didn't even know herself.

We embraced briefly and kissed lightly.

"No Roman collar or cassock?"

"Those things are out of fashion in Rome these days. Turtleneck and sport coat is in."

"You look great in it."

The table I had reserved was outside in the Piazza, in front of the house that had once been the home of the Borgia clan, unpretentious enough as Roman *palazzos* go. It was a warm autumn evening, crisp and clear, the eternal city at its most numinous.

"So what's this about a travel agency?"

"I've bought my own and am already making money with it. I figured I'd come to Rome and see what kind of a tour I could put together for Country Club Irish who want something special that ordinary tours don't provide. Will you make suggestions?"

"I sure will."

Roman women are in my experience the most beautiful in the world and there are always plenty of mini versions of Sophia Loren around Polesi's. But my West Side Irish date was the loveliest of them all.

"I guess you know that both of my parents are dead. They left me a lot of money, some of it in a trust fund for the kids' education and some to me outright. But I want to live as best I can off money that's my own and save the rest for the kids if they need it. So I used some of my own money to buy the agency. I try to make it an upscale enterprise, travel boutique. So far it's going fine."

"Phil approve?"

"He doesn't figure into it," she said smoothly as she refilled my wine glass.

"Oh?"

Was she going to talk to me about her marriage? I found that I hoped she wouldn't.

"He's not very good with money. I'm afraid he's going to run through everything his father left him. That's one of the reasons I'm concerned about the kids . . . but now tell me what you're doing in this city? How long have you been here? Ten years?"

We paused while I ordered the dinner, including the Cushinetta della Lucrezia (a pun because it means both a cushion and a session of love-making in bed). I noted that Jane was following every word of Italian very carefully. Trying to learn the language. Not as quick at languages as Leo.

"Eight actually," I continued the conversation. "Well, I'm working for the birth control commission. Doing the final report that will provide the Pope with the reasons he's looking for so he can change the teaching."

"There's really going to be a change! How exciting! And how wonderful for you to be part of it!"

The wine was making my head spin but not as fast as her wide-eyed admiration.

"It's the kind of situation in which you can feel the Holy Spirit working. I'm sure that a majority of the bishops and the theologians on the commission came firmly convinced that change even on the pill was impossible. Then as we discussed the past practices of the Church and our new knowledge about human sexuality you could almost sense the change in the room. The laypeople like Pat and Patty Crowley from Chicago and Mercedes Concepcion, a Filipina demographer, made a tremendous contribution." I could feel my excitement rising. "Now the plurality for change is overwhelming. Only a few Italian cardinals and a young Polish bishop named Karol Wojtyla are against it. At least we think he's against it. He's a very smart man with a great smile and frosty blue eyes. But you can't tell what's going on in his mind. Cardinal Heenan of England came over completely opposed and has gone back to England and assured everyone that there would be change."

I paused for breath.

"How marvelous! And you're writing the final report?"

"Right."

"It says we can use the pill?"

"We decided early on that the pill wasn't the issue, contraception was. And if rhythm is all right so too are some of the other methods."

"It will make a lot of married people in America happy . . . is there any chance the Pope won't approve your report?"

"Not a chance. He wants change too."

"It's too late for him to turn back, Pack. Everyone my age has made up their mind. So have the women younger than us. It's over. Does he realize that?"

I hesitated. "I don't think he does. People over in the Vatican have no idea what's going on even in Italy, much less in the United States. But it doesn't matter on this issue. The Pope would not have convened the commission unless he wanted change."

Looking back on that night I realize what a ham I was, a teenager showing off for his girl.

And what a fool.

We dug into our vermicelli pasta.

"It won't make much difference to me," she blurted.

Had she said what I thought she said.

"Jane . . ."

"Phil doesn't find me interesting any more," she said easily. "Hardly any sex. He's been fooling around since our honeymoon. Can't help himself, poor man."

She continued calmly to eat her pasta and drink her Frascati.

"There are some new norms for annulments coming along," I stumbled over the words.

"I knew what I was doing, Packy. I'm an old-fashioned Catholic and I believe that if you make mistakes you live with them. We were married. I have four kids to show for that. I don't want them to become bastards in the eyes of the Church."

How many times since then I've tried to argue that objection with laity who seem to want to remain in the prison of their mistake, unwilling to forgive themselves even if God and the Church were willing to forgive them.

"They explicitly would not be illegitimate, Jane. The new norms are based on what they call psychic incapacity—one or both parties lack the emotional maturity to contract a marriage that is a sacrament, that is an image of the love between Christ and the Church. It's a valid marriage but not a sacrament, so the Church declares them free to marry again."

She shook her head slowly, "Rationalization, Monsignor."

"No, Jane, sophisticated psychology."

She thought about it—and went on eating her pasta.

"Maybe . . . finish your vermicelli."

"Yes ma'am."

"What if someone doesn't want to marry again? What if someone assumes that she tried marriage once and doesn't want to try it again? What if someone figures her first obligation is to take care of her children, to protect them from their father?"

"An annulment is a possibility, not an obligation."

"Exactly . . . I'm sorry I ruined our dinner by even mentioning my own problems."

"I don't think you did, Jane. You wanted to be able to talk to someone about them.'

She grinned. "Someone besides that cute little witch from Philly."

We both laughed.

"All right." She refilled our glasses. "I did want to talk to you about it. I guess I needed a priest and you're the only one I know well enough to trust."

"Fair enough."

"He's not around the house much and when he is, he's usually harmless," she went on. "He's messed up young Philly, the only one he's ever cared about. Can't endure Brigie because she stands up to him. Philly adores his father and wants to live up to his father's standards so as to earn his love. He breaks down every time Phil criticizes him."

"My God!"

"He's sophomore at New Trier . . . Phil talked him out of a Catholic high school . . . and he wants to volunteer for Vietnam as soon as he graduates so his father will be proud of him and he can keep up the family tradition of military service during war time."

"At a supply base in Wisconsin?"

"That isn't the way Phil tells it. I think he really believes that he was a combat hero. I can talk Philly out of it. A lot of the kids at New Trier are anti-war, kids he admires because they're good at all the things he's not good at, poor boy."

My triumph on the birth control commission didn't seem all that important any more.

Jane saved the night of course. We laughed a lot, aided by the second bottle of Frascati, and talked about the old times at the Lake and our friends—avoiding all memories of the awful tragedy of 1948. Then we turned to music and literature and Rome and the travel business. My first sweetheart at almost forty was a superb dinner companion without a trace of self-pity.

An amazing woman.

Would she be as beautiful naked now as she had been nineteen years before?

Maybe even more beautiful, not that I'd ever be able to make the comparison.

By the time I took her back to the Hassler, Jane and I were friends again and I was her priest confidant, a flattering and satisfying role.

The lobby of the Hassler was empty. We kissed each other good night. A very modest kiss.

"Ever hear from Lee?" she asked lightly.

"Christmas card."

"Is he happy?"

"I doubt it. He has a daughter about Lucy's age. Laura, I think is her name."

Jane nodded. "No one ever promised happiness in this life, did they Packy?"

"I guess not."

We kissed again, a little more intensely. For a brief moment there were other possibilities, like a scene caught in a blink of an eye as a train races by. Her eyes were soft and vulnerable, her body limp. She was lonely and needed love.

Why not?

Then the blink of the eye ended and I was a priest and she a woman who trusted me.

Yet I walked back to Humility Street happier than I had been in a long time. I saw her twice more before she left Rome and each time returned to my room with laughter in my heart, a stupid grin on my face, and erotic love images in my fantasy.

The day after my last dinner with Jane at Polese's I was sitting at the same table with Professor Leo T. Kelly of the University of California at Santa Barbara. Same old Leo, funny, bright, enthusiastic, red hair as thick as ever and now matched with a piratical red beard. Apparently he had shaken off the effects of the POW camp. When I heard his voice on the phone I thought for a couple of crazy seconds that somehow he and Jane had met each other in Rome.

But his presence in Rome at the same time as Jane was a coincidence. I thought about inviting both of them to dinner and then decided that it wouldn't be such a good idea.

Leo was in Rome for some kind of international meeting on trade at which he was presenting a paper. He listened attentively to my description of the work of the birth control commission and nodded at all the right times.

"It's time and past time, Packy. They've got to get out of the box that their Aristotelian science has got them into. Nothing wrong with Aristotle for his own time. He tried to study human nature from the scientific perspective. But we know a lot more about science these days than he did. Your friends over at the Vatican," he inclined his head in a classic West Side Irish political gesture in the general direction of St. Peter's, "have got a lot of catching up to do."

"This time they're going to do it."

"I sure hope so."

"You going to show me a picture of this kid of yours?"

"You bet." He pulled out his wallet and produced a snapshot of a pretty blonde woman and a five year old who seemed a carbon copy. "Laura! The woman of course is her mother Emilie."

I didn't like the sound of that.

"Forgive me for asking, but is the little girl baptized?"

"Sure she is! We're both Catholics, even if we weren't married in church. She's in a Catholic school in Santa Barbara."

"Not married in church?"

"Yeah." He frowned. "Emilie didn't want a church wedding and at that time I was angry at the Church like everything and everyone else so it didn't make any difference to me."

"Now?"

"Since I've been taking Laura to Mass I find I kind of miss Communion and I'd like to straighten things out. Emilie is less enthusiastic about it than I am."

"I see."

"She's a brilliant young woman, Pack. First-rate mind. Finishing up a book based on her dissertation. Pareto and Gramesci. Having a hard time with it. But she'll knock it off this year and the department will give her tenure. Then it won't be so difficult for her to be a mother and a scholar."

He had said not a word about how much he loved her. Rather he seemed to be apologizing for his wife and answering questions I hadn't asked.

Not good at all.

"Isn't Santa Barbara a step down from Stanford?" I asked.

He shrugged. "You can do good work anywhere and it's beautiful country. They made an offer for the two of us and that's important when you have a two-scholar family. It's not that places like Harvard aren't chasing me."

Not good at all, at all.

As we were leaving the restaurant, huddled under my umbrella because the autumn rains had come to Rome, he said, "Do you mind if I stay in touch with you, Packy? I mean more than before? It'd be nice to be able to talk to a priest once in a while. To say nothing," he laughed, "to the best friend I ever had."

"Be my guest."

I wasn't quite as ecstatic in my room on Humility Street after my meal with Leo as I had been with Jane. But nonetheless it had been great to see him.

I was also a little uneasy. In two weeks I had become the confidant of both Jane and Leo, neither of whom it seemed were happily married. The final chapter of their story perhaps remained to be told.

I wasn't so sure I wanted to be the storyteller.

1978

Leo

I awakened in the middle of the morning, shivering from the cold wind that had pushed its way into my room. I bounded out of bed to close the window and, pushing aside the shutter for a momentary peek, saw that an unexpected rain storm had swept across Wisconsin and was pelting the Lake, what one could see of it in the mists and the low-lying clouds. A good morning to sleep in.

I had put on swim trunks and a University sweatshirt, *not* the one with the names of our Nobel Prize winners on it, shaved (as the proper provost should,) and groped my way downstairs to the table where the woman of the house and her aides (sons and daughters) would have laid out the breakfast buffet. As I had expected that worthy was drinking coffee and reading a psychological journal. Trim and fresh in a pink sweat suit with matching ribbon, Maggie was an attractive early morning picture.

The breakfast room was at the opposite side of the house from the "ballroom" and offered an equally dramatic view of the Lake. Now the only view was of clouds and rain and spray.

No matter what the time of the day or night, Maggie Ward Keenan was always perfectly groomed and impeccably dressed, always a lovely little dish—a very chauvinist reaction, I admit, to such a distinguished scholar and clinician.

"Thunder wake you up?" She had poured my coffee with her eyes on the coffeepot.

"Didn't hear it."

"Help yourself," she had glanced up at me and added with an amused smile, "to our modest brunch."

The smile said in effect, you've been lusting after me since the first time you saw me thirty-one years ago and I'd be disappointed if you didn't—just keep it respectful.

"Yes ma'am," I had said aloud.

"What are you reading?" She had nodded at the book in my hand—Laura had explained with long-suffering tolerance to young Jamie Keenan that her father was an academic and hence *always* carried a book lest he waste a moment of precious time.

She had it wrong. In fact, it was merely a pretense that I was a serious person, a fact of which I have never quite been convinced.

"William Manchester's *American Caesar.*"

"Any good?"

"He leans over backward to be fair to the bastard. Good technique because the result is all the more devastating. When I finally came home and heard about the grand reception the country gave him after Harry Truman finally fired him, I was astonished."

"And furious."

"And furious. And sick to my stomach."

"Are we getting close to writing that book on Korea?"

"Yes we are, Doctor."

"I hear you reenacted a bit of it last night, Captain."

"Does everyone know?"

"Bet on it. The other children are doubtless asking Laura, such a wonderful young woman by the way, what her father is really like."

"And she'll say he never talks about Korea."

"Doubtless." Maggie had put aside her journal, buttered a roll for me, and turned her full attention to the morning's first client. "And the rest of your eventful date?"

Packy had arrived just then and, as I had often seen him do, he had lifted his adored sister-in-law out of her chair, spun her around in the air, kissed her, and then deposited her back in the chair.

"Woman of the house," he had announced, "good morning!"

Flustered and pleased, as she always seemed to be by this greeting, she said, "Thus does the celibate male prove his superiority by reducing the woman of the house to the role of an amusing girl child."

"Which she is," Pack and I had said in unison.

"Don't you dare try that," she had warned me.

"That's an invitation, woman of the house, that before the end of this remarkable summer, I will surely accept."

"Nonsense . . . Monsignor, your brother is still a slugabed. If you want to play golf with him, you will have to roust him out yourself. Our mutual friend here will play mixed doubles with his daughter and my youngest son. The rain will clear away within the hour and it will be a pleasant if somewhat cool evening for our little party on the deck."

So it had been decided by our matriarch with the pink ribbon around her ponytail and so it was.

Just as I was leaving the breakfast room—or "brunch center" as it was called—Judge Keenan appeared. His kiss was not as wild as his brother's but infinitely more serious: a touch of lips that told of a life of love, tragedy, conflict perhaps, sweet reconciliations, and passion that would never end.

I pitied myself that I did not have an extended family or even really a family such as the Keenans with their delicately balanced and powerful network of affection.

My siblings had scattered to the far corners of the country to escape our mother. Now that both my parents were dead I was the only one in Chicago and none of the others were ever likely to return. All of them would be absolutely uninterested in a visit from me. I was still the outsider.

In the course of the tennis I discovered that it had been an age-old custom for the Clares to gather with the Keenans on the latter's boathouse deck to watch the fireworks display from the Club, just down the shore. So I would see her again.

Later we gathered on the deck over the Keenan boathouse, wearing sweaters or sweatshirts because it was a pleasantly cool evening, watching the fireworks display from the Club. I did not particularly enjoy it. Jane in tight fitting white slacks and equally tight fitting white sweatshirt was sitting on the bench next to me. Somehow in the darkness, my hand had found its way to her long and lovely thigh. And somehow she did not banish it, though she did gasp softly a couple of times as, inspired by the spectacular illuminations in the night sky, my ministrations became briefly more intimate than they had the night before.

Then the kids—Lucianne and Jamie Keenan especially—deftly turned the conversation to my exploit at the Bijou the night before and Jane's long and lovely leg disappeared from my immediate environment. She had not, however, changed her seat but merely shifted away from me—temporarily, not permanently, out of reach.

Later, when the show was over and the yellow lights on the deck had been turned on, Packy nodded towards a quiet corner.

"I talked to the old fella this afternoon."

"Oh?"

I noted that Lucianne and Laura were in an animated conversation with Jamie Keenan and another good-looking lout called "Roger"—last name not given. Another seminarian, I presumed.

Despite big changes, some things don't change.

"He sends his best. Will be happy to see you again when they come back as soon as Mom's art festival is over and tell you what he knows."

Fleetwood Mac was blaring again as they had all afternoon. If it was them. One rock group sounded pretty much like any other to me.

"How much does he know?"

"Typically, more than he's telling me and less than he lets on. He did say that the State Police got some of the money, which may be his source, an old cop rumor."

"Why would the Murrays permit a cover-up? Their kids were killed, their family wiped out for all practical purposes."

"Because they were afraid of the truth, which might have been even more horrible."

"I suppose."

"Do you still think Phil might have been involved?"

"Not any more. I can't see him as bright enough to organize a conspiracy."

"Don't underestimate his shrewdness. He won the woman, you know."

"With the help of the People's Liberation Army, but I take your point . . .

did your father say where he thought the money came from? That was a lot of hard cash in those days, maybe worth three million in today's shrinking dollars."

"He hinted that he knew, but he didn't tell me anything. You'll have to pry it out of him yourself. And don't figure that he knows more than he does."

"How do you know how much he knows?"

"That's the problem. About any subject."

"It will be an interesting conversation."

"One more thing." Packy glanced out at the moon bathed waters of the Lake. "He said to be careful. That wasn't Tom Keenan being wise, it was an honest statement about present danger."

"What could be dangerous? Almost everyone who was involved is dead."

"It was a serious warning, Lee. I told him what the prize was and he said that she was probably worth it, but you still should be careful."

"Probably?"

"His word."

It sounded like one of Tom Keenan's beloved mysteries.

"Why didn't you guys stop the marriage?" I blurted a question over which I had agonized for a quarter century. "There must have been other men she could have married."

Packy was quiet for a moment.

"We tried—Jerry and Maggie and I and my parents in their own way. She didn't hear us, Lee, simply didn't hear us. She didn't hear a thing from the time your death was announced until her first child. Oh, she kept up the Jane front. But there was no one home in her head or her heart."

"Strange."

"Not so strange. Long-term trauma is what Maggie called it. Maybe not over it completely yet. Your death has been the big event in her life."

"I didn't die," I said again.

"For her you did."

"I'm alive now. For her."

"I'm not sure she believes that yet. One more thing," Packy hesitated. "Little Phil was born six months after the wedding . . . I mean the wedding had been scheduled for at least six months, so it wasn't a shotgun marriage. I guess our old friend couldn't wait."

"The bastard!" I said. "She was an emotional wreck and he virtually raped her!"

"I quite agree," Packy responded, his normally serene face wreathed in an angry frown. "Whatever has happened to him since, he richly deserves."

Packy's rare lack of charity inspired me to vent my own feelings.

"In spades . . . Dickie told me that he was chasing on their honeymoon."

"Everyone knows that."

"Why did Jane wait so long to toss him out?"

"Old-fashioned Catholic, trying to make the best of a mistake. Thank God she's learned finally there's an upper limit."

"Just at the time I've appeared on the scene to claim my belated prize."

"You might say that," he grinned happily, "you might say just that."

I bade my good-byes to the prize as she and her brood prepared to leave.

"I hope I see you again, Lee," she said as she brushed her lips against mine, "before the summer is over."

"You can count on it, Jane." I hugged her fiercely. "You'll see me again."

I thought I saw—or perhaps only imagined I saw—Lucianne and Laura grinning happily.

1946

Leo

"You want to go down there, Lunkhead?" Jane asked.

I gulped. We were at the edge of the road looking at "Skinny-dip Beach" just barely visible through the trees.

"Huh?"

"There's no one there."

"Are you serious?

"I think," she said virtuously, "it's an experience everyone should have once while they're growing up."

"There's not much light," I observed, "just the moon once in a while through the clouds."

"Do you want more light or less?" she laughed.

"Both."

She laughed again and darted through the trees. Not altogether sure that this was a good idea, I followed less rapidly.

It was the summer of 1946. Jerry Keenan had returned from the wars but not yet to Chicago. He was looking for "a girl he found and lost," Packy explained. Packy himself was about to enter his fifth year at Quigley Seminary, the last before he was swallowed up by the major seminary at Mundelein in which, in those days, seminarians were incarcerated for seven years. Jim Murray, his worried frown deeper than ever, and Phil Clare, his bland smile, more bland than ever, were both at Notre Dame. Jane had graduated from Trinity and, over strenuous objection from her parents and brothers, had entered Rosary College. Eileen and Angie were about to enter their last year of high school at the Convent of the Sacred Heart. I had finished my first year of college and had put in my required six weeks sweating in the sun at Quantico where Naval ROTC units did their first summer duty before embarking on ships in their second year—an adventure I dreaded because of my queasy stomach.

When I came home from Quantico, I was in a somewhat different position than I had been before. The Navy paid me a salary. I had money of my own, which my mother could not confiscate from me. I didn't have to push a lawn mower any more. I could buy a beat-up 1939 Ford of my own. I could spend as much of the month of summer vacation that was left to me as I wanted to at the Lake without having to explain my behavior to anyone— least of all to the elder Keenans who were happy to have me around the house even when Packy wasn't there.

The only price I had to pay for this freedom, for such it seemed to me then, was that the United States Navy would own me for a couple of years, how many not clear, after my graduation. Most ROTC programs had been absorbed in officer training programs during the war. The services, not sure how many officers they would need in the postwar world, opened new programs up and closed them down with dizzying rapidity. The one I joined at Loyola, for some strange reason managed to survive. I was able to stay in by agreeing to choose the Marines as my branch of service when I would graduate and receive my commission.

My mother had not really forgiven me for leaving the seminary. She insisted that there was not enough money to pay for my college education and at the same time send my younger siblings to "good Catholic high schools."

There was even then either enough money or the promise of it to refute that argument and my father tried, unsuccessfully as always when money was the issue, to overrule her. But I wanted no part of family support. ROTC and the United States Marine Corps promised me freedom from the family, a life in which I could finally call my own shots all the time and not merely when I was with the Keenans at the Lake. I would receive a free college education and earn G.I. bill benefits for my graduate school education in political science. (Without even knowing what it was, I had chosen that as my field.) In return the Government would merely require two years of service from me. Well, maybe four.

Everyone knew that there would not be another war for a long, long time. If ever.

It turned out to be three years in the service, two and a half in a POW camp. I paid also with two of my fingers and a lifetime of bad dreams and intermittent rage. On the other hand I also have a lifetime pension and a lot of experience of human nature, including my own—stubborn, stubborn, stubborn for all my phony professorial wit and charm.

Mean too.

A reasonable exchange? Today I think I probably ended up with more gain than loss, though if I had known in 1946 what I know now I would not have made the deal.

It is kind of interesting to watch the old sixteen millimeter film that my adoring sister Megan made of my funeral Mass, especially of Jane's agonized face as they sing "my" *Ave* and then *Panis Angelicus.* For years I would not watch it. More recently I have had it transferred to video tape. Some day I will show it to Laura.

I watch it every once in a while. Just to remind myself that I live on borrowed time. Even if it had not been for Korea, that would still be true, but a film of your own funeral, or more precisely, your own memorial Mass kind of makes the point, doesn't it?

Anyway I was now on my own and would, I said proudly to my family, work to earn my own living for the rest of my life. I don't know whether that was an accurate prediction because I'm not sure whether being a professor is work.

So I turned up at the Lake in the August of 1946—without my uniform of course because even as a Marine I was not much of a militarist.

My first stop after checking in with the Keenans had been the Rose Bowl—so I guess I must have known about Jane's job.

"*Lunkhead!* Is it you?"

She had thrown her arms around and hugged me fiercely.

"You really have changed! What have they done to your hair! Gee, you're really strong! How long will you be here! That Ford out there really isn't yours, is it? Want a malt!"

"You bet, the bigger the better!"

I had seen her at Mass in Chicago before I left for Quantico. Yet she seemed to have changed astonishingly in a few months. Even in the "cute" soda jerk uniform, she looked like a full-grown woman and an incredibly beautiful one.

"Cute," which was synonymous with "adorable" in Jane's lexicon, meant a pink and white dress with a very short skirt, a very tight bodice, and two open buttons—the last being her optional modification.

She took my breath away. She did every time I saw her for the first time at the Lake. But this summer she was something really special. We were all growing up. Or at any rate getting older. I wasn't sure that I had liked that.

That summer, though I was only eighteen, I had begun to think like an adult, as had the men of the same age born a few years before me during the war. A year of college and six weeks at boot camp had not made a man out of me by any means, but I was at least addressing questions from which the seminary had protected me.

Such as: when would I marry, what kind of a woman would I want to marry, where might I find this woman.

In that embrace in the Rose Bowl, for the first time I had begun to think that the woman I might marry was the girl down the street, now turned elegant woman in my arms.

It seemed at the moment like a very good idea. It was moreover an idea that changed the ambiance of that summer and the two that were to follow.

None of the others was around, but they'd all be up on Friday night and we would have a great time this weekend.

And she would give up on "Lunkhead," she informed me, except sometimes, if I would give up on "Milady."

"OK, except sometimes."

She howled at that and offered me yet another large malt, which I could hardly refuse because she said it would be on the house.

"Take me to a movie tonight?"

"What is it?"

"Does it matter with me for a date?"

Instead of answering like I would have only the previous summer that I would not go to a rotten movie even if Linda Darnell was my date, I replied, "Not really."

"Hey you have changed . . . it's called 'Death Takes a Holiday.' "

"Never heard of it."

"1934."

"Ugh!"

"It's supposed to be real good."

"Well, at least it's not 'Girl of the Limberlost.' "

The Bijou, then as now, did not book the most recent films. In those days we said that there was a rule of thumb that they would never present anything made after 1940. "Girl of the Limberlost," surely one of the first "talkies," was an annual. We all knew the lines by heart and acted out the roles.

So we had made a date for the evening. She would walk over to the Keenan house and collect me and we would *walk* to the Bijou. She didn't believe in people our age driving to the movies. I could pick her up and drive her home after work, however. Coming home from work was a different matter, I was assured.

Once again, I was not permitted anywhere near her family.

That night Jane wore a pale green light summer sun dress—high neck, low back—instead of her usual blouse and shorts. She seemed to me more dazzling than ever, an almost uncanny contrast to the eerie film. The movie, which you can still see occasionally on television, is now a kind of classic. Death wants to be loved and comes to earth to find out why he is not loved. Then he falls in love. It is a comedy of sorts but with some wry comments on the human condition. We had drifted over to the Rose Bowl after the movie in thoughtful reflection.

Jane did not smell any longer of chocolate and stale milk and cigarette smoke and sweat. Rather she smelled like the state forest after a fresh rain, mysterious and magical and enchanting.

Midweek in August, the soda fountain was not crowded. Everyone in the place, however, knew Jane and she had worked the room like a precinct captain, smiling, patting on the shoulder, punching in the arm, a word of greeting for everyone. She had always done that and I had never noticed. Now I noticed and approved. The jukebox, as best as I can remember, was playing "It Might as Well Be Spring" from *State Fair*.

That night I would have approved of anything Jane did.

"I'll get even fatter if I keep eating these things," she had said as she settled down with her malt. She glanced at me. "You on the other hand are too thin."

"You're not too fat, Jane," I had permitted my appraisal to linger as I considered her.

She had blushed and lowered her eyes. "You shouldn't look at me that way, Lee."

"Why not?"

"Well," she had concentrated on her malt, "of course you should, but not quite so obviously."

"I don't know if I ever did tell you how beautiful you are," I had mumbled, "but if I did you're twice as beautiful now."

It was not a very creative gallantry, but I was not used to being gallant.

She had blushed again and covered my hand with hers. "You're such a sweet boy, Lee, really you are."

I drifted upward on a fluffy pink cloud.

Then, while Bing Crosby crooned "Ole Buttermilk Sky" on the dilapidated, pre-war jukebox, our conversation had turned serious.

"We're both going to die someday, Lee."

"Not for a long time."

That exchange would stick in my head during the two years in the POW camp.

"But eventually."

"I suppose so."

"What do you want to do with your life?"

"I want to be a good professor of political science."

"I'm not sure what that is exactly but I just know you'd be good with college kids."

"I hope so."

"You'll marry eventually?"

"People do."

"When you're a stuffy old man?"

"As soon as I find the right girl."

That seemed to satisfy her.

"And what will you do, Jane?"

She shook her head. "What does a woman do? Marry, have kids, be a good wife and mother."

"You sound like that's not enough."

"I'd like to do something else too. Write stories maybe."

I tell my classes that if one does not want a civil rights movement in the sixties and a woman's movement in the seventies, one does not send blacks and women to college in the forties and fifties. Looking back on that conversation, Jane Devlin was already some kind of proto-feminist.

"Write stories?"

"Mysteries stories, like the Bobbsey Twins or Nancy Drew."

God or an archangel or someone of similar clout must have intervened to prevent me from making fun of the idea that she could be a writer and that she thought such stories for girl kids were literature. After four years at a Catholic high school.

Instead I had managed to say, "That would be a lot of fun."

"Or maybe G.K. Chesterton . . . do you know who he is?"

"Sure. We read *Orthodoxy* and *The Everlasting Man* in the seminary."

"I never heard of them. I saw a paperback of some stories about a priest named Father Brown in the Dime Store and so I bought it. They're wonderful. I have all the books now."

"I'll have to read them."

"I'll lend them to you."

Nancy Drew and G.K. Chesterton!

"I suppose it's a silly dream," she had continued, "but I'd really like to write stories . . . do writers make much money?"

"Some of them make a lot of money."

"Good!"

It was our first serious conversation. Jane was not only beautiful and smart, she also had a serious streak. What more could one want of a woman?

"Are you afraid to die, Lee?"

"Death is on your mind a lot tonight."

"It's not just the movie." She had finished her malt. "I think about it a lot."

"Why?"

"I don't know. I just do. I'm not exactly afraid of it, but I don't think I want to die. Yet sometimes I wish life was over already. Do I sound crazy?"

"You never sound crazy, Jane." It was my turn to put my hand over hers. "You sound thoughtful and intelligent."

"Is this ever a good night for me to collect compliments!" She had become her laughing self again. "Come on, Lunkhead, lets go home—unless you want your fourth malt today."

"No, Milady."

"Oh, oh! I slipped. I'm sorry."

The jukebox announced that it was "A Grand Night for Singing" as we left the Rose Bowl. It was indeed.

She had chattered happily as we ambled down the dark road toward the Old Houses. Angie Nicola and Jim Murray were really "serious about one another"; Phil was drinking too much again and not doing well at Notre Dame; he was taking summer school classes at "the pier" (Navy Pier, the site of a state college, which would eventually become the University of Illinois at Chicago); Eileen was dating a couple of different boys but she wasn't serious about them; Packy was still Packy, working in a Negro parish on the South Side this summer.

"Isn't he wonderful, Leo? I mean I think he's a lot like Father Brown, so good and so wise and so kind. Isn't he?"

I had agreed. Later when I read the Father Brown stories for the first time I saw no resemblance at all. No one could have looked less like Chesterton's detective than Patrick Keenan. Still later when I reread them, I realize that there was indeed a similarity.

"Won't he make a wonderful priest! I'm so happy that he's going to be a priest, aren't you?"

"You bet." I put my arm around her waist. "Eliminates a rival."

"Silly!" She snuggled close to me. "We're not playing the rivals game."

"Not yet."

"Not for a long, long time." She had paused. "Besides, you don't have any rivals."

A commitment? A promise? An invitation?

"I am glad to hear that."

She slipped out of my grasp, perhaps feeling that she had said too much.

Then we had come to "Skinny-dip Beach."

I caught up to the silhouette just as it discarded what might have been a panty and dove into the water.

"Come on, fraidy cat," she shouted. "The water is great!"

With considerably less enthusiasm, I undressed and dove in after her, a tense mixture of curiosity and embarrassment.

It was too dark to see anything except shapes and outlines. We were both clothed in the night.

I stood on the muddy lake bottom, looking around for her.

Someone emerged from the water next to me in the glow of a brief shower of moonlight—a sparkling Venus arising fully formed from the foaming sea, and, rather less serene than Venus, pulled me under water. In return I wrestled her under with me. Our play was uninhibited yet cautious, neither of us wanting it to become something else. Finally, panting and laughing, we climbed up on the decrepit old pier at the end of "Skinny-dip Beach" and lay next to one another. We both became quiet, closer together than we ever had been yet alone with intimate thoughts to which we could not give word and which we would not have expressed even if we had the vocabulary.

I began to sing. I don't remember the songs, but I suppose I must have sung "Always" and "How Deep is the Ocean" because those were our songs that magical summer. Jane hummed along with me in an off-key accompaniment. We were alone in the world. No one and nothing else mattered. The moon appeared intermittently, cast light like angel wings on her, and then, as if shocked, rushed back behind the clouds.

She put her hand on my chest. I rested my fingers on her belly. Neither hand moved from its appointed station. When the moon made one of its quick appearances, I saw that her hair was slicked down on her head and her body wet with sparkling diamond water drops. The whole world belonged to me that night and all the joy and the love and all the laughter. It was an erotic experience all right but a religious one too. The cool water, the warm night, the naked girl told me in terms so vivid that I would never forget them, not even on the coldest nights in Korea, that life was good and love possible.

"Fun," she said.

"You bet."

"I like being wicked," she sighed.

"Mildly wicked."

"*Of course.*"

"I like you mildly wicked."

"Me too. I mean I like you when you're mildly wicked."

We both had a fit of giggles.

"We'd better go home," she sighed on the pier.

"Yep."

She stood up and dove into the water. For a brief moment I saw a wonderful womanly outline against the clouds.

On the beach we shivered. "Should have brought towels."

"Especially since you planned it all along."

"I did *not* . . . Oh, Lee!"

I had taken her naked body in my arms and pressed it against my own for a quick instant and kissed her decisively if briefly.

For that interlude of a few seconds I thought I was in paradise.

Why did we not make love then and there? We were Irish Catholics and it was 1946. But even if the circumstances were different that was not the point of the event. Sexual love would come later. This was a promise, chaste but erotic, not only of sex but of something even more wonderful that might lurk beyond it, a love stronger than death.

"Wow," she breathed as I released her. "I think we'd better get dressed now."

"Good idea."

"Hook my bra for me?" she asked a few seconds later.

"Delighted. I'll button the back of your dress too."

"Thank you very much."

My fingers trembled only a little as I performed these delicate tasks.

Back on the road, she said, "That was very nice. I'm not sure what we did or why we did it, but it was really great."

"Sure was . . . Maybe we can do it again."

"Maybe," she hesitated, "but not very often."

"Only once more."

"All right."

"Promise?"

"I promise."

It is a promise on which I have yet to collect. But I haven't given up on the possibility of demanding that she redeem it.

Leo

"I'm worried about him, Lee," Angie Nicola sighed, the movement in her luscious breasts sending a shiver through me. "He's so serious, so . . .""

"Melancholy?"

"That's right. His heart just isn't in the fun we are having this weekend or any other time. He pretends to be part of everything. But his mind is far away somewhere else thinking about God and death and other depressing things like that."

Like her mother, Angie wore two-piece swimsuits. While they were nothing like the bikinis of today—in fact they were solidly constructed girdles and bras—they still revealed a lot more than did other swim fashions, particularly when the woman in question, like Angie, combined a china figurine delicacy with a succulent body.

The white outfit with lace trim she was wearing that day hinted at lingerie, which made her all the more appealing.

Maybe I should take her to "Skinny-dip Beach," I reflected. Then I decided that it wouldn't be a very good idea.

That night, while we were sitting on the deck, I asked Packy about Iris Clare.

"I think she's just a lonely and unhappy woman who tried to drown her misery in drink. Now that she's given it up, she acts a little strange."

"Why is she so lonely and unhappy? She has a rich husband and all the possessions a woman could want. She's beautiful and men admire her. What's missing?"

"I don't think," Pack chose his words cautiously, "that Doctor Clare pays much attention to her. She was a pretty nurse from down-state that he married at the same age that his father and grandfather married pretty nurses. Philly is his world and vice versa. It's like the wife and mother doesn't exist—a decoration in the house of which you must be careful, nothing more."

"That's what your parents think?"

He laughed. "I couldn't make that up myself, could I?"

"You agree?"

"Pretty much. She's a bit of a tease, but she doesn't mean anything by it."

Having left the seminary because I didn't want to have to deal with people and their problems, this was my summer for dealing with people and their problems. Phil was worried, in a sincere but stupid kind of way, about his mother's infrequent Mass attendance. I reassured him that it might be a different matter for converts than for cradle Catholics—especially, as I did not add, if one became a Catholic because one wanted to marry Doctor Philip Clare.

Then one night in the forest while we were drinking beer, he asked me another favor after he had explained at great length how his father and Mr. Murray and Mr. Nicola were going to make big money in the upcoming economic boom from a shopping plaza they were planning in a northern suburb of Chicago.

When he had explained to me that a shopping plaza was a group of stores around a big parking lot, I told him that it might be a good idea but it would never work—which goes to show you what a brilliant prophet the future author of *The Big Change* really was.

The favor? Would I please ask Jane for him if she would mind becoming engaged the following Christmas? He knew she loved him and wanted to marry him and would I mind kind of breaking the ice?

"She's very young still, Phil," I temporized.

"Yeah, but we won't marry for a couple of years and she'll be old enough then. Please, Leo, she likes you and she won't mind you interceding for me. I love her so much."

Phil was good at playing the poor, pathetic role so I let myself be manipulated into playing the game—though I had grave doubts about the outcome.

The next night as I was driving Jane home from the Rose Bowl (we usually walked but it was a rainy night), I thought about Phil's plea and decided that tonight was not the right time. Perhaps only because I wanted to kiss her.

I parked the car near the gate of the Devlin Old House—an imitation Georgian country manor—with a large "park" around it, mostly trees and underbrush, a form of landscaping not approved by the other inhabitants of the "Old Houses."

Hand in hand we walked up to the gate.

"Doesn't the warm sand feel good under your feet?" Jane asked, taking my hand in hers.

Once she had acquired her "lake feet" (after the first week of summer) Jane refused to wear shoes, save at Mass and at her job and on dates with Phil.

"It sure does."

"I do so love this place."

"So do I . . . I also love the young woman who lives at this house."

"Sure," she said skeptically.

"I do." I enfolded her in my arms to confirm if not my love at least her desirability.

"Hey," she protested weakly.

I had never kissed her quite that way before. There was not only intensity in that kiss—we were old pros at the intensity game—but demand, a demand that was all the stronger because I would have to carry a message from my rival to her tomorrow or the next day.

I came up for air.

"Lee," she moaned. "I don't know . . ."

"I do."

I returned to my task of telling her with my lips that she was my woman and I wanted her . . . a message to which I was not yet fully committed.

Finally I let her go. She leaned against me, breathless and exhausted.

"That's the way Marine officers kiss their women?"

"It's the way this Marine officer's candidate kisses this woman."

"I see," she gulped. "Well, you always were a good kisser and you've gotten better. Now I'm going into the house and don't try to stop me."

"I wouldn't dream of it."

"Yes you would," she whispered in the night as she ran up the driveway to her home, a driveway that was forbidden ground to me.

I watched her long white legs in the darkness. I wanted all of her.

But I still had promised a favor to Phil.

Leo

"I will die young, Leo," Jim Murray shook his head gloomily. "I know that. I'm resigned to it. Then I will go to hell. I'm doomed. I have no choice."

We were walking through the woods of the State Park. The trail on which we were walking (wearing shoes I hasten to add) was wet and muddy. We dodged an occasional small puddle. Leaves and tree branches on the forest floor, blown off by the ferocious night storm, and the glowering gray sky above the forest arch were all signs of autumn, signs of the end of summer, which I hated then and hate even more now.

"Bullshit, Jimmy. No one is doomed. No one knows when they're going to die. You should forget that stuff."

We had arranged for a tennis match, but the courts were too wet to play. Jim proposed that we walk in the State Park instead. He was tired of tennis anyway, he said, tired of everything.

So we ambled down a trail, stepping over the fallen limbs of the great oak and maple and occasional pine trees that the Chicago lumber companies had somehow missed.

How had such amiable and fun-loving parents produced such a morose child?

"Have you ever screwed a woman, Leo?" he asked suddenly.

"No," I said, "not exactly."

No, not even inexactly.

"I have. All summer. It's heaven. It also means hell for me. I don't care. I'm going to hell anyway."

I had no response ready for that.

"It's not poor little Angie."

"I didn't think it was."

"She's just a child."

"Damn pretty child."

He waved his hand. "Pretty if you like that type, but not very interesting."

"If you say so."

"Do you want to know who it is?"

"If you want to tell me."

Clearly he did. He was both proud of his conquest and terrified by its portents for his eternal damnation.

"Iris!"

"Mrs. Clare!"

How many eighteen-year-old boys, I wonder today, would be able to resist seduction by a beautiful and skillful older woman?

Would the eighteen-year-old Leo Kelly be able to fight off her enticements?

Probably, but because of meanness, not virtue. And stubbornness. Like I say the eighteen-year-old Leo was a very stubborn kid. Very mean too. Which is probably why he's still alive.

Also probably why he sleeps by himself at night.

And he hasn't grown any less stubborn since then.

"I see."

"She's a wonderful woman, Lee. Those bastards don't treat her right. They patronize and freeze her out. Doctor Clare can't . . . make love most of the time."

"I'm not surprised."

Packy had hinted at that. But if the woman was hungry for a lay, why couldn't she pick on someone her own age? Why a kid and a kid who would suffer terrible guilt over what he was doing? Were her pants that hot? Or did she enjoy being perverse? Or did she have a couple of lovers on the line?

Today I would withhold such judgments, partly for reasons of ideology and mostly I hope for reasons of wisdom, the little bits of it that I have.

"Someone has to love her," he continued.

"Why you?"

"Because she loves me."

"This summer."

"We don't think beyond this summer."

"Then it will stop?"

Certainly it would stop. Matrons turning forty soon lose interest in their youthful conquests, especially when they're sad sacks like Jimmy.

"I don't care about the future . . . the present is so wonderful. We do all the things that men and women do to each other, Leo. *All* of them."

I wasn't sure then what "all" comprised. I'm not even sure that I'm sure now. I didn't want to know then and I still don't want to know.

Well, maybe I do a little bit.

"How do you get away with it, Jimmy?"

"When they're out playing golf. The servants don't care because they like her and they hate the other two."

"I see."

"We do it almost every day, Leo. Some days several times. One day we did it ten times."

"Sounds exhausting."

"It was, but, oh God, Leo, it was so wonderful. She's an incredible lay."

"I can believe that."

I had heard other men brag about their sexual conquests, but none with such awe for the woman.

He wanted to brag so I let him brag.

"She taught me how but now I'm in charge, Leo, I can do whatever I want whenever I want. She's kind of my slave. There's nothing like it. No pleasure in the world can match it. It's worth going to hell for."

"You're not going to hell, Jimmy. Forget that bullshit. God still loves you."

"If there is a God."

"If there isn't, how can you go to hell?"

"I'm pretty sure there isn't."

"Then why worry? Fuck her to your heart's content and enjoy it."

"But what if there is a God after all? What if God is playing a trick on me to punish me for my lack of faith?"

"Then it will be all over by September anyway."

I was becoming exasperated by his self-indulgent inconsistency, his sick mixture of pride and fear.

"God won't forgive me."

"That's heresy, Jimmy."

So the argument went on, a bootless argument at that. Jimmy wanted to talk about his woman (though he avoided clinical details) and he wanted to feel he was damned. All I could do was to hope that he'd get over it.

I don't think the poor kid is in hell, if there be such a place. Packy says that there's a German theologian named Urs something or other, who contends that everyone is saved. Seems reasonable enough to me, though there's a couple of Asian camp guards I wouldn't want to meet in the heavenly city.

They're long since dead because Mao and Kim, intent on destroying evidence, liquidated them all. And Peng, the commander of the Chinese Army in Korea, was tortured to death during the Great Cultural Revolution. I resist feelings of satisfaction in both matters.

I did outlive the bastards, however.

But poor Jimmy Murray was right about one thing: he didn't have long to live, only two more years, almost to the day.

After we had escaped the woods, I drove him home in my rumbling Ford and then stopped by the Nicola house to report to Angie who, in charcoal gray slacks and a frilly pink "New Look" blouse, looked like she had stepped out of a fashion magazine. We walked to the gazebo halfway down their huge front lawn.

"Any luck, Leo?" she asked hesitantly.

"It's a bad summer for him, Angie. I think he'll be all right next summer."

"Are you *sure?*"

"No guarantees in life, kid." I took her hand in mine. "But give him time."

"I'm going to St. Mary's the year after next and I'll be right across the road from him and able to take care of him. But what will he do till then?"

"Not a very good idea even to think that way, Angie. At our age we can't take care of anyone besides ourselves. And that not always very well."

"You wouldn't say that if Jane were in the same kind of trouble."

"I don't know what Jane's troubles are, if any. I do know that if she has them I can't solve them. Moreover, she wouldn't want me hanging around trying to help her unless she asked me to. And I'm pretty sure that Jimmy hasn't asked, has he?"

"No, but . . ."

"No," I said firmly squeezing her hand.

"*But*," she insisted, "you have to take care of those you love, suffer for them."

"Only when they're ready for it. Till then you wait."

"I suppose so," she agreed reluctantly. "But I know I'm not going to date next year."

"It's your senior year in high school, Angie, you should enjoy it."

"Look who's talking," she giggled, "the guy that was never a senior."

"That," I insisted, happy that I had made her laugh, however unintentionally, "is beside the point."

She thanked me and kissed my cheek. I was pretty sure that the enthusiasms of the senior year would sweep away her crush on Jimmy. Anyway Iris might have spoiled him for a fresh and gentle young woman like Angie, worse luck for him.

I also wondered, briefly, where she had picked up that notion of suffering for those you loved. Probably from her mother. Up to a point, it was sound religion, I suppose, but somehow it didn't fit the case.

I made up my mind that, although Jimmy had not imposed secrecy on me, I would tell no one about his love affair with Phil's mother. It was the sort of story that ought to be kept secret and would not remain secret for long if I told anyone else.

If he wanted to brag about his conquest to someone else, that would be his problem not mine.

Then I collected Jane at the Rose Bowl, and after consuming my usual malt with four butter cookies, I walked her down to the car, carrying her tennis racket, which she had used before going to work.

Filled with virtue and proud of my sympathy for poor Jimmy and reassurance for poor Angie (both of which were hollow triumphs) I decided I'd discharge my obligation to Phil.

Mistake. Big mistake.

"I want to talk about Phil for a minute."

"That slob!"

"Jane, *please* sit down," I gestured toward a bench under a streetlight above the parking lot across the street from the pier.

"Oh, all right!"

This was not the time to talk about Phil. I would certainly offend and anger her. But there would be no good times for the conversation and I might just as well get it over with.

She sat down and slammed her racket against her tennis shoe. "What about him?"

"He says he loves you."

"I know *that*. He's been saying *that* for years. All it means is that he lusts after me."

"He may not be the only one."

"You're different," she patted my shoulder.

"Don't be so sure."

"I *am* sure. You lust after me respectfully. He doesn't."

"I hope that's true."

I had decided that if I were to do Phil's favor for him, the only way was to play it straight. I could not beat around the bush with her as he wanted me to. You didn't beat around the bush with Jane Devlin.

"*Well*, what does he want?"

So I'd play it straight and God help me and protect me from her fury.

"He wanted me to ask you if it was all right with you if you and he became informally engaged this year at Christmas?"

"What!" She exploded from the bench. "What!"

"He wanted me . . ."

"I heard what you said. All he really wants is to sleep with me. I won't do that, not ever! Go tell him that, do you hear me, tell that asshole that he can wait till the day after the last judgment and I won't sleep with him! Do you hear me!"

"He thinks you love him and will marry him eventually."

"Two days after the last judgment and tell him that too!" She punched her tennis racket dangerously close to my nose.

"I was just doing him a favor by asking," I said meekly.

"Don't ever do that kind of favor again or I'll break this tennis racket over your head!" She waved the racket threateningly.

"Yes ma'am."

"And wipe that silly grin off your stupid face."

"Yes ma'am."

She stalked away.

I followed after her at a safe distance, feeling very happy despite the failure of my foolish Miles Standish mission. She turned on me and swung the racket again. "I can walk home, thank you very much."

I followed her with my car.

"Lunkhead," she shouted as I pulled alongside her. "I *said* I wanted to walk home."

"Yes, Milady."

How wonderful she was when she was angry.

Leo

So I told Phil that he ought to back off for a while. Reluctantly he agreed. Jane phoned me the next morning and apologized.

"I'm sorry I shouted at you. I know you were only trying to make that asshole feel good. He's so good at making us not want to hurt his feelings. But don't do it again."

"No ma'am."

"But if you do I won't swing my tennis racket at you."

"Fair enough."

"What would you have done if I said yes?"

"Maybe died or at least broke down with inconsolable grief."

She giggled. "You can take me to the Bijou tonight."

"I'm forgiven?"

"I'm the one who needs to be forgiven for losing my temper."

So our romance continued for the rest of the summer, a glowing summer love that would never die, but which I often felt in the depths of my soul could no more survive the winter of life than do the leaves of the crab apple or jasmine trees.

Back in Chicago I lived on campus instead of with the family—my mother would not tolerate the purchase of yet another and bigger house—and saw very little of the summer crowd during the school year. Even Packy drifted out of my life.

I lived in two different worlds, summer and winter, and never did the two meet.

Why did I keep my two worlds separate? Mostly I suppose because I didn't think I belonged in the summer world, that it was a temporary fantasy that was not real and never could be real. Jane was the love of my life at the Lake. But back in the city she was an utterly unattainable dream.

Looking back on that reaction it was evidently pure folly, my mother's veto in the depths of my unconscious. But then my behavior seemed completely rational, a decision made in the clear light of day after a night of indulgence in illusions. Hence when I would later storm away from the Lake in a fury of injured pride it was easy to believe that it all had been inane illusion, a daydream that had never really happened and could never really happen.

Crazy, absurd, idiotic? I admit it. But I guess I went to the Lake each summer with my fingers crossed, hoping against hope that the fantasy had survived another winter and knowing that it could not endure.

For some reason my friends at the Lake accepted this bifurcation of my life. Perhaps they took it for granted that I was just a little crazy.

One night after Christmas on Rush Street I encountered Angie, dressed in the tight-waist, full skirt, frilly bodice and phony hints of lingerie, which had been dubbed "The New Look," looking like she was twenty-four instead of seventeen. Her date, who on sight didn't like me, listened impatiently as we gossiped.

"Eileen is going to St. Mary's with me. Phil is leaving school in January to work on the Board of Trade. Jimmy seems a lot better. We never see Packy. I guess his brother finally found that loathsome Maggie person, right here in Chicago. I suppose they'll get married. No, I haven't seen her yet. I'm sure she's ugly. Jane loves college, but that terrible drunken woman is giving her a hard time about it. Two years at the most she keeps saying, like she is some kind of family disgrace. And you've heard the news about Phil's mother, haven't you?"

"What news?"

"She's *pregnant,* can you imagine that? At her age!"

"When does the baby come?"

"In May, I guess. Doesn't that amaze you?"

"It certainly does."

"All right, Roger, I'm coming," she said to her impatient date.

"Nice to meet you Roger," I said pleasantly.

He glared in return.

Somehow I didn't think Roger would be lucky enough to have another date with Angie.

Phil's little sister was named Norine, for reasons that escape me.

Why a child? Was it just an accident or did she want a memory of her sweaty summer afternoons with Jimmy Murray?

Women like her, Mary Anne Keenan would say the following summer, don't have accidents.

I couldn't be sure that Jimmy was the father. Maybe there were other men that summer. But maybe there were not.

The child, born just before Packy graduated from Quigley in June of 1947—what has happened to her?

She's an M.D. now, just like her putative father, and is a medical missionary nun in Central America.

Who says God isn't a comedian?

Or comedienne.

1978

Leo

"I suppose you wonder why I belong here instead of the Chicago Club, where I understand the University sends you, or maybe the Mid-America Club."

"Or the Chicago Yacht Club, they have the best pastry table in town."

"Oh, I belong there, but I thought you'd like the cinnamon rolls here. I see that you do."

He gestured at the roll in my hand and revealed a large diamond ring on his right hand, the kind that affluent political lawyers always wear.

"You have a great memory, Tom."

"Not all that bad for pushing eighty . . . anyway I joined the Union League just to see all those conservative Republican bastards wince when I come in the dining room. It does my old heart good."

"A lot of Irish Catholics from the commodity markets, I'd wager."

"I have no personal objection to gamblers!"

Tom Keenan was still several years away from eighty and wore his seventy odd years very well indeed. Despite a barely visible quiver in his right hand, he was trim and alert and did not wander in his conversation—though since he was always an opaque Irish political lawyer it was sometimes hard to tell. Mary Anne, whom I had seen when the Keenans threw a party to welcome me back to Chicago, was still a striking woman, not the erotic beauty I had first seen in 1942 but still appealing.

Did they still make love, I wondered.

Probably.

I prayed that they did. Maggie would tell me that it was a good Catholic prayer.

"Hope you don't mind a breakfast meeting, but I wake up pretty early these days."

"Not at all. I have a full day at the University."

"Seems like we're always moving from one condo to another—Taos, East Lake Shore Drive, and then up to our coach house at the Lake next door to Jerry and that little witch he found back in '47."

"Where's the best service?"

"At Maggie's Motel," he guffawed. "Thank God Jerry married a good cook."

"And an impeccable housekeeper."

"Obsessive-compulsive she calls herself. Mary Anne isn't that way by a long shot."

"Most Irish women aren't."

"For sure."

Joan had married, to everyone's initial dismay, a young actor and moved to Los Angeles (Beverly Hills to be exact). He has enjoyed a remarkably successful career and they have produced four children and live now in Taos to escape the Hollywood scene.

"Well, it's about one such that we're supposed to talk . . . have another cinnamon roll. They're good for you."

"I doubt that . . . How much did Iris Clare sleep around?"

Tom raised an eyebrow, not to indicate surprise—nothing I might say could, as a matter of definition, surprise him—but rather to suggest that my question might be an odd way of beginning.

"A fair amount I suppose."

"Was Doctor Philip Clare Sister Norine's father?"

"I doubt it . . . do you know who her father really was?" He raised both eyebrows and put down his coffee cup.

"He's dead."

We were both silent.

"I'm not going to tell anyone," I added. "Maybe one more person, but I'm not sure about that."

"That's good," he smiled expansively. "I didn't think you would."

"Does Norine know?"

"I doubt it. No need. Poor old Phil adored her, even more than the son he so desperately wanted. You see, Lee, his father and his grandfather before him were doctors too. The grandfather served in the Union Army in the Civil War, the father went up San Juan Hill with Teddy Roosevelt, Phil quit medical school to join the army in 1917. Unlike me he never made it to France. He wanted, the worst way, for a son to keep the family tradition of medicine and military service alive. But he could see that young Phil wasn't cut out for either . . ."

"He played at being a soldier during the war."

"And acted like a war hero afterwards . . . but as I was saying Phil rolled with the punch. He never blamed young Phil for not being what he wasn't. So he ends up with a daughter who is an M.D. and a nun and a missionary and he's proud of her."

"And a grandson . . ."

"No thanks, no more coffee. Mary Anne permits me only two each morning. Decaf after that. But I'll have another glass of grapefruit juice, please."

"I presume he wasn't Phil's father either."

Tom shifted uneasily. This kind of cross examination did not appeal to his Celtic legal soul.

"I don't know that to be true."

"Not for sure."

"Right," he smiled back in his own world of indirect and allusive conversation. "Boy didn't much look like his father did he?"

"No."

"You just figure this stuff out?"

"I knew about Norine back when it happened."

"Did, huh?"

"Yep . . . I guessed about Phil only recently."

"How does this fit in with your pursuit of the lovely Jane?"

"I'm not sure. I knew something was wrong back then. Iris's love affairs might not have anything to do with the accident. That tragedy, however, is and has always been a problem for Jane and me. We've got to crack that mystery open."

"Why?"

I hesitated. Better not tell him I was trying to remake the past by reinterpreting it.

"We both feel responsible for their deaths."

"Leave it," he said firmly.

"Why?"

"No good will come of it. Neither of you were in fact responsible. Let the dead bury their dead."

I paused. It was solid advice.

"I'd like to, Tom. I can't. What happened that day?"

"If I knew I would have done something about it long ago. It was our car, after all. I could see what it was doing to you two and Packy and poor little Angie. I had my hunches and my suspicions but nothing more than that."

"It was real money?"

"That's what the retired State Police Captain told me. He said some of the cops got a hefty cut of the money. He didn't know who made the decision or where the rest of the money went."

"Someone pretty powerful . . . more powerful than anyone we know," I murmured.

"Probably. At least powerful in the world of people who can do those sorts of things."

"Any leads for me to follow up?"

"You're not a detective. Pretty smart scholar and able administrator. If you really want to reopen the past, hire a pro."

"I might do that eventually."

"About Iris?"

"Yes?"

He frowned, unwilling to say anything evil about the dead.

"Well, some people thought she was a . . . what's the word that cute little witch from Philadelphia uses?"

He knew damn well what the word was.

"Nymphomaniac?"

"Yeah. But, you know, I don't think that she was, not really. Just a beautiful and lonely woman with a lot of time on her hands."

"Time and money."

"Fair enough. She must have loved old Phil back there in those days after the war, our war, I mean, the first one. She became a Catholic for him, though she never did take it seriously."

"Did she come on to a lot of men?"

"The women folk said she did. Even Mary Anne. I said they were just guessing. And that flirting doesn't mean necessarily that you're sleeping around, if you see my point?"

"Uh-huh."

"I used to say she never tried to seduce me. And Mary Anne used to laugh at that. Kinda hurt my feelings," he grinned amiably, "not that my hands weren't already pretty full—in a lot of ways, I guess."

A discrete allusion to his wife's well-developed breasts. From a man of his generation? Why not?

"Still are."

"That's for sure . . . I don't say this to many people," he glanced around to make sure that there was no one near him, "but I don't think you'll be shocked or surprised: there is a certain kind of woman a man can't keep his hands off, no matter how old he or she is. Matter of fact the woman only gets more tempting as she gets older. See my point?"

"I'm glad to hear it's true. It gives me hope."

"Did Iris go after you?" He abruptly turned away from the personal revelation, but not as though he were embarrassed by it.

"No. Kind of hurt my feelings too. Nor Packy."

"She wouldn't have tried it twice with that one . . . but, as I always said, she was more to be pitied than blamed."

"I'm not blaming."

"I know. You're just trying to reinterpret the past. Not a good idea."

Shrewd old guy had figured out exactly what I was up to. He probably had *me* figured out too.

"How do Phil and Sister Norine relate to one another?"

"She's seen right through him since she reached what we used to call in the Catholic Church the age of reason. She's one of those modern nuns, Lee, thinks a woman has the right to a divorce if she's being pushed around. I can't say she's wrong either."

"So she supports Jane?"

"Best she can from Central America."

Jimmy's child a missionary nun! Yeah, God was definitely a comedienne, though one with a strange sense of humor.

It was time, as I circled round and round the questions, to return to the accident. Or murder as I had always thought it was.

"I understand . . . do you have any idea where the money came from?"

"Who usually has that kind of money?"

"The Mob?"

"Who else? And some of their rich friends in the banking world. Most of the Chicago banks have a connection into the Mob. It's good business."

"What were they doing shipping the money up to the Lake?"

He rolled his eyes. "Who puts geographical limits on them?"

"And what was it supposed to be for? To whom was all that money being delivered—and in your car?"

"That's the big mystery, isn't it?"

If he understood the mystery he was not about to tell me.

"I've always wondered," he continued, "why the police were not more interested in the fact that it was our car. But no one asked me any questions about that, except about the brakes."

"Cover-up?"

"Sure looks that way."

"Either Phil or Jimmy or both were acting as couriers."

"Sure looks that way. Maybe they didn't know what was in the metal box."

"Maybe, but still why use them?"

"Good question. They had professional couriers even in those days. Not the art that it is now . . . there's too much water over the dam, Leo. You'll never crack that one. I know—I tried and couldn't get anywhere. Not even with my friends on the West Side who had friends, if you see my point. And I've had a little more experience poking around in mysteries than you."

"I understand. But why did the Murrays not try to find out what happened?"

"That's easy. They thought it was a terrible accident and no one had cause to tell them any different. Maybe they didn't have to pay for the money that was lost. They fell apart after it; they were never up to asking any hard questions, poor people. Like I say, give it up, Leo."

"Maybe I will eventually, Tom."

He sighed heavily as if he understood. "Well, she'd be a good woman to spend the rest of your life with. She never was properly married to that fella. He didn't know what marriage meant."

"I mean to have her," I said firmly—and with more confidence on that subject than I usually felt.

"I suspect you will, I suspect you will. Be a good thing too."

I snatched another cinnamon roll.

Tom Keenan was watching me intently. "You knew, of course, that you weren't supposed to go to Korea!"

"What!" I dropped the roll.

"I had a little experience as a shavetail lieutenant of infantry in the old

A.E.F. during the Great War as the Brits call it, Chateau Thierry. I couldn't see you as that kind of Marine at all—which just goes to show you how wrong an ex-officer can be, if you see my point."

"I was a lousy line officer."

"That doesn't seem to be what anyone believes except you. Anyway, I thought I could ask a few questions in certain places. Maybe, I say to myself, even the Marines will recognize that this guy can talk fluent French and Spanish . . ."

"Not really fluent."

"Better than most of them . . . and he should be either in Washington or at some embassy instead of commanding a platoon."

"At Inchon and Wonsan," I said, mentioning the X Corps' famous landings, "I didn't do a thing except get seasick. My sergeant had to take over. Then up at the Chosin Reservoir . . . I was only a platoon commander for a few days."

"And got all your men out. I see you're wearing that little blue medal with the white stars. About time I'd say. Part of your life . . . well, like I say," he fiddled again with the large diamond on his right hand, "I was wrong about that but I say to these friends, are you going to send that bright redhead off to the Western Pacific? And they say we need people like him in Europe more than out in the foxholes. If you take my point?"

Impulsively and without knowing the reason why, I had put on the ribbon that morning.

"When was this?" I could hardly believe what I was hearing.

"Maybe July 1950. After Stalin's guys crossed the 38th parallel."

"In August I was on a C-54 headed for Japan. In September I was on a LSV off Inchon."

"Something changed, huh?"

"Something changed . . . They knew about the landing in Washington when you talked to them?"

"They weren't sure. MacArthur carried that out pretty much on his own, if you remember. Give the devil his due."

"He was lucky."

"Very. Anyway when I find out from Packy that you've been shipped out I call my friends and ask them how come. They say there was a change in plans."

"Ah."

"I think to myself someone changed their plans."

"Who?" I whispered. "Who could possibly have done that?"

"Someone, son, who wanted you in a position where you might well get killed, if you see my point?"

"Who would have wanted to do that to me?"

"Who would have gained?" he asked.

"Philly I suppose. He wanted Jane. But he didn't have that kind of clout."

"Maybe his father did."

"But the doctor didn't particularly like Jane, or so I was told."

"That seemed to be the impression around the 'Old Houses.' Terrible family. Not suitable for a high class kid like young Phil."

"I can't . . . I can't quite believe it."

"I wasn't trying to use my influence to keep you out of the fighting. Mind you, I might have if it had come to it. But it seemed that you were all right. Shows that you shouldn't mess with God. If you weren't there at the Reservoir your whole platoon would have been wiped out."

"Half of them were killed later anyway," I said, my tongue tight and my lips thick.

"Which is better than all of them being killed. And that's what would have happened. Or so they said."

"Maybe."

My latest cinnamon roll lay untouched on the dish in front of me. I felt like I was in a time warp, standing outside of myself and watching my life stumble on.

"I can't believe it."

"Oh, it's true enough all right," he said, casually sipping from a glass of ice water. "Someone wanted you dead. Fifth Marines in those days was a good place to get yourself dead."

"But they don't seem to want me dead any more."

"Maybe not. But that's why I told that kid priest of mine to warn you that you should be careful. Don't stir up sleeping dogs."

"Phil isn't capable of doing anything to me now."

"Maybe it wasn't Phil."

"His father's dead. Who else is there?"

"Just don't go jumping to conclusions."

"Two and a half years in a POW camp, two fingers lost, nightmares for the rest of my life, Jane . . ."

"I know, son. I know. But getting even won't change that."

"I'm not so sure."

"Take my word for it."

I shut my eyes to blot out the horror of what they—whoever they were— had done to me. I felt like I had been raped, exploited by the rich and powerful for reasons of their own. I wanted to get even with them.

"I suppose you're right, Tom. I don't want to fight God. Maybe it will all work out. I've got to learn more about how it all happened."

"I can understand that, son. Only don't dig any deeper than you have to. If I were in your position," he sighed, "I'd concentrate on Jane. You'll never regret that."

"I quite agree."

I thanked him for breakfast, asked him to remember me to Mary Anne, promised him that I'd see him at the Lake before the summer was over, and said good-bye. He took a cab back up East Lake Shore Drive and I walked towards the South Shore Station.

Instead of boarding the train to Hyde Park I strolled up Michigan Avenue under the hot morning sun like a man in a trance. I phoned my office and told them to reschedule my meeting with a possible recruit for our Biology Department.

I knew his kind. He would stride in, filled with his own importance as a potential Nobel Prize winner, and lay out the conditions he'd need before he would consider favoring us with his presence. The decision really wouldn't be mine. If the biologists and the Med School people wanted him badly enough to find the money for him and his colleagues and his laboratory that was their decision. They knew full well that we would not expand their budget, not even for a man who had been rumored for several years to be on the Nobel short list.

However, if he acted in my office like he had at the cocktail party the Med School had arranged for him at the Faculty Club the night before, I would submit a memo to the president in which I would recommend the appointment but raise (indirectly) the question of whether we wanted to continue to mortgage ourselves for celebrities who had little interest in anything except their own careers.

"As a devout Irish Catholic, do you think you are qualified," he had asked me, "to sit in judgment on my work?"

"I'm not sure I'm devout," I had replied, "and I know I'm not qualified to judge the details of your work. That's up to the Department and the Division through the Dean."

I believe in God's love and the survival of the human person after death and of the enormous importance of the Church and the Mass. I go to Mass regularly, but I don't take the funny little old man in Rome very seriously. I'm also beginning to believe in Catholic summers in which hot air and cool lake water can revive old loves.

Does this make me devout? I'm not so sure that it does or that it doesn't.

"Yet a biologist," he had sneered, "would be qualified to judge a political scientist."

"He might think he was."

"Your people can't explain much variance, can they?"

"Humans are a little more complicated than laboratory rats," I had replied.

"All mammals are fundamentally similar."

"Are they? Do your lab rats organize universities? Do they covet Nobel Prizes? Do they lust after young female rats who are their students?"

Our potential prize winner had a reputation for chasing graduate students. As I say, I can be both mean and stubborn when pushed into a corner.

"That's your Irish Catholic heritage. You can't possibly approve of my work on evolution."

I had sipped my Irish whiskey, straight up—the waiters at the faculty club had learned about my poison and delighted in putting a glass of it in my hands before I asked for it.

"Your ignorance of Catholicism astonishes me. We are not biblical fundamentalists. As long ago as St. Augustine, which was a millennium and a half ago, we were already open to the possibility of evolution. We weren't the ones who are responsible for the monkey trial."

I had never read the passage in St. Augustine, but that was beside the point.

"You mean that you don't have to believe that God created the earth in seven days? I thought Catholics had to believe that."

"I would not tolerate such bigotry if it were racial and I will not tolerate it when it is religious."

I turned my back on him and walked away.

"Do we really want that bastard?" I asked the Dean of the Medical School.

"I'm beginning to have doubts myself," he sighed. "There's an upper limit to what we have to stomach even for a Nobel Prize—and I'm not sure he'll ever win one. He's bound to be a disruptive influence in the school. Personally I think we can do without him. I hope before he's finished here, the Department will agree with me."

"He's the kind of *wunderkind* who has never taken time to grow up. A full professor at thirty-two and the maturity of a fifteen year old."

The Dean grinned crookedly. "I see why they made you Provost, Leo. In a time when we can't pay for any more bullshit at this University, your bullshit quotient is zero."

That wasn't true. It's substantially higher than zero, but it is not infinite. Anyway I thanked him for his compliment.

"He'll be upset, Mr. Kelly," my assistant informed me, "that you won't be able to see him till this afternoon."

"He is perpetually upset. Too bad for him."

"Yes sir," she giggled. "You want me to rearrange the rest of your schedule?"

"Mañana, Mae. We'll do it all tomorrow."

In the summer our faculty disappears to the various watering places it has found for itself, leaving summer school to poorly paid graduate students. The administrators, however, have to keep working. But you can always put almost anything and everything off till tomorrow or next week or even till the departments reassemble in the fall. My job, I tell people, requires little more than some skill at intelligent delays.

If you put off some decisions long enough, you don't have to make them.

"Are you all right, Doctor Kelly?" she asked me. "You sound kind of strange."

"I'm fine, Mae. It's the phase of the moon. Full moon last night."

"Half moon, Doctor Kelly."

"Just goes to show you."

Still in a daze I walked up the Magnificent Mile, beyond Oak Street Beach, which was teeming with people even in mid morning on this scorching summer day, and then on up Lake Shore Drive and into Lincoln Park, which was swarming with lightly clad humans of all ages and sexes. The mighty Lake, flat as a sheet of ice, was crisscrossed with motorboat wakes and weaving water ski wakes. An occasional yacht drifted by, its sails drooping disconsolately in windless air. I marveled at the incredible beauty of the city. Dick Daley had done his job well. I was less happy about the prospects under Jane Byrne, who seemed to me to be a woman driven by hate. Still it was an incredible city, the best in America for all its problems.

I turned back at the zoo and, hardly aware of the heat, ambled back down North State Parkway, by the house of the Crazy Cardinal, as Packy always called him, at State and North Avenue.

I can't recall the confused jumble of emotions and ideas that raced through my head. I was milling, as the collective behavior people call crowds, just before they become violent.

I found myself at eleven thirty on Oak Street and in front of a small but elegant shop—"Clare Travel Tours for Intelligent Tourists."

Just the kind of snobbery my colleagues at the University would love—any university for that matter.

I strolled in. What the hell!

Leo

Clare Travel was decorated more like a prestigious law office than a tourist bureau, oak furniture, plush carpet, comfortable leather chairs. Two young women were sitting at desks talking to customers sitting across from them. I bet the customers were called clients.

"Good morning, sir," one of them glanced up from her computer terminal as her clients rose from their chairs, the couple, maybe a few years older than I was, smiling happily. "Can I help you?"

"Doctor Kelly to see Ms. Clare."

"Do you have an appointment, Doctor Kelly?"

The emphasis of Clare Travel was surely on Ireland. The black-haired young woman spoke with a clear West of Ireland brogue, probably Kerry.

"No, not really."

Her lips tightened in mild disapproval. "I'll tell her you're here Doctor Kelly . . . good-bye now," to the departing clients, "hope you'll have a wonderful trip to Ireland."

"We thought we will," the woman enthused.

"Can't miss," I agreed. "Especially west of the Shannon. The real Ireland begins at Athlone."

They beamed happily. The "travel counselor," as the plaque on her desk entitled her, smiled at me.

"Of course, you gotta watch them Kerry Folk. There's a little bit of larceny in all them and you can only believe half of what they say, the trouble is finding out which half."

The couple and the two travel counselors guffawed.

"I suppose, Doctor Kelly," the one who was about to tell Jane I was here said, "that like most of these Chicago people, you'd be a Mayo person?"

"God help us."

"God help the rest of us you mean." She sailed out of the office to seek out Ms. Clare, under the full sail that Irishwomen break out when they have just definitively put down an obstreperous male.

She returned in a moment, still triumphant. "Ms. Clare says you're not the kind of doctor that takes care of sick people, so she's not going to interrupt her conference call to talk to you, but if you want to take her to lunch I should make a reservation at the Cape Cod Room of the Drake."

"All right."

"She also said that you could read our brochures while you're waiting."

"I'm sure that will be good for me."

The brochures, little pamphlets really, were well done—good copy and superb pictures, though the latter gave the impression that it never rained in Ireland. The tours were "educational"—Irish History, Irish Castles, Treasures of Ancient Ireland, Irish Literature, Irish Music, Ancient and Modern, most of them presided over by faculty members of one of the Irish universities. Jane's travelers would work hard and come back feeling that they had learned something, experiencing a contentment like the pious satisfaction of religious pilgrims returning from Lourdes.

My faculty colleagues would like this kind of travel. Visiting Erin would be not unlike an "educational" trip to New Guinea!

"Ms. Clare will see you now, Doctor Kelly."

I thanked her politely in the Irish language, a bit of which I can manage, especially when it will make a pretty woman blush and smile.

"Talking dirty to my colleagues?" Jane rose and extended her hand professionally.

I shook hands with her, just as solemnly. "In a language that is so short on vulgar and obscene words that it must import them from English, which it does with considerable skill . . . and I note you've discovered that education does help one to make money."

She grinned at me. "Knowledge can be an end in itself even if it has other ends."

She was wearing a blue skirt and a white blouse with long sleeves, light weight, but still business-like, a silver Brigid cross around her neck, and small pearl earrings. No rings. Certainly no wedding rings.

"You look lovely in professional clothes," I said. "I'm so used to seeing you only at the Lake that I almost didn't recognize you."

"It was a resort relationship, wasn't it?" she said calmly and we both sat down.

I thought about trying to explain why and realized that I didn't know. So I postponed the hunt for an explanation to another time.

"You look so lovely," I went on, "as a professional woman, that I'd much rather have you for lunch than bookbinder soup."

"Leo!" Her face flamed. "What a terrible thing to say!"

"'Tis true," I sighed a phony Irish sigh.

"I heard you out there," she tried to sound like she was exasperated with me, "disrupting my staff with your phony Irish charm."

"It's only partially phony."

"You must have swallowed the Blarney stone instead of kissing it."

"Might have." I picked up a copy of *Ulysses* from her desk. "You really *are* serious about this stuff, aren't you?"

"We're doing a Bloomsday tour next year. The Irish will make fun of us but that's their problem. I want to know what it's all about."

"Like it?"

"Harder to read than *Portrait* but," her eyes widened, "a wonderful book. I am having a tough time with 'Night Town.' It's supposed to be erotic, but even with a commentary it doesn't seem very sexy to me."

"Wait till you get to the end."

"I read that first," she smiled, "and I don't want to talk about it."

We chatted for a few moments. She had moved down in from Lake Forest to a co-op a couple of blocks north on the Drive, she was near to work, Lucy was close to school, Charley and Linda were only a few blocks away on Webster Avenue, the memories of the suburban home she did not want to keep. She went on the first of each of her Irish tours, to make sure that everything went off smoothly. People paid enough for them and were entitled to good service. Irish faculty were by and large wonderful, charming, intelligent and responsible. At least as long as they were sober. On the whole, they did not make passes at the women tourists, even the attractive ones.

"Not even at the gorgeous tour managers?"

That, she told me primly, was none of my business.

I did not observe that a striking woman like herself—long legs, thin waist, flat belly, shapely breasts, unbearably lovely face—without a wedding ring would be fair game for faculty members in Ireland or this country or any other kind of male too as far as that goes. I presumed she knew this. And thought she could take care of it.

"Shall we have lunch?" she asked, reaching for the jacket of her suit.

"That seems like a good idea."

"Take good care of the place while I'm gone, Nessa."

"I sure will Ms. Clare."

"You can call me by my real name when Doctor Kelly is around," she laughed. "He's really quite harmless."

"Yes, Jane."

"God keep all who work in this place," I said in Irish as we left the shop.

"And Jesus and Mary and Patrick go with all who visit this place," the lass from Kerry said solemnly as we departed.

"What did she say?" Jane demanded when we were outside.

"It was a chaste Irish blessing, nothing more."

"I'm not sure that the Irish are capable of chastity," she sniffed, "except maybe their clergy."

"You're probably right. And I wouldn't bet all that much on the clergy either."

"It might be argued that their ancient culture is the most obscene in Europe."

"Most erotic anyway."

"Dirty jokes and breast fixation," she said primly.

"So I'm told . . . I note that the two young women in your office would appeal to that latter cultural trait."

"You would note that."

"Yes ma'am, I would . . . Dickie and Mickie have been meeting with our lawyers about the Devlin chair," I said, my heart pounding rapidly, as we walked down Oak Street toward the good, gray Drake.

"And you are astonished still?"

"Maybe because I have been away so long—thirty years."

"You were here in the late fifties working on your doctorate."

"Not at the Lake, not till this summer."

"No," she said softly, "not till this summer."

Jane attracted attention on Oak Street—a striking woman with long legs, slim hips, and a slender waist, she did not try to hide her height. Instead she defiantly wore high heels. She wasn't quite up to my height, but still seemed tall enough to be a power forward. Either she did not notice the turning heads and the delighted eyes or she took them for granted.

A man might feel proud that she permitted him to be seen in public with her. I suspect that was the general idea.

Naturally the maître d' and the headwaiter, and the table waiter at the Cape Cod Room, resplendent in their old-fashioned naval officer suits— blue jackes with gold stripes and white trousers—knew her by name.

As we were escorted through the dark room and up a staircase with brass ship rails to an even darker corner, she was greeted by a chorus of respect.

"Good morning, Ms. Clare."

"Nice to have you with us again, Ms. Clare."

"Your usual booth, Ms. Clare?"

"Royalty," I sniffed. "For a Kerry person too."

"Just goes to show you," she chuckled. "The Big Change at work!"

Her booth, black leather against a straight back and overlooking the Lake Michigan and Oak Street Beach (through a tiny window) was in a corner of the Cape Cod room, almost a private alcove.

"Nice for assignations," I said as we sat down.

"That's *not* what we're having."

"Maybe not today."

She sniffed. "Maybe not ever."

"Maybe."

"I notice," she tried to change the subject, "that you're wearing your blue ribbon."

"Huh?" I pretended to glance at the little blue pin with the white stars. "Oh yeah, it intimidates faculty."

"You're ready to acknowledge that you are a hero?"

"A sort of hero, Jane. An accidental hero maybe. It's part of my life, I guess."

"I'm glad you finally see that . . . *must* you continue to look at me that way?" she demanded after we had ordered our iced tea, bookbinder soup, and Crab Maryland.

"What way?"

"You know what way."

"Tell me."

"Like you're taking off my clothes. It embarrasses me."

"That's the way men tend to look at women like you. It's programmed into the species."

"I understand *that*. But you make it too obvious," she was talking herself into discomfiture, though of a mild variety.

"I told you that I would rather have you for lunch than bookbinder soup. I now amend that to read I would rather have you for lunch than bookbinder soup and Crab Maryland."

"Well, you'd better be content with your soup and your crab."

"I will. For today."

"Forever."

"I intend to have you, Jane my dear, before the summer is over."

She stiffened as though she were angry. "Is that a warning or a threat?"

"I would never dare threaten you, it's a statement of fact."

"I told you that I didn't want a man in my life."

Now she was no longer half fun and full earnest as the Irish would say. She was all earnest.

"I know." I paused while the waiter delivered our iced tea—with the lemon in a net bag—this was, after all, the Drake. "But because you're so desirable and so smart and so much fun, men will pursue you and eventually out of loneliness and maybe a little desire of your own, you'll select someone. I lost out last time through no fault of my own. I don't intend to lose this time."

Her lips tightened and she considered me with a hint of displeasure, even perhaps anger.

"That's a clear enough statement of intent."

"In the meantime I will continue to enjoy romantic thoughts about you as a prelude."

"Romantic?" she sniffed. "I'd call them out and out obscene."

"But you don't storm away from the lunch table."

She grinned. "You're impossible . . . no, I don't. I guess I still like you looking at me that way. But I have to protest for the record. Irish fixation indeed! . . . now tell me why this unexpected lunch? Is it merely to serve notice that you propose to seduce me before the summer is over? Or," she was her happy self again, "to stare hungrily at my boobs, like an adolescent boy? Or did you merely want an opportunity to talk dirty over bookbinder soup and Crab Maryland?"

"Could I respond, all of the above?"

"Certainly."

"And none of the above?"

"What does that mean?"

"I need someone to talk to. I've been wandering around Chicago all morning trying to figure some things out. I guess my unconscious led me to your doorstep."

"Unconscious indeed. Probably your id, but talk, my darling, please. I'll try to help if I can."

Now the matriarch was a solicitous mother with an injured boy child. Had she not called me her darling?

I told her what I had figured out about the accident and what I had learned from Tom Keenan. I even told her about who I thought had fathered Norine. I left out Tom's final revelation.

She drank her bookbinder soup very slowly.

"Dear God, Lee, were we part of all of that?"

"More or less. What did you think of your mother-in-law?"

"She was always kind to me, a little too kind maybe. Doctor Clare was tolerant but I knew that he thought his son had married down. I suppose he blamed me for the problems Phil created for himself. If I were a good wife, his son wouldn't have chased so many skirts. For a while I thought that was true. Then common sense took over. I wasn't the one who had problems in bed."

"How did you stand it for so long?"

"I got used to it . . . but back to Iris . . . I don't like to say this, but we're trying to be candid about those days. I used to think, even back in the forties, that she . . . well, sometimes, not always, she liked women more than men."

"Lesbian?"

"I didn't have the word then, Lee. I certainly don't condemn the reality it describes now. But she looked at me kind of funny. And after Phil and I were married she would look at me or even touch me in ways I thought strange and didn't like. Not often and not overt enough for me to be able to say anything, but still . . ."

"My God!"

"There are women who like to feel up other women and still enjoy sex with men. Maggie says that women can be more truly bisexual than men. Obviously it's easier physiologically."

"You think that was going on at the Lake?"

"It was a cesspool, Leo. The only question was how deep it went."

"Too bad we didn't compare notes."

"How could we . . . but look at it this way, Leo. You're a beautiful woman turning forty. Your husband is too busy for you or is really not able to love a woman. You have nothing to do except loll around in the sun. There are some other attractive women who are in the same situation and you find their bodies, shall we say, interesting. You develop a teenage crush on them, then the crush becomes really powerful. You fantasize about doing some things with them, just to find out what it's like. One hot day, after everyone has had a little too much to drink, you start to play a little and the first thing you know you all find that you enjoy it. You pinch an ass, you grope at a boob, you pull off a strap, you French kiss, you feel a pussy, then . . . then the fun begins. Maybe two of you hold a third down and work her over."

"You should write fiction, Jane."

"I am." She set aside her soup.

"No!"

"Yes."

"Am I in it?"

"Of course, you're in it. How could I write a novel without you being in it. Actually I'm really doing a combination memoir and journal as the first step in the novel . . . thank you, Arthur, it looks delicious."

"Am I the hero?"

"That," she said pertly, "remains to be seen. Anyway there's nothing about lesbian love in the story. Till today I was afraid even to think about it. Mind you I don't think they were real lesbians, not even Iris. Rather they engaged in some adolescent groping and pawing and playing and discovered that there were lots of kinks in those activities and that they enjoyed them as a passing amusement."

"What did you see?"

"I saw the three of them coming out of the Clare house one afternoon when I was walking to work. They were all tipsy and laughing kind of funny and looking like they had some wonderful secret. Besides they wanted me . . . Dear God, Leo, I had forgotten all about it. I never told anyone."

"You think they might have . . ."

"Raped me?"

"Well . . ."

She hesitated. "I don't want to be harsh. It was on their minds. When they were drunk enough they might have talked about it. If I gave them the opportunity, they might have even done it. I wouldn't have used the word rape in those days, but that's what was on their minds or in their imaginations anyway."

"Why didn't you tell me?"

"It was never quite that bad; and, as I say, I didn't know the right words. I thought about it a couple of times. I almost spoke to Mary Anne Keenan too. But then the summer was over."

Despite the harrowing conversation, we had disposed of our Crab Maryland.

"Would you mind if I drank a small class of white wine, dear?" she asked.

I was startled for a moment that she called me dear. Second word of endearment.

"Of course not. Nothing stronger?"

"No, I have to talk to Dublin this afternoon." She glanced at her watch. "You need all your wits about you for that."

"One white wine, one Jameson's on the rocks, please."

My erotic feelings for Jane had vanished completely in the horror of what she had described—a young woman in her middle teens being stalked, there was no other word for it, by three hungry women.

A little summer game all right, but a truly sick game.

"I would have fought like hell," she said. "And I was stronger than any of them, maybe all of them put together. They were all soft and kind of flabby."

"Jimmy was a victim and you almost were a victim. Thank God there were no more."

"That we know of."

That possibility shocked me.

"What do you mean?"

"We don't know who else they might have tried to seduce or rape—a black servant, a girl from town, maybe even Eileen or Angie . . ."

"*No!*"

"I saw the look in their eyes, Lee. You didn't. They were women on fire with their game. Go after a daughter? Probably not. I can't recall any signs in Eileen or Angie. Teenage moods, but what do they mean? And I certainly didn't think about it in those days. But now I'm convinced that there was so much evil in that group that they might have done anything. Then it stopped."

"They might have seen the deaths of Eileen and Jimmy as divine wrath coming down from heaven to punish them."

"I'm sure they thought of that. Do you believe that's the truth?"

"Certainly not," I said crisply. "Our God doesn't play it that way."

"He would forgive them?"

"He loves everyone, Jane. We have to believe that. Maybe nothing else, but that at a minimum."

She smiled. "If you believe that, Lee—and I do—than you might as well believe a lot of other things too."

"Did you ever talk to Maggie about any of this?"

"Sure I did. She didn't like the way they looked at her either. Later on when she knew all the words she said they were involved in an interlude of predatory homoerotic play. She said that two of them might have victimized a third and won her over to the game, a very dangerous game she called it. They might then go looking for more victims. Hopefully they didn't find any."

"Sexual abuse of children."

"Of young women anyway. With terrible potential, Maggie said, for doing very great harm to them."

"Yet you accepted one of them for a mother-in-law."

"By then, Leo, I think she was afraid of me."

"But you must have been afraid of her at first."

"I should have been, Lee, I should have been. But I was so numb I didn't care."

"No thought ever of getting out of the marriage before the wedding day?"

"Some," she sighed, "no thanks, no dessert, not today . . . you knew of course that I was pregnant at the time of the marriage?"

I nodded.

"I hope you don't think too badly of me."

"I'll never think badly of you at all, Jane."

"I finally got tired of saying 'no' to him. It didn't mean anything any more. After he'd made love to me a couple of times, he kind of lost interest in me. Conquest is the name of his game. For a long time I was furious. Then I realized that I was fortunate that he chased after other women. I didn't have to put up with him."

"Bastard."

"Never any ill will in him. Just an overgrown spoiled brat."

"I'm growing a little tired of hearing that excuse, Jane."

"Tell me about it."

She drank her wine rather quickly. "It all seems too bizarre, Leo." She put down the glass. "Infidelity, illegitimacy, murder, large sums of money disappearing, women playing at sex together," she hesitated, "threatened rape of a girl by the women . . . and our lives at that time seemed on the outside to be so serene and happy."

"So it seemed. And so it was some of the time."

I did not know whether I would tell her about Korea. There was something I had to say first anyway.

"I owe you an apology, Jane. It's a funny kind of an apology, but I'll call it that anyway."

"I'm sure you don't," she said firmly.

"I do, actually. When I came home from Korea I was a mess emotionally as well as physically. Most men who've been in combat feel they've been abandoned by those they left behind. All the more so when you've been a POW. Then when you find out that you're officially dead . . ."

"I can't see how it would be any other way, Leo."

"Yeah, well I finally got rid of most of it—time, therapy, stubbornness. What's left is mostly in my dreams at night."

"Oh?"

"They're one of the things you'll have to put up with when we finally share the same bed. I can generally be calmed down by the usual means and I'm not dangerous."

She shook her head in amused astonishment. "You never give up, do you?"

"Just making a prediction . . . anyway, I came back angry and stayed angry for a long time. I think I'm pretty good now, all things considered . . ."

"*Pretty* good," she smirked, "I don't see any ill effects, none at all. Except when you're standing in a movie line . . ."

"OK, but I'm talking about then, not now. I never tried to put myself inside those who thought they had lost me. I never tried to understand the trauma of death and the second trauma of resurrection. I figured they'd just be happy I was back. I couldn't figure out the odd reaction when I returned."

"A lot of guilt maybe and a lot of anger."

"I suppose so. I love my brothers and sisters, good people all in their own way, even the naive ex-priest married to the naive ex-nun. But I don't see them all that much and I'm certainly not close to them."

"Your mother could not wait to tell you about me."

"First words when they came to the hospital in San Diego. First words . . . well that's over and she never forgave me for not being a priest. But I didn't like the reaction of any of them and I never tried to figure out why. I guess I have some catching up to do if it's not too late."

"They adored you, Lee. More than you ever knew. I think they even understand why you had to leave them. Megan, you remember, was there in the hospital when your mother told you the good news. It's not too late."

"It'll be interesting to try to put things back together with them. But worst of all I didn't understand what it all did to you."

"How could you?" She was dangerously close to tears. They would be coming before long.

"I don't know what I could or couldn't do. I know what I didn't do and that's what I'm talking about."

Her eyes brimming with tears, she reached out for my hand.

I stumbled on. "I didn't try to see what you had suffered, were suffering, and would probably suffer for the rest of your life. Not even at the beginning of this summer."

"What difference would it have made, Lee? You couldn't have said any- thing to me anyway. Not till this summer. Now you're saying it and I'm very grateful. I don't think I ended my marriage because you were free again and back in Chicago. It wasn't the only reason anyway. But it was certainly in the back of my head, as you probably guessed."

I hadn't but I thought I'd better not say it. It was as close as she had come yet to saying explicitly that she still wanted me as she always had.

"You must have gone through hell, worse hell than that prison camp," my voice choked.

She tightened her grip on my hand. "I'm sure not. I survived and I'm all right. Maybe I'm a better person for it. I hope I don't let Lucy down."

"Lucianne is what she calls herself."

"I forgot." Tears began to spill over on her cheeks. "Damn, I'll ruin my make-up."

I gripped her hand, now pliant in my own. "Anyway, I'm sorry and I'll try to look at all that has happened from inside you in the years ahead."

"I hope that is not a suggestive promise," she burst out laughing.

My turn to blush. "Freudian slip. Take it any way you want!"

We both laughed and much pain was exorcised.

"All right, Leo," she said, composed and confident again, "I understand what you are trying to tell me and I appreciate it and am grateful for it. I hope it's a turning point in your life and my life. Though I repeat that I'm not available at the moment or for the foreseeable future . . . and you should phone poor dear Megan before the day is over."

She freed her hand from my grasp.

"Yes ma'am."

"Now may I go back to my job?"

I glanced at my watch. If I took a cab back to the University I would have forty-five more minutes to talk to her and still make my appointment with the biologist.

I made an impulsive decision. "One more thing, if you can spare me a few minutes."

"To judge by your expression, Lee, this one is dreadfully serious."

I slumped against the back of the booth. "The most terrible truth I have heard in all my life."

I told her Tom Keenan's story about Korea. She turned pale.

"May I have another drink, please?"

I signaled the waiter. "Another white wine and Jameson's, please."

"Two Jameson's," she said. "Why, Lee, why?"

"Someone wanted me dead."

"Why would they want you dead?"

"That's the question, isn't it?"

"Phil?" She winced in horror. "I don't think he's that evil."

"Or his father?"

"Maybe."

"Lee, they changed our lives, came damn close to ruining both of them."

"I fooled them, whoever they are. I came back from the dead."

The waiter brought our drinks.

Jane swallowed a large gulp. "Resurrection is the ultimate revenge?"

"That remains to be seen, Jane."

"It does indeed . . . do you feel manipulated, violated?"

"I sure do."

"Why," she asked again, "would anyone be so evil? We were two kids in the process of falling in love. Why intervene in our lives to destroy them?"

"I know why they'd intervene in your life, Jane. You're a prize worth having. Maybe someone wanted that prize more than anything in the world."

"That doesn't sound like Phil. He's not capable of that kind of hunger."

"Perhaps you're right. Maybe it was someone who out of sheer perversity could not tolerate the happiness we were stumbling toward."

"Who would do that?"

"There are strange people in the world, Jane. We know that from what you said earlier."

"I can't see anyone we knew in those days doing such a thing, can you?"

"No . . . I figure I was incidental. Someone wanted you and I had to be cleared out of the way. I was just a poor kid from the neighborhood on the fringe of things."

"Do you really think that's how you seemed in those days, Lee?"

"Didn't I?"

"I don't believe you could have been so unperceptive . . . still be so unperceptive. A big redhead with charm and brains and a clever tongue, you were destined for greatness and everyone knew it after the first fifteen minutes talking to you. It's easy to see why someone would resent you and want to destroy you."

"I'm not exactly what you call great."

"I won't argue now. You're the only one that's ever on television. That's enough for the moment . . . dear God, Lee, unseen powers and forces intervened in our lives and changed them completely . . . for evil reasons . . . I feel utterly fragile."

"They used us, Jane, like a little boy uses his marbles or a grand master his pawns."

"Rich and powerful and absolutely evil." She drained her drink and grabbed my hand. "I'm frightened. Are they still out there plotting against us?"

"They might be, Jane. They might be. I intend to find out. If they are I'll destroy them."

She looked at me intently. "I believe you, Leo. Promise me you won't take any chances."

"This time I know there's enemies out there. And I have even more to lose than the last time."

"Reinterpret the past and thus change it?"

"More than that now, Jane my love. Eliminate the evil that has imprisoned both of us for so long. Then the past will be transparent and we can take an honest look at the future."

"Fair enough," she glanced at her watch, "now I really have to get back to work. The rules of the game dictate that the yank be punctual even if the micks are not."

"I'll get the bill."

"It's on my account."

"What?"

She shrugged. "This is my turf. On my turf I pay. On your turf, you pay. If you ever invite me out to that high-toned faculty club of yours, you can pay."

We rose to leave.

"Count on it, Jane. And thanks for the lunch."

"Anyway, I make more money than you do."

"I doubt it. Your salary from your company might be more than mine from the University. However, when I came home from Korea, I put my back pay and my disability pension every year since into a commodities account. I don't have to work a day for the rest of my life." ·

"Why do you work?"

"I kind of like it."

"Being provost?"

We left the Drake and walked into the solid wall of heat on Oak Street.

"It's not really work the way most working people would define work. I wanted to come back to Chicago and the offer was not to be a professor but to be a professor who was also provost. So I took it."

"You think you're worth more than I am?"

"Arguably. We can postpone that subject till a later encounter."

"When you can see the perspective from inside me?"

We both giggled. "You're not going to let me forget that?"

"Certainly not . . . Why did you want to come back to Chicago?"

We waited for the traffic light on Michigan Avenue to change.

"I had some unfinished business," I said, knowing it for the first time. "A tall, striking, bossy woman whom I still wanted. I wasn't about to break up a happy marriage. But I heard it wasn't happy and was probably nearing an end . . ."

"A certain witch from Philadelphia whispered in your ear?"

"The Good Witch of the East . . . So I came back to claim the woman who was by rights mine anyway."

The light changed. I took her arm to guide her across the street because she was paying no attention to the traffic turning from Oak.

"Red-haired buccaneer scheming to carry off the woman."

"That's *your* erotic fantasy, Jane my love."

"Romantic."

"I'll grow a beard if you want."

"That would be cute but you don't have to."

In front of her shop, I kind of apologized. "I'm sorry if I've been offensive, Jane."

"You couldn't possibly offend me, Lee." She touched my cheek with her fingers. "I'm flattered by everything you say, even if I have to keep the banter up. I just need time, a lot of time."

"Fine," I said. "But I still mean to have you by the end of the summer."

As I signaled for a cab, however, I watched her delicately shaped rear end disappear inside Clare Travel, and hungered for it and the rest of her; I thought that I wouldn't wait more than a month.

It was a pleasant intention with which to console myself as, my head buzzing from the two drinks, I drowsed on the ride back to the University and my confrontation with the biologist.

Jane

I walked unsteadily into their office. Nessa and Nulla, the intelligent young women with the appealing Irish lilt and the cute Irish boobs, I had hired to operate and decorate my office, did not even bother to hide their curiosity. Who is he? He is *so* cute. Sweet too. And funny. Damn matchmakers.

They also knew that, for the first time since they had come to work for me, I was tipsy.

No point in pretending.

An old friend, girls. Nothing more elaborate than a friendly lunch.

They snickered skeptically. They would watch me with probing eyes for weeks to come.

I sank into my chair. Why with all the terrible things we had talked about did I feel so elated?

I shouldn't feel elated. The bastard had not offered the slightest apology for running out on me. He had apologized, quite intelligently, for being an asshole when he came back from Korea. But not for being an asshole before he left. Somehow he doesn't see the problem. Blind shit!

Why so much stuff about blame and guilt? I don't know what his excuse is, but I know mine. I don't want to run the risk of being inadequate like I was for Phil. Lee thinks I'm gorgeous now, but what if I'm a failure in bed? I'm not sure I can be anything else. Otherwise I'd have let him have me back in June.

So despite all that, like a big wave at Oak Street Beach, Grace has hit me over the head, clobbered me, knocked me to my knees, and is threatening to drown me.

I melt when he looks at me with that reverent hunger. Absolutely melt. If I'm not careful some day soon he'll simply carry me off and I'll go along with only the mildest of protests, none of which I will believe.

It is a pleasant romantic fantasy after a lunch at which I drank too much. Erotic fantasy.

I need time to think it out. I don't want another man in my bed. He's right though. I'll probably have one eventually. I should say it might as well be him and let it go at that.

I'll never find a better one.

I'm afraid I guess. Afraid of grace. Grace. Whatever.

If he had suggested that we go to my apartment just around the corner I would have said yes. Some day—soon—he will suggest something like that and I will gladly agree.

But then what if I'm a dud in bed? I couldn't stand to fail a second man.

I'm damaged goods and I know it. I don't want to be damaged again.

What will happen when he finally makes his move? Will I resist like I did that night he proposed to me? Will I lose my nerve again? Or will I be generous like I want to be?

Why do I have to make up my mind at all?

I can't think too well when I'm drunk.

I should concentrate on those terrible things that happened. Who killed our friends? Who sent him to Korea and ended our love?

He thinks he ought to find out. Reinterpret the past to make the present better.

Male bullshit. The only thing that really matters is whether he's inside me like he said in that Freudian slip of his.

Maybe that's female bullshit. Maybe we have to find out so they can't hurt us again. Maybe the record has to be set straight.

I just thought of something. I can't remember what it was. It was terrible. The worst thing yet. Truly awful.

I have to remember what it was.

I don't know what to do. Yet I feel happier than I have been in years. Not much sign of the woman who was so close to suicide a few weeks ago, is there?

Silly bitch.

But I still don't know what to do.

I must remember that petrifying picture I saw in imagination for just a second or two.

It's important.

And dangerous.

Leo

My tipsy condition was not a problem in my conversation with the biologist. There was only one subject about which he wished to talk—himself. I needed only listen and nod occasionally. In between nods I could give myself over to semi-inebriated fantasies about Jane—a pleasant enough exercise, God knows.

When he had left, being somewhat more sober, I phoned the dean.

"Your friend was just here."

"No friend of mine . . . What do you think, Leo?"

"What do *you* think?"

Iron rule of the provost game: buck questions back to lower levels whenever you can.

"I'm not sure he's as good as he thinks he is or as his allies in the Department think he is. His sort of narcissism gets in the way unless you are a complete genius and I'm not sure he is quite that."

"The Department?"

"Some of them are having second thoughts. Right now the sentiment is that they still want him but without the responsibility of making the decision."

"OK. I will tell you this: if you receive any sort of recommendation from the Department and transmit it to me, even without your endorsement, I'll pass it on to the president with an annotation that I personally feel he'll be disruptive but it's the decision of the Department and we must honor it and put the responsibility on their shoulders."

Rule two for the day: don't let them buck it back up to you.

"I am to convey this reaction to them?"

"Why else would I be giving it to you?"

He chuckled. "I see the picture, Leo. Very clever. Very Irish."

"Naturally."

"They'll have to live with their choice, huh?"

"And they'll not be likely to get a line for another distinguished appointment for a long time. So they'd better make up their minds carefully this time."

"Got you."

"What bothers me most," I added, with less prudence than I usually display, "is that ten years ago he and his kind were proclaiming that they were the new breed of academics who were going to reform not only the academy but the whole country. Now all they care about is their own careers—and they're still as self-righteous as ever."

"Isn't that how most radical academics end up?"

So we'd both been imprudent.

In the end my strategy didn't work. The "young guard" in the Department turned the offer to this man into a crusade for their own influence and power. The Department insisted even though it would be years before they got a shot at another potential Nobel Prize winner if he were appointed.

It was, as my father would have said, their funeral.

But a funny thing happened. The dean went on vacation. Then I was away for a while. Then the president had to attend a meeting in Brussels. By the time we had put together all the pieces of a complicated offer (and funny how complicated it became) Leeland Stanford Junior Memorial University had made him an even better offer, which he promptly accepted.

There was some muttering among the "young guard" about the slowness of administrative processes at the University. But not much because even they were happy that he didn't arrive in their china shop.

Was this delay an accident?

Is the Pope a Unitarian?

Even a clever provost who was not Irish would have done the same thing. Maybe not so deviously perhaps.

Right after my conversation with the Dean, while I was thinking of calling Megan, Mae, my matronly black administrative assistant walked in.

"A Mr. Clare to see you, Doctor Kelly. Philip Clare."

Indeed. This was my day to strike it rich.

I hesitated, not wanting to see the man.

"All right, Mae," I glanced at my watch, "but tell him I have only a few minutes."

"An appointment in a quarter hour. Phone call from Washington?"

"Anything that sounds important. Make it the White House."

"Hi, Lee, good to see you again." Phil Clare strode into my office as though he had seen me many times since Packy's ordination in 1954.

I accepted his outstretched hand.

"Good afternoon, Phil. I'm happy to see you too." I glanced at my watch. "I do have one of those annoying but critical phone calls coming in a few minutes. I'm sure you know what they're like."

Smooth, huh?

The years had not been gentle to him. He looked ten years older than I was instead of two—and a rough ten years at that. He'd lost some of his hair, put on weight, and gave the impression of being seedy, despite his expensive clothes. Too much drink. Too many women. Yet he somehow managed to radiate the same old genial affability. Even prepared for it, I was close to being drawn into his trap.

"Do I ever? I won't take more than a couple of minutes. Say, nice place you got here, expensive office."

The University provides the provost with the kind of office that would be appropriate for a mildly successful commodities broker who thought that solid and expensive dark furniture and deep colors meant elegance and who was content with secondhand materials left over from his predecessor's term. Trouble was that all the stuff was new. I had held out for a house for the provost and had been assured by the trustees that they would keep the matter "under consideration." It had been a mean and stubborn ploy on my part because I didn't know what I'd do with a house of my own. But, mean and stubborn person that I am, I would keep pestering them about it—as a matter of principle (which is what we academics say when we're being gratuitously nasty). So we had settled for a condo and a totally refurbished office.

"You should see the president's office," I said to Phil.

"I suppose you'll be a university president some day, won't you Lee?"

"Possibly. If I want it and about that I'm not sure."

"Yeah, well we're all really proud of you. Everyone knew that you'd be a great success at something."

So his wife—ex-wife—had said. I would not argue with him that being a university provost was not all that impressive an accomplishment.

"Thank you."

"We sure did have a lot of fun in the old days at the Lake, didn't we?"

"Those were great times."

"Get back there much?"

What the hell did he want, this miserable bastard, who could not remain faithful to one of the most beautiful women in the world, not even on his honeymoon?

"Only a couple of weekends. Say hello to my old friends the Keenans."

"Great people, really great."

"I might buy a house up there," I added for pure mischief. "My teenage daughter Laura loves the place."

Laura's mother had rejected a home on the Cape because she didn't want "sand all over your floors and stupid people visiting you on Sunday afternoons." So it was. I might indeed eventually buy a house up there. Right now I intended to marry into one. Your house, Phil. Your bedroom, which you dishonored so often.

"Yeah, I have a kid about that age. Lucy. Great kid."

Lucianne.

"We sure were surprised when you came back from the dead," he continued. "That was great news."

"I was surprised to know that I was dead. You can't really enjoy resurrection unless you know that you are dead."

What hell was he up to? Was he stupid as I once thought or slick as I now believed possible? Or some weird combination of both? Had he lived a half century manipulating or trying to manipulate the world as he had beguiled his father?

"I suppose so, I suppose so," he laughed. "It must have been an interesting experience."

How much did he know about my erratic pursuit of his wife?

"I see you're wearing your ribbon."

People do notice it.

"Yes, I don't wear it all the time."

"I'd sooner wear this medal than be President of the United States," he said wistfully.

"That was him." I nodded toward the picture of Harry Truman on the wall. "Ike didn't say it when he presented it to me, but I figure they gave it to me when Truman was on the bridge."

"Well," he shifted in his chair and crossed his legs, "I suppose the Keenans told you that Jane and I are having a few problems."

"They said you had sued for divorce."

"Well," he shifted again, "that's not altogether true."

"Really?"

"I mean, you know what women are like." He sighed in a tone of a man talking man-to-man, about a problem with wives that all men understood. "She kept accusing me of playing around, and I thought I'd put a stop to it."

"Ah?"

"Mind you, I haven't been perfect, not by a long shot. But I still love her and always will."

He sounded so sincere that if I didn't know better I would have almost believed him. Maybe he almost believed himself. But what was the point of it? He couldn't be asking me to plead his case just as he had a couple of decades ago, could he?

"I'm told the divorce is final."

"Yeah, that's true I guess. But I think we could still get back together if she'd only talk to me for an hour or so. You see, I've got a little legal problem, nothing serious. Some guys I know got into a difficulty with some stock market stuff and implicated me. I didn't know what the hell was going on and still don't. I won't have to do time or anything like that, but it's kind of a mess, you know?"

"I think I read something about it in the *Journal*."

"You can't believe everything you read there."

"I suppose so."

"Anyway, it's sure hard to fight this kind of shit when you don't have your woman at your side."

"I can imagine that."

He truly did want me to plead his case with Jane. Same damn thing. Moreover, while I knew that I wouldn't do it, just at that moment I felt sympathetic towards him and even eager to help him.

Damn clever.

"These things cost a hell of a lot of money too. I mean I've got a lot of reserves but nothing liquid. Jane could be a big help to me in every way. After this is all over if she still wants to be free, well I won't stand in her way."

He didn't want Jane so much as he wanted her money to pay legal fees. He couldn't get at the money in the divorce settlement so he wanted to get it by exploiting her sympathy. And mine.

"As I understand it, she's free now."

"Not in the eyes of God or the Catholic Church. She wants an annulment, I guess. They tell me that I can help her get that."

Ah, that was the trick. If Jane stood by him, especially with the money, he wouldn't stand in the way of an annulment. Nor in my way either. Blackmail of a highly particular sort.

He was neither naive nor dumb. This was a very clever if vicious ploy.

"I see."

"I heard it makes things a lot harder if the spouse won't cooperate."

"Not all that much, I'm told."

I was not about to play horse to his Lady Godiva.

"I was kind of wondering," he uncrossed his legs again, "whether you might make a pitch for me to her. For old times sake, you know. Like you did for me in the old days."

A masterful performance—vulnerable appeal and veiled threat.

"I'm not that close to her any more," I lied. "I haven't been back long enough to spend much time up at the Lake, so I don't see her very often. I'm hesitant to talk to her about what she might consider a personal matter."

"I can see that."

In his vague, unfocused eyes there was a glow of pure terror, a man at his wits' end. Why should he feel that way? The Feds would let him walk. He still had a fat salary from the Devlins for doing almost nothing.

"You know how Jane is," I continued. "When she doesn't want to talk about something, you can't get her to open her mouth."

"I sure do know that." He shook his head despondently. "She's a tough woman to share life with."

"I can well imagine."

Now I understood Phil Clare's problem. He had skimmed through life by exploiting his own seeming vulnerability. When an attempt at exploitation failed, he was frozen in panic. Maybe the magic was eroding.

It had no more power over me. But I wanted to be rid of him.

"Look," he said, "if you happen to be talking to her and this kind of comes up, could you put in a good word for me?"

Not on your life.

"Mr. Kelly," Mae buzzed me, "it's that call from the White House."

"OK, Mae, tell Mr. Mondale's aide I'll be with him in a minute."

Phil was a bastard, but a poor pathetic bastard. His world was unraveling and would continue to unravel. Jane had probably kept him stitched together. Why not say something harmless to reassure him without making any commitments. I almost did just that.

Instead something snapped inside me. I was angry, not Korea angry, just plain West Side Irish angry.

"You know Phil, I should have thrown you back into that car," I said calmly. "Saving your life was the worst mistake I ever made. You killed two of my friends. You betrayed me in that police station. You stole my woman from me. You raped her when she was vulnerable, knocked her up and forced her to marry you."

"I didn't mean . . ." he gasped.

"I don't care what you meant, you stupid bastard," I continued to be the professional provost, cool, poised, wise. "You found out she was too much of a woman for you, so you dishonored your marriage vows from the beginning and ran out on her whenever you felt threatened."

"I didn't . . ."

"Shut up till I'm finished. You're worthless, Phil. Worthless as a man, worthless in bed, worthless as a husband, worthless as a father. You make me sick to my stomach."

I stood up to dismiss him.

"I tried . . ."

I grabbed the lapels of his coat and shook him.

"Now let me tell you what I'm going to do," I snarled into his ear. "I'm going to take my woman back. I'm going to make love with your wife on the marriage bed you betrayed. I'm going to move in with her and stay with her for the rest of my life. I'll beat the shit out of you if I ever hear that you're harassing her again. Do you understand?"

"You're hurting me," he whined.

"Not nearly as much as I will if you don't leave Jane alone. She's mine now, do you hear me. MINE!"

"Please . . ."

"Now get the hell out of my office and don't ever come back."

He left, shoulders slumped, head bowed, the hang-dog rejected.

"Odd man," Mae observed a few minutes later when I had calmed down and entered the outer offices.

"All of that. I had some odd friends in the old days."

"At his wits' end?"

"Far beyond them. Would you see if you can scare up that other odd friend, Monsignor Patrick T. Keenan."

She laughed. Packy had already charmed her in a couple of telephone conversations. "I'll try. He's almost as elusive as you are."

"Who, me elusive?"

"The Monsignor is with the teenagers," she informed me a few moments later. "Is it important?"

"Yes."

"Father Keenan," a warm personable priestly voice said a few moments later.

"Temporarily leaving his teenagers."

"It's *you*."

"Sorry I'm not a teenager."

"They didn't say who it was. I'll leave word that you can disturb me any time, even when I'm doing something important, like arguing with the kids on the front lawn."

"I feel privileged . . . you'd never guess who paid me a visit out here today?"

"I'd give odds it was our friend from the good-old days, Phil Clare. What did he want?"

"He wanted me to talk herself into funding his lawyers in this case in which he is embroiled."

"Poor stupid bastard."

"A common opinion. He also hinted that if she didn't he might block an annulment."

Silence for a moment.

"Look, Leo, he can delay it for a bit, but he can't stop it. You're not going to pass that on to Jane are you?"

"No, certainly not. It is an interesting approach to blackmail, isn't it?"

"Neither you nor Jane are to let it interfere with your wishes and plans," he informed me crisply. "That was never a sacramental marriage. She is therefore free to contract marriage again in the eyes of God, even by the current canonical standards. There's a lot of different ways to handle it . . ."

"Should it become an issue."

"Right. Should it become an issue, neither of you ought to delay merely to keep the ecclesiastical bureaucracy happy, understand?"

"We're nowhere near that yet, Packy."

"Such matters have a way of picking up momentum. It should only concern you if you want a public Catholic marriage."

"I can't imagine that being an issue."

"The thing to keep in mind is that you and Jane are both free now in God's eyes to contract a marriage . . ."

"With each other?"

"What the hell else are we talking about? Moreover you have the perfect right to do so. Church law cannot stand in the way of that right if it creates a grave inconvenience for you. Given what the two of you have been through for the last thirty years, waiting once you make up your minds would be a grave inconvenience. Right?"

"If you say so, Monsignor."

"I say so," he chuckled. "Now can I get back to my teenagers?"

"Only after I tell you what I said to him."

I was disgracefully proud of myself.

"Oh?"

I told him. He was silent for a moment.

"Did you mean all that?"

"About making love with Jane?"

"That in particular."

"Of course I was speaking metaphorically."

"Of course."

"It remains to be seen how the matter works out in practice."

"Of course."

It's odd, I thought, that Pack is not enthused by my doing what he has wanted me to do for a long time.

"So, can I go back to my teens?"

"Heaven forfend that I should stop you." I laughed.

"Be up at the Lake soon?"

"Not till the middle of August when Laura comes home from Boston and New Mexico."

"Not till then?"

"Not with my present schedule."

"See you then."

Come now, Monsignor, one can pursue the prize in Chicago if one has the nerve.

I dismissed Packy's odd reaction from my mind. It was most unlikely that he wanted Jane for himself.

Later at my apartment, my head aching from a mild hangover, I put some mixed vegetables into the microwave and, a glass of iced tea in my hand, settled back to watch the MacNeil-Lehrer report, a matter of obligation under pain of mortal sin for an academic. After they were through analyzing the world, I would try to analyze my own eventful day.

The University, in lieu of the Provost's house, which I had demanded (as I say, out of stubbornness and meanness rather than real need) provided me with a large and rambling penthouse in an art deco apartment building on the edge of the Park, a fashionable place for senior faculty with a fair amount of money. It was on the sixteenth or top floor and was reached by my own private elevator, which Laura had said, "Like totally blows my mind."

Mine too.

Unfortunately in the twenties when the Castles (as it was called) was constructed, they didn't know air conditioning. The six window units that the University, in its wisdom, had installed, provided just enough cooling for all but the hottest days of the summer. On which days you might just as well turn off all the machines, give them a rest, and let in the fresh air. I thought about opening the windows but not with enough energy to actually do it.

The phone rang.

"Kelly," I said irritably.

"Would you rather talk to your cute daughter or listen to Robin MacNeil?"

"No choice."

"Good. I hear you had lunch with Jane today."

"Who?"

"Whom, Daddy."

"I meant who told you?"

"Lucianne, who else? She calls her mother's office and like Nessa, goes your mother has gone to lunch with this really gorgeous man with red hair and some flakes of white in it."

"So Lucianne has to call you."

"Really!"

"Do you still call Mrs. Clare, Jane?"

"Sure. She said I should. Like I told you. She's like one of the kids anyway. Even Lucianne goes that her mom is like one of the kids. Still she's mad at her a real lot and I go Lucianne you're an asshole to be so mean to your mother."

"And Lucianne goes, er, I means says?"

"Gotcha, Daddy. She goes, yeah I know I am but I can't help it."

"Does she call her mother Jane?"

"Behind her back, sure. Not to her face yet but she'd like to, you know?"

"I'll take your word for it."

"But, *Daddy,* you didn't answer my question."

"Which was?"

"How was lunch with Jane?"

All right, my beloved was one of the kids.

"Laura, how could lunch with Jane be anything else but a fun experience? You know, she's like one of the kids, really!"

"*Daddy!*"

"Actually I had a very nice time. Drank two glasses of Jameson's!"

"*Daddy,* you *didn't!*"

"I did so. Now I have a headache."

"Serves you right!"

"Jane had only one. And a glass of white wine."

"I'm sure."

Huffy because I wouldn't spill out my personal life to her.

"All right, it's too early for you and Lucianne to start ordering presents, but I imagine we'll have lunch again."

"Great! Because, you know, Lucianne wouldn't dare ask her mother anything about it."

Time for candor, real candor not academic candor.

"Laura, I know that teenagers tend to be embarrassed at the thought that their parents, though doddering and decrepit, still have a sex life. Do I hear you saying that you would not be offended at the possibility of your ancient father in bed with a woman?"

"Not if it were Jane. *Of course* not."

"No promises," I concluded our conversation.

She merely giggled.

When I had hung up I could hardly believe that I had permitted the little bitch to trick me into a confession of intent.

So I gave up on MacNeil-Lehrer and tried, like a good professor of the social sciences, to order and analyze the data I had collected during the day.

I had missed a lot of implications in my three conversations. There were patterns and possibilities lurking in the data that I couldn't quite tease out. There were null hypotheses that I should try to test. Somehow there was a hint of an explanation that I saw for an instant or two and then faded away before I could pin it down.

I did come to one conclusion however: Jane wanted more time. Fine, I would give her till the middle of August. No longer.

With that happy thought I put aside the *APSR* (*American Political Science Review* to the uninitiated) and decided to treat myself to a good night's sleep.

1968

Patrick

"The Pope," I exploded, "is a sick little faggot."

The two adjectives and the noun were accurate enough in my judgment but they were irrelevant and I should have had more respect for the Pope. Moreover his sexual orientation was none of my business.

Jane, Jerry, and Maggie (the latter living just down the street) had come for supper the night before. My poor parents had to listen to another one of my diatribes against the Pope. After my outburst our dining room was as quiet as an empty funeral parlor. Maggie opened her mouth as if to say something and then shut it—most unusual behavior for my beloved sister-in-law.

"We're all worried about you, Packy," Jane said firmly. "That terrible place has destroyed your wit and your serenity. You're not the warm, wonderful priest you used to be. Don't go back there. Please. Be a parish priest again. You were never happier than when you were that ten years ago."

I had become Jane's confidant during the year, offering her advice, reassurance, encouragement, and affection by mail and an occasional phone call. Now she had deftly turned the tables on me. Our relationship had become more intricate at that moment—and more intimate.

The rest of them had waited expectantly, Maggie biting her lip to keep her mouth shut.

"You're right, Jane," I sighed. "Sorry for blowing up. I'll get over it."

"We know you will, dear," Mom had nodded. "It was a terrible disappointment."

"But not the end of the world," Maggie had added.

"No," I agreed. "But it will make things more difficult."

"It won't affect us laypeople," Jane added. "We're all are on your side."

So indeed they were.

But many laypeople would suffer terribly because of the encyclical *Humanae Vitae*.

A year ago I had assured Jane and everyone else that change on birth control was inevitable—just as poor Cardinal Heenan had assured everyone in England. Then the Pope double-crossed us.

He had sold out the leading Cardinals of the Council who had been on the Birth Control Commission—Suenens of Brussels, Döphner of Munich. Heenan of Westminister, the best of the moral theologians—Häring, Fuchs, and DeReitman—lay demographers like Tom Burch from the United States and Mercedes Concepcion from the Philippines—and the laity of the world. He had betrayed us under pressure from the Italian curialists who wanted revenge for what the Council had done to their power. Led by Cardinal Alfredo Ottovianni, an old man and almost blind (who had the reputation of possessing the Evil Eye), they had waited to prey on the Pope's conscience till the commission had disbanded and gone home. He was, they told him contemptuously, violating the teachings of Christ and destroying the credibility of the Papacy. He would be the first Pope against whom the gates of hell had prevailed. Good Catholics would go into schism. History would judge him a coward and a failure.

These were his old enemies in the Curia who had made his life miserable when he was Under Secretary of State and had voted against him in the Conclave. Yet through all his years as Pope he seemed more afraid of them than of anyone else.

The Pope gave in, rejected our report, and wrote *Humanae Vitae* renewing the traditional birth control teaching. He said that in twenty years he would be hailed as a prophet and was dismayed when many of the hierarchies around the world were lukewarm in their support. Our own gloriously reigning psychopath had someone write him an innocuous statement and then went off to Alaska the day the encyclical was issued.

Paul VI had listed in the encyclical some of the reasons we had advanced for change. He dismissed them rather than responding to them. There could be no change, it seemed, no matter how good the reasons. The encyclical ultimately was not about sex but about power, the power of the Vatican and the Pope over the sex lives of the laity. It seemed to me then and it still does that to interfere with what goes on in the marriage bed in the name of your own power is demonic. Ironically, far from protecting the power of Church leadership, the encyclical destroyed it because the laity decided that the Pope and his advisors did not know what they were talking about on the subject of marital sex.

A few of us in Rome tried to mobilize opposition in the months before *Humanae Vitae* was issued. We knew that the curialists had defeated us on the possibility of change, but we hoped to head off the encyclical, which we were sure would do exactly the opposite of what Ottoviani and his crew of mafiosi had told the Pope. Maybe Paul would settle for a compromise: an encyclical that said in effect what the Holy Office had told the French hierarchy in the nineteenth century: Don't trouble the consciences of the laity.

But like many passive-aggressive personalities when they dig in their heels, the Pope turned stubborn on us. We warned him that neither priests nor laity would obey and papal credibility would be shattered. The Holy See, trapped in its Aristotelian view of the nature of human nature and indifferent to what scientists since Aristotle had discovered about human nature, had dug a trap for itself.

Ted Hesburgh, a personal friend of the Pope, had come over to try to talk him out of it. But, passive-aggressive man that he was, the Pope had dug in his heels. At least we persuaded him to take out the line that would have made the teaching infallible.

Some day I'll do a book about the whole disgusting business. The letters I wrote to Jane during that year will make an excellent source for describing how hope gradually turned to despair.

I had stayed on in Rome, teaching a seminar at one of the colleges and trying to figure out what to do next. My friends told me that my career was finished because I was the one who had drafted the rejected report. I would become a non-person, just as would the members of the commission. I didn't care about that. I had not come to Rome looking for a career. However, I did not want to return to the insane asylum, which Chicago had become under our new Cardinal. At that time I had no thought of leaving the priesthood and displayed contempt for many of the weepers and complainers who had.

When the phone rang the next day, I was sitting on the front porch of my parents' home on Lathrop Avenue in River Forest on a rainy autumn afternoon in September 1968, still trying to figure out what had gone wrong. Only three years ago, the Church had seemed embarked on historic and exciting changes. Now the whole process of growth and development had ground to a halt. The changes would continue of course, but the Vatican was no longer directing the course of events. It was either trying to play catch up or pretending that everything was normal again.

Mom came out on the porch and told me that the Chancellor of the Archdiocese was on the phone. I hated him. He had sat at the same table as I had when the Cardinal was in Rome and was the first one to say bluntly that the man was crazy. Yet he served him with total fidelity.

"The Cardinal wants to see you this afternoon," he began bluntly. "Get down to the house on North State this afternoon at four-twenty."

"Fuck you and fuck him too."

"What!"

"I'm busy this afternoon. Tell him I'll be there tomorrow."

"Who the hell do you think you are?"

"Whoever I am, I have not sold out to evil like you have."

I had nothing to do that afternoon, but I was not about to be treated like a cog in a machine. I was perhaps too harsh on the Chancellor. He would have argued that he was trying to protect the Archdiocese from worse harm.

The Cardinal was an hour and twenty minutes late for our appointment the next day, which meant that for him he was early. Astonishingly, he did not charge in with his usual bluster.

"Pat!" His fat face relaxed in a happy grin. "Great to see you again! I want you to know that I think you did a great job over there. It was a big mistake. I told the Pope he'd live to regret it. Don't worry about your career, I won't let them do anything to you."

I was quite sure that he had told others just the opposite and that he had supported the Pope completely.

"Thank you, Cardinal."

He was, I feared, much more dangerous when charming. What did he have up his sleeve?

"This is a terrible job I've got here. Not enough good priests to go around. You know St. Regina's parish."

"Sure."

It was by many accounts the finest parish in the Archdiocese, a suburban community of college-educated business men and professionals. The people were reputed to be generous, enthusiastic, dedicated.

"The old man up there is something of a saint. But he's senile too. Crazy. The people like him but they don't want him as pastor any more and I can't blame them."

"I've heard there are problems."

I still didn't see what was coming.

"So I wonder if as a personal favor to me you'd go up there and take over for a while. It might be good to get back in touch with a parish again. Only till we get your career back on track."

I was astonished. He was offering me just what Jane said I needed. Later I would realize that he wanted to keep me out of Rome, just as he wanted to keep all his priests out of anything that would bring them attention. Moreover, he thought that he would look bad if someone coming back from an important assignment elsewhere was not rewarded with an honorable appointment. Crazy, but for me grace.

"I think that's just what I need, Cardinal. Sure I'll accept the assignment. As Pastor, not as administrator."

I was not so astonished as to trust him completely.

"Absolutely," he said. "I'll get the letter off to you tomorrow."

Out in the chill rain on North State Parkway, I felt wonderful. I would be able to see Jane often. And my family. Get to know my nieces and nephews. Play tennis with Maggie and Jerry. Spend some summer time at the Lake.

With Jane.

I did indeed play tennis with her often and also helped her to hold on through the agonies of the loss of her two children. I fell even more in love with her, but the thought of leaving the priesthood for her would remain deep in the subterranean cellars of my consciousness for the next several years.

I continued to hear from Leo with increasing frequency in those years as he moved from Santa Barbara to Brandeis and then to Harvard. His marriage was on the rocks, if it had ever been off the rocks. Yet stubborn Catholic that he was, he stuck with it to the bitter end; giving up when Emilie in effect threw him and the luminous Laura (as he described her) out of the house.

Leo could verbalize about it—he could verbalize about anything—but he could not comprehend a wife who defined herself in competition with him and was envious of his success.

I did wonder occasionally whether eventually Leo and Jane would find for themselves a second chance. Part of me hoped they would and part of me resented the possibility.

1978

Jane

An ambulance siren woke me in the middle of the night. Some poor person being rushed to the medical center after a heart attack with a family desperately praying for life.

Briefly I joined my prayer to theirs.

The siren had jolted me out of a terrifying nightmare—an infrequent event in my nights. I had glimpsed the terrible reality of my hidden insight.

An insight about what?

And why do I have this headache?

Our lunch conversation rushed back into my consciousness. What an incredible mess. But somehow exciting too, filled with promise of maybe making some bad things good.

I hadn't told him that I suspected that Martha and Iris had virtually raped Elizabetta Nicola. Elizabetta had always been extra nice to me in subsequent years, as if she were making up for something. At best she would be a reluctant recruit to such schoolgirl games—enjoying the pleasure perhaps but far more repelled by it than the other too.

My nightmare somehow had been about the Nicolas. There had been something very wrong in that charming family too. A different kind of wrong.

But that didn't seem relevant. There was something else in the nightmare.

Maybe I should tell him all about my suspicions concerning the Nicolas. It would be silly to be too delicate now. We must somehow find out the truth.

But that wasn't the secret insight that part of me was trying to hide. It was in the nightmare too, mixed with my fears for Angie.

I put on a robe and walked over to the window. I would have to invest in something more erotic in the next few days. Just in case.

I opened the drapes a couple of inches and looked out on the Drive. Even in early morning hours there was a steady stream of traffic. Beyond in the darkness the flat Lake was ominous and still, a great force threatening to erupt at any time when the promised squall line came through.

A new robe. New lingerie. Sexy in an understated and elegant way. A man around the house. Apartment. Whatever. A man with his distracting presence and his persistent demands, with his monumental insensitivies and his foolish fears.

Conceited vulnerability, that's what a man is.

I opened the window. The outside air was stale and motionless, a heavy hand on the city. In the distance however faint flashes of lightning crackled across the sky.

I closed the window and drew the drapes.

He's different though. Has been since that day I tried to buy him the ice cream bar. Special delicacy combined with special passion. It was good he was wearing that medal finally. Maybe he was coming to terms with the truth that he was a hero. A sweet and tender hero.

Well he might do. On approval.

I grinned. All things considered it wouldn't be bad to have him here right now because it be would a while before I fell back to sleep.

Was he a heavy sleeper? How would he react if I woke him with an insistent sexual demand?

Well, that wouldn't matter. He'd make love to me anyway. No more of this business of a man who isn't interested in love in the middle of the night.

No way, José.

Otherwise he'd get no TLC when he woke from his bad dreams.

This was silly nonsense. Life with my funny little redhead wouldn't be like that at all. The real question is whether I would ever dare to wake him for early hour sex. What if I were not good at it? Phil said I wasn't.

Then I gasped. The truth from which I had been fleeing flooded my consciousness. Of course. Why hadn't anyone seen that. Not even Maggie. But it was obvious. Once you knew that his assignment to Korea was the result of a plot.

I reached for the phone to call him and realized that I didn't even know his number. Or his address. How many Leo Kellys were there in the phone book? And he probably wasn't listed.

I'd call him first thing in the morning.

What would he think when I told him what had really happened.

Leo

Rain was beating down on the Quadrangle as I hurried from an early morning meeting with the president at the Faculty Club (about a fund-raising appeal) to my office in the administration building.

I had not slept well. For hours I had tossed and turned, unable to sleep and unable to think clearly. Then I had finally collapsed into an exhausted sleep from which I was soon awakened by the lightning and thunder—or by the memories of the bitter cold nights at the Reservoir, which storms always recalled. I heard the bugles and screams as the Chinese charged.

I sat up stiffly, reached for my weapon, then for Jane. Neither was there. Of course not.

I could not go back to sleep. Nor could I sort out any of the pieces of the puzzle that had been spread across my card table the day before, pieces deliberately cut, it seemed, so that they did not and would not fit together again.

As I rushed across the mostly empty and rain-drenched Quad (without an umbrella, naturally; wives and umbrellas inevitably correlate) I thought of Phil Clare again. The bastard. Never again would I call him a poor bastard.

Yet Phil would not knowingly send anyone to Korea, would he?

Soaking wet and irritable, I charged into my office at ten o'clock, an hour after I had hoped to be there.

"Mr. Kelly," Mae scolded me, "you're soaking wet."

I almost lost it, almost took out my anger on her. Instead I leaned against the door and laughed.

"Is it raining!"

She shook her head in dismay. At least she didn't say I needed a good wife to take care of me.

"A Ms. Devlin called this morning at nine. No message, she said she'd call back at ten-thirty. A very pleasant woman, full of fun."

"Ah . . . I imagine she'll call back."

I had time to phone my sister Megan. It was eight o'clock in California. She'd already be up with those kids. I found her number in an old address book I had tossed in the bottom of the drawer.

The number, I was informed, had been changed. I frowned at the picture of Harry Truman that stared at me from the wall and tried the new number.

Megan answered.

"Megan, Leo."

"Leo!"

There was music in her voice.

"Megan, in the words of my teenager, I've been an asshole."

She laughed happily, "No you haven't, Leo, no you haven't."

After that our conversation was pure grace. I agreed that I would spend some time with her family when I was in Carmel after Labor Day on a fundraising venture.

She asked, guardedly, about Jane.

"I'll tell you more about that when I see you. There might be more to tell by then."

"Really!"

"Maybe," I said, hedging my bets.

"Give her my love."

"I will indeed . . ."

"Are you going to call the others?"

"Before the day is out . . . unless you tell me not to."

"Oh, no, you'll make them as happy as you've made me."

I spent a few minutes bringing my emotions under restraint and thanking incoherently whatever powers preside over family reconciliations.

"Any calls come in while I was talking to my sister?" I asked Mae.

The phone rang. Mae picked it up. Hand over the mouthpiece, she nodded, "Ms. Devlin, right on time."

"Naturally, I'll take it in the office."

Devlin, huh? Back to her maiden name. That was a good sign.

"Leo Kelly," I said formally into the phone, reaching for a letter opener to start on my mail while we were talking.

"Lee, Jane. I have something horrible to say."

I put the letter opener down. "Say it."

"The killer wasn't after Phil or the Murrays."

"Oh?"

What kind of nuttiness was this? Had she been talking to the Good Witch of the East?

"I mean it's so obvious that we didn't even think of it, not till Tom Keenan told you about Korea."

"What are you driving at, Jane?"

"Whose car was it?'

"Packy's of course. But he was away at camp with the orphans or whatever they were."

"Right. So who was driving it most of the time that summer?"

"I was. Who else?"

"Who should have been killed then?"

The horror of the phantasm she had seen reduced me to total silence. It was the same dark vision I had been seeing. Both of us had seen it at the same time.

"Lee?"

"I'm still here Jane."

"Whoever weakened the brakes wanted you dead. When Phil borrowed the car without even asking you that day, he and the two Murrays were not only accident victims, they were accidental victims. You were the target."

"Why would anyone want to kill me, Jane?"

"Why would anyone want to change your assignment so you'd be a platoon leader at Inchon and Wonsan and the Chosin Reservoir?"

"Someone wanted me dead the worst way."

"What other reason?"

"Why?"

"I haven't figured that out, Lee, but I'm convinced that it's true."

"It is, Jane. I've had the same insight striving to be born."

Hail pounded against the window of my office, a warning of horrendous forces lurking in my peaceful world, far more horrendous than narcissistic biology professors.

"Do you or did you know something that someone might want to keep a secret?"

"Nothing I can think of now."

"Are you convinced I'm right, Leo?"

I thought for a moment or two.

"I think so, Jane. It makes sense. I'm just not able to absorb it."

"Did you call Megan?"

"Yes I called Megan and we both had a good cry and I'm going to spend some time with them after Labor Day when I go out to California to see a major donor."

"How wonderful!"

"She said she knew it would work out eventually. I didn't even know till you told me there was something to work out . . . she sends her love to you."

"Good old Megan, classy, classy lady."

"You bet."

Then we were somber, life giving away once again to death.

"I feel like a pawn, Lee. Like a piece in a game someone else is playing."

"I do too, Jane. A pawn for most of my life. From now on, however, we make our own moves. The game is about over and they're going to lose."

"Be careful, Lee," she begged. "Please be careful. Promise me. They might still be out there."

"I will certainly be careful," I replied, a prediction of my future behavior, which was unfortunately not accurate.

1947

Leo

"Maggie, these two are urchins who hang around during the summer, so you'd better meet them. Leo Kelly and Jane Devlin. Lee, Jane, my wife Margaret Mary."

"She's probably worth hunting around the country," I said to Jane.

Margaret Mary Ward Keenan was dressed impeccably in a gray dress that conformed to all of the requirements of Dior's "New Look"—tight bodice and waist with a hint of lingerie lace at the tantalizing V neck, wide, flowing and long skirt, matching gloves and purse, and even a matching hat. She was definitely sexy in a diminutive way with pert breasts and deftly carved body, and had the glint of mischief in her eyes.

"Not really loathsome like I thought she'd be," Jane agreed.

"I think Jerry should keep her."

"Yes, I think so too—if she can play tennis."

You don't greet strangers that way usually. But Margaret Mary Ward Keenan was the kind of stranger that you knew on sight would not only not mind, but would love such a breaking of the ice.

Jerry Keenan was bursting with pride over his apparently solemn waif-child with pale cream skin, vast gray eyes, auburn hair, and a slow and magic smile. When they had come into the house, Packy had swept his new sister-in-law off the ground and into the air and planted a kiss on her giggling lips.

"Welcome to the Lake, Sis!"

She had giggled happily.

Packy had deposited her on the ground and, after she had also kissed the elder Keenans, Jerry had introduced her to us.

Jane and I had instinctively recognized a kindred spirit.

"I think her eyes are really sweet," Jane continued our dialogue. "And such pretty hair."

"And a slow and magic smile."

"All of us women are going to have to buy new clothes to dress that impeccably. Note that her ensemble matches her eyes."

Maggie and Jane hugged enthusiastically. Looking over Jane's shoulder at me, she asked, "Do people use that hair of yours for cleaning pots and pans?"

General laughter.

"The Marines," Jane said, "use it for cleaning latrines."

"I have the feeling that suddenly I'm outnumbered."

"And Packy is teaching me to play tennis," Maggie said.

"Good. Tomorrow morning?" Jane promptly set about scheduling. "You can come too, Jerry if you don't think you're too old to play with us young folk."

Jerry was then about twenty-four, a second year law student with two Navy Crosses and Lieutenant Commander's gold leaf cluster tucked away somewhere.

"I think I'll hobble over, just to keep an eye on my wife." He grinned happily at the thought of keeping an eye on his wife. "I might bring a racket along."

So entered our lives one of the most important friends either of us would ever have. When I was supposed to be buried in a nameless grave near the Chosin Reservoir, Maggie and Maggie alone, refused to believe I was dead. She and she alone was not surprised when I turned up, unlisted, among the prisoners who were released in August of 1953.

" *Well,*" Jane commented as I walked her home, "thank God she's married. I wouldn't want competition with that one."

"You look very pretty in that green dress, Jane. It's sort of half new look."

"Why, thank you! I had to dress up, even put on a girdle, nylons, and shoes to welcome the new bride. I'm glad I did. I suppose I'll have to wear a girdle now, but no corsets, not ever!"

"You'll be at the party tonight?"

"I sure will, wait till you see my dress."

"I can hardly wait."

During the remnants of that summer, Jane and I were much more formal with each other. We both understood intuitively that we were in a new phase of our relationship. Shallow petting and kissing were definitely not appropriate. We would exchange affection less often and more passionately. We never spoke of marriage and rarely of love, but we both knew that we were embarking on a path that by next summer would make those questions too demanding to ignore.

I was nineteen, she would be nineteen in mid-August, August 15th, Lady Day in Harvest Time. At the end of the next summer, I'd be twenty with only a year left of school. Unless she dumped me I might well ask her to marry me, either after I received my commission the following year or at least to make a commitment for marriage when I was released from active service, probably in the summer of 1951. By then she would have graduated from college and we'd be twenty-three. I'd have enough money from my saving and my G.I. bill benefit to support her as I struggled through graduate school.

I pondered this schedule as we walked down the road toward her home. It was nice because I could think of her as mine and I would not have to risk myself in a proposal.

So I viewed our friendship that summer as a possibility for the future. I'm not sure how she viewed it, but she showed no signs of dumping me. Unaccountably she seemed to like being with me.

"You keep growing up on me, Lee," she said as we arrived at the gate to the Devlin grounds. "I feel I have to run to catch up."

"And I feel that I'll never catch up with you."

We both laughed.

"See you tonight," she said.

"I'm waiting to get a look at you in that promised dress."

"I hope you don't think it's two extreme."

"Not a chance."

Leo

Jane's dress was indeed worth waiting for. Low cut in both front and back, it hung from her shoulders by the thinnest of straps and ending just above her knees—in total defiance of the "New Look"—its off-white fabric seemed to blend gradually with her alabaster skin and to cling to her by only the most fragile of restraints.

"My eyes are popping," I commented.

"That's what they are supposed to do, Lunkhead. "Do you like it?"

"Love it, Milady. It and you."

"Humph," she sniffed, pleased and (was I imagining it?) not troubled by the hint of love. "Will you look at that little witch? Isn't she too gorgeous?"

Maggie's forest green, off-the-shoulder dress—which fell way below her knees and hence honored the M. Dior's rules—left no doubt about her delectable little figure either.

"How do you know she's a witch?"

"She knows everything. Just look at the way she takes in the room."

We were in the massive parlor of the Keenan home, once a small ballroom for formal dances and still capable of serving that function when necessary, at a cocktail party officially welcoming Margaret Mary Ward Keenan to the Lake.

The parlor or ballroom was covered with throw rugs that could be discarded for big events to reveal the parquet floor. A massive crystal chandelier—rarely lighted save for special events—spread misty illumination on the room and its occupants. The declining sun had painted the dark Lake a rich, royal purple and sent rays of colored lights through the stained glass windows (Tiffany windows I now know).

The guest of honor and her husband, feeling at ease with the "kids" apparently had drifted over to where Jane and I were standing, glasses of champagne expectantly in our hands.

"You look lovely, Jane," Maggie said. "Dazzling."

"Only one woman in the room outshines me, Maggie."

"Already thick as thieves," I protested to the beaming Jerry. "This bodes ill for the future of all the men in the community."

"It will do us no good to fight it."

"If I may have your attention," Tom Keenan's voice boomed out. "I have been warned by my wife and my two sons that I am not to engage in the lawyer's propensity for long orations. Therefore I propose a toast to the newest member of the Keenan family. Maggie, we're happy to have you with us here at the Lake. We are sure that the brightness of your beauty and your wit and your goodness will make all our summers to come even happier than the past ones have been. Your very good health, Margaret Mary . . ."

"Hear! Hear!" Packy bellowed.

We toasted the beaming bride.

Then, utterly calm, she moved to the center of the room to respond—something that I don't think had been in the program.

"Thank you, Tom. As I look out on your beautiful lake and see the sun setting so terribly early and think that this most beautiful summer of my life is ending so quickly, I drink to the Keenans—Tom, Mary Anne, Jerry, Joan, and Packy—whose graciousness to me, this weird little kid from Philadelphia who talks so funny, makes me realize that as long as they are around me with their life and love, it will always be summertime for me."

Eyes shining she lifted her glass to her husband and his family.

Loud applause. Sniffles from many of the women. Including my companion.

Joan was not there but she was included anyway.

"She's too much," Jane sniffled. "Absolutely too much."

As the evening wore on and the crowd mixed I noticed that the guest of honor was shrewdly taking in everything and everyone. Jane didn't miss it either.

"What do you think of them, Margaret Mary?"

"Which ones?"

"Angie Nicola?"

"Sweet and very troubled, poor pretty little thing."

"Her date, Jimmy Murray?"

"Haunted. And not by her either, worse luck for him."

"Eileen Murray?"

"Hollow. Ditto for that big guy. Phil, is that his name?"

"Their parents?"

She pondered the three couples who were chatting happily.

"Pretty, brittle, and empty. And their husbands are charming and crass."

There was no harshness in her voice, only soft, almost melancholy statements. Long before she had finished even her undergraduate training in psychology, Maggie *saw* things.

"And the two of us?"

"My wonderful new brother and sister? How could I possibly find anything wrong with them?"

"Brother and sister?" Jane said suspiciously.

"Well," Maggie said easily, "perhaps I should say my wonderful adopted brother-in-law and sister-in-law."

"Huh?" I asked.

"Packy is my real brother-in-law and you're my adopted brother-in-law and sister-in-law, aren't you?"

"The Keenans haven't adopted us, Maggie," I said. "We have parents of our own. We're not really urchins."

"Oh, no," she replied. "I didn't mean that. I meant you've adopted them. They're your summer mother and father. Of course . . . Now Jerry why don't we start dancing. We don't want to hurt the feelings of those three nice men your father brought to play music."

They were playing music from "Blue Skies," indeed at that very moment, "How Deep is the Ocean."

"What the hell!" I led Jane to the newly polished dance floor from which the Keenans had temporarily removed the carpet.

"She's right, Lee. I've never thought of it that way before but that's exactly what we have done. We barged in and made ourselves part of their family . . . shows good taste on our part, doesn't it?"

"But how did she pick it up?"

I was so baffled by Maggie Keenan that I was distracted from the mostly undressed woman who was relaxing so sweetly in my arms.

"I told you she was a witch . . . why are you staring at me that way?"

"I was wondering whether your dress is a modified nightgown."

"That is a terrible thing to say," she blushed. "I don't deny that the designer probably had that in mind, but it's not gallant of you to say it."

"I can notice it but not say it."

"Well, you can say it so long as I have a chance to pretend that I'm shocked and displeased."

"You dressed up like that to please me?"

She wrinkled her nose. "Certainly not. I didn't want to be outshone by the bride. Or Angie either as far as that goes."

"I see."

"Please you, just because you'd been away on your silly old destroyer all summer? Certainly not! What would ever give you that idea?"

"Well, I'm pleased anyway."

She leaned her head against my shoulder, briefly. Very briefly.

"I'm so glad you are, Lee. Thank you."

"Can I dance with your date during the next dance?" Packy asked.

"I don't have a date, Pack. This is just Jane."

"Just Jane doesn't mind," she said.

"I don't think seminarians should dance with anyone this beautiful."

"They shouldn't," Packy said. "But I'm going to just the same."

On the train ride that afternoon I had heard Mr. Murray and Mr. Nicola and Dr. Clare, unaware that they were not the only ones in the car, talk about their conquests, how they cheated on their wives, bilked prostitutes, and exploited the women who worked for them. Doctor Clare—who was, I strongly suspected, impotent—went into rich detail about what he and his colleagues did to nurses. Tino Nicola told with glee how he would trap women guests at his restaurant into one of the private dining rooms and then, after they had drunk too much, turn them over to his friends. They would never dare complain, he chortled, because their husbands wouldn't believe that they had not "wanted it."

"Hell," he laughed loudly, "they usually love it."

I thought then that it was mostly locker room talk and I'm even more certain today of that about the Doctor and Mr. Murray. Tino Nicola, genial charmer that he was, might do almost anything.

While Packy and Jane danced—and I thanked God for Packy's vocation—I watched the male guests, and not merely Larry, Curly, and Moe of the afternoon train, ogle my alleged date who was really just Jane.

They had no right to look at her that way; she was mine. It was all right for me to ogle her, but no one else could. My hand knotted into a fist when I saw Tino Nicola's hard little eyes examining her from head to foot. Hands off buster. I've learned a little bit about hand-to-hand and the instructor says I'm a natural and you so much as lay a hand on her, I'll break your wrist.

I was good at hand-to-hand because I was—and am—mean and stubborn.

After Packy, Phil danced with her and then Mr. Keenan, and then Jerry, and then Mr. Nicola. He seemed perfectly proper and respectful, but I didn't like the sight of his big paw on her naked back.

"Mind if I cut in," I said, "I'd like to have one more dance with my date."

He frowned at me. "Can't you wait till the next dance?"

"I was thinking of how much this parlor reminds me of the private rooms in your restaurants with all the couches around."

He recoiled as if I had stabbed him and retreated quickly to his wife.

Bastard.

"What was that about?"

"I'll tell you some other time."

"Thanks anyway. I didn't like him holding me. There was something a little strange about it."

"Yeah."

"He's an odd man, Lee. Sometimes so charming and sweet and other times, well, kind of brutal. Angie says he's terribly moody."

"I wouldn't be surprised."

As I walked home with her that night, I sensed that there was no need to wait two or three years. I could propose marriage to Jane this summer and she would accept me enthusiastically. We could be married next summer. Twenty was perhaps too young, though there were lots of people who had married at that age during the war. Including Maggie.

Moreover, Jane and I were not total strangers. We'd grown up together. We'd known each other all our lives. Why not?

I didn't have to decide that night. I had two weeks, but why wait when you know you love and suspect that you are loved in return. The girl holding my hand so firmly in her own certainly loved me.

What would have happened if I had followed up on that impulse?

Both our lives would have been different. Better beyond any doubt.

Well, maybe not.

Who knows?

For the last quarter century, those thoughts have lingered in the back of my head for a moment or two every day.

Like Packy says, it didn't work out that way; so why fight the Holy Spirit?

Is it fair, however, to blame the Holy Spirit for the night we went to see *Oliver Twist*? During the two weeks Maggie and Jane could talk us into only two films. *The Red Shoes* was the other.

Anyway whatever the night was that we saw *Oliver Twist* I did a shameless act at the Rose Bowl, holding up my dish as Oliver had done in the movie and pleading for more ice cream.

"The boy asked for more?" Packy exclaimed his disbelief.

"The boy asked for more," the rest replied in chorus.

Then Jane, who still worked some of the time at the soda fountain and had loads of clout, picked up my chocolate sundae bowl, strode behind the counter, and, in high dudgeon, whipped up what was quite possibly the biggest hot fudge sundae in human history.

"More," she said planting it in front of me with an impatient frown as the jukebox played "I'll Dance at Your Wedding."

Vigorous applause from *omnibus*.

"Is that all?"

She threw up her hands in dismay.

That's the night I should have proposed to her. Made it a joke.

I decided I'd put it off till next summer.

We went back to Chicago on the Tuesday after Labor Day and Jane and I had almost no contact. We exchanged Christmas cards, but not Christmas presents. I called her twice; both times she seemed uneasy. I continued to study languages and military science and politics and collect my A grades. I had a knack for languages my C.O. told me. The Marines really needed someone who could get along in French, Italian, Spanish, and German.

Later I would learn enough Korean and enough Chinese to understand our guards, though they didn't know that I could figure out what they were saying. I suppose that helped me to survive.

I occasionally surprised a Korean colleague by digging up some phrases out of the past.

"That is very good, Professor Kelly, but a strange dialect. Where did you learn it?"

"A long story, Dr. Kim."

I had no idea what Jane was doing during the school year, certainly not home pining for me, I figured.

I was relieved that I had not proposed that night. If we did not care enough about each other to stay in touch during the winter months, why should we think of marriage?

I knew all along, however, that it wasn't a very good argument. We had good reasons, our respective mothers, for staying apart for the time being.

But there was more than that. I was afraid of marriage and its responsibilities, not sure that I would be very skillful in bed with a woman (and if you're a man you have to be a superb performer even the first time, don't you!), and uneasy about sharing my private life with anyone. Even Jane.

Without knowing what one was exactly, I was drifting toward being a typical Irish bachelor. When Jane was around I wanted to be married. When she wasn't around, I thought about her, analyzed the possibilities and dithered. Already on the way to being a professor.

Now I look back on those few weeks at the end of 1947 and wonder what I can find in them that will help me understand not only the terrible mistakes I made, but what other forces were at work, capitalizing on my mistakes.

I know I shouldn't have picked a fight with Tino Nicola. That was stupid Marine exhibitionism on my part. How much of what happened later, I wondered, was the result of my mean and stubborn remark that night.

1978

Leo

"Doctor Keenan speaking," said the soft, smooth professional voice.

"Dr. Kelly calling, Doctor Keenan."

"Ah, Doctor Kelly, how are you?"

"Breathing in and out, Doctor Keenan, breathing in and out."

I put aside the *New York Times*. Speculations about the upcoming Papal Conclave could wait.

I had called her earlier and was informed by her answering machine that Doctor Keenan was with a patient and that I could call back at eleven. It was only fifteen minutes, so I glanced over the arrangements for the signing of the deed of gift for the Devlin Chair of Irish Studies. It would be a remarkably generous gift. The press release was the usual undistinguished stuff that our P.R. people could grind out in their sleep and probably did. The facts were there, if not the sense of the Big Change, which the chair represented. Well, that was all right. We could hardly tell the world that the late Herbert Devlin and his two brothers were thugs who had been civilized by success, affluence, and wise marriages.

Probably marriages arranged by their shrewd and dominating mother who knew the way to respectability.

Nor would we say that the "distinguished military service" of the brothers during the war had been in desks in Washington, Seattle, and San Diego, for Herbie, Mickie, and Dickie respectively.

I corrected a couple of typos in the press release because, like I say, I'm mean and stubborn. Then I called Maggie again.

As the phone rang I noticed that the release did not mention Jane. Perhaps they didn't want to taint their generosity with the scandals affecting her marriage.

Would she come to the signing of the deed? She wanted time and I was giving her time. If I wanted to see her before the middle of August at the Lake, I could always call her, could I not?

Somehow I was reluctant to pick up the phone. I wanted to see her face and measure her reactions when I spoke to her.

"You are continuing your exhumation of the past."

"Digging around. Remember the night we saw *Oliver Twist?*"

"Indeed yes, it was just about then I think my first pregnancy began. As I recall you and Jane put on quite a show."

"Yeah, I should have proposed to her that night."

Pause.

"Possibly, possibly not. However, Lee, you may be able to reinterpret the past, you can't change its facts. You did not propose to her then or, if my understanding is correct, ever, except in one very inconclusive effort. Unless you have done so in the past several weeks."

"No, I haven't."

"Yet."

"That's right, not yet."

"If you are calling to ask me whether I think you should, you must remember that therapists do not give advice to either their clients or friends, but my answer is that you should do so without delay."

"That's pretty non-directive."

"Like I always am . . . now what is it that you are afraid to ask me?"

"You never believed I was dead, isn't that true?"

Another pause.

"Belief does not figure. I *knew* you were not dead. It is foolish to ask how I know what I know. I simply know. So I was the only one for whom your return in 1953 was simply a return and not a resurrection."

"And you tried to tell Jane that?"

"Of course."

"And she didn't believe you?"

"She couldn't believe me, Leo. She had this terrible compulsion to feel responsible for what had happened to you. Matriarchal guilt or something of the sort. Note that she feels responsible for the death of her son Phil, for the loss of her daughter Brigid, and for the apparent deterioration of her daughter Lucy."

"Lucianne."

"I stand corrected."

"As to Brigid, I assure her that the child will return eventually, marry an Irish Catholic—arguably a commodity trader—and probably vote Republican before she's thirty-five. But she cannot accept that promise of good news, because her compulsion to punish herself is so strong. So it was with your temporary disappearance."

Two years of hell a temporary disappearance.

"She's much too hard on herself."

"She expects the worst to happen in her life because she believes she deserves the worst. Alas, the course of events tends to fulfill that prophecy."

"Incurable?"

"Nothing some happiness and reassurance that she can be sexually satisfying to a man would not hold in abeyance. I want to emphasize again, Leo, that I am gravely concerned about her. The *persona,* however valid it may be in some important respects, is fraying at the edges. I assume that you thought she was extremely healthy at that rather romantic lunch the other day?"

"I don't know that I'd call it romantic."

Naturally, I did not question that she knew about it. Of course, Jane would tell Maggie all about it.

"A matter of terms perhaps. The question is about her health, mental and physical."

"Candidly, she seemed fine, the vivacious smartass that she's always been."

"I never discuss, as you well know, the emotional condition of my clients or my confidants. So I will not say to you that she's in very grave jeopardy. Nor will I add that it will not take much to push her off the deep end. One more blow."

"If you say so." I sounded dubious.

"The point is that I do not say so. Nonetheless at a more general level where I may speak with less need for artifice, you thought you had plenty of time that night in the Rose Bowl in 1947 when she made you that obscene hot fudge sundae. In fact, you did not. Is that not a correct statement?"

"It sure is."

"Don't commit the same error again."

"Before her birthday, Maggie. Before her birthday."

"A promise?" she said suspiciously.

"An intent."

"Hardly the same thing."

"One more question, Maggie."

"The important one you save as everyone does till the end."

"Who tried to kill me twice?"

Again I assumed she had been told of our reinterpretation of the events.

"I cannot say."

"Cannot or will not?"

"I do not use whatever these creepy powers of mine are, Leo darling," she was soft and sweet, Maggie the old friend instead of Doctor Keenan, "to solve mysteries. My convictions that you were not dead and that Brigid will surface were and are simple and elementary and beyond doubt. Any instincts I might have about the mystery are much more problematic."

"Should I lay off that?"

"I don't know, Lee, I don't know. It may in some sense be necessary to resolve that once for all. I do know that Jane does not have much more time."

"I hear what you're saying."

I really didn't hear it. Not clearly enough. I couldn't comprehend that Jane was as disturbed as Maggie seemed to think she was.

Professors, you see, think they know everything.

1977

Patrick

It was in December of the year before last that I finally realized how much in love with Jane I was. I knew that I'd always loved her. But when she took me to supper at Tuffano's, a little Italian restaurant on Taylor Street, the week before Christmas and told me what was happening to her, my heart flooded with love and I knew that I wanted her as my companion for the rest of my life.

"I want one of those annulment things, Packy," she began in her usual businesslike manner. "Can you swing it?"

"It shouldn't be any problem. But why now?"

Her lips tightened. "My husband wants a divorce. His latest mistress wants to get married. To hear him tell it, I owe him a divorce so she can get on with her life and have the children she wants."

"Wow!"

"So I said fine, so long as he provides evidence for an annulment. That would help wouldn't it?"

"It would help but it's not absolutely necessary."

"At first he didn't want to, but when I made it clear that it was a condition, he agreed. I want to be rid of him, Packy. Permanently rid of him, in the eyes of God and the eyes of the Church, and in the eyes of everyone."

"High time," I agreed.

I told myself that this would force me to make up my mind about staying in the priesthood. Saint Regina's had been a wonderful experience. The old pastor was delighted to see me and the parishioners liked me at once, mostly because I was good to the old man. It was a busy, exciting, challenging, rewarding parish. I loved it and I loved them.

It was also exhausting, especially because I never seemed to find time for a vacation. I told myself that overnights at the Lake were enough. They were for a while. But then I found that I was becoming impatient and irritable.

"Boss, you need to get away from this factory," my young associate told me when I had lost my temper with him.

"I'll spend some time at the Lake this summer," I simmered down, knowing that my exploding at the kid was unjust. "Sorry I blew my top."

"Be my guest," he grinned. "But the Lake will do only if they cut down all the telephone lines."

I don't know when I began to think about leaving the priesthood. Maybe only a year or two ago. But the idea had become a full-blown possibility that night on Taylor Street. If I were to leave as a burned-out case, I should do it when I was young enough to enjoy the rest of life—and now a companion with whom to spend the rest of my life.

Jane had become dependent on me and I on her. When the news came of Philly's death in Vietnam, she called me before she tried to find her husband. She leaned on me during the arrangements for the wake and the funeral. Phil was useless, drunk both nights of the wake and absent at the funeral mass—though he did show up at the cemetery, still drunk.

"I told the stupid punk to keep his head down," he said over and over. "But, no, he knew it all. He never would listen to me. God, what a disappointment he always was."

I felt like slugging him. Jane ignored him, which was the better strategy.

When Brigie ran away from home to join a commune a couple of months after her brother's death, Jane finally lost her cool and sobbed in my arms.

So why not spend the rest of my life with her? I had paid my dues and more than my dues to the priesthood. I'd wait till the annulment was granted and then talk to her about it.

I wondered anxiously what she would say. Might she turn me down? Would I never be anything more than a priest to her?

In the spring of 1977, while we were gathering materials to support her petition for a decree of nullity, my sister-in-law phoned me.

"Packy, you'd never guess who's coming back to Chicago."

I knew instantly and with a sinking heart and guilt for my regret.

"Tell me."

"Leo T. Kelly. *Professor* Leo T. Kelly."

"Who says?"

"Rosie O'Malley. Her husband, Charles E. O'Malley, reports that Leo will be the new provost at the University. And as Rosie said her Chucky Ducky is sometimes in error but never in doubt."

"Interesting."

"Isn't it?"

The next day Leo himself called.

"I've done an interesting thing, Packy." He sounded sheepish. "Maybe an impulsive thing."

"Doesn't sound like a cautious academic to me."

"I've, uh, accepted an invitation to become provost at the University. Effective in September."

"What university?" I said, tongue in cheek.

"You know what university. *The* University."

"You're coming home again?" I said very gently.

"It would seem so. I hope it's not a mistake."

"I'm happy for you, Leo. Very happy."

And I was happy. To hell with ambivalence. My best friend was coming home.

1978

Leo

"Good morning, General," I said to the man at the Pentagon who owed me a favor. "I need a favor."

An Irish Catholic like me, he understood about favors. I had done a favor for him at Chuck O'Malley's request. All in the family. Or at least all in the parish.

"Name it, Leo, and you've got it."

"I'm interested in my records from the United States Marine Corps."

I was calling him from my office in the University, oozing the kind of confidence I should have used to speak to Jane.

"That was thirty years ago, Leo."

"Twenty-five when I was finally discharged."

"That's right."

"Can you get them?"

"It might be a little difficult. We haven't computerized that far back yet, though we're doing a little bit each year. But that medal of yours makes you different. I think we have a special set of files for those who have won it. What are you interested in?"

"Someone who has reason to know tells me that my first orders were not to Korea but to either a carrier or an embassy and that they changed my orders at the last minute."

"That would be unusual."

"So I thought. Would an examination of the file reveal such a change? And the reason for it?"

"Hard to say. It might reveal the fact of such a change. Not likely the reason."

"Good. Could you check it out for me?"

"It'll take a few days, maybe even a week or two, but I'll hunt it down. Why are you so interested?"

"My life would have been a little different if I had not been sent to Korea."

"Yes . . . It's been a very distinguished life, however, has it not?"

"If you say so, Tim. I want to know, nevertheless, if someone has been screwing around with it."

"I guess I understand that. I doubt very much that anything of the sort happened. But, as a favor to you, I'll look into it."

"Great. I'll be looking forward to hearing from you."

He thought I was crazy. In his perspective Korean service, POW, the medal—all made my career distinguished. I should have been happy that someone might have changed my orders at the last minute.

I asked Mae to see if she could find Judge Angela Nicola Burke in her chambers at the Dirksen Federal Building.

Angela was one of the last of the survivors of those summers. Angela and her father. Perhaps she would remember something—if indeed she remembered someone she had not seen or heard from in thirty years.

"Judge Burke is on vacation, Mr. Kelly," Mae informed me. "She'll be back after the 15th of August."

"We'll call her then."

August 15th. The Feast of the Assumption of Mary. Mary's Day in Harvest Time. Jane's birthday. And the day of the accident.

Just thirty years ago this summer.

Mary's Day in Harvest Time

I adorn all the earth.
I am the breeze that nurtures all things green.
I encourage blossoms to flourish with ripening fruits.
I am led by the spirit to feed the purest streams.
I am the rain coming from the dew that causes the
grasses to laugh with the joy of life.
I call forth tears, the aroma of holy work
I am the yearning for good.

—Hildegard of Bingen

Now welcome, somer, with thy sunné softe,
That hast thes wintres wedres overshake
And driven away the longé nightés blake!

Saint Valentin, that art ful hy o-lofte,
Thus singen smalé fowlés for thy sake:
'Now welcome, somer, with thy sunné softe,
That hast thes wintres wedres overshake!'

Wel han they cause for to gladden ofte,
Sith ech of hem recovered hath his make;
Ful blissful mowe they singé when they wake:

Now welcome, somer, with thy sunné softe,
That hast thes wintres wedres overshake
And driven away the longé nightés blake!

—Geoffrey Chaucer

1948

Leo

I see all the summers before 1948 through the prism of that summer, indeed I view all the events of my life, the joys and the tragedies and above all the mistakes through the lens of the sweetness and the sorrow of that eventful two months.

The United States military was in chaos. Congress had forced a merger of the War and Navy Departments into a single Department of Defense and established a United States Air Force, which was independent of both the Army and the Navy. The Navy had fought the merger with all its considerable bureaucratic skills and was still resisting with a fierce guerrilla war inside the new department. The Navy eventually won the battle and internal rivalries have plagued and on occasion paralyzed the Department ever since. The first phases of the battle provided me with a summer off between my junior and senior year, a summer I proposed to use in pursuit of my beloved Jane.

Maybe.

In its preoccupation with fighting the Air Force (which wanted to expropriate all of naval aviation) and the Army (which wanted to abolish the Marine Corps, a good work I must say in retrospect), the admirals had little time to worry about their sagging ROTC programs, which were prime victims of congressional appropriations cutting.

The Loyola program survived but just barely. There was only enough money for two weeks of summer service and that at Great Lakes, not at sea. However, since we were technically still members of the Navy we would receive full salaries but we were not to spend the money on tuition for summer school classes.

None of this made any sense. If we were to be paid, why not give us something to do? However, as the commanding officer of our program put it, "The Navy does things its way and that's the right way."

Yes *sir.*

So I was to have the summer off. With pay. I figured I would pile up a stack of books and devour them in my hot apartment in Rogers Park near Loyola—no air-conditioned apartments for students in those days. I was conscious for the first time of how much I had imposed on the hospitality of the Keenans in previous summers and I vowed I would not do it again.

But I was going to pursue Jane at the same time, wasn't I?

In truth I changed my mind about that subject every day.

Packy, home from the Major Seminary at Mundelein and assigned again to an orphanage north west of Chicago (now in fact a residence for kids from broken families), called me on the phone.

"Summer off with pay, Lee? That's a boondoggle if I ever heard of it. And on tax payers' money."

"I stand ready to protect our republic."

"Yeah, well you can do it just as well up at the Lake. Get your lazy ass over to Northwestern Station and on up here. I'll be around on weekends."

"I don't want . . ."

"No arguments. Anyway, someone has to take care of Jane."

"There's that," I agreed.

So I became a permanent resident at the home of my adopted family that summer.

During the week I had Jane pretty much to myself. Maggie was, as we might have expected, pregnant, and temporarily withdrawn from athletic competition—though I think she deliberately left the two of us alone so that our still shy and tentative romance might blossom. All of our other friends were busy with summer jobs or, in Phil's case, a permanent job. Their mothers spent at least half their time in the city.

So Jane and I were left alone to eat ice cream at the Rose Bowl (where she was now assistant manager), talk about *Cry the Beloved Country* and *The Loved One,* watch Laurence Olivier in *Hamlet* and Orson Wells in *Macbeth,* and sing together "Buttons and Bows," her voice as off-key as ever.

As I remember it—and I know I see the first six weeks through the tinted glass of romantic love—the weather was perfect: warm but not humid, sunny days and cool nights with brief thundershowers towards morning. We played tennis every morning and swam off the Keenan pier every afternoon or evening depending on Jane's schedule. We hiked through the woods of the State Park and discovered together how alive and beautiful nature is in the summer. We held hands and kissed and cuddled in each other's arms and caressed each other's fascinating bodies.

Our passions were stronger than ever, but our affection continued to be focused by respect or fear or some combination thereof. We knew we were being swept along by powerful energies and we did not want to hurt one another.

At night we would often lie in each other's arms on the Keenans' pier and kiss each other tenderly and gently as if we were the only persons alive on earth and our kisses the only activity that mattered.

Jane was my whole life. I think I had become her whole life. My pile of books diminished only slowly. Karl Marx and Max Weber, admirable gentlemen that they were, could not compete with Jane.

We talked endlessly, but most of the words do not come back when I search for them in my memory. Young lovers have much to say, I suppose, and all of it very important to them. However, they can talk all day long and say nothing that would mean much to anyone else.

Yet we did talk about our hopes and our plans for life.

"I don't know what I want to do," Jane sighed one warm afternoon at the edge of a small meadow in the forest with the smell of honeysuckle on the air and lacy white clouds drifting by overhead. "I suppose I'll graduate from college. You were right about that, as you're right about everything, Lunkhead. I do like it, though I don't see much point in it as far as making money goes. At least I'll be able to get a job teaching and support my family if my husband should die."

"I think you're hooked on reading, Jane. That may be the only reason to go to college."

"Maybe."

"Home and family is still your main goal?"

"I think so. I want to do something great besides. I still think I'd like to write. The nun who teaches creative writing says I have some talent, but I'm not sure. There are so many people who want to write. I don't know how much I'd earn."

"Do you have to earn money?"

"Of course, I have to earn money when I work. What's the point of working if it's not for money?"

"For the fun of it?"

"That doesn't make any sense at all. What does fun have to do with it?"

I helped her to her feet and we strolled back to the car, Packy's battered old Lasalle, which was mine during the week since my Ford had gone to whatever reward waits good Fords when they expire of old age.

"Isn't it enough that I want to be a good wife and mother? That's hard work, isn't it?"

"And when your kids are all raised?"

"I'll sit on the porch and sip martinis like Mrs. Nicola and Mrs. Clare."

"No you won't."

"I know I won't . . . Lee, I have big dreams but they're kind of vague. I want to do something important, something that's fun and exciting and glamorous. I just don't have the slightest idea of what it is. Do you think I could do that and still be a good wife and mother?"

"Not a doubt." I took her hand in mine.

"I have time yet."

"You certainly do."

We walked along in the cool silence of the giant trees on either side of the path.

"You're going to graduate school when you get out of the Marines?"

"I don't think I'll ever serve in the Marines, except in the reserves for a couple of years. The rumors are that next summer they won't have enough money to do anything but give us our commissions and put us on inactive duty."

"They'd pay for all your education and you wouldn't owe them any time."

"The way they look at it, the reserves are time."

"That would be wonderful for you."

"It sure would. I could go right into graduate school and finish my Ph.D. in a couple of years."

"I think you'll make a wonderful teacher."

"I hope so. I want to write books too."

"I'm sure you will; and you'll make money on them too . . . do you think you'll have time for a wife and family in all that activity?"

A seeming casual and innocent question, was it not?

"They'll come first, obviously."

"How old do you think you will be when you marry?"

Less innocent and less casual.

"I don't know. I don't think age is the issue. I'll marry when I meet the right girl and she and I think it's the proper time to marry."

"That makes a lot of sense."

So it went. The days and nights flew by. We were both supremely happy. We both knew that by the end of the summer, after many cautious explorations, we would reach an understanding about our future. We both also knew what that understanding would be. What else could it have been?

Our friends appeared on the weekends and kidded us about our dreamy eyes when we were with each other—all except Phil. He continued to invite Jane to dances at the Club and she went with him once or twice when I told her it was all right with me.

The last one I feared was Phil Clare.

I didn't have much time to consider the changes that were occurring in our group. Jim Murray seemed more morose than ever. Phil Clare was proud of his baby sister. Angie Nicola continued to brood over Jim. Eileen was as flighty and fidgety as she always was. I'm sure I engaged in deep and serious conversations with each of them, but I have no recollection of what they said. I had other things on my mind.

I don't think poor Jimmy ever mentioned his affair with Iris. Nor, as best as I can remember, did he seem particularly interested in pretty little Norine Clare.

When Phil and Jane went to the dances, Angie would invite me, I suppose so Jane could keep an eye on me with a date she considered as safe as her own.

Angie and I would kiss and hug at the end of the evening fully aware that we were only exchanging pleasantries and that both our interests were elsewhere.

"Are you going to marry Jane?" she asked me one night as I was driving her home in the clunky, noisy Lasalle.

"Blunt question."

"I'm sorry if it is, but I want to know anyway."

"Should I?"

"You certainly should."

"If you say so, Angie, I guess I might."

She pounded my arm. "Admit it, you're both in love."

"Could be."

"I think it's wonderful."

"We'll have to see what happens."

"I know what will happen."

I thought then that I could be happy with Angie too, but not as happy as with Jane.

When Maggie was at the house, she would always raise an eyebrow or even two when I came in after a session with Jane, but she never asked any questions. I guess she didn't have to.

The older generation continued to seem to have troubles of its own. Iris was drinking again. Doctor Clare, James Murray, and Tino Nicola huddled constantly on the weekends, though I thought that as the summer wore on their worries seemed to fade away and they were enjoying themselves as they had done before that train ride which had so shocked me.

Their wives were now five years older than when I had first seen them, but if they were fading at all it was hard to notice the change. Despite my obsession with Jane, I was still very much aware of their mature appeal. They continued to be restless and odd.

All of these people and events I observed out of the corner of my eye. Most of my attention was focused on Jane—her wit, her laughter, her lovely face, her intelligence, her flawless body, her sense of fun and the funny. I thought about her when I woke in the morning and even more when I was slipping into pleasant dreams at night.

She became more passive and submissive to me. She was still a very tough and strong-willed young woman. Now her strength was focused on me and what I wanted. I had no illusions that she would ever be a pushover.

Even on weekends her role as mistress of the revels seemed to diminish, until I told her that everyone expected her to organize our activities.

"You think I like that?"

I pondered. "You seemed to."

"Someone had to do it."

"It's up to you, Jane."

She kissed me. "You're right as usual, Leo. I should take charge. But not with you. I'll do whatever you want."

"Half the time," I insisted.

"A little less than that," she grinned impishly. "It's all right if you think it's half."

She was, in retrospect, too absorbed in me to pay much attention to anything else. As I was absorbed in her.

It was your classic summer idyll for young lovers, pleasure, fun, obsession, hope.

Finally we had to talk about marriage.

On a night in early August we were lying on the Keenans' pier under the starlight, bundled up in towels against the cool night air after we had climbed out of the water, her head on my thigh, my hand under her swimsuit touching her breast and the hard nipple that had risen to meet my fingers.

"Should we talk about marriage, Jane?"

"Why not?" she said airily. "It's an interesting subject. What aspect of it do you want to discuss?"

"Our marriage."

"Really? Are we going to be married? I didn't know that."

"I think it's a possibility."

"Oh, well that's an interesting notion. You haven't mentioned it before."

"I'm mentioning it now."

"Is this a proposal, Lee?"

I should have said "yes" and that would have been that. Life would have been very different. Instead I said, "It's a proposal that we discuss the prospect like sensible people who won't rush into something precipitously."

Still a long way from my doctorate, I was already talking like an intellectual.

"That seems reasonable," she sighed. "Well, I think you're nice enough to spend a lifetime with, if that's what you mean. You'll require some shaping up, but you'll probably do. It's not that we've just met each other, you know. The only problems I see are our families who won't like it at all."

No time wasted beating around the bush, not a second.

"I worry about them too."

"Your mother thinks I'm worthless Shanty Irish. She'll never like me. I'm not and never will be good enough for you."

"What makes you think that?"

"Megan tells me about your mother."

"She shouldn't."

"Sure she should. The poor kid has to tell someone."

"My mother doesn't run my life, Jane. I've moved out on them."

"But you still love your family. It will be hard to have her against us and your father and your brothers and sisters caught in between. She'll be a great one for creating scenes, I imagine. We'll have scenes as long as she's alive and that's likely to be a long time."

"I don't think it will be that bad."

"Yes it will. You're the one that wanted us to be sensible," she shifted her position and rested her face on my thigh, depriving me of her breast. "I'm not saying that she would control our lives but she will be a problem and we ought not to deceive ourselves about that."

I wanted to be sensible, but I wanted the sensibility to be romantic. My woman was an incorrigible realist.

"Now *my* mother will be even more of a problem. She pays almost no attention to me. She spends a lot of time conniving about my brothers but, being a girl, I'm not worth that much effort. Thank God. She sits at her desk overlooking the Lake all day long and pores over the family books and receipts. She'll call Daddy in Chicago because of a two dollar and a quarter difference in the books. She runs everything they do from up here by phone. She was a sweet and pretty young woman once, lots of laughter and singing, and fun. But now she's, well, I guess the word is avaricious. She's addicted to money the way poor Mrs. Clare is addicted to gin. It's her whole life, nothing else matters. My daddy and my brothers are terrified of her. She pushes them all the time. They'll do anything she wants. Anything. They'd like to relax and settle down and enjoy their success. She won't let them. She tells them what to buy and what to sell and who to order supplies from, even where they can buy the cheapest towels for the washrooms in their gasoline stations."

My love's wonderful body was stiff with rage.

"Jane . . ."

"I'm trying to be sensible. My three brothers are married, as you probably haven't noticed because as far as anyone up here knows, I don't have a family. They never see me with a family unless it's at the seven o'clock Mass on Sunday and then they say what horrible people the Devlins are. Anyway, she picked out the women for each of them and made them pursue the women, all respectable women who will bring respectability to our family. They're nice girls, I suppose, certainly sensible and loyal. They've learned to do what she tells them to do and probably hope that she'll die soon of meanness and greed—and gin because as everyone in the village knows she's a drunk in addition to everything else."

"Jane . . ."

"Money and marriage, that's how the Shanty Irish are supposed to become respectable."

"I don't think you're Shanty Irish, Jane."

"You think my family is. Everyone does. What I'm telling you now shows just how Shanty they are."

"Jane . . ."

"Be quiet until I'm finished being sensible. She is determined, absolutely determined that I should marry Phil Clare. That would crown her search for respectability. No one is more respectable than Doctor Clare."

"That's a very narrow picture of the world."

"I am well aware of it." She pulled away from me and wrapped her towel around herself more tightly. "Nonetheless it is her view. She lets me live up here and work at the soda fountain only because I'm in contact with Phil here. She's too busy to notice what I do with my time and doesn't care enough about me as a person to ask questions. I'm just a piece of goods to trade for respectability."

"How horrible!"

"Oh, I get along. She leaves me alone because she thinks that like the rest of the family I am obedient and therefore I am doing exactly what I'm told. She rarely asks about Phil, only once or twice a month . . . have you wondered why I don't let you pick me up at the door of the house and I let Phil do it when he takes me to dances and the Club?"

"Yes."

"If she sees Phil dressed up in his white flannels and blazer a couple of times a summer, it's enough to keep her happy. She thinks I've about sewed him up and I let her think it. When she finds out I've been deceiving her all these years, she'll hit the ceiling."

"I don't think . . ."

"I'm still being sensible, Lee dear. My brothers do exactly what she tells them to do. So does Daddy most of the time. I deceive her and get away with it. So does he up to a point. He has a woman in Chicago. Nice lady. Polish. If Mom dies first I'm sure he'll marry her. I don't think Mom knows or, if she does know, would care. But she'll care when she finds out that I wouldn't marry Phil if he were the last man in the world."

I drew her into my arms. "My poor Jane."

She pulled away. "I'm all right. I'm just being sensible, that's all. Maybe we can work it out. Maybe not. There are two terrible mothers who will make our lives hell from the day we tell them that we're thinking about marriage until the day both of them are dead. They'll never give up, they won't quit, they'll keep coming after us, and they won't be content until they tear us apart. And there's so much of them in our souls that they'll be trying to tear us apart after they're dead."

"It wouldn't be that bad."

"Yes it would. Worse maybe. Can you imagine a baptism when both of them have given us the respectable name for the new baby and one loses or the other loses. Or maybe, because we're both crazy, the two of them lose?"

"I hadn't thought of that."

Romantic dummy that I was, naturally I hadn't thought of that.

"Well, I have . . . I don't know, Lee. Maybe I should have said these things before. Maybe it would work out. Maybe we can move to South America, though Mom would pursue us wherever we go. I'm glad you wanted to be sensible. We ought to talk about these things. Only I don't think this blissful summer romance will have a happy ending."

"God damn it, Jane. Those two women can't run our lives."

She stood up. "They'll try, Lee. Oh they'll try while there's still a breath of life in them. We'll have to fight them off all the time. If we get tired of the fight, we may get tired of one another . . . take me home now I want to cry myself to sleep."

"I'll never be tired of you, Jane."

"That's what you say now. But it won't take you long to be tired of her. I hate her, Leo, oh, how I hate her, but she has a lot of power over me. I still love her too and feel sorry for her. I'm not sure how long I can fight her off. Otherwise why would I have deceived her about Phil and you for so long."

"Let me digest this, Jane, and we'll talk about it again."

"If you want to," she said wearily. "Please think about it sensibly first, because we will have a war in heaven on our hands if we try to marry one another."

I walked her home and kissed her gently. "We will talk again."

We didn't have a chance to talk again.

What if I had demanded that night that she agree to marry me, regardless of our mothers?

I didn't and in another week, on her twentieth birthday, I lost my chance.

Leo

We never renewed that conversation on the pier. I thought there was plenty of time. In fact, there was almost none.

I can't remember in any specific detail the combat in Korea. The most I have are vague, disconnected, and terrifying memories of the landings at Inchon and Wonsan, the horrible motion sickness, fear, the sound of rifle and automatic weapon fire, the booming of artillery, the screaming of our jets as they came in to cover us, even the feel of the cold, up at Chosin. All of these come back to me in a montage, a kaleidoscope in my dreams. But no details.

However, the two days in mid-August are branded into my memory in rich and precise detail. Even now as I try to sort through those detailed images and put some order into them I cannot make sense out of any of it. It was like forty-eight hours in an evil Wonderland in which the Mad Hatter and the March Hare both turned diabolic.

"No wonder you ran away," a psychiatrist would say to me after I returned from Korea. "Even allowing for exaggeration on your part, it sounds like an interlude in Franz Kafka."

Maggie Keenan, many years after that, said sadly, "I was busy having a baby in Chicago. When they told me what had happened it made no sense at all. It still doesn't."

And Tom Keenan who was listening solemnly to our conversation added, "There was a cover-up going, Leo, from day one. Crooked state and county police. You didn't have to leave, however."

"I know that now."

"Yes, you did have to leave," Maggie insisted. "To save your sanity, you had to leave. You may or may not have been right about what happened— I suspend judgment on that—but as I told them when they finally gave me the details, you should have run."

"I lost a lot."

"I quite agree but you didn't lose it then. You lost it when you didn't come back. Why didn't you come back? Why didn't you call Jane?"

"I tried to call her before we shipped out."

"Two years later. What happened to those two years?"

"I don't know," I said. "I simply thought it was all over."

That was a lame answer. But it's the best I could give then. Or now. I just assumed that what I thought was my disgraceful performance at the police station, my wild accusations, my deliberate insults would have made me a permanent *persona non grata*. I know now that it was an absurd reaction. But it was the way I felt, so powerfully that there seemed to be no reason to question it. Yet the horror of those days affected everything I did until I received orders assigning me to the Fifth Marines.

It all started with Packy's old Lasalle, which was my car for the summer— Packy somehow having come into possession of a new Olds convertible with hydromatic drive as they called it in those days, like his mother's, except a discreet clerical black instead of bright yellow.

The day after Jane and I were "sensible," I noticed that the brakes were loose and didn't grip as they should when I came down the high hill on the gravel road from Warburg that runs from the end of the Lake at the far opposite of the town, through the newer subdivisions and opens up to the road to town where the recent and indifferent asphalt paving, soft and gooey on a hot summer day, begins.

The Old Houses where the very wealthy lived were on small hills of their own, except for the Devlins'. Theirs was at the very top of the large hill, which a glacier had gouged out of the ground ten thousand years ago. The rest of them stretched out for a mile and a half on the north side of the Lake. Each of the homes was approached by an upward grade because the road that ran behind the homes was flat. The "big hill," as we sometimes called it, was high enough and the road flat enough that crude skiing was possible in the wintertime before the county got around to plowing it. It was also, I imagine, great fun for kids on sleds.

In the summertime, when we would venture over to Warburg, ten miles west of the Lake, we used to coast down the hill and see how far we could glide along the flat before having to use the accelerator.

It was a harmless enough game because even if a car was coming from the opposite direction you could see it from a distance and there was room to pass.

Neither Jane nor Packy would accept the crazy suggestion that we race down the hill at full speed to discover whether we might be able to coast all the way to the outskirts of the town. It was, as Jane insisted, just plain silly.

Since we didn't go to Warburg often because, as we said, it was Hicksburg, U.S.A., we didn't use the hill all that much.

Mrs. Keenan, all aflutter about the imminent arrival of her first grandchild, asked me to deliver a package over to the post office at Warburg. It was coming back that I noticed the brakes seemed to be looser than usual. So I drove right into the tiny auto repair station in town.

The mechanic, a slow-talking rural type named Al Winslow with little love for people in the Old Houses, looked at the car dubiously.

"You should be able to afford better than that, kid."

"Family heirloom."

"Well, let's see about those brakes that are worrying you so much."

He pumped them up and down, climbed under the car, muttered a few obscenities, and crawled out again.

"Well, they could stand a little tightening all right, nothing serious, but you probably have to get it done unless you're gonna throw this one away and get a new one."

"How much?"

"Twenty dollars."

"Come on."

"All right fifteen."

I suppose I could have got him down to ten.

"When will it be done?"

"Can't get to it till late today."

As far as I could see there was no car on which he was working.

"What if I come back about this time tomorrow?"

"Yeah, might have it ready then."

So I turned the car over to him and walked back to the Keenan house.

If I missed an appointment with Jane, I could not call to explain it to her because I was strictly forbidden ever to call her home. We understood that she would not hold it against me if I failed to show up. I didn't catch up with her that day, until I found her at the Rose Bowl.

"Sorry, Jane . . . yeah I'll have a massive malt, why not? . . . I had to run an errand for Mrs. Keenan and then the brakes were sorta loose so I brought them in for repair."

"I'll forgive you in a thousand years. I had to play singles with Jimmy and Eileen."

"Are they up here to stay?"

"Two week vacation."

"How are they?"

"Same as ever. He's a drip, she's a dope."

"Jane!"

"I'm a little tired of our friends. Then stupid Phil showed up and wanted to play doubles, me and him against them. I said I had to work. I'm also fed up with stupid Phil."

"He on vacation too?"

"Traders don't get vacations. They take their own time off. He said something about restructuring his capital. He made it sound like a big deal, like he had made some kind of huge killing, but I think he went broke and has to borrow more money from his dad."

"You are not in such a good mood today, kid."

"I was till I met them. Don't worry, I didn't tell them that you and I were going to the Bijou tonight, so we won't have to put up with them."

"I didn't know we were going to the Bijou."

"I didn't tell you either," she grinned, "but I am now. OK?"

"Wonderful."

The Tarzan film that night was something less than wonderful and Jane, my Jane, not the one in the film, was still listless. We walked home quietly and I kissed her good night gently. Tonight was not the night to talk of love.

She told me she had promised that we would meet the Murrays at the tennis courts the next morning at ten for mixed doubles.

"I hope you don't mind, Lee?"

"Not at all. They're our friends and it will be good to see them again."

The next day I picked up the car, paid Al Winslow his fifteen dollars and accepted his receipt, laboriously scrawled out on a half sheet of loose-leaf note paper with his signature at the bottom. I knew Packy would insist on picking up the tab, so I wanted to have documentation.

It might have been a lifesaver for me the next day because it was my way of proving that I had taken care of the brakes. Yet I don't think that mattered. Even without the receipt a decision was made that I didn't matter one way or another.

I drove back to the Keenans' to grab my tennis racket. The Polish woman who was in charge of the place—and found all of us vastly amusing—told me excitedly that Missus go to town for baby.

I responded with the few "happy words" she had taught me in Polish.

I was excited too. If Maggie was my adopted sister that meant I was an adopted uncle.

We played only one set of tennis because the Murrays were planning a trip of some sort with Phil in the afternoon.

"Want to come?" Eileen said. "We'll have a great time. Maybe drink some suds on the way back. Whataya say?"

I'm afraid that the poor kid's notion of a great time in those days was nothing more than drinking some suds.

"I'm working," Jane said, clearly relieved that she could decline.

"I'll stay here to keep Jane company."

"You don't have to," she said glumly.

"I want to."

Eileen giggled at our romance. Jim said nothing at all. During that idyllic summer he hardly opened his mouth.

Thank God, I had an excuse.

"Swim before or after work?"

"After. I'm off at five. At the Keenans'. We can water-ski. You're bound to get the hang of it eventually. Call me at the Rose if you hear anything about Maggie."

The thought of Maggie's baby brought a little more life into her disposition. She still hadn't recovered, I told myself, from her explosion on the pier. I'd wait till she calmed down.

I walked back to the house. My Polish friend greeted me with a vast smile. "Missus call. Young Missus have fine girl child. Both fine. Baby named Maria Margarita."

We hugged each other and sang a Polish song, I phoned the house in River Forest. Packy answered the phone, deliriously merry. "I'm an uncle!"

"And I'm an adopted uncle!"

We chattered happily. Then I told him about the Lasalle.

"Good thing you fixed it. I wouldn't want you and herself banging into a tree. How goes it with her by the way?"

"A difficult period, Pack."

"Oh?"

"We're trying to talk seriously and we encounter the enormous problem of what we do about both our families."

"Ignore them."

"That may well be what we'll have to do eventually, but they won't ignore us."

"You'll beat 'em."

As it turned out we never got the chance.

After I hung up I thought about the Lasalle. Did I see it in the driveway when I came in?

I went to the back door. Sure enough, the car was gone.

"Missus," I asked her, "where car?"

"Young doctor come, borrow car, say he need car, his not work, he bring back, hokay?"

"Hokay Dokay Pannia!"

"Pannia" being Polish for "Mrs."

But it wasn't. We left the keys to the old tub on the front seat because no one would want to steal it. But it was there only for the Keenans and their guests. No one else was supposed to borrow it. What was Phil's rush? He could have waited to ask me. Or even driven by the tennis court.

I would have warned him to test the brakes on the hill as I would have.

Maybe he knew I would say that I couldn't give him permission and I didn't think he should take it on his own authority.

I called the Rose Bowl.

"Rose Bowl Soda Fountain, the best ice cream in the world, Jane Devlin speaking."

"I bring good news, one Maria Margarita Keenan. Mother and daughter doing well."

"Maggie knew it would be a girl! How wonderful! How much did she weigh?"

"Maggie?"

"No, Lunkhead, little Maria!"

"I didn't ask, Milady."

"Typical man. Pick me up at five o'clock?"

"Can't. Phil borrowed the Lasalle."

"With your permission?"

"He didn't ask."

"Typical. All right, I'll be there about five fifteen and today you're going to master the water-ski thing, right?"

"Right!"

And I did.

We had a glorious time on the Lake—it was long before there was a rule about a third skier in the boat, then went back to the house, ate a couple of Missus' "good Polish sandwiches, ain't it?" and went back for more swimming as the sun set and the harvest moon rose in the east.

"You know what day tomorrow is?"

"Feast of the Assumption of Our Lady, Mary's day in Harvest Time, August 15, a Holy Day of Obligation."

"And?"

"A day on which all Catholics must attend Mass under pain of mortal sin."

"*And?*"

"A certain young woman's birthday."

I reached in the pocket of my beach robe and produced a box.

"*OOOOH!*" She ripped it open. "A peridot pendant, my very own birthstone."

Tears poured down her cheeks and she hugged me fiercely. "Thank you so much!"

"It's not very big."

And I could barely afford it but after sponging off the Keenans all summer I had a little extra money.

"You're so thoughtful, Lee, so thoughtful. No one ever gave me a birthstone before."

As I write these words, I am furious at myself that it was not a ring. It would not have had to have been an engagement ring. Just a small peridot. A promise for the future.

So many regrets, so very many regrets.

We went back into the house, changed to dry clothes, made more congratulatory calls to Chicago, and listened again to the "Kiss Me Kate" album. Jane insisted that we sing along—a hard task for me distracted as I always was by her off-key voice.

It didn't bother her. Never did.

Then she said, "Walk me home, Lee, I want a good night's sleep before my nineteenth birthday."

"Big party tomorrow?"

"Not with the family. My mother probably won't remember it's my birthday. We don't have time for celebrations. Besides they cost us too much."

So I walked her home, wished her a happy birthday, and kissed her good night, the last kiss until Memorial Day of 1978.

Jane

Mary, my mother, my real mother in heaven, I failed him. I let her drag me away from him when he needed my help. He's too hurt and too shocked to realize what they're trying to do to him. Mr. Keenan won't let them. But he's not here. I'll call their house in River Forest in another hour or so and beg him to come right up.

That doesn't change it, my heavenly queen, I failed him. I know that I'll never see him again. I lost him tonight.

No, that's not true. He'll forgive me because he is so good.

I didn't know that Mom was on to us and watching us all summer. When she heard me rush out of the house and looked out the window and saw I was in my pajamas, she thought I was rushing out to make love to him.

She knew I had been seeing him. She hit me and shouted, "What are you doing, young woman, in public in your pajamas with that trash? You have disgraced our family and all I've worked my fingers to the bone for."

I tried to explain that Phil was in the car and he had saved Phil's life.

She slapped me again. "You're a goddamn liar. I know what you've been up to," she said. "I've known it for a long time. You went out to make love with him."

"I came back to call the police about the wreck and put on my clothes."

"After you laid him!" She hit me with a broom handle. "Trash!"

I wish that was the reason I went out and not the death of my two friends. Mom seemed utterly unaware of the wreck. She had seen only me and Leo.

As I lay on the floor trying to protect myself from her blows, she hit me again and again with the broom. There was no point in fighting back. There never was.

Finally she stopped. "There, that should teach you. Never speak to that trash again."

She poured herself a glass of gin and drained it in a single gulp.

I dragged myself here to my room to pray for Eileen and Jim. Dear God, I can't believe it. They're not dead. They can't be.

I didn't deserve Leo. I never deserved, him. I am not good enough for him. But I do love him. Since I can't take care of him, please, you take care of him. On this my birthday and your feast day and the most unhappy day of my life I offer all my sufferings for the rest of my life to you so that you will take care of him.

I also want to pray for poor Jim and Eileen. I can't believe they're dead.

Grant them peace and happiness. And even poor dumb Phil who killed them.

By rights, I should be dead.

Ask your son to forgive all my sins.

Amen.

Leo

"You were drunk and you were driving the car," Sheriff Black insisted, "admit it and we'll stop hitting you."

"I wasn't in the car," I muttered through swollen lips. "I didn't kill anyone."

Omer, the little cop, giggled happily and hit me again.

I had been in the lock-up in the crumbling old nineteenth century Warburg County courthouse for hours, I had lost track of how long and couldn't focus on the clock on the wall. There were no Miranda rights in those days. Rural cops thought that they were perfectly within their rights to beat a suspect into a confession.

Thirty years later I think I can understand the whole Kafka-like scene. By then the cops knew that I was not in the car. Or at least Joe Miller had told them and they perceived it in some dim fashion. But they were under enormous pressure to solve the deaths, both from the people in the Old Houses and from those shadowy forces that were also at work. They wanted a confession from me so they would have some breathing space, even if later, in the next day or two, they would have to release me. Moreover, they had a rare opportunity to take out their resentment against someone from the Old Houses, someone who didn't quite have the protection other kids did. Finally they enjoyed beating people up—a pleasure many cops indulged in during those days before the Miranda ruling. I think this final explanation accounts for the brutality of the beating.

That model at any rate seems to fit the data.

At first they had locked me in a dark cell in which the stench of urine filled the air and left me there to wonder what they would do. There were no formalities, no filing of charges.

"We're going to beat it out of you, punk," Omer laughed. "We're going to make you confess and we're going to have fun doing it."

My handcuffed hands, useless and tortured appendages, felt like they were about to fall off my arms. I wished I could loose them so the pain in them would no longer be mine. My head throbbed, my body was burning with fever. I could hardly remember who I was and what had happened.

Then they had dragged me out of the cell, sat me in a chair in the sheriff's dusty, humid office; while the two state cops had watched, Sheriff Black and Omer smashed their fists against my head and body. All four of them had laughed enthusiastically as the county cops beat me unconscious, threw water on me, and started in again.

Hope that Tom Keenan would appear and save me had long since faded. But my determination for revenge had not diminished. I would get these phonies if it was the last thing I ever did.

They had taken my wallet and removed my Navy I.D. card.

"This fucker ain't no fucking Marine," the sheriff chortled, "he's a fucking midshipman whatever that is."

"A fucking midshipman!"

"Hell, he ain't gonna need this shit, not where he's going," the sheriff howled with glee and tossed the card into his wastebasket.

As the day wore on I began to believe that maybe I had been the driver and maybe I had killed my friends.

"How much did you have to drink?" The big cop punched me in the head.

I almost passed out again.

He hit me once more. "Answer me, fuck face, how much booze did you have?"

"I wasn't drinking."

The little cop hit me in the stomach. "You did drive the car?"

"I was not in the car."

"You knew the brakes were no good, didn't you?"

"Winslow fixed the brakes!"

"Funny, he doesn't seem to remember it."

The little cop hit my burned hands. I screamed with agony.

"Don't like that, do you now? I'm asking one last time, are you ready to confess that you killed your two friends?"

"Go to hell!" I shouted.

Still stubborn, still mean, still plotting revenge.

The door of the sheriff's office burst open and five more people pushed in—the Murrays and Dr. and Mrs. Clare and Phil who seemed none the worse for wear.

"He killed my babies," Martha Murray jumped on me and tore at my face with her fingernails. "I want him dead, do you hear me, I want him dead! Kill the bastard!"

Jim Murray jabbed weakly at me with his fists. "You filthy, murdering trash," he wailed, "I'll see you in hell!"

I tried to kick at both of them but my feet would not move.

"Maybe we ought to stop it," one of the state police muttered.

"Hell," the sheriff snorted, "he's got it coming."

"Stop it!" a voice at the door commanded. "Stop it this minute!"

Tom Keenan. And Packy, his eyes blazing with fury. I became light-headed again and almost fainted. I tried to focus my eyes to see if Jane was with them.

She was not.

Packy jumped across the room and pulled the Murrays off me, hurling them back against a wall. Omer approached Packy, saw the look in his eyes and his clenched fists, and backed off.

"Release him at once," Tom ordered.

"Well, Mr. Keenan, sir," the sheriff laughed nervously, "we can't quite do it. You see sir he drove the car last night . . ."

"You're a crook, sheriff, we all know that. You think you control the justice system in this county. I don't care what venal things you do. But when you assault one of my guests, you run the risks of publicity in the Chicago newspapers to say nothing of suits that will destroy you. I said release that boy and release him now."

"He killed my babies," Mrs. Murray moaned.

"Martha," Tom turned on her, "you have my sympathies, but your pain does not excuse this injustice. Leo was not in the car."

"We think he was," the sheriff said uncertainly.

"Louie, I tried to tell you last night," Officer Joe Miller had appeared next to Tom, "this kid wasn't in the car. I saw him walking down the road with the Devlin girl not five minutes before. He burned himself trying to save the people that were in it."

"Faulty brakes," the sheriff grunted.

"He had Winslow fix them yesterday."

"Winslow says he didn't."

"We have a receipt," Tom held up the piece of paper. "We have the testimony of witnesses that Philip Clare IV borrowed my car without permission yesterday afternoon, that Leo Kelly was not in the car, that he had seen to the repair of the brakes, and that the car was seen driving at a high rate of speed before it careened down the hill."

"Well," the sheriff temporized, "we have a crime on our hands here and we've got to find out who's responsible."

I was a spectator watching this confrontation from a great distance. I did notice, however, the tense worry on Doctor Clare's face. I began to understand some things. Phil seemed mildly bored. I'd fix him.

"This young man saved a life last night. Either you release him this minute or I'll put a call through to my friends at the *Chicago Daily News*."

The sheriff worked his large jaw thoughtfully. "Well, we might release him, seeing as how Joe here tells us now he wasn't in the car . . ."

"I told you that last night, you crazy fool, only you were too drunk to listen."

"Shut up, Joe. Omer, release this punk. We may want to talk to him later."

Omer gave my hands one last twist as he opened the cuffs. I screamed.

Packy would have hit him if his father had not reached out a commanding hand. "I don't propose to forget any of this, Sheriff, even if we don't sue you and don't turn the Chicago press on you, you'll never be re-elected, I promise you that."

I struggled to my feet, intoxicated with pain and rage. I jabbed my finger at Phil Clare. "You killed them, you drunken bum! You took the car, you got drunk, you drove too fast, you knew the crash was coming, you jumped out and escaped. I saved your life while they burned to death. You're the murderer and you stand there hiding behind your rich father and your adulterous mother while they beat me!"

"Tom Keenan," Jim Murray bellowed, "you won't get away with this. I'll kill this bastard with my own bare hands. You'll not soft talk him out of it."

Martha Murray was wailing hysterically. "My babies! My babies! He killed my babies!"

She meant me, not Phil.

Mean, stubborn, half-mad and still speaking in crude periodic sentences, I raged on.

"I didn't kill them, you goddamn fool. Your friend Dr. Clare's son killed them. Just because I'm not rich and he is, you can't get away with blaming me."

"Leo," Tom said softly, "stop it, please."

"My mother's no whore!" Phil sprung into action and smashed his fist against my face.

It was a weak blow from a weakling. And a mistake too. Packy threw him against the opposite wall.

"I should have let you die, fucker!" I yelled. "I shouldn't have ruined my hands pulling you out of the car. You deserved to die with them."

"Leo!" Tom Keenan's voice was peremptory. "Please stop!"

I ignored him.

"You're all up to something crooked," I shouted. "There were thousands of dollars of counterfeit money in that car. Phil, you were bringing it back from somewhere. That's why you had to borrow my car. You had to pick it up yesterday. You're a cheap crook and a killer, just as much as your mother is a whore."

"There was no money in the car," one of the state cops said nervously. "We didn't find a thing."

"I saw you take it out this morning, coming home from Mass. You said they were real good fakes."

"Leave it, Leo," Tom begged me. "It's not our fight."

He was right. I was making a fool out of myself.

"Phil Clare is a drunk, and a thief, and a killer!" I yelled. "And his father is a phony and his mother is a whore. You're letting them all get away with murder."

The Murrays were cringing in the corner of the room, in their grief unable to understand the scene I was creating.

Doctor Clare, his thin face white and tight, his nostrils flaring, strode up to Tom Keenan.

"I've never liked you, Keenan, and you've never liked me," he spoke in the measured, disciplined tones of a doctor in an operating room. "I warn you that if you don't shut this piece of filth up I will destroy you."

Tom stared at him from his six feet two inches of towering strength. "You're incapable of destroying anyone, Phil. Don't mess with me."

"My wife and my son have been calumniated. I hold you responsible for it. You have brought this trash into our lives. It's typical of your pinko values. Get him out of here now."

Tom considered him thoughtfully. "You'd have a hell of time proving calumny, Phil. A hell of a hard time. Come on, Leo, let's leave these fools to their folly."

"They're covering up murder," I shouted. "He killed Jim and Eileen because he wanted the money for himself. He deliberately caused the accident."

The office was dead silent for a moment. Phil ducked behind his father. The eyes of the various cops shifted nervously. Packy's fists were still clenched. He desperately wanted to hit someone.

And I had hit pay dirt. Or close to pay dirt.

"That's a pretty wild charge, son," the sheriff said mildly.

"Come on, Leo," Tom insisted, "it's not our fight."

Packy helped me out of the office, down the steps of the courthouse, and into the Keenan Packard.

"Take us home, Alvin," Tom said with a sigh to the chauffeur. "You may be right, Leo. There certainly is a cover-up of some sort, but I don't think we can prove it. If we could, perhaps we should. But, as we can't, I don't think it's our fight. Let's get you some medical care."

"I think I should go to the hospital at Great Lakes. My dog tags are in my bag. They'll get me in."

"If that's what you want," Tom said mildly.

"I'll drive you in," Packy offered.

Back at the house he helped me find my dog tags and pack my bag. "You'll be coming back, won't you, Leo?"

"Not this summer."

"I guess I understand that. Do you want to say good-bye to Jane?"

"No."

I did say good-bye to "Missus" and a few words of thanks in the Polish she had been teaching me. I thanked Tom for coming to my rescue, congratulated him on being a grandfather, asked to remember me to the others, and promised that I'd see them soon in Chicago.

"You did well, son, under terrible pressure."

"Maybe."

"We'll see how it sorts itself out."

"I don't want any part of it any more, Mr. Keenan."

I had made a fool out of myself. Even if there were worse crimes than drunken driving and vehicular homicide, I had no proof. I should not have called Iris a whore, even if we all knew she was. I also knew that I would not return to the Lake for a long, long time—if ever.

"I hope you want part of us."

"Sure," I grinned. "You won't be able to get rid of me."

"And you won't be able to get rid of us," Packy said grimly.

The three of us knew, however, that our summers were finished. If I ever came back, it would be in the deep distant future.

They patched me up at Great Lakes; and, after a couple of days of observation, let me go back to Loyola. The scars on my hands are almost invisible now.

I did stay in touch with Packy. Or he did with me. He told me all the news. The Murray kids were buried amid much weeping from St. Mary's parish in Lake Forest. Joe Miller was elected sheriff. Maria was a delight. No charges were brought in the Murray deaths, which were ruled accidental. The Murrays sold their home at the Lake. Jane seemed like a lost child.

"You've got to come back next summer," he insisted.

"Maybe."

I was angry at the cover-up and ashamed of my outburst. I had acted like an injured child instead of an adult male.

"You were not yet an adult male," my therapist told me years later. "Why put such demands on yourself. Surely no one of any consequence remembered your behavior or judged you by it. The doctor was not the whole community."

He was right. Now I am told that I am remembered from those times as a hero.

Indeed, during my final year of college I had already begun to realize that perhaps I had exaggerated the importance of the scene in Warburg. Perhaps. Perhaps I should try again. There was always Jane, was there not? The beautiful princess imprisoned in a tower by the wicked witch of the west? Was there not a good witch of the east to help me?

Yet I could not go back to the Lake or to Jane in the summer of 1949. I graduated from Loyola, *summa cum laude* (not even *summa* satisfied my mother). The Defense Department commissioned me a second lieutenant in the United States Marine Corps and assigned me to inactive duty. I enrolled in graduate school at the University and prospered. The academy was where I belonged. What I couldn't achieve there by intelligence and hard work, I could achieve by glibness and guile.

During the spring of 1950, I thought often of Jane (whom Packy no longer mentioned in his increasingly infrequent phone calls). I also thought of how much the Keenans meant to me. I had never seen Maria, never congratulated Maggie, who was now expecting a second child and finishing up her college work. I had been told I'd receive orders to a European post in late June. Why not return to the Lake to say farewell to my old friends and, maybe, to Jane too?

Then Kim Il Sung sent his armies across the 38th parallel and my orders were to the Fifth Marines. I knew the mortality rates in combat of second lieutenants and assumed that I would come back in a casket, a pessimistic prediction, which fitted my mood in those days. I would not burden anyone with heartache over my death.

With an icy feeling of doom in my stomach, I called Packy, home for another summer from the seminary, the first time I had initiated the phone conversation since August 15, 1948.

"I've been given my orders, Pack."

"Paris?"

"Western Pacific."

"Korea?"

"Most likely."

"Good God!"

"I was thinking of coming up to say good-bye until the orders came. Now there won't be time."

"Yeah. Well, we'll see you when you get back."

"If I come back."

"You will come back."

"I don't think so."

"Call Jane."

"I will."

And I did. No answer.

After I recovered from my POW traumas and got on with my life, I stayed in touch with the Keenans in later years, sometimes sporadically, sometimes less so. I saw Maggie and Jerry again and became "Uncle Lee" to their kids. When I traveled through Chicago I would usually call them from the O'Hare madhouse. I'd eat a meal with them when the political science meetings were in Chicago, although Emilie found them "tiresome" and would not join us for lunch or dinner. I talked to Packy when I was in Rome and signed on as a member of his extended parish.

We almost never talked about Jane. What was there to talk about?

They did tell me that Ita had died just before I came home from the POW camp—a long death from cancer during which she blamed her children for her illness and cursed them literally to her dying breath.

May she rest in peace.

Joe Devlin remarried within the year and lived five more years, like Herbie dying before he was sixty.

I still don't know why I did not try to talk to Jane again during the two years between the wreck and my orders to Korea. As I try to figure out what was going on in my head then, I think I was on automatic pilot, nursing my hurt and my humiliation—as I saw it—and thinking that in a year or two I could straighten it out. I was not angry at her because she wasn't around when I needed her. I knew what her mother was like. I guess I still loved her. No, I know I still loved her. Maybe I thought that I had more time, that I could renew our love after I graduated, and that it would take a couple of years for the memories of those terrible days and nights to simmer down, both inside me and in the community at the Lake. I didn't have the time.

Thus did that part of the story end.

1978

Patrick

The Pope is dead. I regret all the bad things I've said and thought about him. In his own way he was a nice man. In his presence you could not help but feel his gentle appeal. He was very kind to me when I met him with Mom and Dad at a private audience—and particularly nice to them—though he must have known I was on the other side.

He made a terrible mistake but he meant well. We are all so limited. I'm in no position just now to judge anyone. I don't think that I've done anything to stand in the way of a new beginning for Leo and Jane. But my ambivalence and jealousy are both very strong. I want them both to be happy and I see that as they spar with each other they are happier than they have been in a long time.

I want to be happy too. I don't want to lose Jane.

Which statement proves how daft I am. She's not mine to lose.

My hunger for her is worse than ever. I want her in bed with me, more than I've ever wanted anything in my life. Lust, I suppose. Terrible lust. Yet I still think I would be a good husband. After a couple decades in the priesthood, I know the damn fool mistakes men make with women and I wouldn't make any of them. I'd be tender and kind and sensitive. I'd never make fun of her.

Whom am I trying to kid? How many of my married classmates have made good husbands?

Not all that many.

Anyway, true to his indecisiveness to the end, the Pope, poor man as Maggie would say, backed off on getting rid of our sociopathic Cardinal. He called Baggio at Fumicino Airport in Rome at the last minute and told him that the whole program depended on the Cardinal's voluntary acceptance. Baggio had a big shouting match with the Cardinal up at the House on the Hill at the seminary. I would have loved to have heard that!

Now the new Pope will be saddled with the problem. We need more than a new Pope. We need a whole new structure for the Church so it is not run by men who will sell their souls, such as these may be, for a place in the Papal power elite.

August 15 is Jane's birthday. And the anniversary of the accident. I don't see how she and Leo can resist the drama and the sentiment of that day.

Leo

The day before my mid-August trip up to the Lake was a frantic one. I took the South Shore downtown to buy a peridot ring for Jane. It was not a grossly expensive present, but the stone was substantially bigger than the one in the pendant I had given her long ago and which she had probably long since lost. I was supposed to meet Laura at O'Hare at three thirty and thus get a head start on the weekend traffic.

I confess to considerable unease at the prospect of my sexual encounter with Jane. I was less afraid that she might reject me than I was uncertain of my own behavior in the critical moments. The naked body of a woman, simultaneously glorious and earthy, is a delight, a challenge, and a terror. Wedding night folklore pays little attention to a man's fears, but John Ruskin, the English writer, was not the only man to be vanquished by the sight of his undressed bride. I did not think I would go Ruskin's route, but I was less than confident about my performance—should we get that far.

The Feast Day was on Sunday this year and in any case it would not have given us a long weekend—though Laura had announced that she didn't care, she was going to take a long weekend anyway. I had tentatively scheduled an extra day for myself too.

So I had two days' work to clear off my desk in a half day of office time with delightfully obscene fantasies and fears of embarrassment contending in the sub-basements of my brain. Normally that would not have been a problem, not if I avoided conversations with various faculty worriers or malcontents, my principal activities during the summer it seemed.

It is a rarely violated rule that professors never come to the point in the first half hour, a trait they share with Irish politicians.

Unfortunately for my plans, the faculty malcontents and worriers crawled out of the woodwork that day, as did some of the rarely noticed crazies. I don't mean crazy like all of us academics are a little mad (maybe everyone else in the world is too), but truly crazy.

Then there was the call from my friend at the Pentagon.

"Leo, Tim."

"Yeah, Tim."

"We found the damnedest thing in your jacket."

"Oh?"

"You never went to Korea."

"I thought it was all a dream."

"The orders they cut for you in July 1950 are there in the file. Paris. Assistant to the naval attache. You ought to be a general today instead of a provost. You might have my job."

"I doubt it." My stomach was churning in excitement.

"You don't happen to have a copy of your orders to the Western Pacific, do you?"

"Somewhere."

"Would you mind sending them to me, not a copy you made, but the orders you originally received."

"I think I can dig them up."

"We know who actually went to Paris. Very prominent man in the Corps today. He won't like us poking around in his past, but that's his problem."

"You pull his jacket yet?"

"Nope. We've got to get authorization to do that, but we'll get it. What do you think we'll find?"

"His orders to the Western Pacific?"

"I wouldn't be in the least surprised . . . it doesn't follow that he knows anything about this. He's not the kind of man we'd normally suspect of such a trick. But you never know."

"I see."

"We have to go after it now, Leo, whether you want us to continue or not. This could have been a major crime, even if the statute of limitations has expired. You will send us your orders?"

"You bet your life."

My guess was that the general, who as a young man went to Paris instead of me, was innocent. I still had no clue, however, as to who would have the power to change my orders. No, it wasn't a change. It was a forgery of new orders.

My head had been whirling with images of the summer of 1948 during the past several days. Again I felt like a pawn who had been maneuvered around the chess board of life by the rich and powerful at the Lake. I began to wonder about the possibility that two events had combined in accidental concatenation on that hot August night—an attempt to kill me and an attempt to bring money from the Mob or their financial backers either to Dr. Clare or Mr. Murray. Both projects had backfired, perhaps because they were not related. Or maybe they were related because the same people were involved but the projects were different. Thus perhaps Tino Nicola had decided for reasons of his own to dispose of me and Jim Murray and Phil Clare sent their sons to pick up the money and the latter took the wrong car. It was a reasonable model. All I had to do was to prove it—and then link it to my changed orders. Nicola had the clout to do that too, didn't he?

Alternately, Ita Devlin certainly wanted to get rid of me so that Jane would marry Phil. But would she go so far as murder? And where would she get the clout with the Pentagon?

Rich people determined to have their own way and to destroy any poor kid who happened to get in their way. My old social class paranoia.

I understood now that they were not really rich or powerful, not by the standards of the truly rich and powerful. Nonetheless I had been their pawn.

I also understood that I should have been in contact with Jane after our lunch at the Cape Cod Room, on the phone at least if not in person. My old fetish about our relationship being confined to the Lake was absurd now that both our mothers were dead.

Yet I wanted to resolve our past and begin our future on site, a silly and romantic notion like the yellow-green stone that was burning a hole in my jacket pocket.

Also part of my character defect of postponing final decisions if I possibly could.

I shuffled through one of my file cabinets while I talked on the phone with a certifiable faculty crazy, the kind of man whose subjects and predicates fit together but whose sentences don't cohere one with another.

I found my file of "memories"—degree from Loyola, commission, various sets of orders, the citation for my medal—while I listened to the man babble. I could put him on hold and he would continue to babble. Sure enough there was my assignment to the Fifth Marines in the Western Pacific, a death warrant, so to speak.

I pulled it, waved to Mae in the outer office and whispered to her, my hand on the phone, "make a copy of this and send it to my friend at the Pentagon. Send the original and give me the copy."

She nodded in agreement.

While the madman raved on, I tried to find some coherence in the images that had rampaged through my mind during the past weeks, some meaning to the bizarre events of my first summer life at the Lake. Sometimes I thought I briefly saw a pattern and then I lost it.

I also fantasized about Jane. She would turn fifty on Sunday. I resolved that she would be mine that day or perhaps even the day before. Or the night before that. This time there would be no evasion. I would no longer tolerate evasion.

Big talk, I told myself. You may not do anything at all this weekend.

You're the one who is evading. Why haven't you called her, coward?

If you evade again, you'd be a damn fool. You just say to her, Jane I won't wait any longer. She'll cave in right away.

Would she really?

Probably.

Maybe.

Who knows?

What would she be like in bed? Her marriage to Phil could not have been a very useful training camp in lovemaking. Well, that didn't matter, I was no prize either as far as that went.

Maybe together . . . and besides there were some things that would be interesting experiments which I had never tried with Emilie . . .

I finally got rid of the pest and ordered my fantasies to leave me alone. I had work to do.

Laura's plane from Boston was an hour late. We were caught in the Friday afternoon rush to the countryside.

"Hi, good looking," I greeted her.

She was wearing jeans and a T-shirt and looked dazzling, to my admittedly prejudiced eyes.

"*Daddy!*" She wrapped he arms around me. "You look like totally happy!"

"Do I?"

"Have you talked to Jane lately?"

Never a moment's respite. "Well, not in the last couple of weeks."

"*Shame* on you!"

"We'll see her this weekend."

"*Big* deal," she sniffed.

I was in trouble.

"How is your mother?" I asked her when we got into my Volvo.

"Same as always."

"Which means?"

"Sad, lonely, angry, pathetic."

"So."

"It's not your fault, Daddy. You did your best."

"Did I?"

"No one," she said judiciously, "ever does their *total* best, but even if you did, it wouldn't have made any difference. You did more than most men would."

"She was so sweet and so fragile when we first met, Laura."

"Terrible need to dominate by preying on your sympathies."

"Uh-huh. Sounds like something Aunt Maggie might say about someone."

"She might even say that she's a lot like your own mother."

"She might indeed . . . are you planning on being a therapist like Aunt Maggie?"

"Probably."

"I'll be surrounded."

"That would be good for you."

"Maybe."

"Her birthday is this weekend."

"Sunday."

"You *did* remember."

"I'm not completely senile."

"Buy her a present?"

"Yes."

"What?"

"None of your business!"

She clapped her hands and laughed.

"Is it anything I can see?"

"It's not an engagement ring, little Miss snoopy!"

She laughed again.

Well, not exactly an engagement ring.

Jane

Fifty years old. I don't feel that old. Maybe I don't look that old. As I see myself naked in the mirror I think I am still a pretty good prize for a man. No, an excellent prize.

Even better, there is a man who thinks I'm the greatest prize in the world.

I took off those extra five pounds so I'd look really sleek for him. He probably won't notice, but that's all right. I'll know. If he does make love to me, I promise I'll never put them on again.

I better get in the shower. Shouldn't have dirty thoughts about myself.

Thirty years ago this week we talked about marriage. Sensibly, we said. Stupidly, I'd say now.

Hum. The shower feels good. I must look my best and smell my best for him. All he'll have to say this weekend is that he won't take no for an answer. I'll surrender. I want to surrender. And if he doesn't try, I'll go after him. Lee, my dearest, haven't we waited long enough?

Will I really do that?

I don't know. I just don't know.

I might.

I become horny even thinking about it.

I'm entitled to a little happiness am I not?

He's such a romantic, he's probably put everything off till this weekend. Anniversaries, a couple of them. He wants to redo the past. That's fine but it's the future that matters.

The son of a bitch hasn't talked to me for almost a month! What the hell is he up to?

I wish he'd let go of the past. Maybe he's right, maybe we have to get rid of the demons, maybe we should destroy those who have treated us like pawns. But they can't take away our future happiness if we make up our minds that we will be happy, come what may.

I'm afraid. I've always been afraid. I'm not much of a lover, I know that. I'll disappoint him. But he's a kind person. He'll help me improve, won't he?

I should get out of the shower now.

My delight is mixed with terror, my terror with delight.

I hope Lucy doesn't act up.

Lucianne as she wants to be called.

Even if the mirror wasn't steamy, I'd still look pretty good. If I were a man I think I'd want me.

We both want each other. Please God, please Mary the Mother of Jesus, help us this time not to blow it.

Leo

"Lucianne is, like a total asshole," my daughter announced to me.

"Really?" I looked up from Barbara Tuchman's *A Distant Mirror,* a libelous attack on our ancestors of the fourteenth century. Someone was playing Mozart piano music on the stereo in the Keenan ballroom.

"I go, Lucianne you are suffering from a terminal case of assholeism."

I closed the book. There were perhaps more serious issues at stake than Ms. Tuchman's arrogance.

"I see."

"I mean, she really blew it this time, you know?"

When dealing with Laura's generation, you must become accustomed to listening to a number of highly charged symbolic statements before they are able to tell you what is really troubling them.

"She, like, took her mother's brand new Mercedes out and totaled it."

"Is she all right?" I said anxiously.

We had arrived at the Keenan compound, for such it was now, late for supper. Maria Reilly, the oldest of the grandchildren, had welcomed us.

Maria was a tall slender woman with her father's height and fair skin and her mother's auburn hair, gray eyes, and whimsical smile. In her arms squirmed her own happy girl child, Margaret, known to the young people as "Maggie Two."

"Hi, Uncle Leo, welcome! Everyone is out somewhere. You know what it's like here on summer weekends. Laura, Jamie, and Roger, and Lucianne are around somewhere looking for you."

"Great!" Laura had bounded out.

"Shouldn't you eat some supper, Laura?"

"I ate on the plane," she shouted as she thundered out the door.

"There's some sandwiches in the fridge," Maria had continued, "and blueberry pancakes or just plain blueberries for cream or ice cream."

"Fine. Happy birthday, by the way!"

"Thank you, Uncle Leo, I don't feel like I'm thirty."

"I hope I look as good as you do when I'm thirty, Maria. By the way, I found this box on the road and I thought I might give it to you."

I gave her the Chanel Number 5 I had purchased at Fields at the same time I had bought the ring for Jane.

"Oh, Uncle Leo, how thoughtful! Do you mind if I don't open it till the birthday party for me and Jane tomorrow evening?"

"Am I invited?"

"Of course you are . . . how very sweet to remember." She had kissed my cheek.

Nice old uncle.

I was not likely to forget the day of her birth, August 15, 1948. Not ever.

I had put on white slacks, running shoes, and a University sweatshirt and found the ham and cheese sandwiches, the blueberry muffins, and the plain old blueberries and efficiently disposed of them, the latter with a large scoop of ice cream—from the Rose Bowl of course.

I then had settled down on the porch with my book and a glass of cognac and Mozart (Alfred Brendel playing, I thought) and a light breeze to keep me company.

It was too late and I was too tired to take on Jane tonight. Tomorrow would be plenty of time.

Then Laura burst in upon my peace with her tidings of doom.

"Well, like she's under observation at the Warburg hospital and maybe has a brain concussion and her eyes are really black and she looks totally terrible."

"Nothing worse?"

"The doctors say she'll be out in a day or two and poor Jane really lost it."

"Oh?"

"Yeah, like she went into orbit. I never saw her do that. She's usually so cool. She was like hysterical. Jamie was worried about her. Really."

"Jamie?"

"We like found the car where she had driven it into the ditch and took her to the hospital and Jamie goes to me like you'd better call her mother, so I did and she lost it even then."

Slowly the story was emerging, backward perhaps but not without a certain vividness of narration.

"You found her?"

"And like, Daddy, she isn't even legal yet."

Laura was striding up and down impatiently, like her father has been known to do when he's upset.

"No driver's license?"

"And she'd been drinking too. Not too much but you could smell beer on her breath."

"If you did something like that I would like go into orbit too."

"Not the way Jane did," my daughter said firmly. "I mean she really lost it."

"I see."

"We wanted to drive her home, but she goes, no she can drive herself, so Jamie goes we'd better follow her, because she looks like she might kill herself."

"Jamie is a therapist too?"

"No, he's going to be a priest* . . . but I think he's right. Daddy, she

---

* *The Cardinal Virtues*

was like totally incoherent . . . and Aunt Maggie says that she's been on the edge for a long time. Years."

"That's what Aunt Maggie says?"

Laura nodded vigorously. "And she's always *right*, you know that."

"So I've been told."

"She was really terrible, Daddy. I mean Lucianne is a total asshole and they already lost poor Brigid, but like she was more mad at herself than at Lucianne."

"That's the way parents tend to be, dear."

"I wish you'd go over and see her, Daddy." Laura turned and faced me head on. "I really think you should. She's like totally terrible."

"I will, Laura, first thing in the morning."

"Now, Daddy. I mean tomorrow is her fiftieth birthday too and you know what that did to *you*."

"A telling point," I murmured, remembering all too well my morose response to that event.

"Jamie goes I'm not sure that poor woman will survive till she's fifty. Someone has to do something. But Aunt Maggie won't be up till really late. So I go I'll tell my Daddy and he'll talk to Jane."

"Tomorrow morning," I picked up my reading glasses and Barbara Tuchman.

"Tonight, Daddy, please."

"I'll think about it."

"Tomorrow might be too late."

"Maybe I'll walk over in a few minutes."

"Great, promise?"

"*All right!*"

I was of course acting like a jerk. A coward. I was the same guy who hadn't called her for two years, repeating the same mistake all over again. Worse still, this time part of me knew it.

Laura bounded out of the house, doubtless to tell Jamie that her all-powerful father would wipe away all of Jane Devlin's story of suffering.

I would finish the book and then, if it were not too late wander down the road.

Jane

I can't take any more. I'm losing Lucy like I've lost the others. Everyone I have ever loved. Except Charley. I never did love him as much as the others, poor kid. That was bad too.

I'm a failure, a worthless little shit. I don't want to live any longer.

She looks at herself in the vanity mirror, a hysterical old woman in her underwear with a glass of vodka in one hand and a bottle with little green pills in the other. Who could possibly love her?

What an ugly worn-out, mis-shaped body at that. Who could possibly want it?

No one ever loved her, not really. No one will ever love her. God would not mind her ending her worthless life. He never loved her either. She wasn't worth loving.

She pours the sleeping tablets out of their bottle. All of them. It would be just like a long sleep. One that would never end. And no dreams. No guilt. No regret.

Jane, she tells the woman in the mirror, you are being hysterical. You frightened those poor kids half to death tonight. Good old Jane, one of the guys, everyone's big sister, loses it. Goes into orbit as they say.

I'm tired of being good old Jane. I can't do it any more.

How many pills would it take, I wonder.

It doesn't matter. If I drink all of them down with my vodka, that should be more than enough.

Leo

Still acting like a terminal asshole, I put aside Ms. Tuchman and wandered out into the fresh night air. Thousands of stars hung just above the treetops. No one could end their life on such a night. Could they?

Teenagers exaggerate. Don't they?

I walked around to the drive. My car was blocked by several others.

It was only a short walk anyway.

Then I hesitated. It was ten o'clock at night. I had no right to burst into a woman's house at this late hour. My pursuit of Jane should be gentle and sensitive. If she was distraught over poor Lucianne, I should leave her some room to recover. I shouldn't come bumbling in on her late at night when she was recovering from a long bout of tears.

Especially not because of the exaggerated fears of well-meaning but hyper-romantic kids.

I wandered around to the front porch, walked inside and picked up my reading glasses.

Damn, that brat Laura was right. I was in terrible shape the day I turned fifty. Got over it the next day all right, but if I had acted out that day, I don't know what stupid thing I might have done.

I replaced the glasses on the wicker end table and hurried out the front door.

On the road, the same road where Jim and Eileen Murray had died, I found that I was running.

Jane

Just swallow them and be done with it. It will be a nice long sleep. Nothing more. You can forget everything, especially how you ruined your life. God gave you so much and you didn't use any of it. Your mother was a fine excuse but she's been dead more than twenty-five years and you still haven't straightened out your life.

She pours all the pills into her hand.

Maggie says most attempted suicides are only a plea for help. The person doesn't really want to die, only to scream that someone make all the pain go away. Sometimes, she says, they miscalculate and die before anyone can help them. A person who really wants to die, doesn't make any mistakes.

I don't know whether these little pills, about the same color as the pendant I put on this morning, will kill me. Maybe I'm only crying out for help. That would be a stupid thing to do.

You look terrible after they've pumped out your stomach. I look terrible enough as it is.

Isn't that silly! I'm thinking of ending my life and I'm worried about my vanity if I should fail.

Just do it.

Leo

The back door was locked, damn it. Only one light on in the house. Bedroom probably. I have no right to go charging into her bedroom.

I pounded on the door.

No answer.

Where's the bell? Why don't they have doorbells on these damn palaces!

I dashed around to the front. The door to the porch was ajar. Should I push my way in?

Damn it, why not? If I make a fool out of myself I can blame the kids.

I shoved the door aside and bolted up the stairs to the second floor. The light at the end of the hallway must be her bedroom.

The door was open. She was sitting at her vanity table, startled and frightened, a pile of green pills in her hand.

Jane

He charges into her room like a Viking berserker and knocks the pills out of her hand. He grabs her by the shoulders and shakes her and tells her that she is his woman and he will tolerate no more of this hysterical nonsense. She is too important to too many people and too wonderful a person and woman even to think of it.

Do you understand, he shakes her again, furious in his fright.

She wants to laugh and tell him that she had decided not to kill herself, not out of virtue but out of vanity, and that she was about to put the pills back into the bottle when he charged in like a demented rapist.

Instead she sobs in his arms. He enfolds her and they cling to each other on the side of her bed. He continues to give her firm orders. She belongs to him now. No more of this foolishness. When she wants to cry, she should cry with him instead of alone with vodka and sleeping pills. Do you understand?

Oh yes she understands. She knows what he means. She does belong to him. Always has. She wants to laugh and cry at the same time. The laughter can wait. She has a right to weep in the arms of someone who loves her. She hasn't done it for a long time.

Still it is all kind of funny. He's funny and she's funny too. The whole world is funny.

She collapses completely in his embrace and permits herself to cry her heart out, something she has not done for a long, long time.

Yes, she tells him, I won't ever do it again. I won't ever think about it again. I promise with all my heart. I won't be a dumb little shit.

Then she cries some more. He is gentle and consoling, almost like a mother. I suppose he's had practice being a mother with that adorable kid of his.

As her tears diminish, his embrace changes. It becomes hungry, demanding. Not tonight she thinks.

Why not tonight?

He kisses her, first lightly, then voraciously. He's an even better kisser than he used to be. His hands roam her body, challenging her, devouring her. His teeth sink delicately into her boobs, first one then the other.

Yes, why not tonight? Get it over with. Find out how good you can be with a man who loves you.

Impatiently he brushes aside her bra and panty. She wishes, quite irrelevantly, that she had time to fix her make-up. His insistent lips probe everywhere. Everywhere.

Please God, grant that he enjoys me.

It will be a solemn high fuck, all the trimmings, kissing, playing, biting, licking, setting me on fire with foreplay. Take a long leisurely time to turn on the poor frigid bitch. That's all right, who's rushing?

Who's hiding anything?

Oh my darling, I am yours now and forever, do to me whatever you want. Please! No! Oh! Don't stop.

I wish I was a better lover. All I can do is submit. Maybe I'll learn more. I'm pretty good at submitting anyway. He likes me. He dotes on me. He'll never grow tired of me.

"I told you I'd do this before the summer was over," he crows triumphantly, a big red-haired pirate exulting in his captive.

The fire inside her burns out of control. Her body, moist and eager, yearns for unity. Still he prolongs the play, teasing her, tormenting her, eating her up with pleasure.

I can't take it much longer.

"Please, Leo, I can't keep this up."

"You can and will," he chortles. "I've been waiting for this for thirty-five years."

"Solemn high fuck," she says and they both laugh. They keep on laughing as the fun continues.

Yes, I can keep it up as long as he wants it. I love it all.

Finally, oh dear God, finally he enters her, the proud conqueror. She wraps her long legs around him. How long I have waited. How long both of us have waited.

Her body, a time bomb ready to explode, arches up to meet his thrusts. She twists and squirms and screams in repeated paroxysms of ecstasy. Super solemn high fuck for the fifty-year-old woman.

Still he continues to thrust. She screams again. His warmth flows inside her. He collapses on top of her, a big solid, demanding man, terribly proud of himself, who now belongs to her as much as she belongs to him.

Happy birthday, Jane, she smiles to herself as she sinks into a peaceful sleep.

Leo

The folk wisdom, I thought to myself, says I should be peacefully asleep. But she's the one who is sleeping. Poor woman probably needs it.

I glanced around the room. Perfect Georgian country house bedroom—dark red fabric, trimmed in gold, on the walls, thick blue drapes, four poster bed, hunting prints, period furniture. Packy said the Devlins had someone do a historic reconstruction. This must have been her mother's bedroom. Any bad vibrations here? I don't feel them; but I wouldn't. I'll have to ask Maggie sometime.

Sure enough, there's the Our Lady of Fatima statue Packy told me about. You've been watching us through our little game, haven't you? To judge by your smile you don't disapprove.

What a prize this woman is; and, with proper loving, which I propose to provide, she'll only get better. She was worth waiting for, no doubt about that. Thirty years? Only a few moments. She understands that this is forever from now on. I won't let her get away ever again.

Long, slender body, fiercely disciplined muscles—no wonder her serve is so fast. Lines and flesh pockets that didn't use to be there but they make her all the more appealing. She's taken good care of herself. Genetic luck and pride. A great lay!

And a lot of power to put into that tennis serve!

She was wearing, I noted, the pendant that I had given her thirty years ago. She's as much a romantic as I am. Maybe more so. Well, we'll match it before morning.

Should I slip out of bed and go back to the Keenans'? None of those matriarchs do bed checks. But Laura will snoop. The word will get around the house and everyone will wonder whether I'm in bed with Jane. Even if I wasn't, they'd think I was. Maybe I should try to protect our privacy.

To hell with that, I closed the argument. I'll stay here till the sun comes up. I'm not finished with the woman. We have some catching up to do.

A happy smile lingered on her contented face. I touched the cheek, the smile, the neck, the upturned breast. So very lovely.

I traced gentle Book of Kells lines on her belly and then played lightly with a breast, softly teasing its nipple.

She stirred in her sleep and her smile deepened.

Not much sexual experience in all those years with Phil. She's a novice, but, as in all things, Jane is the great improviser. She figures that she should respond passionately to my passion and she does, surprising even herself. That was quite a show at the end.

This is going to be a lot of fun.

She slept a lot longer, opened her eyes, seemed surprised, and then sighed blissfully. "Oh, it's you, Lee, I thought it might be."

"Who else?"

"Some terrible berserk redhaired Viking pirate." She closed her eyes. "But it's only Leo T. Kelly. Irish Catholic provost."

"I'm not finished with you, woman."

She opened her eyes. "I should hope not."

"I mean tonight."

"That's what I mean too." She hugged me, her nipples quickly hard against my chest.

"You know," she said as I was covering her body with quick kisses, "as far as I can tell, you are a very experienced and skillful lover, in addition to all your other admirable traits."

I paused. "Not really, Jane, not really."

"Well you certainly suit my fantasies, which is all that counts right now."

"Let's say that as an empiricist, I rise to the occasion?"

"Is that a pun?"

"A Freudian slip."

Her giggle turned into a moan as I proceeded in my second assault.

"Am I any good, Leo?" she asks, foolishly anxious.

"You are yourself, Janie, totally generous. A man could ask nothing better."

"Good enough to wait thirty years for?"

"Thirty-five to be exact. And well worth the wait. Now forget your worries and pay attention to what I'm doing."

She sighed softly and paid attention.

Jane

Oh my what a night!

The man is insatiable. He can't get enough of me. How wonderful!

Thank You very much for sending grace charging into my bedroom. At just the right time. I owe You.

Dawn light. I'll make us both some coffee. What will they think at the Keenans'?

I know damn well what they will think and I don't care.

I hope Lucy is all right this morning. Lucianne. She must be or they would have phoned me this morning.

She slips quietly out of bed, so as not to disturb her exhausted, complacent man.

Such a dear.

She reaches for her robe.

No. There are times for modesty, she smiles to herself, and there are times for other things. She hangs up her robe, retrieves her bra and panty from the floor and stuffs them into a vanity drawer. Must surely buy sexier lingerie for him. She folds his clothes neatly, glances around the room and sees the sleeping pills on the floor. Messy. She gathers them up, returns them to their bottle and puts the bottle on the bedstead. There will be other amusements at night now. She picks up the half-empty vodka glass, shakes her head at her sloppiness, and then tiptoes downstairs to make the coffee.

What if anyone should come up to the house and see me now.

She shivers and then decides it wouldn't matter in the least.

He wakens as she creeps into the room with the coffee and cinnamon rolls.

Do I smell breakfast?

You do, she puts the tray on the bed next to him, so there's room for her on the other side of him.

A gift you should expect only some mornings.

Two gifts, he rests his hand on her bare belly.

She bites her lip as her physiology begins to spin out of control. His hand slips slowly downward to her loins. She gasps. Her body quickly prepares to receive him again.

The second gift, she says thickly you can have any time.

I will cherish it always.

And, here, she hands him the bottle of pills, is a kind of third gift.

He looks at the bottle, smiles, and gives it back to her. I trust you, Jane.

Another touch of grace. But then grace should be graceful, shouldn't it?

Now climb in next to me, he adds, so I can feed you some of your own coffee and cinnamon rolls and play with you.

Yes, master, she says and quickly hops in beside him, snuggling close.

They eat and drink and play with each other and giggle happily.

You still have the pendant, he says, touching it when she removes the tray and sets it on the floor next to the bed.

Time enough later to bring it downstairs.

Naturally she says.

It should have something to match it. I think there's a box in the pocket of my slacks. Would you mind reaching for it?

She wants to tell him that he shouldn't have, but she's too eager to find out what it is.

She gives him the box, he opens it and takes out a ring with a huge peridot stone.

He puts the ring on her right hand, another graceful touch.

She stares at it in wonderment.

And moves it to her left hand.

Leo

"You're not wearing any clothes, woman." I moved my hands from her shoulders to her thighs. "Only those two glowing stones."

"You've noticed?"

"I have."

I rose from bed, lifted her up and slung her over my shoulder. She was astonishingly light.

"What are you doing!" She screeched.

"Carrying you downstairs and outside."

"Stop it!"

"Nope!"

"Why?"

"I want to make love to my woman under the old oak trees as the sun comes up by the side of the pool."

"Oh."

"Catholic summer idea."

"The old Monsignor wouldn't approve."

"You seem to." I arranged her on a chaise at poolside, sat next to her on the edge of the lounge, pressed her breasts against her ribs, and kissed her.

"Not much choice," she said when I gave her a chance to speak.

The first rays of the sunlight turned her flesh rose and gold. I began my ministrations to her with all the tenderness and delicacy I could muster.

"I suppose you think you can do this to me whenever you want," she sighed.

"Yep."

The birds were singing around us. Jane murmured something I could not understand.

"Hmmn?" I raised my mouth from her belly.

"Chaucer," she said as she moved my lips to her loins: "Well have they cause to be often glad, /Since each of them recovered hath his mate; / Full blissful may they sing when they wake."

"The birds?" My tongue probed into forbidden country.

"Not just the birds."

When we were finished with our sunrise ecstasy, covered with dew and sweat and the fluids of love, she pushed me off her.

"Did you ever swim in a pool with a naked woman after you made love at poolside?"

"Only in my fantasies."

"Now's the time, Lunkhead," she propelled me toward the pool, "to do it for real."

Without waiting for an answer she shoved me into the sparkling blue waters and dove in after me.

Later, our wet bodies glistening golden in the rays of the summer sun, we climbed out of the pool, giggling and holding hands like children.

Maggie would have compared us to the newly baptized on Easter morning.

Leo

I swung Maggie Ward Keenan into the air, just like her real brother (as opposed to her adopted brother) did. She blushed and giggled happily. Everyone else applauded.

"Thirty years and he's finally done it," Jerry grinned. "Better late than never."

"She's been wondering whether you'd ever try," Packy laughed.

"Should I put her down now?"

"Yes, you may!" Maggie insisted but not too seriously.

"You see, dear," Mary Anne Keenan explained, "she really enjoys the role of the poor little waif child that the Keenans took in, as untrue as it is."

I finally put my captive back on the floor. She promptly served up a plate of bacon for me and kissed my forehead.

The five of them were sitting in the brunch room, discreetly reserved about where I had been before I walked into the room.

My exuberance with Maggie must have resolved any doubts—as well as my voracious appetite.

"The waif child isn't all of me," Maggie insisted, passing cinnamon rolls that must have come from the same bakery where Jane had purchased hers, "but it's some of me. And the Keenan family is the Church that rallies around us waifs and protects us and gives us life—complete," she jerked her finger at Packy, "with its own built-in cleric."

The Keenans with their generosity and their strength and their love a metaphor for the Church? Not a bad image at all.

I realized that all my anger at Jane had been exorcised in our romps. It would never come back. How could you be angry at a woman who muttered a quote from Chaucer while she was in the advanced stages of arousal?

"Will someone preside over rearranging the cars?" I asked when I had demolished my second breakfast.

"You can use mine if you'll be back by noon," Packy said. "The key is in the car . . . I have to go in for the afternoon Mass at the parish, so I can come back for the birthday party tonight. Mustn't miss that."

"I think I'll stay around for it," I said, looking for smirks but not identifying any. "I'll be back long before noon, Pack, I'm going over to Warburg to have a word or two with Lucianne Clare, notorious asshole. I'll be back for your noon Mass here."

"Be kind to the poor child," Mary Anne pleaded.

"Give her hell," Maggie insisted. "That's what she needs."

"I know that, dear," Mary Anne replied, "but do you think Leo can do it right?"

"Now he can."

I didn't wait for further discussion.

Leo

"Lucianne," I hugged briefly the small child with the huge black eyes and the bandage on her head, "you are an asshole."

"Don't bawl me out, please, Uncle Leo."

It was a brand new, modern Warburg hospital, at least new in regard to me. Its sleek corridors and bright rooms and smiling staff were not at all like the place where I had come with burned hands.

"I agree with the received opinion that you might be suffering from a terminal case of assholeism."

"I know I goofed up," she said listlessly.

"On your mother's birthday weekend. You wanted to ruin it for her."

"I'm sure Aunt Maggie thinks that."

"Aunt Maggie, I'm told, is always right."

"I like Laura a lot," she said squirming on the bed. "She's really neat."

"She has her problems too, Lucianne."

"But you're so good with her."

"I try," I said cautiously.

"I mean, Laura goes it's a lot easier for someone to be a father and a mother to a daughter than it is to be a mother and father."

So.

"You know what I mean?"

"Kind of."

"I love my mother. I adore her. She's one of the kids. I'd like to call her Jane, but I'm afraid."

"Ask her if you can. She'll be flattered."

"Really?"

"Really."

"Are you and she going to get back together again, Uncle Leo?"

"No comment."

"I sure hope so."

"If you love your mother, why do you do bad things to her?"

"Because I get so angry at her. She can be a real dork, you know that, Uncle Leo?"

"Sometimes we all are."

"I don't mean that, I mean about him, I mean about that man. He's tried to ruin her life. He messed up Philip and Brigid. And the only reason he didn't ruin me is that he wasn't around often enough."

"I thought you were against the divorce?"

"I go I don't want to be fought over in court, you know? But then I call Aunt Norine, you know, down in Central America and she goes like it's time your mother led her own life. And I go he's trying to ruin me and

Aunt Norine goes, he's a sad man, dear, but he can't ruin you unless you let him."

"So you're going to ruin yourself?"

"Pretty dumb, huh?"

"So because you are angry at your father, you take it out on your mother, that's pretty dumb too, isn't it?"

"Really dumb . . . he called her at the office yesterday morning and made her cry."

"About what?"

"About how he would go to jail if she didn't help him."

"That's not true!"

"She knows it's not true, but he's so good at messing her up."

"So you were angry at her because she will give him the money?"

"No, she won't give him any money. I was angry because she let him make her cry."

So. All very neat.

"Lucianne."

"Yes, Uncle Leo?"

"Drop it. Your mother is ending a relationship that has been both intimate and long. She will finish it in due course and in her own time. Let her finish it her own way and support her instead of making her life more difficult."

"Are you sure she's ending it?"

"Bank on it. There'll be some difficult times, but it's all over."

She sighed. "What should I do?"

Aha, I wasn't doing too badly.

"Join her side, make up with her, hug her. Cry in her arms. Tell her how much you love her. Promise that you'll be no worse than any other teenager. Tell her you want to be friends."

"Can I ask her if I can call her Jane? Really?"

Another very important symbol.

"Absolutely."

"If I try to make up with her, she'll just lecture me. That's all she ever does is lecture me."

"Parents are for lecturing but if you try to become friends with her today, I promise: no lectures. I'll forbid them."

She seemed skeptical. "Really?"

"Like I say, bank on it."

Lucianne smiled complacently to herself.

"Will you kiss me on the forehead, Uncle Leo, like you do with Laura?"

"Absolutely.

Everyone was making guesses.

Let them guess.

Later in the morning, Jane appeared at the Keenans' dressed in blue slacks, a blue blouse, and a blue ribbon around her hair.

Blessed Mother blue, naturally.

She was wearing the ring, on which no one chose to comment, but which everyone saw.

What the hell, so they know.

"I'm off to the hospital to visit my youngest. Anyone need anything from Warburg?"

She was instructed to bring more ice.

"I'll drive you."

"I don't want to trouble you, Lee," she frowned.

"I said I'll drive you."

"OK," she shrugged, "have it your way."

I took the keys of her big, long, red Chevy convertible from her hand.

"Relax. It's your birthday."

"And a happy one." She touched my arm.

I admit that I was a little distracted during the drive. My right hand had some strange ideas about what it wanted to explore again this morning. The woman who was riding shotgun did not seem to mind its presumptions.

"I don't assume, Jane . . ." I said as we pulled into Warburg.

"Yes," she laughed, "what don't you assume?"

"I don't assume that the renewal of our love gives me any right to tell you how to raise your daughter."

"Nonetheless, you are about to give me strong advice on that subject."

"Which you are free to ignore."

"I won't ignore it, Lee, believe me."

"No lectures today."

"I don't lecture her."

"All parents lecture."

"All right, I guess I do lecture . . . I'm so worried that she doesn't understand the kind of trouble she could get into."

"Maybe and maybe not. My point is that telling her what you know about the world will not have any effect at all at this point in her life."

"God knows," she sighed, "I've made enough mess of my life."

"I don't think that is true either. In any event, dear God do I sound like a professor, Lucianne is ready for big reconciliation. Let her talk and love her. A lot."

"Really?"

"Really."

"I feel I have a lot more love to give today."

"I should think so."

We both laughed.

"You've set this up, haven't you?"

"Certainly."

"You do move in quickly, Leo."

I pulled into the hospital parking lot.

"Are you coming up with me?"

"Absolutely not."

"Do you mind if I take off the ring before I go in? I don't want to have to explain everything at once."

"Go right ahead. There's more holding us together from now on than a ring."

"So I noticed," she chuckled and touched my arm. "Wish me luck."

"Happy birthday."

She grinned. "Thank you."

Unquestionably, the ineffable Laura had already been on the phone about "Jane's" new ring. Lucianne would phone as soon as she left and they would ponder in great detail why Jane had not worn the ring into the hospital room.

That was their problem.

I opened Iris Murdoch's *The Sea, the Sea,* not the most appropriate reading for my present exalted mood, but, as an academic, I had a certain obligation to read "intelligent" novels by other academics.

It wasn't Professor Murdoch's fault, but my spirits plummeted while I waited for Jane. *Tristis post coitus.* It was all too good to be true. The enemies were still out there. They would still try to take it all away from us, unless I found out who they were and, one way or another, disposed of them.

The worst enemy had been dead for twenty-five years. But she was still an enemy. This time I would beat her.

All I really wanted to do was to make love with Jane for the rest of time and most of eternity too.

What if I should lose her again in my battle to unmask those who had made us pawns for so many years?

I didn't see how that could happen. Yet I had an uncanny feeling that the battle for the fair matron whom I had stormed in her phony Georgian castle the night before was not yet over.

When the fair matron joined me in the Chevy convertible an hour or so later, she was glowing.

"She wants to call me Jane! Can you imagine that? It's a very big deal with her. Isn't that astonishing!"

"Did she say why?"

"Because she wanted to be able to relate to me as one of the kids like everyone else does."

"And you said?"

"Why, naturally I said yes. I told her I was flattered and I'd try to be one of the kids for her. And she asked me if we could still fight once in a while and I said I sure hoped so. Then she embraced me and cried like a baby and swore she loved me more than anyone else in the world and she would do her best never to act like an asshole ever again."

"Really!"

"It was very moving. So I promised her I'd try not to lecture her any more and told her if I started, she should stop me and say I wasn't being Jane. She howled at that."

She pulled her new ring out of her purse and put it on again. "Last time it ever comes off. She probably knew about it anyway."

"I'm sure she did . . . sounds like a good conversation to me."

"It was glorious!" she exulted. "Simply glorious. I have my lovely little Lucy child back again. Oops, Lucianne child . . . she even told me where I could find the birthday present she hid for me."

"What is it?"

"She wouldn't say. I'm afraid," she blushed, "it is some thoroughly improper article of lingerie. Those connivers will never give up."

"I will wait eagerly to see it."

"So you shall my dear, so you shall."

"Will she be coming home for the party?"

"Not till tomorrow, which is the actual birthday anyway." Her left hand began its own guileful explorations. "Now lets go back to the Lake. I'd like to play a set of tennis before Packy's Mass."

"Tennis?"

"I want to see whether a night long orgy improves my game or ruins my game."

"It was only a demi-orgy."

"Truly? I can hardly wait for the real thing!"

Her game was much better. Her serve faster than it had ever been. She beat me 6–0 in two sets.

"Can you imagine how good my game would be after a total orgy!" She hugged me at the end of the second route.

"The problem is the deterioration of my game."

"So much the better."

Patrick

"To say that Mary's body is in heaven, my friends, is nothing more than to say that the human body is destined for glory. Our bodies with all their weaknesses and frailties, their propensity to weariness and sickness and eventual deterioration are nonetheless sacred. There is nothing in the human body that is not sacred, neither birth, nor growth, nor love, nor aging, nor death. In Jesus all creation is saved, in Mary that salvation is celebrated. Moreover she represents for us God's life-giving, life-nourishing love, the blessings of the flock and the field, of the womb and the breast, the flourishing of life and love in all creation. Mary tells us about God: 'whose glory bare would blind / or less would win man's mind / through her see him / made sweeter, not made dim / and her hand leads his light / sifted to our sigh.'"

Leo

She was radiant at the birthday party that night in a blue summer dress, draped off one shoulder, which made her look like a Greek Goddess or a Roman Empress or a Fairy Princess.

Again.

Packy proposed a toast—to be drunk in the usual prohibitively expensive champagne—to his "first niece and his first girlfriend, long ago turned by the marvelous alchemy of our grinning little witch from Philadelphia to my adopted sister."

Applause.

Maria yielded the response to Jane.

"To the Keenans," she said, "all of them, in gratitude for not letting me ever get away."

Much clinking and laughter.

And much truth.

Cake was cut, presents were opened, dancing commenced.

"Did Leo give you anything, Jane?" Packy, all phony innocence asked. "He gave Maria some very expensive perfume."

"A little ring," she held out her hand, champagne glass in the other. "Matches my pendant he gave me long ago. He's such a romantic."

"Takes one to know one," Maggie sniffed.

More laughter.

"I'll take you home," I had said when the party broke up.

"You don't *have* to."

"Yes I do."

"Oh, all right."

"We don't need the car."

"Get in," I shoved her rump.

"Leo, what are you doing, this is not the way to my house."

"It is the way to Skinny-dip."

"You're out of your mind!"

"You promised!"

"That was thirty-two years ago."

"A promise is a promise."

"You'll ruin my dress."

"No, I won't."

We turned off the road and down the path to the beach.

"What if someone is there?"

"We'll leave."

"You may remember that I do have a pool at my house. We did use it this morning."

"Not the same thing."

"I suppose this is an important symbol," she said with feigned reluctance. "You're not about to try to make love to me here are you?"

"No. I'll arouse you and make you wait till I take you back to your house."

"All right," she agreed, "sounds like fun."

Nonetheless, she shivered as I carefully undressed her next to the car and wrapped her in a huge towel I had packed in the car for just such a purpose.

"You figured this all out."

"Sure. Just like you did a few years ago."

"I'm cold."

"Just nervous. The water's warm."

"It had better be . . . hey, put me down."

"No way."

"Stop it, monster," she pounded against my chest. "Brute, rapist, Viking berserker . . ."

"Actually your first berserkers were Irish. Finn MacCool and that bunch."

"Add professor to the list of accusations."

"That's a given."

"I suppose your Irish berserkers were high on breast fixations," she sighed.

"Totally obsessed."

I put her down on the pier, tossed off my own remaining clothes, unwrapped her, jumped into the water, and delicately guided her after me into the water.

"Hey, it *is* warm! I can't imagine a woman turning fifty is doing this."

"A woman whose ivory body glows in the moonlight with the glamour of the rising sun."

"How lovely." She sunk all the way into the water and began to swim. "Naked in the water by both moon and sun. How delicious! Thank you so much, Leo my dearest, for being my Finn MacCool."

We swam and played and swam again. Then I bundled her up, took her to the car, and deposited her inside.

"Don't I get even to put my panty on?"

"No."

"All right master."

Then we went to her house for our second night together.

I worried that I could still lose her.

Leo

Back in her bedroom I thought I was about to lose her. I lovingly lowered her, still wrapped in a towel, on the bed, which had been carefully made up since our previous romp. I noticed a frown on her face, a warning of a thunderstorm. Before I could take cover, she bounded off the bed, pushed me away, swept a terry cloth robe around herself, and poked an angry finger at me.

"Fucking bastard!" she screamed.

"Me?"

"You! Why did you run away on me?"

"I know I should have called you, Jane, but things were busy at the University and I had to sort some things out in my own head."

"Dickhead!" she wailed. "I'm talking about 1948. You saw what a monster that woman was and you never came back to save me from her! Never! You went off to war and left me here!"

My heart sank. I had never thought of it that way.

"Jane, I'm . . ."

"Don't 'Jane' me, you worthless pile of shit. You were the big romantic. I was the fairy princess and you the brave knight. Well, you left me in this castle a prisoner of the witch and went away forever because your precious little lower middle class ego had been hurt by a bunch of dumb cops and a few sex-crazy idiots. You never called me, not once!"

"I tried when . . ."

"That doesn't count!"

I was sitting on the bed listening and she was striding around the room, white with fury. Her long, lovely legs mocked me as she swirled by me, her robe trailing behind.

"You never called me either."

"You knew goddamn well that I couldn't call you."

"I suppose so."

"You *suppose* so? You goddamn well *know* so!"

"I don't know what to say." I was hurt, confused, angry.

"Are you going to walk out on me again?"

"Of course not."

"How do I know that?"

"I love you."

"You told me that shit thirty years ago. Why the hell did you leave me?"

The enormity of her charge—and its fairness—hit me like a brick wall.

"I . . . don't know, Jane. I don't know."

"YOU DON'T KNOW!"

"I thought I'd have more time . . . I didn't."

"What about my time? Two years of hell and then nothing but a memorial mass?"

The wall collapsed on me, buried me, obliterated me. I was weeping, sobbing, overcome by pain and regret.

Jane stopped shouting and leaned against the crimson walls, breathing heavily, her robe coming apart. She stared at me, her face a harsh mask.

"I was afraid," I choked on my own sobs.

"Of *what?*" She sounded a bit more calm, the eye of the hurricane.

"Of you, of me, of our families, of life, of my own terrible inadequacies as a man, of my failures, of my resentment, my hurt, my anger. I wanted time to get over my fears."

"And, like you said, we didn't have any time?"

"Not enough."

"Gosh, Lee," she said softly. "Is that all? I was afraid that way too. Still am."

She knelt beside me on the bed and cuddled my head against her breasts. Then we both wept together.

"It's over, Lee," she whispered finally.

"Over. We are free from it all."

"Not completely," she warned.

"Enough to go on?"

"More than enough. This time, buster, I won't let you go away."

"Nor I you."

"Fair enough . . . by the way. I almost never use that kind of language."

"Be my guest."

There was no sex that night. We huddled in each other's arms, like very old people or very young children. We were both confident that it was over.

But it wasn't.

Labor Day

Glory to thee, thou glorious sun,
Glory to thee, thou sun
Face of the God of life

The Eye of the Great God,
Pouring upon us
At each time and season,
Pouring upon gently
And generously

—Gaelic Hymn

Leo

"Judge Burke will see you now, Doctor Kelly."

"Thank you."

The bailiff, like an acolyte leading a priest to the altar in the old church, ushered me into the chambers of Judge Angela Nicola Burke of the Federal Court for the Northern District of Illinois.

Shedding all judicial solemnity, despite her solemn robes, she flew across the room and hurled herself into my arms.

"Lee! How splendid! Let me get a look at you! You haven't changed a bit! As handsome as ever! Do you ever see Jane? I haven't heard from her the last couple of months! I read that that idiot is divorcing her! What a laugh!"

The years had been reasonably good to my ceramic doll. She had put on a few pounds, her hair was streaked with gray, and there were lines, more of suffering than of age on her face. But she still was a lovely little woman with an appealing body, a pleasure to come home to for the sports columnist who was her husband and who, according to legend, had not touched a drop of booze since the day of his first date with her.

He is reputed to have said, "She's worth more than all the Scotch in the world!"

Fair comment.

Hers had been a hard life—from wealth to poverty and then back if not to affluence at least to comfort.

The summer after she had graduated from St. Mary's, apparently over the trauma of Jimmy's death, she, her sister and her mother were in the family Cadillac, preparing to drive from the Lake back to Chicago. Angie raced back into the house to get a book she'd forgotten. As she came out the door, her mother started the car and it blew up.

Her father raced down the stairs at the sound of the explosion. His first words to her as he sobbed hysterically at the flaming rubble, were "Why didn't you die with them?"

It was a reaction, however spontaneous and unintended, from which neither of them ever recovered.

The bombers were never found. The press reported, as Tom Keenan had told me many years later, that her father was moving in on a chain of restaurants that were Outfit fronts. The Boys warned him off and he laughed at them. So with the simple philosophy according to which those people worked, they decided to blow him up.

There was perhaps some regret out on the West Side, that the Outfit, basically a male chauvinist organization that prides itself on its respect for women (except for the prostitutes they own), had killed a mother and a daughter instead of the father. But the outcome was the same. Tino abandoned his Chicago interests, sold all his companies, and retired to San Diego where, in some six months time, he married a woman only a year older than Angie.

There were certain whispers that his wife had been the target all along and that he had put out a contract on her and both his daughters.

"Did he?" I had asked Tom.

"Personally I doubt it. His new wife, if one were to judge by the pictures, is a Sophia Loren type beauty. Tino would do a lot for a woman like that and she apparently said marriage or no dice. But kill your family? I think he had too much of an Italian regard for family to do that. Screw around, sure. Laugh at fidelity, sure. Push around your wife and daughters, yeah. Cheat every chance you get, you bet. But kill them? I don't think so. Probably he meant nothing more than he couldn't figure out how she escaped the blast and in a crowning bit of irrationality blamed the survivor."

"He was a strange man, Tom."

"Oh all of that. Every inch the courtier and the aristocrat. Rather like Cesare Borgia might have been, as you suggested a few summers ago. I liked him. Couldn't escape his charm or his good taste in wine. But I never wanted to do business with him. He came to me a couple of times and invited me into what we'd call ventures now." Tom had smiled. "Funny thing, I never quite had the capital available."

He had disowned Angie completely. "She's got an education," he had told his friends. "Let her take care of herself. I'm going to start a new family. Get me some sons."

His callousness shocked everyone that knew him. But the shock was not enough to move them to help Angie. "Her mother must have left her something," they said. Or, "surely he'll give her a little money."

Not one red cent from either source.

Angie didn't quit. She got a job running an elevator at Carson's Department Store in the loop, moved into an apartment with some classmates who had graduated from St. Mary's the same year, and enrolled in night class at Chicago Kent Law School.

She led her class, although in the mid-fifties women were not all that welcome in the profession. She clerked for a federal judge and then went to work for the State's Attorney. In those days women were sent to the Juvenile Courts, which was a hell hole then, though not as bad as it is now. She was as effective as anyone can be there and eventually, with some reservations, they transferred her to Criminal Court. She won a couple of spectacular cases. Dick Daley heard about her intelligence and ability and probably about her history and decided that she was one of the women he needed on the bench. So in 1964, in the landslide with which LBJ crushed the unfortunate Barry Goldwater, she was elected to the Cook County Courts and was sent back to Juvenile Court.

For one week. Until Daley heard of it. Then she was put back in the Criminal Court where she stayed for four distinguished years until in his last batch of appointments in the terrible year of 1968, Lyndon Johnson appointed her to the Federal Bench. At the age of thirty-eight she had shown her father just what she was made of, not that it would have made any difference to him. In the feature articles that began to appear about her, she refused to discuss her father or the death of her sister and mother.

She dated on and off but apparently was shy of marriage, not without some reason I thought as I read the clippings on her. Then, right after her appointment to the Northern District of Illinois, she married Joe Burke, a gifted but erratic sports writer, a perennial Irish bachelor her own age, and appeared at Cubs games with him. It was said he proposed to her on the first date and she promptly accepted him because he was such a gentle and loving person.

No one else had thought so, but she must have been correct because, by all reports it was a marriage of mutual adoration, now shared by their son Joey who was born a year after the marriage.

Burke's writing, always clever, became brilliant. The judge, hitherto somber, was known to smile often, even to laugh.

A tough magic woman, our Angie.

It was now being said that she was in line for the next appointment to the Seventh Circuit.

"First of all, Angie," I began, as she poured me a cup of tea, "I should have called you long ago. I heard about what happened to your family when I came back from Korea, but I was too much of a mess to feel any compassion for anyone but myself."

She nodded, "I know the feeling, Lee. I didn't get in touch with you either."

"Then I became involved with my career and my marriage and I drifted away from Chicago. I always wanted to write you or send a card at Christmas time. I found out about your marriage long after the fact and thought about writing you and never got around to it."

"All the things you hear about the courtship and marriage are true," she smiled. "He did propose on the first date, he did swear a solemn oath that he would never drink again, I did accept him, we were married in three weeks, and I am very happy with him. I have had a little easier time keeping up with you. I run into Maggie often because Jerry is a colleague and she tells me about your life and career. Congratulations on your election to the National Academy. Not bad, not bad."

"Not as impressive as a judicial appointment."

"No invidious comparisons permitted or possible . . . now tell me about you and Jane."

"Well . . . ?"

"I mean do you see her ever?"

"Just this weekend up at the Lake!"

"Wonderful."

"Maybe, Angie."

"Definitely," she smiled benignly. "I've never been back there since the deaths, but I've begun to think that's silly. We had such good times. You know, I tell my husband that I fell in love with him because his eyes were so kind, like those of the only other boy I ever loved. As you imagine he wants to meet you. We must get together soon. With Jane."

"I'm flattered. I hope he is."

"Naturally. He's so much like you."

She loved me? But what about poor Jimmy?

Don't ask.

"You see Jane around town too?"

"Sure, how can you miss her? She's lovelier than ever, isn't she?"

"So I've noticed."

"What's on your mind, Lee?" she asked sharply. "Something's bothering you."

Bright lawyer.

"Let me put three pieces of evidence before you, Judge."

She smiled her approval.

"One: there was a half million dollars of money in that car Phil Clare drove into the tree. Real money, not counterfeit. The police lied when they denied it."

Her jaw tightened. She nodded at me to continue.

"Two: it seems very likely that I was the target of the weakened brakes. Under ordinary circumstances, I would be the only one driving the car. Packy had his Olds convertible by then."

She became grim. "Go on."

"Three: the Defense Department records show I was ordered to Paris, not the Fifth Marines. My orders were changed at the last minute by a forgery."

She leaned forward and blew air out of her lips, now very definitely a judge on the bench.

"You've shared these data with Jerry Keenan and his father."

"Of course."

"There were a lot of strange things about that accident, Lee." She closed her eyes thoughtfully. "Even then it screamed cover-up. There were so many odd accusations and suspicions. Some people swore for years that you were in the car when all the evidence was in the opposite direction. I heard the rumor about the money. I heard it denied. But there were no arrests, no charges, no suits. Nothing. After the two kids were buried, the case disappeared from the face of the earth. As the Murrays did a few years later . . . you're sure of all your facts?"

"Absolutely."

"Still use that word, don't you? I always liked it. Seems to fit you. Well, one thing is pretty clear, someone wanted you dead or maimed a whole lot in those days. Moreover it also seems reasonable that someone needed money pretty badly at the same time, badly enough to cover up a terrible tragedy. That Phil Clare went to collect the money kind of points the finger at people we both knew."

"I hope you don't mind . . ."

She waved aside my scruple. "Go right ahead."

"The best wisdom from the Lake, especially from Aunt Maggie as a new generation of urchins and young people call her, is that I should leave it all alone."

"Let the dead bury their dead . . . not bad advice, you know?"

"So I understand. Your friend Jane agrees. Yes, I am in love with her all over again."

"I knew you were. I could tell by the expression on your face."

"I feel they may still be out there."

She did not ask whom I meant. Rather she nodded, "There are a lot of *them* out there, Lee; and they're all dangerous. But they only kill when they have reasons. It's hard for me to see what the reasons might be after all these years."

"I feel like a pawn that has been moved for all its existence around a chess board by unseen and dangerous powers. I want to be free of them."

"I understand." She nodded slowly. "I understand. Yet you have Jane now or, to be discreet, you will surely have her soon. What else do you need?"

"I have her now Angie," I said bluntly.

"I know," she laughed, "I could tell. Give her all my love and my very best wishes."

"I will."

"Then what is the problem?"

"I lost her once and I don't want to lose her again."

She pursed her lips. "I can understand that fear."

"I don't want to punish anyone, Angie. I merely want to know what happened and to make sure it never happens again."

"Some garbage dumps are better left untroubled."

"What can I tell you?"

"Well," she became very businesslike, "if you tell me that money of that size was floating around at the Lake in 1948, I would say it was almost certainly from Organized Crime. And I would add that my father was probably involved in some way. He was never quite part of Organized Crime. But he had certain liaisons with them. He thought he could be both outside and inside at the same time. He learned," she grimaced, "that it was not possible."

"Phil was bringing Mob money to his father for some project that your father and his had in common. Phil or Jim. Or maybe both."

"It would be the kind of angle my father would work . . . he was such a strange combination of affection and terror. But let that go . . . When the Mob found out what had happened, very likely they demanded a cover-up, which the local police handled clumsily and then effectively."

"Murray went along?"

"He assumed that there was an accident. As perhaps did my dad and Phil's father. Perhaps that was all there was."

"Except my orders."

"Except your orders," she sighed. "The two phenomena might be totally unrelated, you know."

"I've considered that."

"My father and Doctor Clare and Mr. Murray put a lot of money into a shopping mall as we call them now in the northern suburbs. It was not a bad idea, just a little too early. They lost everything they put into it eventually, though neither of them were anywhere near bankruptcy. Subsequently the Old Orchard center replaced their plan and, as I'm sure you know, has been a huge success. In 1948 their idea still seemed viable. I would imagine that Daddy might well have invited his friends who had friends into the action. Perhaps on an urgent basis. After the accident, they might have pulled out or might have taken over completely. They would be capable under the circumstances of doing either. The mess itself would have given them one more reason to think that my father was too clever for half."

She recited these facts quietly and dispassionately, as though there was not terrible heartache beneath them.

"Pieces fit together."

"Some pieces, Lee, and they fit together hypothetically. Personally I would worry very much about your own safety if you become involved in further exploration."

"Some of the Boys might still be alive."

"Or their heirs. They don't like anyone digging."

"So I'm told."

For the first time in my poking around, I now felt fear, a cold terror such as I experienced in the LSV as we rode in on the huge tide at Inchon.

"As should be obvious, Lee . . ." she stood up, "I have a court call in a few minutes . . . as should be obvious, I do not like my father. I invited him to our wedding with a personal letter. He ignored it. You may wish to discount what I say for that reason. I urge you not to do so. If anyone is capable of orchestrating this sort of treachery, he would be that person. It would delight the dark side of his character. I know very little of his circumstances now. He lives luxuriously off his so-called investments. He's in reasonably good health for a man approaching eighty, very proud of his wife and family. Even now, he would be dangerous if he felt threatened. Very dangerous. Do not go up against him unless you are armed to the teeth with evidence, clout, and automatic weapons. About the latter I do not joke."

"Thank you for your candor, Angie, and for your willingness to renew an old friendship."

"I'm delighted to do so," she said rather formally and then kissed me. "May I call your office at the University and propose a date for dinner— we live in Lincoln Park, near Wrigley field, naturally—after Labor Day?"

"I would love it. It might take a few days to clear it with Ms. Devlin, as I think she calls herself again. I don't quite have access to her calendar yet."

"It looks like you have access to what matters."

I did yesterday, but that was yesterday. It was pretty special too.

As I was walking down the corridor after leaving her chambers, she appeared in the doorway, her face ashen.

"Lee, please come back."

"Something wrong, Angie?"

She waved me into a chair and slumped on a couch across the coffee table from me.

"I just remembered something. It didn't matter until you told me about your orders. Then it fit into place."

"Oh."

"I bumped into Brigie, Jane's daughter a few months ago."

"In Chicago?"

She nodded vigorously.

"At Tuffano's out on the West Side. She was with a nice young Irish Catholic commodities trader."

Arguably the best Italian restaurant in America.

"Really?"

"She's been clean for over a year and a half and can hardly wait to see her family again. She looks wonderful, like a cute little kid again. But she won't go home till she's been clean for two years."

"How wonderful!"

"In the women's room she told me a strange story. One night, when she was living in San Francisco three or four years ago, her father visited her. She said he was drunk, really awful. More awful than usual, which was pretty awful. He bragged about how they got rid of you. Failed once and then succeeded. She didn't know what he meant, but he seemed to think it was pretty funny. She said it had bothered her for a while and she forgot it but then seeing me and knowing you were back in town she remembered and wondered what he meant. Naturally she swore me to secrecy about being in Chicago."

"Did he give her any hint about who 'they' were? Was it first personal?"

"I asked of course. Not for nothing am I a lawyer. She said he was too drunk to be sure. I confess I discounted it. In his cups Phil could say almost any stupid thing. What had anyone done to get rid of you? Now I know. Not once, but twice."

"Not once but twice."

Outside under the Calder mobile in the Federal Plaza I looked up at the ice cream clouds that were drifting towards Lake Michigan.

I had rediscovered an old friend, however belatedly. Old sweetheart, really.

I had realized that I was not the only one who could rise from the dead. Angie too. As far as that went Jane was a resurrection person too. Maybe the bravest of them all. How vile had been my years of self-pity.

I had, finally, found confirmation, however tentative, of what I feared might be true. I should forget about the past and enjoy my new life. With Jane.

If only I could forget.

Jane

At six she prepares to close her shop. As she is about to lock the door, he appears. What do you want she demands. To come in, what else, he grins triumphantly at her.

I think you want more.

She really has no time for him this evening. She must finish some work before her eight o'clock supper with the visiting people from the Irish National Tourist Board. Nonetheless she finds herself opening the top button of her blouse.

He really can't be serious. Not here. Not at this hour of the day.

He does seem to be serious. He grabs her hand and drags her into her office. She should protest, but the words won't come. She also is a little frightened of him. Not terribly frightened, but still uneasy.

He does not close the door of her office. He does not give her a chance to talk. He is all over her. In a few seconds he has disposed of her clothes and her sexy new lingerie. He throws her on the narrow couch and forces her to race with him down the path of love, breathless, surprised, possessed.

Not sweet or tender love. Wild, demented passion. Two wrestling, panting, shouting, clawing creatures tearing at one another in an outburst of hunger and need. He leads the way in their furious ride but she follows willingly.

I cannot possibly be doing this.

You wanted an active sex life, didn't you?

Please! Please! Please! Stop! I can't keep up! It's too much! Too much! You're cleaving me apart! I cannot stand the pleasure! It is killing me! No! Oh!

Yes, yes, now, yes, yes. Oh!

Oh.

Leo

"There's a lot of violence in you, my darling," she stroked my chest.

"I didn't hurt you, did I?"

She smiled and patted my chest. "You'll never hurt me. It's a little scary when you want me that way, but I like it. Obviously."

We were huddled on the couch in her office, she resting in my arms, both of us naked and content, oblivious of Oak Street and the world beyond.

"You must tell me if I ever . . ."

"Don't worry about it," she kissed me. "Your violence speaks to violence in me that I didn't know was there. We're well-matched lovers it seems."

"We're fortunate that we can express our angers in love instead of hatred."

"That's my dear professor speaking philosophy."

"I don't think I'll ever have enough of you."

"I hope not my darling."

"I saw Angie today."

"How wonderful!"

"She says she was in love with me back then."

"Certainly she was in love with you. Didn't you know that?"

"I guess not."

"They all loved you, my darling . . . she finally married someone just like you. Not," she looked up at my face, "quite as cute as you, but maybe a little bit nicer. I bet he never charges into her chambers and practically assaults her."

"I bet he thinks about it."

"I hope he does."

We fell back into sleepy and satisfied silence. It didn't seem necessary to tell her about Phil's conversation with Brigie years before, especially as I felt honor bound to protect the young woman's confidentiality.

"You know what I want?"

"What?"

"I want to go to films and concerts with you, I want to talk about books with you, I want to meet your friends at the University and charm them even if I'm not a professor, I want to talk about politics with you, I want to watch you with people, charming them as you do so well, I want to watch you charming me despite me, I want to see you pulling the wool over the eyes of those poor teenagers who worship you, I want to know your ideas about everything, I want to eat breakfast with you, I want to seduce you when you're working at your computer, I want to fight with you sometimes just for the pure hell of it, I want to beat you at tennis, I want all of you, do you hear me," she pounded my chest, "all of you."

"Do you?"

"Yes . . . is that all right, my darling?"

"To want all of those things?"

"To insist on them, to demand them, to settle for nothing else?"

"You propose to push your way into my life and take it over, is that it?"

"Yes, damn it," she twists around so she can pound my chest with both her fists.

"Sounds like an offer no man in his right mind could possibly refuse."

We laughed together.

A demanding lover, my mistress, my wife.

Dear God, don't let me lose her this time.

"I have to leave, I really do." She struggled up. "I've got to get dressed and go off to supper with these damn flannel mouth micks."

"Let me help you dress."

"All right, that will be fun."

I did, and it was.

After I had helped her into a cab and she had blessed me with a wicked grin, I walked down Michigan Avenue in the fading August light.

I had the whole resurrection paradigm wrong. Korea wasn't death. It didn't figure in the equation. Death came long before in our families. Angie had risen from the dead. Poor Jimmy and Eileen never had much of a chance. Phil had a chance but a slim one and had not been able to break away from the forces that were killing him. Jane and I hung in the balance. The verdict for us was maybe.

Why does family life become so twisted? Five families, six kids about the same age, one authentic survival and that at terrible cost.

On the other hand the Keenans, Maggie Ward's metaphor for Church. Not a perfect couple. Mary Anne was not a woman with great depth; Tom was often so tangled in his Irish political obscurities that he didn't know himself whether he was coming or going. Yet their three children were all fully alive from the beginning, even Joan who at one time seemed so different from her two brothers.

Why are some families life-bestowing and others death-dealing?

Why can't we leave our children alone so that they can be themselves?

Dear God, help me not to blow it with Laura.

Or now, I guess, with Lucianne.

Leo

"Mae, will you make a reservation for me at the faculty club for lunch? For two."

"Should I call someone and confirm the time?"

Mae knew about absentminded professors.

"I don't think that will be necessary, Mae. Ms. Devlin is not a professor and hence is not likely to forget."

"Ms. Devlin!" she exclaimed. "Do I get to meet her?"

"How could I prevent that?"

Jane, I knew without being told, was determined to capture the University in one brilliant attack. Her excuse was that she wanted to meet one of our Joyce scholars about her Bloomsday tour. But she really wanted to see me in action and stake out her claim to the University.

I smiled to myself. It would be a show and a half.

"The general is on the phone."

"Hi, Tim."

"Leo, you've stirred up a lot of trouble down here."

"Have I?"

"The general whose orders were apparently changed with yours is furious. He's had a distinguished career and he sees this charge as a blight on it."

"I didn't make any charges."

"I understand that . . . we have an assistant secretary monitoring our investigation now."

"Should I be impressed?"

"We rarely are this serious about something that happened twenty-five years ago."

"Twenty-eight."

"It would be hard to bring formal charges against anyone, especially if the suspect were no longer in the service. If there is a pension that might give us some leverage."

"I don't want formal charges. I want only to know what happened."

"Well there's no doubt that your orders were forged, sometime after they were cut and before they were sent to you, the names were switched. In fact, the forgeries were crude, but a young officer right out of Annapolis and out of . . ."

"Loyola of Chicago."

As George Orwell had said in his *Animal Farm,* all animals are equal but some are more equal than others.

". . . would hardly notice the crudity. These were your first orders and you didn't question them."

"No."

"Could you come down here for a day next week while we try to figure out what we should do? We're trying to put together a list of those who might have been in a position to accomplish this forgery. The criminal may be dead or long since out of the Marines. It's not the sort of risk a career Marine would normally take."

"Not unless there was a lot of money involved."

"Well, yes."

"What can I do?"

"We'd want you to look over our list of suspects and see if you recognize any of them."

"All right. I have to make some other Washington stops anyway."

What exactly did I want to know? Did I really think they could tell me who switched my orders in 1950? If it wasn't for an irate senior officer who thought his life had been messed up too, they would probably have told me they couldn't find a thing.

Maybe it was all coincidence.

I had tentatively decided not to pursue the Nicola lead. He was dangerous enough, a narcissist with sociopathic tendencies. However, those who might be lurking behind him were more deadly. They'd simply keep coming at you. Maybe you'd win a few rounds against them, but they'd do you in eventually. It wasn't worth it.

Jane, my exuberant, challenging, delightful love, was a distraction from all possible serious worries. Our teenagers were off at a basketball camp and we had one another to ourselves. We had not spoken yet of the next phase of our relationship. Yet we took it for granted that our commitment was permanent. What else would it be?

After Labor Day we would become serious and figure out the logistics and mechanics of our merger. Now, in the waning days of summer, we wanted merely to play.

"Are you Ms. Clare or Ms. Devlin when I introduce you at the University?"

"Either. Both." She punched my stomach. Very gently. "For the moment."

"For the moment indeed," I moved my hand across her breasts, pushing them firmly against her ribs and holding them there.

"Hey, that doesn't mean you can do anything you want to me."

"Within reason . . . I think you gave me that right long ago."

She sighed happily and drew me close. "I sure did. Don't stop. Please."

I heard her chattering in my office with Mae. That nice Ms. Devlin. Co-opting my staff. Gradually taking over my office and then the whole University.

I let them talk. Better that they be on her side.

"Ms. Devlin to see you, Mr. Kelly."

Mae beamed her approval.

"I thought I heard distracting conversation."

"Hi, Mr. Kelly," Jane took in my office at a glance, "not a bad place for a provost. You can look out the window and watch all the kids."

"We don't have any kids at the University, Ms. Devlin."

"I can think of two."

I had prepared myself for her to be devastating but I had underestimated her capacity for anticipating a situation and making the most of it.

The Jane of that morning would be a sight rarely seen at the Faculty Club but not out of place. She wasn't quite part of our world, they would think, but what good taste. Clearly a woman of importance and class, perhaps a major benefactor. Or an opera singer.

She wore a white sleeveless dress, which managed to hang so it touched just the right parts of her generous anatomy, a matching white hat whose blue ribbon matched the scarf at her neck, white shoes and a large white shoulder purse, whose trim somehow keyed the scarf and the ribbon.

"I hope I haven't overdone it," she said anxiously as we walked over to the Club.

"Perfect."

"I thought I might be."

She was wearing both the peridot ring and pendant. Perhaps she never took them off. I would have to buy her matching earrings.

Every head in the dining room of the Faculty Club turned when I walked in with her, even the heads of the Nobel Prize winners at the round tables. The dining room, on the second floor of the Club, high ceiling, gothic windows, red leather chairs, is the most elegant in the country. Harvard isn't in the same league with us. It is a very serious place; you don't hear much loud talk and very little laughter. And rarely does someone like Jane stride in.

I could imagine the whispers.

Is she the Provost's wife?

He's not married. His wife divorced him.

Is that her?

I'm sure not.

His significant other?

She doesn't look the type.

A fiancée?

Maybe.

His new woman?

The way he looks at her, how could she not be?

She'll certainly liven up the campus.

Make him smile more. He's really a mean and stubborn bastard.

I wonder what she's like in bed.

The Joyce man was, needless to say, overwhelmed. We Irish are genetically programmed to cave in to beautiful and intelligent women, especially when they are familiar with our field and have read our work.

I let them talk. Let everyone see this new woman of mine, who is really my timeless woman, talk with a Joyce scholar like she's an expert too.

"Nora is all of the women, isn't she? Gerda, Gertie, the girl on the beach, Molly Bloom, Anna Livia Plurabelle?" she asked.

"Nora was his life. She kept him together. He didn't live very long, but he would have died years before if it wasn't for her."

"It's a responsibility that all we Irish women must bear," she said with an elaborate sigh. "We have so little to work with, you know."

He chuckled. "That's what Nora thought too."

On the way down the steps after lunch, the dean of the Social Sciences, an Irish Catholic like me, whispered in my ear as Jane continued to enchant the Joyce scholar, "Don't let that one get away, Leo."

"I don't plan to."

We strolled out of the Faculty Club and by the tennis courts.

"Nice tennis courts. You play here?"

"Certainly."

"Maybe I should have brought tennis clothes?" she asked cautiously.

"That would create a sensation."

"I shouldn't?"

"Oh yes, you should. Next time."

"I'm going to be permitted to come back again?" She wasn't quite sure of her success. No, that wasn't quite true. She knew she had been impressive, she merely wanted to be reassured.

"I think so."

She beamed. "Great . . . are you going to show me your apartment?"

"Was that to be part of the program?"

"I assumed that it would be . . . hot summer afternoon, quiet day at the University, laughter in the park . . ."

"I'm convinced."

She prowled around my apartment like an Irish "woman of property" who might be thinking of buying it. Or selling it.

"What a strange, charming sort of place—very expensive art deco, deliberately tasteless, but lots of room. Someone could do a lot with it."

"Could they?"

"Beautiful view of the park and the Lake and the museum."

She stood at the window and casually lowered the zipper on the back of her dress. "Hang this up, will you please."

"Are we going to make love?" I asked with pretended innocence.

"I don't know about you, but I am . . . now hang it up carefully and come back and I'll take off your clothes."

"Will you?"

"Yes, I *will!*" She turned to look out on the Lake again. "No voyeurs out there in cruisers that I can see."

I hung up her dress, very carefully indeed, in my bedroom. My heart was pounding in turbulent anticipation. She was learning very quickly the game of love—how to drive me out of my mind at her whim.

When I returned to the parlor, she tossed her lacy, fronthook bra at me. "Now let's get down to business."

"I'm scared," I said honestly enough as she removed my tie.

"My darling, on this nice summer afternoon here at your University, you have reason to be scared. I've been reading a few books about men and what scares them."

It was an exquisite *pas de deux* she made me dance with her.

At the end of our dance I feared more than ever that I might lose her, not to a death that might lurk ten or fifteen or twenty or perhaps even thirty years in the distance, but to a doom that lurked outside the window of my apartment and might invade at any time to take her away from me.

"Foolishness," I told myself as she slept in my arms, enormously proud of our dance. "No one can take her away from me. Not this time."

Yet my dread, dark, brooding, dismal, did not abate.

Which would be worse, I wondered, to let the sleeping dogs lie and to worry about them or stir them up so we can chase them away forever?

Which strategy runs the greater risk of losing her?

None of my computer models could answer that question.

Leo

"Isn't it strange," my love said to me as I lathered her body with thick suds, "that God chose to compare himself with love?"

We were in the vast shower of her co-op in East Lake Shore Drive—black marble walls and gold faucets.

"How so?" I piled the lather on thick in some strategically important places.

"It's so violent and messy and demanding and unpredictable," she sighed as my hands and the soap did their assigned work of stirring her up again.

"Raw impulse toward unity."

She nodded. "Leo, it would never have worked between us thirty years ago. We were too young, too confused, filled with too much passion and too many furies."

I paused in my progression. Jane's insights during foreplay or after-play or whatever it was to be called were almost always distracting and usually important.

"Too tied up with our families' needs and demands?"

"It took us a couple of decades to be old enough to be able to love one another."

"Not second chance, but first real chance?"

"Uh-huh . . . don't stop what you were doing!"

Leo

"I'm offended, Mr. Kelly," the Marine with the three stars on his shoulder frowned, "that you should wait till now to surface this ancient history. Your charges are a grave threat to my record of thirty-four years of service."

We were in the office of an assistant secretary of something or the other, looking out on the inner court of the Pentagon. The general, a hard-charging Marine of the type I had always hated, strode into the office spitting fire. I was his target.

My friend Tim, who had only two stars, and the youngish assistant secretary watched our confrontation with silent interest.

"No charges, Max, just curiosity."

He was a man of medium height at best who strove to look taller by holding himself stiffly erect. His hairline had receded substantially, so his head was shaven. He seemed fit enough, though I thought he had to work at keeping his stomach in place. His chest was covered with ribbons, though he lacked the single ribbon I had remembered to wear, which was worth more than all his put together.

He gave the impression of being your ideal, hell-for-leather Marine who had just charged up a hill on Iwo Jima. In fact, as I had learned from Tim, his Vietnam tours were mostly in intelligence work in Saigon and DaNang, and he had not seen much combat. The kind of intelligence work, I reflected, that had won that war for us.

"Why now!"

"Because I only found out about it now."

"How did you find out?" he demanded.

"I'm afraid, Max, that question is beside the point. What I was told turns out to be true. I want to find out why it happened, if that be possible."

"I hope you aren't suggesting I forged those orders."

"I can't imagine that you did, Max."

"As a matter of fact, I wanted to go to Korea, I would have been much happier there."

Bluster.

"Maybe, Max, but I doubt it. No one was happy there."

"I don't intend to minimize what you did," he mumbled, with a faint hint of apology in his voice. "It was a remarkably brave action in the circumstances."

"Maybe."

"I should have thought that it would have been possible to evaluate the situation in such a way that the withdrawal might have been more orderly."

An armchair general. Would they make this asshole Commandant and put him on the Joint Chiefs? They just might. They'd done dumber things.

"Maybe. I was concerned only about getting my men out of there and back down to Wonsan. It was a long way."

"I've studied that redeployment at some length. Naturally. It was a remarkable feat. Brilliant improvisation by junior officers like you."

"It was a retreat, sir. Very nearly a rout. We pulled it off because we could run faster than they could and had air cover and naval artillery. Not as bad as Dunkirk maybe, but still not a victory."

"I suppose so."

"I was there."

"Yes, you were. And I was in Paris and we both wonder why."

So he had settled down.

Not a bad asshole, maybe; but he would have run that bitter cold day, surely he would have run. He would not have lost his fingers in a POW camp. If they had captured him he would have died. Not stubborn and mean enough to survive.

You don't need to be that kind of person as Commandant. Maybe you need the stubborn, mean kind only as platoon leaders when the world is collapsing all around you.

Well, God had a good reason for putting me there. I wanted no revenge, but I did want to know who *they* were.

"If you had gone to Paris," he continued, "you'd probably still be a Marine officer, a colleague here."

"I wasn't the type, Max. Much more likely I would have married a French girl of dubious morals but great piety and would be loafing in a bar on the Left Bank."

That wasn't very likely either, but it got a laugh and eased the tension.

"We can reconstruct the matter somewhat like this," the Assistant Secretary continued. "The Department has issued orders in many different ways through the years. In those days they were actually cut. It was easier to type mimeograph stencils than to make photocopies, a much slower process then than it is now. Your orders were cut by a clerk typist who distributed them to the appropriate offices and files. Only two copies left this building, one to each of you and one to the commanding officer to whom you were assigned. Subsequent orders in your careers, many for you, General, only one or two for you, Doctor Kelly, were added to your jackets. There was never any reason for anyone to look at your first set of orders."

"I see."

"Presumably the Commanding Officer of the Fifth Marine Regiment received his copy as did the Attaché in Paris. It would be hard to find those at the present time. One must presume that they received the same version as you did, though in those days the Fifth Marines were not looking at documents all that carefully because they were otherwise occupied."

The Assistant Secretary was too young to remember those days.

"Between the time of the duplication of these orders and their actual transmission, almost anyone with access to the Bureau of Personnel could have accomplished a quick and crude forgery. There are four men who might have had especially easy access to them—Lance Corporal Farmer who was the typist, Sergeant McIntosh who supervised the files, Gunnery Sergeant Gorman who was the mail clerk, and Private Crick who was the mail messenger."

"I understand."

"We have investigated the records of all these men. Private Crick subsequently died in Korea. Farmer returned to civilian life after the war and lives in Seattle. McIntosh and Gorman became career Marines and retired after twenty years of service, the former lives in Minneapolis, the latter in Boston. We have interviewed the three survivors and they deny all knowledge of a forgery and indeed all memory of your names."

He paused and looked up at me. "I believe you can understand that hundreds of thousands of names must have flowed through that office in those times."

"Yes."

"Would you mind glancing through these files, both of you, and see if you recognize anything about them or their history in the Corps."

Nothing. Crick was an innocent looking kid. Gorman was your classic Boston Mick, the look of a Kerryman about him. McIntosh seemed more Swede than Scot. Farmer looked like the kind of guy who sells used cars.

"Not a hint of anything," I said.

"Nor I," the general agreed. "I had never been inside the building at that time. I don't imagine you ever had either, Leo."

"Today's the first time."

"It looks like a pretty cold trail to me," Tim suggested.

"Stone cold."

"The statute of limitations has long ago expired," the Assistant Secretary continued his bureaucratic recitation, "we would have a hard time with Farmer. Maybe go after his veteran's benefits, Hospital and such like. McIntosh and Gorman could be in more trouble. We might be able to revoke their pensions if we found evidence of wrongdoing. But we don't have a shred of evidence."

"Tim said someone tried to kill you in Chicago a couple of years before?" the General frowned. "You were only a kid then. Hell, so was I! Who would want to kill a kid?"

"Someone who hated him pretty bad . . ."

"You think they'll try again after all these years?"

"Maybe, you can understand my curiosity, Max."

"I sure can, Leo. Lot of crazy people out there."

Time to end it.

"Gentlemen, I appreciate your time and energy to satisfy my foolish curiosity. I'm sorry to have troubled you. As far as I am concerned the matter is closed."

"No records of this inquiry?" The Assistant Secretary raised his eyebrow.

"None at all."

"Leave your jacket as is?"

"Absolutely."

"Yours, General?"

"No reason to change it now . . . I appreciate your sensitivity, Leo."

"And your understanding, Max."

We all shook hands cordially. I had taken them off the hook.

"I still think you would have made a hell of a Marine officer, Leo."

"Too stubborn, Max. Too stubborn."

He laughed but he didn't deny it.

My visits to the National Academy and the National Science Foundation were no more successful. They weren't supposed to accomplish anything, however. They were merely routine court visits to the modern Medicis.

There was bad weather from the Rockies to the Great Lakes and my 727 was late getting out of National Airport, a nighttime adventure reminiscent of the rides at Riverview in the old days.

I had remembered to phone Jane before I boarded the plane at National. One of the responsibilities of acquiring a person who will worry about you is to let them know what phase of the worry situation they should take into account.

"Good trip?" she asked brightly.

"There are no good trips to this city, some are just worse than others. This one wasn't too bad."

I hadn't told her about the visit to the Pentagon.

"Check in when you're home?"

"It'll be late."

"I don't care."

"Sure."

That comes with being loved.

We landed in rain and low clouds at O'Hare, the kind of weather that makes you wonder whether the airport is really there until you see the white lines of the runway at the very last minute at which time God gets a lot of attention.

It was ten-thirty Chicago time when I found an empty phone.

"Another successful experiment in aeronautics," I said when she answered the phone.

"Always the Professor!" she giggled. "Get a good night's sleep."

"It would be easier if my bed wasn't empty."

"That problem can be resolved easily enough in the near future."

"The sooner the better."

I waited in a long line for a cab. There's always plenty of them at O'Hare until you want one.

On the tedious ride back to the University, through fog and rain, I abandoned any hope of cracking the mysteries of the past. Let the dead bury their dead.

As to the puzzles of the present, they were pure pleasure.

Where would we live? Her apartment presumably. She owned it and the University only lent me mine with the job. We'd keep mine for University events over which a provost ought to preside and for assignations free from snoopy teens.

Thinking of such assignations I snoozed during the final part of the ride. I wakened with a start when the cab driver said, "Here we are sir."

"Thank you," I paid him and glanced at my watch. Almost midnight. Rain still beating down. Autumn rain. So soon. The doorman would be gone by now. No problem. I'd let myself in with my key, ride up to my apartment on my private elevator, fall into bed and dream about Jane.

As I fumbled to get my key into the lock, they hit me.

There were two of them, large dark objects in the rain. Muggers. Give them your money and don't fight, my professorial head said.

Kill the bastards, the POW camp survivor insisted.

Leo

They seemed more interested in messing me up than in getting my money.

"Mother fucker," one of them grunted, hitting me in the gut.

"Fucking bastard," said the other, punching my back.

I spun around and kicked one of them in the shins. Then I buried my fist into the groin of the other.

How quick it all comes back, I thought.

They flailed away at me, amateur alley fighters against a trained killer, no matter how many years away from killing.

I made up my mind to kill both of them

Jane, the University, all the important things in my life faded away. Killing these two muggers was all that mattered.

They kept coming back for more, jabbing and pounding on me, despite my devastating blows. Probably high on drugs.

"I'm going to cut the mother fucker," one of them yelled.

"We're not supposed to do that."

"He gonna kill us."

"Let's get outta here."

"Gonna cut the mother fucker first."

I saw him coming at me in the rain and darkness, an opaque shape with a sliver of metal reaching out for me. I ducked away, felt a sharp sting in my shoulder, grabbed his arm and snapped it.

He bellowed with pain. I kneed him in the groin, threw him to the ground, and stomped on what I thought was his hand. Then I kicked him in the stomach.

"Mother fucker," he moaned.

I kicked him again. He rolled away, scrambled to his feet, and tottered off into the storm. His friend was already gone.

"Mother fucker," he groaned from a safe distance.

I could have killed him, but I didn't. Good sign.

I felt in the general area of the pain in my shoulder. Blood under my jacket. Damn. Ruined a good shirt and suit. I'd better go over to the hospital and have them sew me up.

I stumbled the three-quarters of a mile across campus and into the emergency room of the hospital. I got a little lost at first and maybe fell three or four times. For a couple of minutes I was not sure who I was or what I was up to.

Then I thought of Jane and that I had better not bleed to death from a mugging or I would be in great trouble with her.

I was soaking wet from the rain, dizzy from the blows I had received, confused about what had happened, and dripping blood.

An attractive black resident saw me collapse into a bench in the waiting room. "Mr Kelly! What happened! You're bleeding!"

Injured provosts get quick attention.

"I guess I was mugged."

"Let me see! Oh my, this is a serious wound, you've lost a lot of blood. We'll have to give you a transfusion. Come along with me. Does it hurt?"

"No, Doctor it doesn't. I'm a hero."

She giggled nervously as if I had said something hilariously funny.

A half hour later in the presence of the Director of Emergency Services, the Director of the Hospital, and the Dean of the Medical School, the Chief of Trauma Treatment sewed me up.

I must have been hilariously funny as I lay on the table, blood trickling in through a tube in one arm and antibiotics through a tube in the other arm. They all were laughing at my comments, most of the substance of which has since escaped me completely.

"You were lucky, Leo," the surgeon said. "Nothing much damaged. An inch in either direction and it would have been another matter."

"Did you refuse to give them your wallet, Leo?"

That was the president himself who had just drifted in, a tall, thin lawyer with thick glasses and a whimsical smile.

"They didn't seem to want my wallet," I said, realizing again how strange that was. "Odd, isn't it?"

"Very odd," the Dean agreed.

"Provosts are odd people. Thank God they get first-class treatment, even if they fly coach."

More laughter.

"Dr. Kelly," the resident said, "you sure are funny."

"A real stitch."

More laughter.

A cop was lingering at the doorway. "Be with you in a minute, officer."

"No hurry, Doctor Kelly."

"Can I go home now?"

They looked at one another.

The young woman made the decision, as was perfectly proper. "You're my patient, Doctor Kelly, and I'm going to keep you in here overnight . . . because you're so funny!"

"All right," I sighed. "I know better than to argue."

The rest of the crew drifted out eventually. I answered the cop's questions. Two men, on drugs, one of them with a broken ar. not a very easy search.

"We'll do our best, sir. We might just luck out."

"I understand."

I felt very tired, I wanted to sleep until the day after the Last Judgment.

"Maybe you should take a little nap now, Doctor Kelly," the woman's name I had learned was Diane and she had the tenderness that a male M.D. must work hard to achieve and women have almost for the asking.

"You're right, Diane. I need to nap."

There were a couple of other things I needed to do, but they could wait till morning.

No, one of them could not wait.

"Can I make a phone call, Diane?"

"Sure can."

She carried a phone with a long extension line over to me.

"It's pretty late to make a call now, Dr. Kelly."

"It will be a lot later for me if I don't . . . damn! Diane I can't read the numbers . . . will you punch them in for me?" I paused and struggled to remember the magic number.

It wouldn't come.

"I can't remember it. I must be a real mess."

"You've had better days, Doctor Kelly. Where does the party you're calling live?"

"Near north, Michigan Avenue."

"642-exchange?"

"Right! Brilliant! 642–0913 . . . I hope."

She giggled again and handed me the phone. "It's ringing now, sir."

She slipped away, discreetly protecting my privacy.

"Yes!"

Jane, awake, alert, worried.

"Me. I'm all right. You will hear radio reports in the morning that the Provost of the University has been mugged. No reason to worry, he is surviving nicely."

"He sounds woozy." Her voice was tight with fear.

"Long, hard day Jane. They're keeping me overnight just to play it safe. But there's nothing seriously wrong with me, except that this young resident is so pretty."

"Then there's nothing wrong with you at all," she laughed, but was still worried.

You cannot deprive them of their right to worry, even when all cause for worry is over.

"Not at all. But I realized I would be in the deepest of shit if I was not the first one to tell you."

"Absolutely, to use your favorite word."

"My daughter, the inestimable Laura, is returning from basketball camp early in the morning along with your equally admirable child. Ah . . . ."

What was the brat's name.

"Lucianne?"

"Right. You'd best intercept them so they hear about it from you."

"I will! I will!"

"Then you can all worry together, even though there's nothing to worry about."

She laughed again. "I'm terribly worried right now."

"Your privilege. In a minute I'm going to put the pretty young resident on the line and she will give you an exact description of my case, thus you will have all the details, I repeat all of them. Officially on the record. Thus, we can give some dimensions to your worry. Fair enough?"

"Good idea . . ."

"One more thing before I sink into the sleep of the just . . . let me see . . . oh yes, Jane, I love you. I'm absolutely—sorry—totally and crazily in love with you and I always will be."

"Oh, Lee, me too. Forever and ever. Amen."

"Diane . . . Ms. Devlin on the line. Would you tell her the truth, the whole truth, and nothing but the truth about what my condition is?"

She grinned. "Sure will."

I didn't listen to the conversation.

"All OK, Doctor Kelly. That Ms. Devlin sure is a nice lady."

"She is that, Diane. She is that."

The next morning that nice lady and the others in the gaggle of women who had suddenly become my family were gathered around my hospital bed, still worrying—Laura and Lucianne looking very worried. Lovely women all.

Also, to provide psychotherapeutic support should such be needed, the cute little witch from Philadelphia lurked behind them.

The tone of their comments from youngest to oldest stated that the "mugging" in great part was my own fault for not being more careful. The next time I traveled, the University Livery should bring me back and forth to O'Hare. Their driver would have waited till I was in the building and would have phoned the police when he saw the muggers.

Perhaps he would have, but by the time they came it would have been too late.

I suppose I didn't help matters any by responding with the horrific macho comment, "You should see the other two guys."

They assured me that a wide variety of food and drink would be waiting for me at my apartment. As would Jane too, to make sure I didn't do anything crazy for the next day or two.

Well, not too crazy, I didn't say.

Maggie lingered after the rest.

"Still at Chosin, Leo?"

"I guess so, Maggie. They weren't supposed to knife me. Just beat me up a little. I scared the hell out of them."

"And they didn't take your money?"

"No. They weren't interested in my money. Stupid. If they had tried to take money it would have looked like an ordinary mugging. Our friends, whoever they are, are getting clumsy."

"They're still out there then?"

"Yes, Maggie. They are still out there. They still want to take her away from me."

"This time they will fail, Leo." She touched my hand and I felt healing energy flow from her body into mine. That was a new trick.

"A promise?"

"Absolutely," she smiled.

After she left, I tried again to put the pieces together as I had all summer long. I had more pieces now, a lot more pieces.

I rearranged the pieces several times, like I play with data on my SPSS analysis package. Still didn't fit.

Too much painkiller in me.

I gave up, relaxed, and began to think of Jane waiting for me at the apartment, long legs, lovely face, rich body. Ah Jane.

I should have stayed away from the Pentagon, I told myself as I drifted into a trance-like state. Pentagon. Navy Department. Nothing good came from them.

Pentagon. Navy Department.

Why are those words important?

Is some voice deep down in the sub-basement of my soul trying to tell me something?

Pentagon? Navy Department!

Then the picture erupted in my head. I saw it all, the total and each of the pieces. I played it over, just like I always rerun a correlation that seemed suspiciously high.

It all fit.

Despite the medication, I was now wide awake. My heart sank. It was not good news, not at all.

Well, I must go ahead with it now. Check out the details. I called Tim in Washington and he confirmed a detail with an answer to one question.

"Does that solve it for you, Leo?"

"It does."

"You want us to do anything?"

"Not at the moment."

My brain was churning now, adrenaline exorcising painkiller. I went through the details, listing in my head the evidence I would need. We must not stir "them" up again.

With a little luck we could get it all. We could certainly get enough. I'd do one interview myself, no two, leave the rest to pros.

I phoned Jerry Keenan.

"You all right, Lee?"

"Fine! I've solved it all, Jerry!"

"You sure? You sound kind of strange."

"All of that. But I have it down cold. Listen to me."

I painted my picture.

"Dear God," he whispered. "It sounds right, crazy, but right."

"Here's what I want you to do." I went through the list in my head. Had I missed anything? No, not a thing.

"All right, I guess it can be done, we'll have to be lucky a couple of times."

"Tell your dad, no one else. Except Maggie of course."

"Couldn't hide it from her."

"I need it all quick."

"I can see that. You can't tell what they'll try next."

"I agree. It's too late to turn back now."

"It's always been too late . . . what will you do when you get the evidence?"

"I don't know. I'll have to think about it then."

"There's no statute of limitations on murder or attempted murder."

"Yeah."

The adrenaline kicked out and the painkillers took over again.

Maybe I'd do nothing. Maybe it would be enough to have the evidence. Maybe, but that sounded too easy. High risks either way.

I had a lot to lose either way.

I vowed I would not lose Jane no matter what happened. I would not tolerate that loss again.

Leo

We were in Jane's house on the Saturday afternoon of the Labor Day Weekend. She was hosting a small party in honor of the Devlin Chair, toasts in real and unreal champagne, depending.

She and I had been together constantly during the past week, deepening and strengthening our love.

Her brothers and their wives—presentable matrons in their middle fifties (Dickie's wife was Madge, I reminded myself and Mickie's was Helen)—but not their children were on the porch with us. And the usual crowd: Laura, Lucianne, and the Keenans—Tom and Marie, Jerry and Maggie, Packy.

Jane smiled at me over her glass as she toasted the Chair, a shy, sly lover's smile.

"I have something to say," I began.

"Say it," she grinned at me.

"I want to make some charges."

Her smile faded.

"I intend to charge your brothers with being accessories before and after the fact to the murder of James and Eileen Murray. I intend to charge them with conspiracy to commit murder against me, once thirty two years ago and again the week before last. I further intend to charge them with conspiracy to falsify government documents thirty years ago, though on that charge the statute of limitations has long since expired."

The terror on the faces of her two brothers persuaded me that our hastily assembled evidence was unnecessary. They were guilty on all counts.

"You're out of your mind," Dickie blustered. "Out of your fucking mind."

Her face drawn tightly, her eyes closed, Jane sank quietly into a chair.

"I'm not, Dickie. Hear out my evidence. On all other charges except the assault last week, I believe you were only accessories."

"You can't prove a thing."

I opened the briefcase out of which I removed a stack of statements.

"As to that most recent crime, we have the sworn testimony of the man you hired to pay those two goons to beat me up. You were rather crude about that, boys. Out of practice I suppose. I thought I faced an elaborate and sophisticated conspiracy. In fact I was dealing with crude amateurs, crude but dangerous and potentially deadly. I note for the record, that if that knife blade was an inch to the right I would be dead and you'd be free forever of your past crimes."

"Bullshit."

"This testimony alone would be enough to convict you." I put it aside.

"Then I have a sworn statement from Al Winslow that your brother Herbie paid him five thousand dollars in 1948 to loosen the brakes in the Keenans' old Lasalle instead of fixing them. Mr. Winslow is an elderly man now and afraid of spending the rest of his life in jail. He was only too willing to talk to our investigators, especially since then Officer Joe Miller, now Sheriff Joe Miller when asked of the possibility of seeing someone hanging around Winslow's place after the crime said that he'd seen you there, but had at the time thought nothing of it."

"That kind of testimony won't stand up in court," Dickie argued nervously.

"No, Dickie, probably not, but it confirms for us that we are right in our analysis."

Dickie broke down. "We didn't mean for you to get killed," he sobbed, "just an accident. We didn't figure anyone would drive it down the hill that fast. Anyway, Mickie and I were going to warn you to have another look at the brakes because we'd say we didn't trust Winslow. There wasn't time."

"She made him do it," Mickie agreed. "You knew that she should make us do anything. We were terrified of her. He didn't want to do it either. He carried the memory of what happened to his grave."

"Michael!" His wife spoke sharply. "Don't say anything more!"

"It's no good, Helen." He slumped in his chair. "They have all the goods on us. We knew it would catch up with us eventually."

"It's caught up now. I note in passing that the memory Herbert P. Devlin carried to his grave was of two young bodies incinerated in a car just a few yards away from this house late on the night of August 14, 1948. I do not believe he was in this house when it happened. But I presume the three of you rushed up the next day to see the results of your handiwork."

"She made him do it. You don't know the kind of power she had. We couldn't resist her temper, especially when she was drunk. You don't know what it was like to live with that woman."

"In fact, the car was driven that night by Phil Clare who had borrowed it without permission. He was probably on an illegal errand of his own for his father. The nature of that errand need not detain us."

"Probably" was not the right word. He certainly was on an illegal errand. Sheriff Miller had, as he had promised, confirmed my suspicions when I confronted him with an accurate scenario, when I had finally figured it out. It was a relatively simple scenario once I perceived that the money and the faulty brakes represented two separate plots.

Thinking he was clever, Doctor Clare did not want his car to be seen in Warburg. Deceived as always about his son's maturity and intelligence, he told Phil to borrow someone else's car and pick up a package for him. He had tried to impress on Phil that it was an important task. He had literally sent a boy on a man's job, a boy who brought along two friends to drink with him and risked a joyride down a steep hill in an old car. The Outfit people were dismayed that their potential partners in a shopping mall would be so careless. They demanded all the money back, less what it took to bribe the local cops. The cops accepted what they were given because they did not want to wake up some morning and find themselves dead. The Outfit charged the bribe money to Tino Nicola. When he refused to pay, they conspired to blow him up and killed his family by mistake.

"We didn't mean to hurt anyone," Dickie groaned.

"No one but me. Instead you killed two innocent kids and indirectly their parents. You wiped out the whole Murray family."

"Good God!" Madge Devlin screamed, "Can't you see what you're doing to us!"

"I would submit, Ms. Devlin," I continued calmly, "that rather a lot was done to the Murrays too."

"We have masses said for them every day of the year," Dickie sobbed. "I pray for them for every day too. I really do . . ."

"Herbie drunk himself into an early grave." Mickie wiped tears away from his eyes. "He saw ghosts. They drove him to drink."

"It could just as well have been my ghost."

"You wouldn't have been driven that crazy."

"So you had to try again!"

Jane was deathly pale. I was taking a big chance. Jerry Keenan had said that he hoped I knew the risk I was taking.

I knew it all too well.

"You can't prove a thing," Madge Devlin shouted. "It was all so long ago."

"I was knifed last week, Ms. Devlin."

"We didn't mean that," her husband was pleading with me now. "All we intended was a warning. You fought back and almost killed them. That's why the guy pulled a knife on you."

Jane gasped. Lucianne started to weep.

"Let that be a warning to any more thugs you plan to send against me . . . if I may continue. We also possess a statement from Martin Gorman, late Master Sergeant in the United States Marine Corps that his good friend, Herbert Patrick Devlin, whom he knew in the Bureau of Personnel during the Second World War, paid him ten thousand dollars to see that I was sent to Korea instead of to the Embassy in Paris. In current money that's more like seventy thousand dollars. A lot of money.

"They became friends because they both worked in personnel departments and they were both born to very recent immigrants from the same part of Ireland. Sergeant Gorman was very much afraid of losing his lucrative service pension if he did not tell the truth."

In my altered state of consciousness—or whatever it was—at the University

Hospital I had remembered that Herbie had worked in the Navy Department during Second World War. The Navy and the Marines had started asking questions about me within the last week. It seemed likely that the mugging was the result. They must have hit paydirt without realizing it. I called my friend Tim to find out if Master Sergeant Gorman was the son of immigrants, perhaps from County Kerry. When he had phoned back and confirmed my hunch, not without some astonishment on his part, I told him to go after Gorman. Within twenty-four hours I had confirmation of my suspicions. All the rest was, as we used to say in the Marines, mopping up.

I put Gorman's statement aside. After that lucky guess or insight or whatever, all the rest were certainties.

"She made us!" Dickie groaned.

"Yeah, it was all her idea," Mickie continued. "She hated you. She hated your mother. She wanted Jane to marry Phil. She had to get you out of the way."

I shivered. The evil of that hatred lingered long after the woman, twisted with sickness and anger, had died cursing her children to the end. Yet once she had been a pretty young woman with bright hopes for herself and her children in America.

"You were adult men. You're trying to tell me that your mother had that kind of power over you?"

"She was the very devil! She wanted you out of the way." Dickie held his head in his hands. "She knew Herbie had friends in the Pentagon. She made him keep up those contacts because, like she said, you'd never know when you'd need friends. She told Herbie to get you sent to the war, no how matter how much it cost. We didn't know about it till after he'd done it."

"You would have stopped him if you did know?"

"There was no stopping him when she gave the orders. He was the oldest. He'd do anything to please her. Anything. We all figured you'd come back anyway. Then you didn't."

"Then I did. But too late it seems."

Were they telling the truth about Herbie's responsibility and their own relative innocence? Probably. Not that it mattered either way. Their assault on me the other night was a hamhanded return to the goon tactics of the past, doubtless occasioned by a call from Marty Gorman. They shouldn't have done it. That was the last bit of data I needed to put my puzzle together. They had foolishly overreached.

Dullards, not arch villains but dullards.

"I now have a statement that ties the two attempts on my life, the first two of them at any rate. It's from Philip Clare."

Jane's eyes opened in horror.

My darling, I hate to do this, but it is necessary, absolutely necessary. Absolutely.

"He told me that shortly before his wedding he encountered Herbert Devlin at a place of entertainment in Chicago. Herbert Devlin was intoxicated and feeling guilty over what he had done. Perhaps to expiate his guilt he confided to Philip Clare that he and his brother had made the marriage possible by getting rid of me. They'd tried once, he told Philip Clare, and failed but they were successful the second time. According to Mr. Clare, Herbert Devlin blamed it all on his mother."

I had played a hunch with Phil. I thought that if I confronted him up front that he had known about the plot against me before the wedding, he would want to know how I found out instead of denying the truth of what I said.

My hunch had worked. He collapsed. How did I find out, he begged.

"You talk too much, Phil. Especially when you're drunk. Now you're going to tell me exactly what was said and when and where and you're going to sign an affidavit admitting what you knew. In turn I promise you that the federal prosecutors will not be given information that you were an accessory after the fact to murder."

"I didn't kill anyone!"

"After you heard Herbie's confession or boast or whatever it was you knew about it, you didn't report it to the police. That makes you an accessory."

"You won't use it against me?'

"No."

He had signed the statement. "If Jane sees this you'll lose her again," he looked up at me slyly.

"I don't intend ever to lose her again."

I might not have been as confident as I sounded.

Nonetheless, before I let him off the hook I made him promise to cooperate in the annulment process. He promised he would. I had sufficiently frightened him that I didn't doubt it.

"Herbie was like that," Dickie sighed. "He couldn't fight Ma off, but he had terrible guilt feelings afterwards, especially when he was drunk. God knows how many people he told."

Lucianne was now embracing her mother.

"He had much to be guilty about."

"That's why he died so young. He drank to forget it all."

"I daresay." I placed the four documents on the table. "Read them at your leisure."

"Why did you take the money for the Chair?" Madge Devlin asked.

"The University has taken money from far worse people, I fear. At the point in time the deed of gift was signed I was unaware of these matters. I would never have dreamed that such horror could actually happen in a family. But in any event I would not have turned down the gift. It's not my right to make decisions on such matters."

"You'll have a great scandal on your hands when the trial starts."

"Oh," I stood up, "there will be no trial."

"No trial?" Dickie looked up astonished. "Why not?"

"Why? Let the dead bury their dead. They're all in the hands of God anyway. I will not attempt to arrogate a divine role for myself."

Damn professorial language. "Arrogate."

"But then why this," Madge Devlin gestured at the pile of affidavits.

"So that the truth be told, Madge. Once and for all. So that the past may be put to rest and life may go on. For everyone in this room. So that the evil and the hatred will be forever banished. Something like that anyway."

"Is that what we need?" Jane sounded tired and bitter. "More truth?"

One last homily.

"I accept the explanation that Ita Devlin forced you to do these things to me. I don't blame you and now that she's dead, I don't blame her either. Who knows what terrible energies drove her, energies for which she was not responsible? I can only hope that she's found the peace and joy for which we all seek. I hope that from this day on, the energies of hatred that have caused suffering to all of us will be permanently exorcised."

I felt I could not stand another minute of the terrible currents of tension that were bounding back and forth among the people in the room.

All the demons were there. I glanced at Maggie; her eyes were closed in pain, as if she were absorbing all the hurt, all the sickness, all the misery, all the violence.

The twisted soul of Ita Devlin was there among us and then gone. Left permanently to Heaven, which has promised mercy to all.

I turned to leave the house. I did not care if everyone else remained. What I had done was done; now others might have made of it what they would.

I strode down the drive and out into the road. A hundred yards away at the foot of the hill was the oak tree where Jimmy and Eileen had died. I had done whatever I could to put their souls to rest.

I knew Laura was behind me. I didn't look to see if there was anyone else till I was on the road.

They were all there, the Keenan family church, standing by one of their own.

"That was very brave of you, Leo," Mary Anne said.

"I hope you knew what you were doing," Tom added. "I suppose you do."

"He knew all right," Jerry said. "Just what he was doing."

"Chosin all over again!" Packy exulted.

Summer at the Lake

"Brilliant, Lee, brilliant." Maggie hugged me. "I couldn't have done a better job myself."

Back at their compound we were herded into the elder Keenans' coach house, where wet and noisy grandchildren would not interrupt us. Maggie produced champagne she had, without my knowledge, put in the fridge before we had made the trek down the road. She and Laura poured the bubbly for us.

In the center of the spacious parlor, my adopted sister raised her glass, a slender statue of victory, an angel of light celebrating triumph.

"Confusion to all our enemies," she toasted me. "And God's choicest blessings on all our friends."

Leo

Packy went back for the Sunday Masses at his parish. Our crowd went to the early Mass in the church in the town.

I encountered Jane in back of the church. Laura was behind me. Jane and Lucianne in tow. I dreaded what she might say. It was too early to talk about the scene.

"Why did you do it, Leo? Why in the world did you do it?" She looked much older than her fifty years, the first time I had seen her in that condition.

"The truth had to be told, Jane. It was there and it had to be told."

"What if their children were there?"

"Then I would have put it off to another day."

"You ruined their marriages."

"I doubt it."

"It was hell on earth after you left last night."

She did not seem so much angry as too despairing to be angry.

"It will get better."

"It will never get better. She was my mother after all."

"You knew what she was."

"I didn't need to know all that she was."

"I think you did."

"You had no right to decide that."

"I think I did. The truth had to be told."

"What does that mean? What does it do to Lucianne to know what a heel their father was?"

I saw that Lucianne was about to open her mouth and, teenlike, charge in with an argument. She caught my eye and thank God shut up.

"All of us have been prisoners of hatred. We must at last shake ourselves free."

"Fine sounding words . . . but what about devastating their poor wives?"

"They're the kind that will snap out of it. Probably last night they were already recalling how cruel she was to them."

She swallowed uncertainly. I had hit home. Well, that was good.

"You were very angry at me a couple of weeks ago because I had not freed you from your mother in 1948. In our second summer I had the chance to free you and I risked that chance."

"You risked a lot," she said, her face stony.

"I don't judge her soul, Jane. I really don't. I'm concerned only about the truth and the truth making us free."

"You and your goddamn Irish integrity," she turned on her heel and weeping, stormed away. Not good. Now this conversation itself would become a new focus for her anger.

Lucianne hesitated, as if she had to choose sides. I pointed towards her mother hurrying into the parking lot.

Lucianne nodded and ran after her.

"Nice going, Daddy," Laura said. "You won that one."

"I wish I thought so."

Leo

Late Sunday evening, Laura showed up on the porch where I was trying to read Graham Greene's new novel *The Human Factor*. I had watched the new Pope—John Paul he had called himself—on television at noon. He seemed a wonderful man. The Church desperately needed someone like him. Alas, he would only live for another month.

What had happened to the money? As best as Joe Miller and I could figure it out, the Mob/Nicola/Clare theory held. Tino had made Doctor Clare pick up the money. He in turn had sent Phil to pick it up. The Murrays went along for the ride. Probably Jim Murray knew nothing about the pick-up nor about the money, perhaps not ever. The Mob people wanted the money back, all of it. But the police had it. So they were paid off and Nicola was supposed to pick up the tab. That may have been why his car was blown up a couple of years later. The Devlin attempt on me had coincided accidentally with the money exchange. Two unrelated conspiracies had a single unintended consequence—two young lives snuffed out.

I looked up from the unturned pages of my book to see my daughter in jeans and a maroon St. Ignatius sweatshirt.

"Lucianne goes that her mother is like really totally angry at you, but she goes she'll get over it because she loves you so much."

"That's what Lucianne thinks, huh?"

"Yes, Daddy, she goes Leo was simply wonderful yesterday. Aunt Madge and Aunt Helen think so too. Even Charley and Lin who weren't there but read the papers you left behind. Nobody goes Jane don't be a fool because she's so mad. She's mad at all the Keenans too, especially Aunt Maggie."

"She'll calm down."

"Are you sure, Daddy?"

"No, hon, I'm not sure. But it's up to her."

"You could go over and talk to her, couldn't you?"

Aha, that was the latest Lucianne/Laura scheme.

"I don't think so. Not now."

"Not ever?"

"Maybe, we'll have to wait and see how Jane feels in a couple of days."

"Even Lucianne's Aunt Madge and Aunt Helen go that you did the right thing. I think her uncles are so relieved that they are grateful to you. It's only Jane . . ."

"Mr. Clare was her husband for a long time, the father of all her kids."

"She knows what a creep he is."

"I suppose it's her mother. You don't like to have to face that fact that your mother was so filled with hatred."

"Why was she that way, Daddy?"

"We may never know."

"Daddy, won't you *please* go over and see Jane tonight?"

I hesitated. What was the most pragmatic strategy?

"Not tonight, hon, I won't let her get away again. I promise that."

"How long?"

"Soon."

"How soon?"

"When it's time."

"You and your goddamn Shanty Irish integrity!"

She laughed when she said it. Somehow I had responded properly. She and Lucianne would be reassured. Perhaps they thought I would give up on Jane.

Not ever.

"Jane didn't say 'Shanty.'"

"I know. I just added it for emphasis."

She skipped out of the room, confident that it would be all right. I wished I felt the same.

Yet I had done what had to be done.

Or had I made another huge mistake?

Patrick

"You're on his side, Packy," Jane shook her head disconsolately. "You don't want to see it from my viewpoint."

For almost four decades I had loved the woman. Never had I loved her more than at this moment. And never had I felt more powerless to help her. She was digging herself into a pit from which it would be difficult to emerge.

"I'm on no one's side, Jane. I don't think it's a question of sides."

It was mid-September, a dull rainy day with a chill northeast wind blowing across our suburb.

"You don't see, not even a little, that it might be terrible from my viewpoint."

"Leo is a hero, Jane. We both know that he behaves heroically under sudden pressure and backs off when he has a chance to reflect. This time he was deliberately a hero after reflection."

A wave of raw physical hunger for her rushed through my body.

"How is it heroic to ruin a whole family?"

"He risked everything to free a whole family."

The force of the hunger passed, but my hands were trembling. I dug my fingernails into the palms of my hands to keep them where they should be.

"I don't need any big, brave male hero charging into my life to free me from anything. I can take care of myself. I have for a long time and I intend to continue to do so."

My heart sank. Such jumping from anger to anger, hurt to hurt, from subject to subject almost always reveals a deeper rage that the person will not face.

"We all need help and protection, Jane," I sighed. "All of us are dependent."

"I will not be dependent on him."

"It's your right to make that judgment."

"And I've made it. You were there, you saw what it did to my children, to my brothers and their wives. I'm not defending my brothers. But couldn't he have told me privately and them too? They would never have done anything again. Why the big show?"

"If you can't see that, Jane, I'm sure I can't explain it . . . I put it to you that you're the only one who is angry at him. Your daughter, your son, your brothers and sisters-in-law rather admire what he did. They're free now of the past, at least free enough that they can leave it behind them. I don't see why you cling to it."

In saying that I did see why.

"I hate him," she shouted at me. "I hate him!"

"No, Jane, you don't hate him," I sighed wearily. "You hate your mother. As long as you hate her, you are a prisoner of your own anger. You're not angry at poor Lee whom you love very much. You're angry at her and yourself. It's not him you must forgive. It's Ita and Jane. Abandon your anger at your mother and forgive her, that you'll finally be free of the rage that has eaten at your soul all these years. Maybe you'll then be able to forgive yourself or, even better, listen to Lee when he tells you that you have been long since forgiven."

"A lot you know," she sobbed and ran out of my rectory office.

All right, Patrick T. Keenan, you scored a direct hit. Maggie couldn't have done any better.

Exhausted by my bout of passion and our argument, I watched her run out to her Mercedes, the replacement for the one that Lucianne had totaled, oblivious to the pounding rain.

I didn't like to argue with women. Any man who desired to play the role of a lover to Jane would have to get used to arguments with her. Or like Leo, he would have to enjoy them. Funny I had never thought of that before. Arguments before passion, arguments after passion. Maybe, God knows, even during passion.

What would she do now?

She was an intelligent woman, very intelligent. But intelligence is no help when you've surrounded yourself with impermeable armor, in this case an armor of self-loathing.

Maybe love would do it. Maybe.

Or sexual hunger. How clever of God to link the latter two.

All her other lover could do at this point was hope.

And pray.

And commit her to the care of the appropriate angels.

I was exhausted by the conversation. I had been true to my friendship with Leo and my confidant relationship with Jane. I had been a good priest and a good friend.

Had I lost Jane forever?

Well, so be it.

The next afternoon, she called me.

"I'm sorry, Packy. I was a jerk. Sorry to unload my anger and confusion on you."

"That's what priests are for, Jane."

"You've always been a good priest for me. You're not a man who possesses the priesthood but a man possessed by it."

"That's high praise," I said slowly.

"If I do manage to straighten things out with Lunkhead, you'll still be my priest?"

"Sure will."

"Mine just a tad more than his?"

"A tiny tad."

We both laughed.

"One more thing, Jane," I said before she hung up. "I hear that your annulment will come through no later than the first week in October."

"Oh," she said.

And there the conversation ended.

I thought for a long time before I took my hand off the phone. Like Lucianne I had been a terminal asshole. Of course I was possessed by the priesthood. It was my whole life. I could no more not be a priest than I could not breathe. My fantasy romance with Jane was folly. Comic folly at that, I grinned.

The three of us would be good friends for the rest of our lives. That was better than a marriage between two utterly incompatible people who would never forgive one another for the dream of the priesthood they had blighted.

Jane needed someone as crazy as Leo. And I did not need someone as manic as Jane. I'd made a fool out of myself.

But, fortunately, only in my head.

I put on my sweatsuit and wandered over to the basketball courts where the young priest was playing with teenagers.

"Make room guys," he instructed the kids. "The old pro is coming out of retirement."

"I can still beat the young rookie at twenty-one."

"Boss," he whispered, "you look great, like a huge burden has been lifted off your shoulders. You're smiling again."

"Has it been a long time?"

"A real long time."

"It takes a while to realize that you're possessed by the priesthood."

"Gee, with you it's clear every day."

"The new me might be permanent."

"It will mean a lot of work for the rest of us. But how come the change?"

"Two friends who will keep me smiling."

"New friends?"

"No. Old ones. From long ago."

Jane

The memoir is finished at last. Now I'll have to begin the novel. Would he be the hero or the villain?

Silly question, he was the hero and I'm the stupid little shit.

That Sunday night you should have walked down the road, said a prayer for Jimmy and Eileen by the tree, and fallen on your knees. In front of him. Not in regret, but in thanksgiving.

You didn't. Too proud. Too scared.

Free from her for the first time and you didn't know yet who you were. You didn't want to be free. You screamed at him because he didn't rescue the princess in the castle and then when he did rescue her, you screamed at him for trying to rescue her.

You really can't trust your garden-variety, Shanty Irish princesses these days, can you?

You haven't talked to Maggie yet either. And you ran out on poor Packy. How long you gonna be a stupid little shit?

For the rest of your life, maybe?

I love him too much for that.

You've already wasted a month.

Almost a month. And I am seeing a shrink finally. Someone I heard Maggie talking about often.

You didn't tell her.

I will pretty soon.

You want to screw with him don't you.

Sure I do. It was fun. The man is irresistible. Always has been. Always will be. Doesn't know it yet.

So call him and be done with it. Tell him he's irresistible.

I'm not ready yet.

You're less ready every day

That's true.

She kneels in front of the Madonna, the statue her poor mother brought from Ireland and prays.

> *Hail Mary*
> *Full of Grace*
> *The Lord is with thee*
> *Blessed are thou among women*
> *And blessed is the fruit of thy womb, Jesus.*

Holy Mary mother of God
Pray for us sinners
Now and at the hour of our death.
Amen.

The Feast of St. Michael, Gabriel, Raphael and all the other Angels

Angel of God
My Guardian dear
To whom God's love
Commits me here
All this day
Be at my side
To light, to guard,
To rule and guide.

—Catholic Childhood Prayer

Leo

In September, I had presided over the trauma of Laura's entry into St. Ignatius and then traveled on fundraising missions around the country.

In California I spent time with Megan and her clan and Pete and his family. Three decades of relative silence meant nothing to the love they felt for me.

I didn't deserve it, but I reveled in it.

I heard nothing from Jane. The two week deadline I had assigned to her anger had passed. Should I now make an attempt myself? It would be so much better for our future if she did, but there was no point in being an academic perfectionist.

Laura said nothing. She and Lucianne were still fast friends but had apparently decided on a strategy of noninvolvement, most unlikely given their personalities.

Late in the afternoon on the last Thursday in September, a soft, warm day, which made you think summer was coming instead of leaving, the phone rang in my office. Mae had already gone home so I answered it.

Having discovered I liked flowers, that worthy had provided mums for the office before she left, their scent hinting at autumn, maturity, and maybe death.

"Kelly," I stroked the beard I was growing, just to make sure it was still there.

"I'm calling from Devlin Travel," a hoarse voice I could barely recognize.

My knees shook, my stomach heaved.

"Ah?"

"We're offering some tours of Ireland in October. The days in Ireland are short in October, but usually quite nice. We're planning a historical and political tour, perhaps as long as two weeks. We would begin in Shannon and then go on to Ashford Castle and over to Dublin. We would emphasize West of Ireland history."

Her voice became more controlled and confident as she talked. Purely a business proposition.

"Ashford Castle is pretty expensive."

"Reduced rates because of off season."

"I see."

"The tour would visit Nora Barnacle Joyce's home in Galway."

"Sounds interesting."

"Then it would go on to Dublin to look at Dublin history, particularly as it pertains to the West of Ireland."

"Uh-huh."

She had already said that.

"And of course we would follow Mr. Bloom's famous walk. One could even buy lemon scented soap at Sweney's on Westland Row."

I wasn't sure how that fit in, but it might make some sense.

"Late October is a very busy time at the University."

"I understand that."

"I would be expected to lecture?"

"I assume you would lecture. That's what professors do, isn't it?"

What kind of game was she playing?

"Large tour?" I said, playing along and beginning to hope.

"Quite small actually."

"Double occupancy, I presume."

A sound that might have been a giggle. I imagined her shoulders hunched forward.

"I'm afraid that's required for the special rate. Twin beds if you like."

"Then I wouldn't come."

"Good. The tickets are already on the way to you by messenger. Be sure to wait for them."

She hung up.

I threw back my head and laughed. Jane! Jane! Jane!

The phone rang again.

"Yes?" I knew who it was.

"Leo," she blurted, "I'm driving up to the Lake tomorrow for a quiet weekend. Our daughters are on retreat, doubtless praying for us. It's gorgeous this time of the year. Heat still on in the swimming pool too. So quiet and peaceful. No one's there. I have room for a passenger."

The poor woman was weeping.

"I think I could clear my schedule for that."

"Good, I'll come by your apartment at one o'clock?"

"Why that early?"

"If we start early we'll miss the Friday afternoon rush up to the Lake. You know what that's like."

"How come there will be a rush if no one is up there on these weekends?"

"If there isn't, then we'll get there early. Maybe do some swimming." She laughed gaily. "I'll be at your place promptly at one. Don't keep me waiting, Lunkhead."

Because I am mean and stubborn, I replied, "I'll be at the door, Milady."

"Yes," she said, "yes."

Author's Note

A full account of the workings of the Birth Control Commission can be found in Robert Blair Kaiser's book *The Politics of Sex and Religion* (Leaven Press).

The "Lake" in the story is something like Lake Geneva in Wisconsin, but for the most part it is a construction of my imagination. The University is something like *the* University, but it is also in great part a construction of my imagination.

Thus *the* University has never had an Irish Catholic political scientist as Provost, and there is no Appricot Cord 1935, I am told, on the premises of its administration building.

Worse luck for them on both counts? Ah, that would not be for me to say, would it now?

Chicago
Halloween 1996